Palisades Park

ALSO BY ALAN BRENNERT

Honolulu
Moloka'i

PALISADES PARK

ALAN BRENNERT

ST. MARTIN'S PRESS ✖ NEW YORK

This is a work of fiction. All of the characters, organizations, and events portrayed in this novel are either products of the author's imagination or are used fictitiously.

PALISADES PARK. Copyright © 2013 by Alan Brennert. All rights reserved. Printed in the United States of America. For information, address St. Martin's Press, 175 Fifth Avenue, New York, N.Y. 10010.

www.stmartins.com

Design by Steven Seighman

ISBN 978-0-312-64372-0 (hardcover)
ISBN 978-1-250-02433-6 (e-book)

St. Martin's Press books may be purchased for educational, business, or promotional use. For information on bulk purchases, please contact Macmillan Corporate and Premium Sales Department at 1-800-221-7945 extension 5442 or write specialmarkets@macmillan.com.

First Edition: April 2013

10 9 8 7 6 5 4 3 2 1

FOR NICK AND ELEANOR TIBURZI
and a big stuffed dog named Ruff

Across the water were the Palisades, crowned by the ugly framework of the amusement park—yet soon it would be dusk and those same iron cobwebs would be a glory against the heavens, an enchanted palace set over the smooth radiance of a tropical canal.

—F. Scott Fitzgerald

PALISADES PARK

OPENING BALLY

Palisades, New Jersey, 1922

EDDIE HAD GONE to Palisades Park only once, on a scorching Saturday in June when the temperature in Newark topped ninety in the shade and most sensible residents of the Ironbound had either fled to the Jersey shore or opened up a fire hydrant and cooled themselves in its geyser. The Stopka family more usually went to nearby Olympic Park in Maplewood, which had not yet broken ground on its own proposed swimming pool; and so Palisades' much ballyhooed saltwater pool sounded mighty appealing in this withering heat. Eddie's father had wanted to go the previous Sunday, but Eddie's grandmother, who still held considerable sway over the household, would not hear of it: according to Polish custom no good Catholic could go swimming until June 24, St. John the Baptist Day, when St. John would bless the waters of the seas, lakes, rivers, and, in an apparent concession to modernity, swimming pools, thus protecting bathers from drowning. Eddie's dad—stocky, solid as a two-by-four and equally practical—felt there might be some justification for the practice in Poland, where the Black Sea could be frigid and swimmers might conceivably cramp and drown; but it hardly seemed necessary in New Jersey, in the summer, when you could practically poach an egg in the hot, humid air.

But Jack Stopka lost this argument as he had many others with his mother, and to soften his son's disappointment, the next day he brought home three packages of American Caramel candy. The chewy caramel sticks, though satisfying, were strictly of secondary interest to Eddie, who tore the packs open at once for the revealed treasure of three brand-new baseball cards: Jesse Haines of the St. Louis Cardinals, Ivey Wingo of the Cincinnati Reds, and most exciting for Eddie as a Yankees fan, Babe Ruth, posed in a sepia-tinted photograph holding a regulation ball innocent of the beating it would shortly receive from the business end of the Babe's bat. "Wow, thanks, Pop!" Eddie said happily, adding the cards to his growing collection—most of which had come in packs of his father's Coupon Cigarettes, a godawful smoke that Jack purchased solely for the pleasure of seeing his son's face light up when he handed him a Ty Cobb card, or a Red Faber.

Finally, on Saturday, June 24—after Jack finished his half-day's work at the foundry—Eddie, his parents, grandmother, and sister, Viola, took the maroon-colored Public Service trolley from Newark, across the Hackensack meadowlands. The car clanged its bell at every stop and in between the air compressors huffed and puffed asthmatically, pumping air for the brakes. But eventually they reached Palisade Avenue in Fort Lee, where the amusement park sprawled atop a two-hundred-foot bluff overlooking the Hudson River and New York City. Eddie heard the park long before he could see it: from at least a mile away he could hear the chattering of winches pulling a train of roller-coaster cars up to a creaking wooden summit, followed by the roar of gravity dragging them down the other side and the high-pitched screams of women, children, and even a few men as the cars dove headlong into space.

"Look at *that*, willya," Eddie said as the skeletal shoulders of the coaster appeared in the distance. His tone was one of hushed reverence usually reserved for discussion of Babe Ruth or "Long Bob" Meusel.

His mother, Rose, nervously eyed the height of the coaster and cautioned, "You may not be old enough to ride that one, Eddie."

"But I'm almost eleven!" Eddie reminded her. "If I wait I may be *too* old to ride it!"

His mother found this very amusing and said simply, "We'll see."

As they got off the trolley, Eddie could feel the rumble of the coaster deep in his belly, making him want it all the more. He ran ahead, only to have to wait for the rest of the family to catch up. They entered through the Hudson gate, nearest to the famed pool, a gigantic "inland sea" two city blocks long and one block wide, filled with a million and a half gallons of salt water pumped up each day from the river below. Eddie's eyes popped at the size of it: children, for whom the whole world is big, love the biggest of the big, and this more than qualified. A man-made waterfall churned the waters at the far end of the pool; at the other end, the shallows were fronted by a real sand beach; and somehow, as Eddie would discover, there were even rolling ocean waves in the pool, though he had no idea how this could be. At the pool's green-and-white ticket booth his father purchased tickets, and in the huge bathing pavilion they changed into their bathing suits—all save Grandma, who was appalled by these new styles with their scandalous display of naked leg, and so planted herself on the sand in her long, ruffled black dress (with unfashionable petticoats) and a white babushka that at least afforded her some protection from the sun.

The pool was packed with hundreds of swimmers, the beach overrun by sunbathers and toddlers wielding toy shovels, but the Stopkas found some unclaimed real estate and spent the next several hours swimming and playing in the remarkably clear waters, watched over by rugged life-guards perched atop red-lacquered rescue stations ringing the pool. One lifeguard, named Happy, coached Eddie on his swimming. But even more than the cool refreshing waters on this very hot day, what Eddie would remember were the smells: the salt spray from the waterfalls, a vanilla breeze from the waffle stand across the midway, and the sharp tang of lemons, big as grapefruit, that hung from the nearby lemonade stand.

After their swim the Stopkas left the bathhouse and strolled past a dance hall where a band was playing ragtime, to the main midway graciously shaded by stands of chestnut, poplar, maple, and oak trees. From here the whole park beckoned, dozens of sights and sounds competing for their dimes: the ricochet of pellets striking targets in the shooting gallery, calliope music from the Carousel, the rattle and roar of four roller coasters—the Scenic Railway, the Toboggan Racer, the Giant Coaster, and the Deep Dip Thriller—and dozens of concessionaires, each delivering his "bally," his pitch to the crowd, hawking refreshments, sideshow tickets, or games of chance. What to do, where to go next?

"Let's go ride the coaster," Grandma declared with a wink to Eddie, and Jack laughed and said, "You're on, Lil," her Christian name being Lillian.

The Giant Coaster was situated near the edge of the Palisades, an impressive location not afforded many other amusement park rides in New Jersey or anywhere else. The family squeezed into the first car, Eddie and his father up front, Mother and Viola behind them, Grandma in the third row. The cars started with a lurch, Eddie's excitement ratcheting up a notch with every clack-clack-clack of the climb up the first hill. When they finally reached the top, the height of the Palisades doubled their altitude and made for a dizzying view: Eddie took in the exhilarating expanse of the Manhattan skyline; saw ferries chugging their way across the Hudson like windup toys in a bathtub; felt his stomach flutter at the sight of trolleys and automobiles snaking along River Road hundreds of feet below. Olympic Park had a roller coaster, but boy, it couldn't hold a candle to this! Then the car slid down the other side and all at once they were plunging earthward like a falling plane. Eddie left his stomach behind at the summit, his blond hair blowing into his eyes as he glanced over at his father, grinning beside him—and though his mother and sister were screaming in the row behind, damned if Grandma Lil wasn't laughing as much as she was screaming, even after her babushka was ripped from her head and took off like a flapping gull toward the waters of the Hudson.

After the coaster they took a more sedate gondola ride through artificial canals and a diorama of Venice, Italy, which Mother adored (she had painted a little in her youth; "mostly just bathrooms now," she would say wistfully) but which Eddie found rather slow and boring. Much better were the whizzing, spinning buckets of the Virginia Reel; after which Pop tried his luck in the Penny Arcade and Mother and Viola rode the gently trotting Arabian horses and Indian ponies of the Carousel, which Eddie believed himself too old, or too manly, to patronize.

But the whole family enjoyed the Third Degree, a large castlelike funhouse next to the pool whose floors tilted crazily and in whose mirrored walls they saw laughing distortions of themselves. At the end of this ride a gust of air blew Mother's skirt up over her hips, but one steely look from Grandma Lil to the man working the air nozzles kept her petticoats firmly brushing the floor.

After all this exertion the Stopkas had worked up an appetite, and stopped for a supper of hot dogs, hamburgers, and French-fried potatoes. The latter were thick and crispy on the outside, warm and soft inside, served in a white paper cone. Eddie's dad handed him a saltshaker and a bottle of malt vinegar: "Here. You're supposed to sprinkle these on the fries."

Eddie squinted dubiously at the bottle. "Vinegar?"

"It's good, try it," Jack urged, and since his father had never steered him wrong before, Eddie tentatively sprinkled some of the vinegar on his potatoes. He was surprised to find, upon taking his first hesitant bite, that it was delicious—they were the best French fries he'd ever tasted—and soon he was liberally drenching the fries in salt and vinegar, both of which made him so thirsty he asked for one of the ice-cold lemonades made from those gigantic lemons. This too was delicious, the tops. Meanwhile Pop washed his own meal down with a glass of "near beer," the closest thing to a Polish lager to be had, at least in public, since the Volstead Act.

Later, Eddie's family passed a sideshow, the Palace of Wonders, with bold banners snapping in the wind, announcing such exotic performers as Marie DeVere, a lady sword swallower; Habib, the fire-eater; Population Charlie, a "mental marvel"; Lentini, a boy with three legs; and Carl, the Giant Swede. The "outside talker" extolled the wonders within, as a pair of scantily clad dancers, or "bally girls," swiveled their hips, beckoning the crowd to enter. Eddie really wanted to see the three-legged boy, but his parents balked at the bally girls, judging the children not quite old enough for the sideshow.

Instead they walked the midways as dusk settled over the park—and as nightfall transformed it. Day gave way to night but not to darkness, as somewhere switches were flipped and concession stands were delicately traced with glowing strings of colored lights, like theater marquees. With the coming of evening, Palisades was jeweled with light, from the glittering spokes of the Ferris wheel spinning like a fireworks display, to the soft white lightbulbs strung in the trees like clouds of fireflies. Suddenly the park atop the Palisades was no longer just a park, it was an enchanted island in the sky. Above the Hudson floated the starry constellation of the Manhattan skyline, which seemed a part of the same magical terrain. Eddie wished he could stay here all night, or at least until the park closed at midnight; but Viola was starting to doze and Grandma Lil was tiring as well, and so the Stopka family began to make their way back to the No. 92 trolley that would start them on their long journey home to Newark. Eddie took one last look behind him, trying in those last minutes to absorb and preserve the glittering lights and the sweet smell of candy floss and caramel apples and the sound of people shrieking in delight as they plummeted down the Giant Coaster. Eddie was certain that no place had ever made him as happy as Palisades Park had today; and so it was perhaps just as well that he had no inkling that this would be the happiest day and night he would know for a long time to come.

1

Atlanta, Georgia, 1930

HOBOES CALLED THEM "side-door Pullmans," empty boxcars with one door standing open like an unblinking eye—God's eye, maybe, daring the brave or the desperate to trespass, knowing their journeys could end as easily in jail or in a hospital as in Chillicothe, Ohio, or Casper, Wyoming. Eddie took the dare and ran to the back platform, planting his foot in a metal stirrup and hoisting his six-foot frame up onto the ladder. But before he could step up to the second rung, he felt something grab hold of his shirt collar from behind and pull him, with a violent jerk, away from the car.

Eddie lost his grip and tumbled backward, landing on the ground with a jolt. As he lay there in the dust, stunned and winded, a boot came crashing down on his chest, knocking the remaining breath out of him. He opened his eyes to find a nasty-looking railroad bull glaring down at him.

"You ain't goin' nowhere, bud," the bull declared.

The train whistled twice—a highball—signaling imminent departure.

Eddie held up his hands in surrender. "Okay," he told the railroad cop, "you got me. Serves me right for being sloppy. But I can pay my way, all right? How much is a ticket to New York—fifteen bucks? I can pay."

The bull's eyes gleamed with interest. "Show me."

The boxcar lurched forward as the train began chugging out of the station. Eddie had no doubts that this thug was going to steal all his money as a main course, then give him the beating of his life for dessert.

Eddie said, "Wallet's in my rucksack. I dropped it over there."

The bull, still keeping his foot on Eddie's chest, reached down and picked up Eddie's rucksack. He began to rummage through it for the wallet.

Eddie grabbed the man's foot and yanked it out from under him. He toppled like a felled tree. Eddie scrambled to his feet, snapped up his rucksack. "Sonofabitch!" the bull yelled, but as he started to stand, Eddie jerked up his knee and connected with the bull's chin. This hurt Eddie almost as much as it did the cop: he hoped the satisfying crack he heard was the bull's jawbone breaking, not his own kneecap. The bull quickly crumpled.

Eddie made a run for a passing boxcar. His heart hammered as he ran to keep pace, threw his rucksack inside, then grabbed the door latch and pulled himself up and in. It wasn't until he was safely aboard that he looked back, relieved to see the bull still beside the tracks, out cold.

Soon the car was rattling out of Inman Yards, one link in a long chain of rolling freight headed north. Eddie hadn't lied: he had cash in his pocket for once and could have been eating roast chicken in a posh dining car instead of the bread and bologna in his rucksack. But it was early April and the weather was mild, and after three years of riding the rails, he had grown used to the percussion of the wheels reverberating deep inside him, even the coarse perfume of pine tar and creosote inside a boxcar.

But mostly he liked sitting near the open door, feeling the wind on his face, watching the countryside roll past without walls or windows between. At night, out here in the great empty spaces between towns, the only illumination came from the moon and stars, the train's running lights, and the occasional farmhouses along the way. Whether lit with the warm flicker of kerosene lamps or by steadier, cooler electric bulbs, their windows always looked inviting, and Eddie imagined families sitting down to dinner or to listen to Guy Lombardo on the radio—fathers reading the paper as mothers sewed, girls played with dolls, and boys shuffled baseball cards. The glowing windows, and the images they conjured in his mind, were both warming and painful. He curled up under a cardboard blanket, dozing to the clattering lullaby of the train's wheels and the mournful sigh of the steam whistle.

By the following afternoon Eddie was crossing the Delaware River, back in New Jersey for the first time in three years. Rolling hills gave way to roadside commerce, and then the train was swallowed up by Newark's canyons of concrete and steel. Soon they were passing through Eddie's old neighborhood, the Ironbound, a patchwork of ethnic enclaves girdled by the foundries and railroad tracks that gave the area its name. Eddie longed to jump off—to walk the streets with their smorgasbord of cooking smells, kielbasa on one corner, spaghetti and meatballs on another, borscht on the next. But he didn't, and all he could see from the train was a soup kitchen doling out bread and stew, a long line of haggard men curling around the block like the tail of a starving dog.

Not until they reached the outskirts of Jersey City—the terminus, where cargo was off-loaded onto barges bound for the New York docks—did Eddie finally hop off and begin hoofing it up River Road. On his right the Manhattan skyline greeted him like an old friend he hadn't seen in years; on his left rose the stony grandeur of the Palisades.

Eight miles later he entered the borough of Edgewater, home to companies like Alcoa, Valvoline Oil, and Jack Frost Sugar—the usual harborfront smells of salt and diesel fuel sweetened by the scent of burning sugar and molasses. In the distance stood the latticed steel towers of the new Hudson River Bridge, as yet only a single cable strung between them. At the Edgewater Ferry Terminal, ferries arrived from 125th Street in New York and trolley cars took ferry passengers up the steep cliffs and into Bergen County. Eddie looked up, pleased to find, still crowning the bluffs, a majestic if motionless Ferris wheel; the twisting wooden skeleton of a roller coaster; and a huge metal sign with towering block letters that announced:

PALISADES AMUSEMENT PARK
SURF BATHING

He took a trolley car up winding iron tracks stitched into the granite face of the cliffs, paying a nickel for the short run up to Palisade Avenue and the main gate of the park. The entrance, with its triangular marquee, still retained its capacity to evoke wonder in him. Since the park had yet to open for the season, there was no rumble of roller-coaster cars, no delighted screams or calliope music, just the hollow echoes of construction work from inside. But it still brought a smile to Eddie's face.

A single security guard manned the gate. "Excuse me," Eddie said. "I'm here to see . . ." He consulted a fraying page torn from *The Billboard*, the outdoor entertainment industry's trade magazine. "John Greenwald?"

The guard gave him the once-over. Eddie supposed he must have looked (and smelled) pretty ripe after his travels; only now did it occur to him that he might've gone first to the nearest YMCA for a hot shower. But the guard didn't run him off the grounds, just asked, "You got an appointment?"

"No, I'm looking for work. Mr. Greenwald, he's the park manager?"

"Yeah, come on in." The guard unlocked the turnstile to admit Eddie, then gave him directions to the administration building. Eddie thanked him and started walking toward the main midway.

It seemed strange to see the park so empty of crowds and laughter, but it was far from deserted: everywhere there were workmen wielding hammers, saws, or paintbrushes as they repaired and renovated rides and concessions. He passed the merry-go-round Viola had ridden, where workmen were stripping away the old paint from the Arabian horses and oiling the working parts of the magnificent Dentzel Carousel. Instead of the enticing aromas of lemonade, cotton candy, and French fries, he took in the tart odor of varnish, paint, motor oil, and fresh sawdust. He wondered where his sister was today, what she looked like now.

The nondescript offices of the administration building were at odds with the colorful world outside; the men at work inside wore suits and ties, the women conservative dresses. The amusement business was still a business, after all, and it helped to remind Eddie that he was here *on* business. Approaching the first desk he saw, he told a young man wearing a white shirt and dark tie, "Excuse me. I'm looking for Mr. Greenwald?"

"He's not in right now. I'm Harold Goldgraben, I'm the assistant manager. Can I help you with something?"

"Eddie Stopka. I'm looking for a job."

"Well, you're in the right place, but not the right time. We open in three weeks, and we're pretty much staffed up for the season. Do you have any experience working at amusement parks, Mr. Stopka?"

"Not parks, no, sir. But I've worked plenty of carnivals. I spent the last two seasons with the Greater Sheeshley Shows, a railroad carnival."

"That's Captain John's outfit, isn't it?"

"Yes, sir. We traveled all over the Midwest and South—Ohio, Alabama, Georgia, South Carolina, Florida . . ."

"You don't sound like you're from the South, Mr. Stopka."

"South Newark is more like it."

Goldgraben laughed. "So what brings you back to Jersey?"

"I got homesick, I guess. And tired of traveling."

"Fair enough. What kind of work did you do for these shows?"

"Little bit of everything. Started as a roustabout, lifting and loading the carnival equipment for the jump to the next town. Worked my way up to concessions—Penny Pitch, Skee Ball, Hoop-la . . ."

An older man in dungarees, on his way out of the office, overheard this last exchange and asked Eddie, "You ever done any ride maintenance?"

"Yes, sir. I've torn down Ferris wheels and put 'em back up again. Coney Island Flyers and carousels, too. And I'm good at carpentry."

"You afraid of heights?"

"No, sir."

The man looked at Goldgraben. "I could use another hand to sweep the Scenic. For a few days, at least."

Goldgraben said, "Okay, tell you what, Mr. Stopka: we can offer you two, maybe three days' work. Meanwhile I'll ask around, see if any of the concessionaires can use an extra hand. Can't guarantee anything, but come back first thing in the morning, you'll report to Father Cleary here."

Eddie looked at the older man. "You're a priest?"

"Oh, Christ, no. That's just a nickname, everybody here's got a goddamn nickname." He offered his hand, which Eddie took. "Joe Cleary, I manage the Big Scenic Railway. See you tomorrow at nine, sharp."

Eddie was very happy when he left the office: he had a job at Palisades, even if only a temporary one.

On his way back to the front gate he passed a lemonade stand and thought of the sweet but tart drink he'd enjoyed on that long-ago night. Sure enough, there were those giant lemons hanging in the window, big and close enough to touch. Well, hell, why not? Eddie went up to the stand, reached out to take one of the lemons in his hand . . . and he laughed.

The lemons were made of papier-mâché and plaster.

So *that* was how they got them that big.

After spending the night at the YMCA in Hackensack, Eddie got to Palisades a good half hour earlier than even the security guard. The Big Scenic Railway was an old wooden coaster, its assistant manager a short fellow with a receding hairline named John Winkler, who explained Eddie's job: "You walk the tracks, and wherever you see dirt you sweep, and wherever you see rust you oil down the track with this"—he handed him some rags and a bucket filled with a liquid corrosive—"remove the rust, then sweep it off. You sure you're okay with heights?"

"Yeah, sure, I don't mind."

One of several workers "oiling and sweeping" the Scenic, Eddie ascended the mountain of lumber like a climber scaling a wooden tor. But the harder thing was going back down the other side—walking backward down a steep grade a hundred feet or more above the ground. He would soak the rags in corrosive, then scrub at whatever patches of rust he found on the tracks. After a winter of snow and rain there was a lot of oxidation, but the "oil" loosened it sufficiently that it could be swept away.

Following behind was Winkler, inspecting the tracks. He sounded out the planks, uprights, and timbers with a pick, looking for soft, spongy sections that might have rotted; checked the tracks for warps in the wood, broken screw heads, loose bolts, or worn pins in the chains that dragged the cars up the slope. If he found something not up to par, he marked it with a piece of greased chalk for the mechanics to replace or repair.

At the summit, Eddie paused to rest a moment and let his gaze wander across the thirty-eight acres of park, straddling the towns of Fort Lee and Cliffside Park, spread out below him. The silence up here was profound, broken only by the tinny voices of hammers and saws floating up from below. The great saltwater pool was empty, its green cement bed being thoroughly scrubbed with lime by a squadron of workmen. Across the main midway stood a coaster called the Cyclone, a colossus made of all black metal, its steel peaks steeper than those of the Scenic; Eddie noted that its tracks also seemed to twist like licorice sticks as they ascended and descended. What must it be like riding one of those cars, he wondered, twisting from side to side even as it plummeted to earth?

"Taking in the sights, Eddie?"

Eddie turned to see John Winkler a few yards below him, a bemused smile on his face. "Sorry," Eddie said, quickly dipping a rag in the corrosive.

"S'okay." Winkler climbed up to join him. "It is a helluva view."

Eddie nodded. "And that Cyclone looks like one helluva ride."

"Yeah, too much so. It's all steel, so it has absolutely no give, not like a wooden coaster. People are actually scared to ride the damn thing. And all that steel is a pain in the keister to maintain, we're losing money on it hand over fist." This was the first, but not the last, intimation that Eddie would receive that all was not well at Palisades.

By lunchtime Eddie had worked up a substantial appetite. Sitting at a picnic table with other workmen on break, Eddie turned his attention to the ham-and-cheese sandwich he had brought to work. After one bite he heard a plaintive *"miaow"* from behind him and turned to find a skinny little tabby cat, its big yellow eyes staring soulfully at him, ribs visible beneath its striped fur. Eddie's heart got the better of his stomach; he tore off a piece of ham and held it out to the cat, who scurried over and gulped it down. Then there was another *"miaow"* to his right, and one to his left, and Eddie found himself at the center of a pride of kitties all begging for parts of his lunch.

A tall man with an amused twinkle in his eye sat down beside him. "Don't let these little moochers fool you," he told Eddie as he unwrapped a pastrami sandwich. "They do okay, cadging meals off the steady staff. I haven't seen one starve to death in the twenty years I've been working here."

"Where do they all come from?"

"They live in the woodshop, curling up between the piles of sawdust. Breed like rabbits. The office staff adopts one or two each season, the rest are on mouse patrol." He extended a hand. "Roscoe Schwarz. I blow air up women's skirts for a living."

Eddie laughed, remembering the Funhouse and how his mother's and sister's skirts were hiked up around their waists like umbrellas blown inside out by a storm. "Yeah? What does your wife think about that?"

Roscoe shrugged. "She's not overjoyed. But she knows it pays the bills." He took a bite of pastrami. "Before managing the Funhouse I worked the Ferris wheel for sixteen years. I like the Funhouse better, you've got an audience, you get laughs. Only once a lady got huffy with me, hit me with her purse." He smiled. "She was a natural redhead, by the way."

They shared a laugh. Eddie surrendered the last of his ham and cheese to a calico cat and resolved to pack an extra sandwich tomorrow.

By the end of the day Eddie's legs ached like a mountain goat's, but the next day he finished ahead of schedule and did a good enough job that he was assigned to the park's second biggest coaster, the Skyrocket. In the middle of his third day, Eddie was called down by Harold Goldgraben, who told him, "I just spoke with Chief Borrell, he can use an extra man on his candy concession. Meet him at his hot-dog stand near the pool."

Eddie had worked enough carnivals that he wouldn't have been fazed to be meeting with a full-blown Indian chief decked out in war paint and headdress, but at the stand he found a tall, avuncular man around forty, wearing a police uniform. "Hi. Frank Borrell," he said, offering his hand.

"Eddie Stopka."

Borrell smiled. "I see you've noticed the uniform. No, it's not for show. I'm the police chief here in Cliffside Park."

Confused, Eddie asked, "And you own a hot-dog stand too?"

"This is just kind of a sideline, you know what I mean? I also sell candy floss, soda pop, apples on a stick . . . we got no crime to speak of in Cliffside Park, but a hell of a lot of tooth decay."

Eddie laughed. "So how did a cop wind up selling hot dogs?"

"Lotta cops moonlight here as security guards, but me, fifteen years ago I was walking a beat on Palisade Avenue. I got friendly with the

Schencks, the owners—helped them out with traffic and whatnot—and they offered to let me buy into some concessions as an investment." He looked Eddie up and down. "The Goldgraben kid says you're a damn good worker. You've worked carnivals?"

Eddie rattled off his experience, and Borrell took it in with the close attention one would expect of a policeman. Then, "I need a grind man to sell candy floss and popcorn," not exactly police parlance. "You interested?"

"You bet."

"I can pay fifteen dollars a week plus two percent of the take. But that might not amount to much."

"Why not?"

"We're all holding our breaths to see how this stock market crash affects gate receipts. As it is, I've been just breaking even. The Schenck brothers aren't doing any better—I'm not sure how much longer they're going to foot the bill to keep this place open. They got bigger fish to fry in Hollywood."

"I've worked other shows that were getting by on the skin of their teeth," Eddie said, though saddened to hear of it. "I know what it's like."

"Okay, one more thing. Palisades has an employee dress code: men have to be clean-shaven and wear coats, ties, and collared shirts during the week, a full dress suit on weekends. I'm looking at you and thinking maybe you don't own a suit, am I correct?"

Eddie flushed with embarrassment. "No, but I can—"

"Don't sweat it, I'll front you the cash. Go over to Schweitzer's Department Store in Fort Lee, get yourself a nice suit, couple ties, two or three dress shirts. You could use a haircut, too. Phil Basile's got a barbershop here on the park grounds, tell him the Chief sent you and to shear off some of that hay on your head, put it on my tab."

"Thanks, that's really swell of you."

"You got a place to stay, kid?"

"Yeah, a room at the Y."

"My cousin Patsy's in real estate, I'll see if he knows of a place. No, wait a minute. Hey, Duke!" he called out across the pool area. "Duke!"

About fifty feet away, one of the men helping to clean up the pool area looked up. "Yeah?" he called back.

Borrell said, "You know the guy, don't you, that manages the building where Lightning lives? Over on Anderson Ave?"

"Yeah, so?"

"So get your wop ass over here, there's somebody I want you to meet." The Chief turned back to Eddie and gave him a good-natured slap across the shoulders. "We'll get you fixed up with something, kid." Borrell then spoke three words that thrilled Eddie more than he could admit:

"Welcome to Palisades."

Johnny Duke was not a sentimental man. "Sure, I'd miss the park if it shut down," he told Eddie. "It's a great place to get laid."

John "Duke" DeNoia, one of the lifeguards at the Palisades pool, was six feet tall, husky, with curly black hair—a rugged thirty-year-old with only his scarred, pockmarked cheeks to detract from his good looks. According to him, that didn't matter much.

"The pool is like a giant magnet for pussy," Johnny expounded as he and Eddie made their way across the park. "Blondes, brunettes, redheads, big tits, little tits, what have you—they all come to the pool. And if you're a lifeguard, sitting on one of them big red chairs, you might as well be a king. Well," he added with a laugh, "a duke, at least."

"Yeah, I was gonna ask," Eddie said, "why Duke?"

"The Duke DeNoia was a nobleman from Naples, sixteenth century. His given name was John Carafa. I'm John DeNoia, ergo, Johnny Duke."

"Does the park let you take girls on the rides for free?"

"Wouldn't know. Never been on one."

"You've never been on a ride here?"

"Never been on one anywhere," DeNoia said.

"Really?" Eddie said in disbelief. "Not even as a kid?"

DeNoia shrugged. "They go up, they go down. What's the point?"

Eddie was at a loss to reply to that.

The "Duke" grinned. "Only one thing I'm interested in riding, and it ain't no friggin' Ferris wheel. Though one gal I knew was kind of a cyclone."

They reached the parking lot where Johnny kept his sporty yellow Oldsmobile Roadster. "Nice car," Eddie said.

"Thanks. Great for getting laid. Climb in."

Johnny opened the throttle and drove to a redbrick building with Tudor-style gables in the 700 block of Anderson Avenue. Eddie thought it looked too swank for him, but Johnny disagreed: "Times are tough, everybody's willing to negotiate. C'mon, let's see what they got."

Johnny made introductions to a rumpled-looking manager: "Eddie here's working for Lightning and the Chief. You got any singles available?"

"Yeah, I got one backs up on the alley. No fancy view or anything . . ."

"I don't mind," Eddie told him.

As they followed the manager down the hall, Eddie said in a low voice to Johnny, "Who's . . . 'Lightning'?"

"The Chief's partner at the park, that's his nickname. He lives in this building, I'll introduce you. Hey, come to think, you're gonna need a nickname yourself. Stopka—is that Russian?"

"Polish."

"'Eddie the Polack'? No, wait, we got one of those already . . ."

The manager led them into a cramped but clean room with a Murphy bed, a small kitchen with an icebox and coal-burning stove, the promised view of an alley, and a bathroom about the size of a box of Wheaties. But it was a nice neighborhood and right on a trolley line. It rented for ten dollars a month—a bit rich for Eddie's blood, but when Johnny bargained it down to eight-fifty, Eddie bit and paid the first month's rent in advance.

On the way out, Johnny stopped by Dick Bennett's apartment and introduced Eddie to him. "Hey, nice to meet ya," Dick said, glad-handing him. "Lightning" Bennett lived up to his nickname, a fast talker not unlike many Eddie had met in the carny game but a bit slicker than most, sharply dressed and genial. "You play the ponies, Eddie?"

"Not really."

"I've got a tip on a nag called Legerdemain in tomorrow's fifth at Freehold. I'll be at the track, I can place a bet for you."

Eddie demurred again. Dick didn't hold it against him, and he even gave him a bottle of bootleg whisky (at least it looked like whisky). "Welcome to the park, kid. I don't get by as often as I used to—I've got stakes in a couple of nightclubs too—but the Chief's a great guy, you're in good hands."

Leaving the building, Eddie offered to buy Duke dinner by way of thanks for his help. They dined at one of Duke's favorite haunts, Tarantino's on Palisade Avenue, where they consumed hearty helpings of spaghetti and split the bottle of pretty good whisky Bennett had given them. "Dick gets this hooch from a guy at the track," Duke said, "who uses it to spike a nag's water before a big race. Man, I could run a few lengths myself after this." He looked at Eddie, snapped his fingers, and suddenly announced: "I got it!"

"Got what?"

"What is it they say? 'I wouldn't touch that with a ten-foot pole'? You're our Ten Foot Pole! There's your nickname."

Eddie smiled and hoped not.

The next day, with the money the Chief fronted him, Eddie went to Schweitzer's Department Store and bought a blue worsted suit for $14.95 and three white dress shirts for 88¢ apiece. He bought some toiletries at Ghiosay's Pharmacy and groceries at the Big Chief Market—mostly cans of pork and beans, Dinty Moore beef stew, a pound of Hills Brothers coffee—and moved into his new apartment. It was tiny, lacking in niceties—but it was *his*, not a carnival tent or boxcar. Maybe he couldn't go back to his old home in Newark, but he was determined to make a new one for himself.

Like all concessions at the park, the Chief's candy stand—in a good location, halfway up the main midway—fronted a larger stockroom behind what the public saw, crammed with supplies, gaming equipment, or prizes. Eddie was one of two concession agents, the other a short, round man named Lew who never seemed to be without a lit cigar in his mouth. As they shook hands, Lew said, "They call you Ten Foot, don't they?"

"Where'd you hear that?" Eddie said, appalled.

"Word travels fast. I was on the job less than thirty minutes before I became Lew the Jew." He shrugged with equanimity. "Whatcha gonna do?"

Ride operators worked in shifts—four hours on, four hours off—but concessionaires didn't have that luxury, often only having time for bathroom breaks and maybe twenty minutes to wolf down a quick meal. Lew and Eddie agreed to alternate doing the "grind," the pitch to the crowd, while the other worked the counter and rang up sales. They spent the first day inspecting and cleaning the working parts of the candy floss machine—the copper bowl, the spinner with its colander-like holes in its surface, the heating elements—which Lew warned could be a little erratic.

Lew also introduced Eddie to the agent next door, a veteran grind man named Jackie Bloom, who worked a "cat rack"—an old carny game in which marks tossed balls in an attempt to knock fuzzy stuffed cats off a shelf and win plush prizes. Then Eddie made the faux pas of asking, "Where's the gaff?"—the button or lever that threw the game.

Jackie looked at him with a mix of scorn and amusement: "You're not working the carny anymore, kid. Everything here's on the up-and-up. Now, that doesn't mean this is an easy game to win. See all that fuzz on the cats? A ball can sail right through that fuzz with barely a ripple— you gotta hit the center of the cat to knock it down. But that's not a gaff, it's a challenge."

Eddie was surprised to find how much the park reminded him of the Ironbound, where so many nationalities shared just four square miles of neighborhood. Palisades was a similar melting pot: August Berni, an old-timer who ran the Penny Arcade with Phil Mazzocchi, had emigrated from Italy. Plato Guimes, originally from Greece—and looking with his pince-nez glasses like a stuffy European professor out of a Hollywood movie—had operated the shooting galleries and soda stands almost from the park's beginning. Harry Dyer, from Colchester, England, had the mug of a street brawler but the soft heart of a carny; he co-owned many park restaurants, though not the chop suey place above the roller-skating rink, which was run by Yuan Chen. All were struggling to stay afloat after the Crash.

But one concession agent made a particular impression on Eddie.

Directly across the midway was a root-beer stand whose red, white, and blue awnings one day unfolded like a flower opening to the sun. It was run by two women agents—one a shapely blonde about Eddie's age. She had a sweet face with delicate features; he found himself stealing glances at her whenever he could. When she was at work, her wavy blonde hair would periodically get in her eyes and she would blow air out of the corner of her mouth to clear her vision. Somehow Eddie found this very fetching.

"Who's the blonde across the way?" he asked Lew.

"Adele something-or-other," Lew said indifferently. "She and Lois work for Norval Jennings."

It wasn't long before Eddie decided he needed a bathroom break and moseyed across the midway, pausing in front of the root-beer stand. He waited until the girl came up to the cash register at the front of the stand, opening the cash drawer to dust it out. Eddie stepped up, smiled, and said, "Hi."

She looked up. Her eyes were gray—not blue, not violet, but the lightest, most beautiful shade of pearl gray. They stole away Eddie's breath.

"Hi." So perfunctory, she made it sound like less than one syllable.

"I'm Eddie."

"I'm busy."

She clanged shut the cash drawer and turned away.

Eddie's smile sank to somewhere below his knees. He skulked off to the men's room, and when he returned to the candy stand he concentrated on his work, doing his best to put the girl out of his mind.

But she was hard to miss, and every time he looked across the midway he saw her working her stand, her blonde hair getting in her eyes—which Eddie now knew, maddeningly, were as lucid as pearls.

2

Fort Lee, New Jersey, 1930

THAT MORNING, ADELE—still in her bathrobe, hair unwashed, utterly bereft of makeup—had answered the doorbell to find a tall, handsome man, impeccably dressed in a Brooks Brothers suit, standing on the doorstep. He was a dead ringer for Greta Garbo's onetime heartthrob John Gilbert, but Adele, suddenly conscious of an unruly lock of hair in her eyes, feared she looked less like Garbo than Harpo.

"Does a Mr. Franklin Worth live here, ma'am?" he asked.

And he called her *ma'am*. Could the day get any worse?

She blew the hair out of her eyes and replied, "Yes. He's my father."

He flashed a badge at her. "Special Agent Crais. I'm with the United States Secret Service. May I come in?"

Holy Toledo—a real, honest-to-God G-man. "Yes, of course, come in."

Her mother, Marie, appeared just as the agent was showing Adele a letter addressed to President Herbert Hoover. "Have you seen this before?"

Adele immediately recognized her father's handwriting. Her stomach began to coil. "No," she said. "He wrote this to the *President?*"

"Just the latest in a series, I'm afraid," the agent informed her.

Unbeknownst to Adele or Marie, Franklin had apparently been mailing belligerent letters to President Hoover for months. Hoover had served as national conservator during the Great War; Franklin's screeds accused him of killing the East Coast's film industry by withholding coal needed to heat studios. Since Hoover was currently being blamed for all the ills in the country up to and including acne and cloudy days, the White House didn't pay much attention until Franklin's letters became overtly threatening.

Marie was mortified beyond words, but when Adele introduced the agent to Franklin, her father appeared surprised.

"I never wrote this," he said as he examined the letter. Grudgingly he conceded, "I thought I'd only—*thought* about writing it."

"So when you tell the President you would like to, quote, remove his liver with a pair of garden shears, unquote," the agent said, "you're saying that wasn't your actual intention?"

"Oh Good Lord, no! I'd never really do that, not even to Hoover."

Adele caught the agent's eye and mimed the tipping of a glass. Crais took a step closer to Franklin, and to the smell on his breath at eight in the morning.

"I . . . think I understand," he said slowly. "Mr. Worth, may I suggest you refrain from writing any further letters to President Hoover."

"Yes, yes, of course," Franklin agreed gruffly.

As she showed him out, Adele promised the agent that in the future she and her mother would more closely monitor Franklin's correspondence.

He tipped his hat. "Thank you, ma'am, your country appreciates it."

Again with the *ma'am*. Adele forced a smile, then closed the door. Marie, just a few steps behind her, said, "I'm so embarrassed I could die."

"*You're* embarrassed? He looked like John Gilbert, for God's sake!"

By the time Adele got to Palisades to ready the root-beer stand for tomorrow's opening, she felt humiliated, angry, and in absolutely no mood to have some husky blond guy from across the midway put the make on her—so she bit off his head with one bite.

But opening days always put Adele in a better mood. The next day, the park smelled of French fries, waffles, roast beef sandwiches, and sizzling hot dogs; the weather was perfect, sunny but not too hot, and crowds intent on having a good time thronged the midways. Palisades may have been just an amusement park, not Broadway, but there was still an air of theatricality about it: many concession agents not only had a signature bally but a wardrobe designed to capture attention. Kid Fiddles worked the crowd with a cowboy hat and a live horse. Jimmy Feathers, whose grocery wheel paid off in these hard times not with kewpie dolls but with food, did his bally in five different languages, which always drew a big "tip," or crowd. Jackie Bloom wore an immaculate white linen suit, and despite the hundred fifteen-watt bulbs illuminating the prizes in his showcases, he always managed to look cool and composed:

"Knock down a cat, win a prize! Kayo just one fuzzy feline and win a piece of fine imported china!"

"Try your hand at the Penny Pitch, first throw is free, hit the right square with the penny and win a prize!"

"Ride the Skyrocket, see the moon and stars up close, come hurtling back to earth and up again! Just ten cents for a Skyrocket to the stars!"

Adele launched into her own bally:

"Root beer, ice-cold root beer! Only legal beer in the park! Not as much fun as malt, but just as delicious and twice as foamy! C'mon, lift a glass to Carrie Nation!"

It wasn't the Great White Way, but it was still performing—and Adele loved to perform.

From across the midway, Eddie noted that the snippy blonde at the root-beer stand was building a pretty good tip with her grind. But Lew's wasn't half bad either: "Cotton candy, popcorn! Watch it being made, sugar spun into delectable fairy floss right before your very eyes!" Business was brisk and Eddie was kept busy providing pink clouds of candy on a stick for the crowds. Everything went smoothly until late afternoon and the sound of a loud, slurred voice emanating from Jackie Bloom's stand next door:

"Hey! Hey! I godda *great* idea—"

Eddie glanced over to see a man bobbing on his heels like a wobbly ten-pin, who then bent over to pick something off the ground. In his back pocket was a flask, doubtless containing a recent vintage of bathtub gin.

Eddie heard him call out, "Gotcha!"—and when the drunk stood up again he was holding a tiny white kitten in his fist, one of a new litter of woodshop cats stalking the park for scraps of food. Eddie saw where this was heading, and so did Jackie Bloom, who held up his palms and said, "Now, wait a second, pal . . . put the little critter down . . ."

"No, no, thiz great, see?" the man announced loudly. "Use a *cat*—to knock *down* a cat! Oughta get extra points for that!" He laughed uproariously, and a few of the idiots with him laughed along.

The kitten hissed and snarled, but he was gripping her so tightly she couldn't lash out. Now he made a great show of winding up his pitch, like Lefty Gomez about to launch one across home plate.

Eddie vaulted the counter of his stand, and before the drunk could let the fur fly, literally, Eddie reached out and grabbed his right arm.

"Yeah, you're a riot, all right," Eddie said. "Now put the cat down."

Eddie squeezed the man's arm, hard, which caused his fingers to relax their grip on the feline. Eddie reached up with his free hand, grabbed the kitten by the scruff of the neck, and let it spring out of his hand and onto the ground, where it quickly made a run for the border.

The drunk was furious that his joke, his grand stunt, had been ruined. "Who the fug are *you*?" he snapped.

"I'm the guy who just stopped you from making an even bigger knucklehead of yourself," Eddie said mildly.

The man glared belligerently at him but took in Eddie's size and staggered away without further incident. Eddie was on his way back to his own stand when he noted that across the midway, the blonde at the rootbeer booth was staring at him, as if noticing him for the first time. Then, catching his gaze, she quickly turned away and returned to work.

But come midnight, closing time, Eddie was startled to find the blonde standing at his counter, asking, "Your name's Eddie, right?"

"Uh . . . yeah, that's right."

"See? I've got a good memory, just bad manners." She smiled sheepishly. "A girl gets so many come-ons in this business, she starts thinking every guy who looks at her cockeyed is a wolf she's got to beat off with a stick. And I was having a bad day too. Sorry."

"Oh, well . . . that's okay," Eddie said magnanimously.

"My name's Adele Worth. I'm on my way over to the sideshow, we're putting together a little party. You want to come along?"

Eddie was surprised but pleased. "Sure."

"It's potluck, you got anything left over?"

Eddie filled a big bucket with cotton candy and another with popcorn; Adele cadged a tub of fries from the hot-dog vendor. As they made their way to the sideshow tent, Eddie asked, "So how long you worked here?"

"Two seasons. But it's just a summer job. I'm really a movie actress."

Eddie tried not to sound incredulous. "You are?"

"I was in a bunch of two-reelers when I was a little girl. Fort Lee used to be the motion picture capital of the world, didn't you know?"

Eddie had to admit that no, he hadn't.

"I haven't done any pictures in a while," Adele admitted. "The directors say my eyes don't photograph well because they're so light. I'm waiting for Technicolor to become standard, then I think they'll be an asset."

"I think your eyes are beautiful," Eddie said. "Or was that a come-on?"

She laughed. "Probably. But I'll take it as a compliment instead."

They arrived at the tent housing the Palisades Park Circus Side Show—or, as Eddie knew it from the carny, a "ten-in-one," ten acts under one tent. A line of colorful banners flapped in the breeze, each displaying illustrations of the attractions alongside breathless prose:

ALL ACTS ALIVE ON THE INSIDE!

FATTEST WOMAN IN THE WORLD—JOLLY IRENE!

SUSI, THE ELEPHANT SKIN GIRL!

CHARLES PHELAN, STRONG MAN!

VICTOR-VICTORIA—HALF MAN, HALF WOMAN!

HOPPE THE FROG BOY!

They went around back, where Jolly Irene, all six hundred and fifty pounds of her, was reclining on a divan big enough to seat three people, eating pizza pies—she had several stacked up beside her—consuming them as if they were Communion wafers. Her real name was Amanda Siebert, and her husband, George, was the sideshow's inside talker. Amanda was usually a featured performer at Coney Island, but Adolph

Schwartz, the sideshow manager, lured her to Palisades for the season. "I was born in Jersey City," Amanda told them. "I got a soft spot for Palisades."

Adele said, "I like your act. How you joke around with the audience."

"Nobody likes a sad fat girl, honey. I'm not some skinny film star like Vilma Banky and I know it, so why not have a laugh about it? Besides, what do I have to be sad about? I probably make more money than Vilma Banky, I've got a wonderful husband, and I can eat whatever I want."

"And you're a star," Adele said, with noticeable envy.

"Star, hell. I'm a whole galaxy!" Amanda laughed.

Eddie knew that a good fat lady could command a lot of money, even in bad times like these; but it still seemed odd to him that a beautiful girl like Adele should envy the life of a freak.

Soon, three more performers arrived: Charlotte Vogel, aka Susi the Elephant Skin Girl, and Julius and Erna Keuhnel, who, like Charlotte, came from Germany. Julius was Charlotte's manager and she lived with them in their apartment in Manhattan. "You do the magic act, don't you, Mrs. Keuhnel?" Adele said. "You don't see many women magicians around."

"Yes, well, if women now have the right to vote," Mrs. Keuhnel said wryly, "why should we not have the right to saw other women in half?"

Charlotte—Susi—was a young German woman who suffered from ichthyosis, her skin resembling the thick, gray hide of an elephant, though her face was normal and quite pretty. Like Irene, she had performed at Coney, where she said she'd had one particularly ardent fan:

"There was a gentleman, if you wish to call him that, who came to every one of my shows and began loitering around the tents waiting for me to leave. Eventually he proposed marriage. And when I turned him down, he went right to work making time with Lena the Leopard Girl!"

Amanda hooted at that. "Oh, I had a couple guys like that. One wanted me to sit on his face. I told him, 'Are you nuts? I'll kill you!' He said, 'Yes, but I'd die a happy man!'" After a burst of laughter all around, Amanda said, with a tender glance toward her husband, "Boy, was I ever lucky to find George. See what he gave me last year for our eighth wedding anniversary?" She showed off a jeweled wristwatch that glinted even in the dimness. Adele and Charlotte cooed enviously at it, but it seemed to Eddie that "Susi" was envying more than just a piece of jewelry.

After an hour of convivial talk, the party broke up and Eddie and Adele walked together down to Palisade Avenue. "We had an alligator-skin girl on the Sheeshley Show," Eddie recalled, "but she wasn't as smart and sweet as Susi—Charlotte. She just seemed kind of . . . damaged."

"Everybody's damaged," Adele said offhandedly. "Susi just has hers on the outside."

Eddie didn't know how to respond to that, but knew he didn't want the evening to end. He offered to buy coffee at Joe's Restaurant across the street, where they slid into a booth and ordered some joe. Adele talked a little about her family—she lived with her parents and two brothers on Cumbermeade Road in Fort Lee—then asked, "So you're from Jersey?"

"Yeah, Newark. I left home a long time ago, though, to work carnies."

"Your folks must have been happy to see you again."

"I . . . haven't been back." He hesitated, then felt obligated to explain, "My dad is dead. He was killed in a foundry accident."

"Oh God, I'm so sorry."

"S'okay. It was a long time ago—1923."

Such a foolish whim—pulling back the sheet covering his father's body so he could say goodbye. Jack Stopka had been killed when a mold being filled with molten steel broke loose and fell on him. What remained no longer looked anything like Eddie's dad; there was nothing left to say goodbye to. But the image had seared itself into his memory.

Eddie blinked back tears and hoped Adele couldn't tell.

"What about your mom?" Adele asked.

"She remarried a couple years later," Eddie said, the words still bitter in his mouth. "An art teacher at a vocational school. Guy named Sergei."

Just saying the name, he felt again the sting of Sergei's hand across his face, and, later, the pummeling of his fists.

"We—didn't get along," Eddie said. "My grades were never good enough, and I wasn't artistic like my mom and sister—I liked carpentry. One day I was helping our neighbor repair the banister on his door stoop, when Sergei came out of nowhere, his fist slamming like a lug wrench into my face." Adele's eyes widened. "He screamed how I was disgracing his name—I was a Bajorek now, not some 'peasant,' some common laborer. Like my dad." Eddie's eyes flashed with anger. "And *that* was when he was cold sober."

"Your mother—she didn't try to stop him?"

"No," Eddie said quietly. "He never hit my sister. I guess she thought I could take care of myself."

But worse than all the violence was the day Eddie entered his room and saw his bed blanketed with gaily colored pieces of cardboard—like confetti. He quailed as he saw them for what they were: the meticulously shredded remains of his cherished baseball cards. Numbly he scooped up a handful, recognizing here and there a scrap of a favorite card his father had brought home, Ty Cobb or Babe Ruth. He sat there a long while, crying, then carefully gathered up the tatters and dropped them into a wastebasket, where they settled like debris from a long-vanished parade.

That night at dinner, Sergei had said without even looking up from his plate, "Now maybe you will have more time to tend to your studies."

Eddie told Adele, "I caught out on the first train to anywhere else." Anxious to change the subject: "So what does your dad do for a living?"

It was Adele's turn to hesitate. "He's . . . retired. He used to direct movies here in Fort Lee. Worth While Pictures, his company was called."

"And you starred in some of his pictures?"

Her face lit up. "My first was called *Babe in Arms,* I was just six months old. I don't remember a thing about that, but I'll never forget the ones we shot at Rambo's Hotel in Coytesville—at lunch we'd all sit outside under a grape arbor, eating the same meal every day: ham and eggs, biscuits, and fresh apple pie. I even sat in Douglas Fairbanks's lap on one shoot."

"No kidding?"

"I met Blanche Sweet too. And Daddy would always kiss me on the cheek after I did a take he liked. He used to call me his 'little star'—'My beautiful girl who will someday be the whole world's beautiful girl.'" Then, embarrassed, she quickly added, "Didn't quite pan out that way."

"Not yet, anyway."

She smiled at that. "I was Miss Bergen County of 1927, I thought that might help me land some parts, but no soap. I came to Palisades because the Schencks are in the picture business—they don't spend much time here, but you never know when you might be spotted by somebody who knows somebody, so I try to get around the park, meet people." The light in her eyes had dimmed; she looked at her watch. "It's late. I should be getting home."

"I'll take you."

"That's okay. Just walk me to the trolley stop."

As the northbound trolley approached, he told her, "I had a nice time tonight, Adele."

"So did I, Eddie," she said. She squeezed his hand. He took that as a signal and leaned in and kissed her—a light, gentlemanly kiss—on the lips.

The trolley clanged to a stop. Adele said, "See you back on the midway," then boarded the streetcar, which continued down Palisade Avenue and into Fort Lee. Eddie looked after it, a big dreamy smile on his face, and decided it was such a nice night he would walk home.

If he hadn't saved that poor kitten, Adele might never have given him a second glance. But his kindness made her ashamed for how she had treated him. When by way of apology she invited him to the sideshow party, he broke into the sweetest smile, making her very glad that she had.

Now that she really looked at him, too, he was a pretty good-looking guy . . . an open, honest face, wide shoulders, a nice build. The evening lasted longer than she'd planned, but she didn't mind—she found that she liked him, liked being around him. He was down-to-earth, good-hearted, uncomplicated. God knows she had enough complications in her life.

And that smile of his warmed her in ways few things had of late.

It wasn't an easy courtship, since concession agents worked seven days a week, but they were able to share some egg foo yung at Yuan Chen's or a midnight dinner at Joe's. And on days of bad weather and slow business, they could visit each other's stands as much as they wanted. There was nothing so miserable as an amusement park on a rainy day: sheets of mist rippled across the empty midway like watery carpets being shaken out; the roar of the roller coasters, rudely silenced, was replaced by the incessant beat of rain on a concession's wooden or canvas roof; everywhere you looked were the glum faces of concessionaires sitting in their booths, smoking, playing solitaire, and above all, losing money.

On one wet day in June, Eddie was loitering at Adele's empty root-beer stand, making her laugh with some carny story of his, when she suddenly looked past him and said, "Holy cow, will you look at that."

Arthur Holden—the durable, champion high diver who had been appearing at Palisades since 1908—was striding casually up the midway in his white diving trunks. Tall, slender, graying, Holden was trim and fit for his age—fifty-three, though he liked to tell people he was eight years older because it sounded more impressive—and presumably on his way to his twice-daily dive from a 122-foot platform into a tank filled with five feet of water.

"Art," Adele called out, "where do you think *you're* going?"

"It's almost four o'clock," Holden replied. "Time for my first show."

"There's more water out here than there is in your tank!"

"This? This is nothing." Holden took time to walk over to them, smiled. "Back in 1915, I think it was, there was a terrific cloudburst that came out of nowhere. I was standing atop a ninety-foot pole when a bolt of lightning suddenly hit one of the guy wires, threw me off balance, and I fell off the platform like a sack of russet potatoes."

"Jesus," Eddie said. "What happened?"

"I twisted and turned in midair, trying to right myself, but I hit the edge of the tank with my right shoulder and I was knocked cold. Luckily I just dislocated my shoulder, and I was back to work within the week. Now *that* was a rainstorm!" He looked up at the drizzle falling from cloudy skies and scoffed, "This is just nature taking a piss on me, that's all."

They laughed as, trouper that he was, he headed for the free-act stage.

The weather cleared up by evening, and Adele got wind of another impromptu party being planned for after closing. She hurried across the midway to tell Eddie: "Pool party tonight!"

"What?" he said. "But I don't have any swim trunks."

"There's plenty in the bathing pavilion." She gave him a grin. "Or you can swim in your underwear. C'mon, it'll be fun."

The Palisades pool was drained each night, a million and a half gallons of salt water emptied back into the Hudson River from which it had been pumped the previous night. Massive filters purified the water before any bather ever dipped a toe in it. It took hours to drain and employees were technically prohibited from swimming after closing, but the pool manager, Phil Smith, appeared not to notice as Eddie, Adele, and a few other concessionaires, men and women, slipped into the bathing pavilion. Johnny Duke gave them a wink as he left.

The first time Adele saw Eddie in bathing trunks—his lean, muscled body and incongruously boyish face—she felt a thrill pass through her. Eddie was similarly impressed by the way she filled out her swimsuit.

"Last one in's a rotten egg foo yung," Adele said, and raced down the beach. The pool was about two-thirds full; once in the water the men and women paired off, stealing kisses beneath a faint sliver of a moon.

Eddie did the same with Adele. She didn't object.

Adele suggested, "Let's go swim under the waterfall."

They swam to the back of the pool and through the falls, which pelted them like a heavy rain. In addition to its roar they could now hear the hum of the motors that powered the pool's artificial wave machine, and they saw the tangle of pipes that fed water to the falls. There wasn't a lot of room back here but the water was shallow enough for them to stand. Screened from prying eyes by the curtain of water, Adele draped her arms around Eddie's neck and kissed him with a hunger that surprised and aroused him. He slipped his arms around her waist to draw her closer, but she said, "Wait."

She stepped back, and to Eddie's astonishment began to undo the straps of her swimsuit, wriggling out of it until it floated like a jellyfish on the water. She stood there completely nude, the water just covering, though hardly obscuring, her beautiful breasts. They embraced and kissed with an urgency Eddie had never known before. The roar of the falls muted the sounds of their lovemaking, their pleasure magnified by the sensuality of the water as well as the danger, however small, of being discovered.

Finally, Adele slipped back into her swimsuit, then took Eddie's hand as they dove under the falls. As they broke surface again Eddie took a big gulp of the briny air. They looked at each other and giggled. Eddie wished the sun would never come up, that he could feel this way forever.

It wasn't until the next day, when he happened to glance at the calendar tacked up on the inside of his coat closet, that Eddie realized what day it was yesterday. He looked at the date and laughed.

June 24, 1930: St. John the Baptist Day.

In late August, after Adele had missed two of her periods, she went not to her family doctor but to one she picked out of the phone book. When the test confirmed her suspicion, she worked up her nerve over dinner one night and said, "Eddie, I . . . I'm pregnant."

To her relief she saw joy, not horror, on his face. "You're sure?"

She nodded.

"That's swell," Eddie said, breaking into that big endearing smile of his. "That's just terrific." Then, trying to read her face: "Isn't it?"

She smiled. "Yes. I think so."

Eddie quickly proposed marriage. Adele wasted no time accepting.

But now came the moment she had long dreaded: when she informed her parents, they quite naturally wanted to meet their prospective son-in-law.

"So this is the man my little star wants to marry," Franklin Worth said, soberly shaking Eddie's hand. "Pleasure to meet you, son."

"Thank you, sir, I'm pleased to meet you."

Adele was relieved—her father seemed to be on his best behavior. As they sat down to a dinner of ham, biscuits, and sweet potatoes, Franklin told charming stories of his precocious, performing daughter. "Her first featured role was in a picture called *Lost in the Pine Barrens*," he said, reaching for his coffee cup. "Adele was the little girl who leads her idiot parents out of the woods. She was only three years old, but a beauty even then." He took a swallow, added, "We shot it in Coytesville, where one of Edison's so-called 'detectives' tried to shut us down by confiscating my camera."

A shiver of dread spidered down Adele's spine.

"Thomas Edison?" Eddie said. "He invented the movies, right?"

That ignited a spark of fury in Franklin's eyes. "Oh, that's what he'd like you to *believe,*" he said acidly. "But he only created the Kinetoscope, which you had to view like a peep show! The Lumière brothers of France invented the projection process that's used today, not Edison."

Franklin put down his cup, and now Adele, sitting opposite it, caught a whiff of what was in it—and it wasn't coffee.

"That miserable son of a bitch, pardon my French," Franklin said, warming to his subject, "tried to put independents like me out of business. He sent goon squads to disrupt our shooting—one thug split open my camera like a cantaloupe, ruined an entire reel." He took another swig from his cup. "Thomas Alva Edishit, that's how he was known in *this* house."

Adele's hopes foundered in the bitter seas that had once again claimed her father, his conversation degenerating into stinging recriminations about Edison, about Hoover, and how, in the face of the coal shortage, movie companies fled to warmer climes like California and motion picture production in Fort Lee became nearly as mythical a beast as the Jersey Devil.

"Why didn't you go to California, too, then?" Eddie asked innocently.

His eyes not quite focusing, Franklin stared down at his dinner plate and muttered, "I . . . I had obligations. Debt. I had a wife and three children to think of. So I did the responsible thing—stayed here, worked to pay off the debt. And I did it." He threw his wife a sullen look. "Didn't I, Marie?"

Marie winced even as she agreed, "Yes, Franklin. You did."

Franklin pushed away from the table and stalked into the kitchen, presumably for another shot of the bootleg whisky he had hidden there.

Adele glanced at Eddie; the shock on his face was easy to read.

When Franklin returned, Eddie waited an appropriate number of minutes before announcing, "Gosh, this has been swell, but we've got to get back to the park—they only gave us half a day off. Right, Adele?"

The two of them had actually wangled the whole day off, but Adele quickly concurred, "Yes, that's right."

Franklin muttered a goodbye and headed for his den, where, as usual, he could retreat into his bottle like a worm in tequila.

As Eddie and Adele walked away from the house, she thought: *That's it. It's over. And I'm pregnant. Oh God, what am I going to do?*

After walking in silence a long while, Eddie finally spoke up.

"That can't be a picnic for you," he said quietly.

"No," she said. "Not hardly."

He waited a moment before adding, "You must want to get out of there pretty bad."

Tears welled in her eyes. "You can't imagine."

"Oh, I think I can." He stopped in mid-stride, looked at her. "Adele, just tell me straight: do you love me?"

She looked into his eyes, saw the fear and hurt in them, and she said, "I do, Eddie. Yes, I want to get out of there. But I really do love you."

He took her hand in his, and that big smile of his made her smile.

"I love you too," he said. "So let's get married."

When word of their engagement got out, the park's publicist, Perry Charles, came to Eddie and Adele with a curious offer: "Palisades will pay all your wedding expenses," he told them, "ring, bridal gown, license, even a three-day honeymoon in Atlantic City—if you get married on our Carousel."

Eddie laughed, then realized, "You're not kidding."

"No, trust me, it'll be a great stunt. I guarantee it'll make all the papers, and I bet we can get Pathé or Fox to cover it too."

Publicity—which might be seen by his family—was the last thing Eddie wanted. It also reminded him a bit too much of the carny tradition of a "*Billboard* wedding": couples sent a notice to the trade paper that they intended to live together as man and wife, and after the carnival closed for the night, they boarded a Carousel, someone waved a copy of *The Bill-*

board over their heads like a sacrament, and the couple simply cohabited together.

But Adele was transported by the idea:

"Oh, Eddie, the newsreels! What if some producer sees my picture and offers me a part? What an opportunity!"

She was so excited, Eddie couldn't bring himself to say no.

And so that Labor Day weekend, Edward Stopka and Adele Worth began married life at Palisades Amusement Park, with Adele's family in attendance along with a park photographer and a newsreel cameraman. Franklin was stone sober and Marie seemed only slightly mortified as her daughter prepared to take her vows on a merry-go-round.

Adele, in her white bridal gown, sat astride a red-and-gold-painted pony. Eddie, wearing a black suit, and a justice of the peace climbed aboard adjacent horses. Perry Charles called, "Start 'er up!" and the Carousel began turning, with calliope music in place of a wedding march.

"Wait a minute!" Eddie cried out. "We're actually gonna *ride* this thing during the ceremony?"

"Of course!" Perry called back. "It's good action for the newsreel."

"Dearly beloveds," the justice of the peace began, "we are gathered here today to join this man and this woman in holy matrimony . . ."

But he kept rising and falling along with the horse he was riding, as did Eddie and Adele; they could barely hear him over the din of the calliope.

By the time they got to the vows, Adele was coming down with motion sickness and having a hard time maintaining her sweet smile.

"Do you, Edward, take this woman, Adele . . ."

The real trick for Eddie was slipping the wedding ring onto Adele's finger, when they were sitting two feet apart and kept bobbing up and down. "Please hurry," she implored, "before I throw up."

"Maybe I should grab one of the goddamn brass rings instead," Eddie muttered. But finally he got the ring on, the J.P. pronounced them man and wife, and they even managed to kiss without falling off their ponies.

When at long last the Carousel came to a stop, Perry announced, "Now for the wedding photo!"

Adele posed astride her pony, while Eddie held on to a brass pole as he leaned in to kiss the bride. He felt like a horse's ass, but at least he wasn't the most prominent one in the picture.

The wire services captioned the photo:

HORSIN' AROUND ON THE MARRY-GO-ROUND

Mr. and Mrs. Edward Stopka take their vows on the Carousel at Palisades Amusement Park in Cliffside Park, N.J. No word yet on whether the lucky couple will be honeymooning in the Old Mill!

But Adele truly didn't mind getting married on a merry-go-round, because she'd been riding one for years—and now that the ceremony was over, she was finally able to jump off it.

Seven months later, on March 23, 1931, Antoinette Cherie Stopka was born. When she was old enough to use it, her playpen would be a big wooden crate with bits of straw, which once contained the pieces of "fine imported china"—from the Hex Manufacturing Company of Buffalo, New York—that were among the prizes in Jackie Bloom's cat game. But Antoinette would want for little else; Eddie had taken an off-season job at the Grantwood Lumber Yard—only part time, but he was lucky to get any work in this worsening Depression.

It was Adele who picked their daughter's name, wanting something European and feminine, and though Antoinette herself would come to soundly despise it, she would be mercifully unaware of the others her mother considered—Huguette, Twyla, Zéphyrine—and of how much worse, really, it might have been. "Antoinette" conjured images of elegant Parisian ladies wearing taffeta gowns trimmed with lace, dancing to lovely waltzes with dapper Frenchmen. Adele wanted that for her daughter, wanted her to be poised and feminine—she was thrilled at the prospect of having someone with whom she could share all the things she loved, someone she could dress in fashionable clothes, show how to apply makeup and walk in heels, as her mother had shown her. And who knew? Maybe Antoinette would grow up to be an actress too, and they could both make Franklin proud.

She was a pretty, fair-skinned baby with plump cheeks and a wisp of blonde hair that would soon darken to chestnut brown. Adele sometimes brought her to the home of Roscoe Schwarz and his family, whose house on Palisade Avenue adjoined the amusement park, to play with the Schwarzes' youngest daughters. But to Adele's dismay, as soon as Antoinette was old enough to walk she brushed past Hazel and Dorothy's dolls and made a beeline toward eleven-year-old Laurent's set of toy trucks.

As Antoinette began pushing one of the tin vehicles back and forth, she provided her own sound effects: "Vrooom! Vrooom!"

Laurent smiled in bemusement. "That's pretty good vrooming," he said, "for a girl. 'Specially a little one like you."

Getting down on his knees, he began pushing another truck toward hers, veering away at the last moment, rolling the truck end over end while making crashing sounds befitting a two-car collision. Antoinette laughed delightedly and began preparing for another exciting traffic accident.

It was Adele's first clue that perhaps everything might not be proceeding according to plan.

3

Palisades, New Jersey, 1935

In May of 1935, Nicholas Schenck—eager to rid himself of a failing amusement park—granted a lease with option to buy to Jack and Irving Rosenthal, whose careers in amusement began when Irving was all of ten years old and Jack, twelve. At Coney Island, the brothers overheard a pail-and-shovel concessionaire grumbling that he would sell his entire stock for fifty bucks. The brothers promptly wheedled the money from their Uncle Louis and bought their first concession. When a tourist boat would arrive, Irving, at one end of the pier, distributed pails and shovels to every kid who walked off the ferry. At the other end Jack informed the parents, "Your child just bought a pail and shovel, five cents, please." By then the kids were spot-welded to their new toys and the parents grudgingly forked over the nickel. It probably didn't hurt that the two smiling little extortionists were barely out of knee pants themselves. That summer they earned more than fifteen hundred dollars.

They went on to operate rides and concessions at Savin Rock Park in Connecticut, and turned around the fading Golden City Park Arena in Brooklyn. Their earnings paid for their education—Irving studied dentistry and Jack became a concert violinist with the Cincinnati Symphony—but as Irving put it, "I always liked the sound of a merry-go-round better than a dentist's drill," and soon they were back, building the Cyclone coaster at Coney.

Now, at Palisades, they hired amusement veterans Al and Joseph McKee. Al would serve as general superintendent and brother Joe, an expert in roller-coaster design, would supervise the operation of the park's rides. They also hired PR man Bert Nevins, who arranged a cross-promotion with Hearn's Department Store in Manhattan, where thousands of free tickets for children to Palisades were distributed.

Some of the Rosenthals' business decisions were met with skepticism. One was the installation of their niece, Anna Halpin—a tiny but formidable brunette—as manager of park operations. Some longtime employees complained that at thirty years old she was too young to be running a park this size—or maybe just too female. Several ride operators griped that she often came by and watched them like a hawk as they worked.

But the Rosenthals' other decision was one that would have more public consequences.

Eddie and Adele had moved to an apartment house on Bergen Boulevard, an end unit on the ground floor with a small terrace in the shade of a tall oak tree, where the children could play in the afternoon. But in autumn, when the wind gusted through the tree, it shook acorns out of the branches at least once every thirty seconds, strafing Antoinette and her one-year-younger brother, Jack—named for the grandfather he would never know—with a fusillade of acorns that went *Bam! Pop! Bam!* as they peppered the concrete. Far from discouraged, she and Jack would retreat under a wooden crate or cardboard box and pretend they were taking tommy-gun fire from Jimmy Cagney, ducking out long enough to cry "You dirty rat!" and fire their Wyandotte water pistols at the imaginary Cagney.

The apartment was close enough that Eddie could walk to Palisades as Adele took the children to Marie's, who babysat them while their parents worked. Marie adored them, as did Franklin, who remarkably even drank less when they were around. He would hoist Antoinette up into the air and call her "my baby's baby," which Adele found quietly touching. "She's good for him," Marie confided to Adele. "I think she reminds him of you when you were small, before everything started to go wrong for him."

Business at the park had been modestly encouraging since it opened under the new management at the end of May, and Eddie was feeling cautiously optimistic. But his bright mood was dispelled on an otherwise sunny morning in June when, as he was making his way south down Palisade Avenue in Fort Lee, he recognized a familiar figure heading toward him from the opposite direction. It was Arthur Holden.

Eddie felt awkward as hell, but as he drew closer he put on a cheery smile and called out, "Hey, Art, how's it going?"

Holden cut a far different figure from the dashing performer who used to stride confidently down the midway. As Arthur approached, Eddie could see that physically he appeared fine—no limp or any other after-effect from a car accident that had sidelined him last season—but there was a sadness and loss in his face that almost made Eddie's heart break.

"Hello, Eddie," he said with a smile, the two men shaking hands as they met. "Off to the park?"

"Yeah, back to the grind," Eddie said. "You're looking good, Art."

"I feel good. Good as ever. That's the hell of it."

Although fully recuperated from his accident, Holden had not been engaged by the Rosenthals for another season at Palisades. "They think I'm washed up," Arthur said bitterly, "but I'm not. I can still do the act, Eddie, if only they'd give me a chance."

Eddie didn't know what to say, but Holden had enough to say for both of them: "Hell, do you know how many bones I've broken over the years? Both legs, three times apiece! Fractured a dozen ribs, my right foot, my left arm . . . not counting all the times I've been knocked cold hitting the side of the tank. And I always came back from it! Like I can now."

"I know, that's rough luck," Eddie said. "Say, you used to play Olympic Park, didn't you? Have you tried them? Or Coney Island?"

"Nobody wants to take a chance on a fifty-eight-year-old high diver," Holden said bleakly. "Florence and I have been on relief for months."

"Jeez, Art, I'm sorry, I didn't know," Eddie said. "You need some cash? I can spot you twenty bucks if you need it."

Arthur seemed touched by that and put a hand on Eddie's shoulder. "Thanks, Eddie, that's damned nice of you. But all I really need is an-other chance to show what I can do. I guess I've just got to start all over again, like I did in Brooklyn. And if I can't cut it, well, better to be out of the picture than just a sad old relic gathering dust."

He held out his hand again and Eddie took it. "All of you at Palisades, you've been like a family to me," he said with a melancholy smile. "I really appreciate it. Take it easy, Eddie."

"Yeah," Eddie said, feeling the opposite, a vague unease, "you too, Art."

Holden strode away, continuing north on Palisade Avenue as Eddie continued south—disturbed, he couldn't say why, by the whole meeting. It did seem as if Arthur had gotten a raw deal, but he wasn't the only performer the Rosenthals had dropped, and Eddie suspected it was as much about their wanting to bring in new acts as about Arthur's age or health.

Still, it was the man's tone and manner—as if his life were effectively over—that bothered Eddie. And when he talked about starting over, "like in Brooklyn"—Arthur wasn't from Brooklyn, was he? And "better to be out of the picture"—what the hell did that mean?

Eddie walked on, and it wasn't for another ten minutes that it came back to him: the story Arthur had once told him about how he'd gotten his start as a high diver, how he'd made a name for himself.

He had jumped off the Brooklyn Bridge.

Eddie made a fast about-face. Arthur was now a distant figure making his way up Palisade Avenue, already having passed the strip of roadhouses and hot-dog stands, like Costa's and Hiram's, on each side of the street.

Eddie knew with a cold certainty that there was only one place he could be heading and began hurrying after his friend. He called out to him, but either Eddie was too far away or Holden chose not to hear. Eddie quickened his pace, trying to close the gap between them.

Arthur veered to the right, onto a side street.

Eddie ran as if he had a railroad bull hot on his heels. When he finally turned onto that same side street, he knew, of course, what he would see.

He was standing on the shoulder of the concourse that led to the George Washington Bridge, its latticed steel tower looking uncomfortably like a memorial arch in a fools' graveyard.

Scores of cars were being funneled through that arch. Amid the noise and commotion, Eddie saw no sign of Arthur; but there was only one place he could have gone.

Eddie ran up to the bridge, flipped a dime into the toll booth for the pedestrian toll, and hurried up the walkway on the right. He had no idea whether Arthur had taken the right-hand path or the left, so he tried to take in as much of the other side of the bridge as he could through the shifting kaleidoscope of cars whizzing by on the roadway.

Eddie had to stop for breath a few times, having been running flat-out for the past fifteen minutes, but when he was a third of the way across the bridge he saw someone up ahead at about the halfway point— standing at the low pedestrian railing, looking down at the river below.

Eddie redoubled his pace as, up ahead, Arthur began peeling off his clothes, stepping out of his shoes, unbuttoning his shirt.

"Art! No!" Eddie shouted over the traffic noise.

Somehow Arthur heard him and looked up—but though he appeared surprised to see Eddie, it didn't give him any pause. He shrugged off his shirt and began unbuckling his belt.

"Jesus, Art!" Eddie cried again, drawing closer. "Don't do it!"

Arthur's trousers fell, revealing his white diving trunks underneath.

"Eddie," he called out, "I've got to!"

Arthur stepped out of his trousers just as Eddie ran up, winded and pleading, "Art, please, it's got to be a three-hundred-foot drop from here!"

"Oh no," Holden corrected him, "only two hundred and fifty-seven."

"You'll be killed, is that what you want?"

"No, no! I'm just going to show the Rosenthals I've still got what it takes, that's all. Like when I jumped off the Brooklyn Bridge."

"Yeah? How high was that?" Eddie asked, stalling desperately.

"Hundred and nineteen feet."

"My God, Art, this is twice as high!"

"Well," Arthur said brightly, "I'm twice as good as I was then."

Eddie was groping for a reply when he heard the wail of a siren and turned to see a police car weaving in and out of the bridge traffic, cutting off at least two cars before it pulled to the shoulder with a squeal of brakes, just feet from where Arthur stood. A uniformed cop immediately jumped out of the car and called out: "Mr. Holden, stop! Fred Stengel, Fort Lee Police!"

"Aw, hell," Arthur said dejectedly, "what is this, a convention?"

"Don't do it," the officer told him as he approached. "Your wife called us. She begs you not to jump!"

"How did Flo know I was coming here?"

"She saw you put on your bathing suit before you left the house. She doesn't want to be a widow, Mr. Holden."

Holden looked at the cop, and there was a weariness in his voice that echoed the tone Eddie had heard on Palisade Avenue: "I'm just so tired of being out of work. Of feeling worthless."

"You're not worthless, Art," Eddie said.

"Who the fuck are you?" the cop demanded.

"A friend of his from the park."

"The park? Is this a publicity stunt, did they arrange this . . . ?"

"Oh, *shit*," Arthur snapped with uncharacteristic indelicacy, "you've both just gone and ruined this whole thing. Would've been a grand dive, too. I hope you're damn well satisfied with yourselves!"

With that, he picked up his pants and put them back on. When he'd finished dressing, Officer Stengel apologetically took him into custody.

Arthur was charged with disorderly conduct and held a few hours in the Fort Lee jail, then released in the custody of his wife pending a hearing.

Less than a week later he received a suspended sentence in exchange for a promise to the judge that he would not attempt again to dive off the George Washington Bridge. Arthur gladly agreed, since that morning he had been rehired by the Rosenthals to return to Palisades Park.

The day of his triumphant comeback happened to be one on which Marie had brought Antoinette and Jack to the park, and Eddie, wanting to share in Arthur's victory, got Lew to cover for him as he, Marie, and the kids went over to the free-act stage at four o'clock. Eddie lifted Antoinette onto his shoulders so she could see; Marie hoisted Jack up into her arms. They watched as Holden strode onstage in his white diving trunks, basked in a round of applause from the audience, then began to climb the one-hundred-and-twenty-foot ladder.

"Daddy, what's he doing?" Antoinette asked.

"He's going to jump into that tank over there."

Her eyes followed Holden all the way to the small platform at the top. He walked out to the edge of the diving board—and jumped.

Antoinette gasped as he sprang off the platform, doing a backward somersault, his body gracefully turning over in midair, then plummeting down, down—plunging feetfirst into his customary five feet of water.

Antoinette's eyes were wide with amazement.

"Oooh," she said, a sigh of both wonder and delight.

Arthur climbed out of the tank, unhurt and unfazed by his long fall. He raised a hand to the crowd, which burst into applause.

So did Antoinette, her little hands clapping together gleefully as she watched the silver-haired diver take his bows.

Jack Rosenthal showed up for work every morning at eight A.M., always sporting a light-colored suit, spats, and a cane. When Eddie arrived around ten thirty he was amused to hear the sound of violin music issuing from the administration building—Jack, on his coffee break, filling the amusement park not with the sounds of a calliope, but a Mozart prelude.

The Rosenthals were sticklers for cleanliness—insisting that every stand be regularly scrubbed inside and out, even fining concessionaires five dollars for every burned-out lightbulb on their marquee. Irving Rosenthal spent more of his time at first managing the brothers' interests in Coney Island, but when he did show up—always wearing a dark blue or black suit—he would patrol the midways, assuring himself that each ride and concession was spotless and that all refreshments were up to snuff. Anna Halpin made certain that these rules were strictly complied with, and Eddie was beginning to share some of the other men's resentment toward her.

So each Friday morning Eddie and Lew would scrub down the candy stand until it shined . . . until one Friday in late June when Eddie had to do it on his own, since Lew was nowhere to be found. As the morning wore on, Lew continued to be a no-show, and Eddie had to stock the shelves by himself. It wasn't until eleven thirty that Eddie found out why, when Anna Halpin herself appeared unexpectedly at the stand and announced, "You're Eddie, right? Lew's having his appendix taken out. Show me what he does."

"What?"

She entered the stand through the side door. "Show me what he does, I'll fill in for him until Chief Borrell can find somebody else to bring in."

Eddie was momentarily nonplussed. "Uh, Mrs. Halpin, you're going to get your nice dress all sticky and dirty."

She just laughed. "If I cared a hoot about that I wouldn't have lasted five minutes in this business. I've handled a popcorn popper before but not a candy floss machine—show me how it works."

Eddie did as he was asked, Mrs. Halpin observing as he put in a batch of sugar and pink food coloring, then switched on the heater and set the spinner to spinning. Halpin had a plain, serious face, but she smiled a little when the liquefied sugar was forced out of the spinner's holes: "Like a pasta maker," she said, "only with pink pasta." He demonstrated how to capture the pink strands on a stick, making an artful cloud of sugared cumulus. She nodded once, said, "Okay, I've got it," and made the next batch on her own, letter perfect. By the time the park opened at noon there were the requisite number of cotton candies in the display case waiting to be snapped up.

Eddie went into his grind, Mrs. Halpin working the counter, until his throat started to get sore and Anna stepped in and took over, even if she did have to stand on a couple of phone books at the counter:

"Cotton candy!" she cried out to the crowd. "Sweeter than a mother's kisses, lighter than a cloud! Get your cotton candy here, heaven on a stick!"

Goddamn, Eddie thought: she could actually build a tip. The stand enjoyed brisk business for the next hour; finally, during a lull, Eddie told her, "Nice grind. You've done this before?"

"Oh, I've done a little of everything," she said. "I started out working for my uncles at Savin Rock Park as a cashier. I carried change to the concessionaires, but I made it a point to watch every concession agent and ride operator to see how he did his job. By the time I became manager I could pinch-hit on almost anything, if need be."

"The rides, too?"

"Sure. I worked the Whip, the Water Scooter, the Airplane Swings . . . I may be small but I'm no weak sister." Now Eddie realized: she wasn't trying to catch Palisades' ride operators lying down on the job, she wanted to see how they *did* their job. "It's been a while since I've worked a grab stand, though. The past few years I was boxing promoter at Golden City Park Arena."

"You were?" he said, doing his best not to sound disbelieving.

She smiled at the skepticism in his voice. "We had a few comers we brought up at Golden City. Canada Lee, Tony Canzoneri . . ."

"Canzoneri? The guy who beat Lou Ambers for the lightweight title?"

Anna nodded. "Eddie, you know what I was going to be when I grew up? A piano teacher." She laughed. "Imagine that—me teaching kids to play 'Chopsticks' all day. I met my husband at that park too—that cashier's job was the best thing that could have happened to me."

A customer stepped up to buy a cotton candy, another asked for popcorn, and that was their last chance for small talk for the rest of the morning. By midafternoon Chief Borrell had brought in a man from one of his hot-dog stands to take Lew's place until he recuperated from his appendectomy. Eddie actually found himself sorry to see Anna return to the front office.

"Thanks, Mrs. Halpin," he said. "You can work my stand anytime."

"I'm here if you need me, Eddie," she told him—and he believed her. It wouldn't take her long to win over the remaining doubters.

Monday, July 1, was warm and sunny, a perfect day for the fifteen hundred visiting children—white, black, rich, poor—who, in May, had received free tickets to Palisades at Hearn's Department Store. They came from New York City, swarming eagerly over the park, riding the coasters, the Carousel, the miniature train, and flocking to the George Hamid circus troupe two blocks away, to be entertained by clowns, jugglers, acrobats, and the trained animals of Captain Walker's Jungle Wonders.

Most of those kids were at the circus at 4:45 that afternoon when Eddie—having just handed some cotton candy to an eight-year-old tyke, one of perhaps fifty left on the midway—felt his nose twitch at a familiar, ominous smell and then heard the cry most feared by carnies everywhere:

"Fire!"

Eddie's head jerked up. A park staffer was running up the midway, sounding the alarm—as behind him clouds of bilious black smoke rose from the Old Mill, only a few hundred yards down. Licks of flame charred the low wooden roof of the ride as cinders ignited the walls of the squat, rambling structure. In the time it took for Eddie to lock his cash register and jump the counter, the flames were consuming most of the Mill.

Other concessionaires now jumped their counters, the ones closest to the Mill unfurling a long fire hose. It quickly inflated and began spraying water onto the blaze like an elephant spitting water from its trunk.

Eddie looked across the midway to Adele's stand and saw her standing inside, frozen to the spot by the fiery spectacle. He ran across the midway, grabbed her by the wrist and said, "Get out of there! Hurry!"

That shook her out of her daze, and she quickly clambered over the counter. In the distance came the sound of approaching sirens.

But when they looked back at the fire they saw that the flames had spread to the Spitfire ride next door to the Old Mill. It was not lost on anyone that the fire was now blocking the path to the park's front gate.

Among the spectators were dozens of children standing there transfixed, drawn like moths to the raging fire and the billowing clouds of smoke. "Somebody's got to do something about all these kids," Adele said. Before Eddie could reply she ran up to a ten-year-old boy enraptured by the flames, grabbed him by his shoulders, and turned him around:

"Get out of here! Run!" she told him. "There's an exit by the pool, you know where that is?"

"Uh, yeah," the boy said, "I think so."

"Up to the end of the railway, turn left, run straight out! Go!"

The boy did as he was told and Adele rushed up to a young girl, giving her the same instructions. As Eddie got as many kids into the hands of Hearn's employees as he could, the Spitfire lived up to its name and began spewing hot cinders across the midway—where they quickly ignited the fencing around the Whip. From there the sparks jumped to the Fascination game booth next door, its canvas roof erupting into flames with a rush of air like the beating of giant wings. The flames raced down the roof supports as if they were fuses and in less than a minute the entire booth exploded.

Eddie could hear the crackle of timber being consumed and felt the heat being pushed up the midway on an easterly breeze. The smoke was so thick he could no longer make out the Old Mill, or what remained of it.

"Shit," he told Adele, "we've got to get out of here, now!"

They herded together as many kids as they could and led them to the Hudson gate near the pool. There were thousands of visitors hurrying to leave the park, but no panic, as park employees calmly guided people to the available exits. When Eddie and Adele reached the Hudson gate they found a fire company from Fort Lee waiting and left the children in their care.

By now the fire engines of seven communities—Fort Lee, Cliffside Park, Edgewater, Englewood, Leonia, Fairview, and Ridgefield—had begun converging on the park. The engines pulled up to Palisade Avenue, hooked up hoses to hydrants, and began dousing the flames, or trying to.

"There are still dozens of kids in there," Adele told the fire captain.

The smoke had now enveloped much of the midway; when Eddie looked back he could barely make out the rides through the sooty clouds. Captain McDermott organized his squad and asked for volunteers from among the park employees to help find and retrieve the remaining children. Eddie and about a dozen other men volunteered, and he soon found himself heading back into the conflagration.

Adele said, "Eddie, be careful—"

"I will," he promised. "Find a phone and call your mom, tell her you're okay. She's going to be worried when she hears about this."

By the time the firemen and volunteers made their way back to the main midway it was totally blacked out by smoke. In the midst of this false night Eddie and the others could hear the sounds of children crying in the darkness. Captain McDermott had the men put wet handkerchiefs over their mouths, then form a human chain behind him, the last man standing just outside the clouds of smoke, Eddie somewhere in the middle. It was hotter than hell, and the handkerchief didn't do much to filter the air. At the head of the chain the captain groped in the darkness until he found a child, passed him or her to the man behind him, then the next man, until finally reaching the end, where a fireman escorted the child out of the park.

Eddie coughed constantly, wondering if he was breathing in the incinerated remains of his own stand . . . or worse, some luckless person who had been trapped in the path of the flames.

Finally, after twenty minutes of shepherding children along the chain and assuring them everything would be all right, Eddie was relieved when McDermott called out, "That's the last of 'em," and gave the order to leave.

Once back outside the Hudson gate, Eddie coughed up black soot and drank down as much water as Adele could hand him, his throat coarse as sandpaper. They walked around to Palisade Avenue, where long fire hoses sprayed arcs of falling water onto the flames. As the Stopkas approached they saw Chief Borrell talking with the fire captain from Cliffside Park; when the Chief saw Eddie with his face smudged black from the smoke, he hurried up to him and asked, "Jeez, Ten Foot, you okay?"

"Yeah," Eddie said, "but I got a feeling your stand's seen better days."

"It's just wood and money, Eddie," the Chief said with a shrug.

By six o'clock the fire was finally out. When the smoke cleared it could be seen that one-eighth of Palisades was in ruins: a charred forest of smoldering building frames was all that remained of the park's northwest corner. Among the structures burned to the ground were the Old Mill, the Whip, the Spitfire, the Motor Parkway, the roller-skating rink, and fifteen concession stands and storerooms—including the Chief's candy stand.

But though ten firemen suffered from smoke inhalation, there were no serious casualties, and no fatalities. All the children, thanks to the quick thinking and heroism of the fire department, were sent safely home.

Almost as remarkable, no sooner were employees and concessionaires okayed to enter the grounds than a squad of workmen roped off the burnt area and began cleaning the soot from the seven-eighths of the park that was undamaged. Despite the cataclysm, that evening at nine P.M.

Palisades Amusement Park reopened for business. The indefatigable Arthur Holden performed his scheduled high dive, even though the tank he was diving into had been drained of a foot of its water in order to fight the blaze.

Since both their concessions had been wiped out, Eddie and Adele left and took the trolley to Marie and Frank's to pick up their children. There Eddie shouldered a drowsing Jack, who woke up long enough to sniff his shirt and declare, "Daddy, you smell." Eddie laughed: "Don't I know it." Marie, grateful that her daughter and son-in-law had escaped unscathed, drove them all home to Bergen Boulevard. It was only after Adele put the kids to bed and kissed them goodnight that she sat down at the kitchen table, covered her face with her hands, and collapsed into helpless tears—the stress and terror of the past five hours finally taking their toll. Eddie went to her and held her, feeling kind of shaky himself.

"Sssh, sshh," he said soothingly, "it's okay, we're all okay . . ."

"We could've been *killed*," Adele gasped out between sobs. "Antoinette and Jack could've been orphans!"

"But they're not. Everybody got out safe."

"Eddie, what if they'd been there? What if my mother had taken them to the pool today?"

"They still would've gotten out safely."

"I'll never let them set foot in that damned park again!"

"Fires can just as easily happen in apartment houses."

"Oh, go to hell," she snapped, but she only held him tighter.

When Eddie dropped by the park the next morning, he saw hundreds of workmen busily hosing down the midway, tearing down the gutted remains of rides, digging up the blackened stumps of trees, and rebuilding concession stands. Eddie helped out a little with the latter, cutting some corner posts and roof joists, until construction boss Joe McKee wandered by and told him, "If you think you're getting paid for this, you're nuts." Eddie laughed but McKee was serious: "For Chrissake, Eddie, you ate enough smoke yesterday to fill a chimney. Take a break, will ya?"

The park opened as usual at noon, and for the first time since his trip here in 1922, Eddie found himself at Palisades without a job to do. So he did something he'd wanted to do for years: take a roller-coaster ride. The

Big Scenic had suffered fire damage, the troublesome Cyclone had been demolished last year, so that left the Skyrocket. It was a great ride with steep climbs and stomach-churning hairpin curves—and at the summit of the first hill, Eddie looked down and saw again that enchanted island in the sky, no less magical than it had been thirteen years ago.

By July Fourth weekend, Eddie was working at a newly rebuilt stand with a brand-new cotton candy machine and popcorn popper, alongside the same old Lew (minus one appendix). Lew fancied himself a jaded carny who'd seen it all before, but even he was impressed: "Jumpin' Jesus," he said, chewing around his cigar. "These Rosenthal boys really mean *business.*"

After a brisk Fourth, life at the park proceeded as usual. In a publicity stunt, an American Indian wrestler named Chief Little Wolf began training for the world wrestling championship at Palisades and performed exhibitions in the ballroom. The ballroom manager, Clem White, also had a good instinct for musical acts, and "Whitey" belied his name with his interest in black jazz musicians. One of the first such bookings came in August, when the ballroom hosted an all-Negro band fronted by "Mrs. Louis Armstrong"—Lil Hardin Armstrong, Satchmo's wife and the composer of some of his biggest hits. The music drifting out of the ballroom that evening reminded Eddie of the blues songs he had heard down South, and he longed to visit the ballroom on dinner break, if Lew could spare him. "Yeah, sure," Lew said, "but God knows what you see in that nigger music."

There was a time this word, spoken as offhandedly as Lew used it, would not have drawn Eddie's attention. He might've even used it himself in the Ironbound, when players were selected for sandlot softball teams: *Okay, you get the Polack, the wop, and the Mick, and I'll take the nigger and the Jew.* It was, he thought then, more descriptive than derogatory.

Or so he thought until the day he was walking down a street in rural Alabama, and a young colored man walking ahead of him was suddenly set upon, like dogs on a crow, by three enraged white men. "Uppity coon," one of them spat out, "where the *hell* you think you're goin'?"

He punctuated the question with a fist into the man's solar plexus.

Doubled over in pain, the colored man tried to speak between gasps of air: "I—I was just goin'—to the drugstore—"

Eddie came running up and cried out, "Hey! What's going on?"

Cold, hateful eyes glared at him. "You takin' this *nigger*'s side?"

The word no longer sounded descriptive. It sounded like a cocked gun, ready to go off.

"But—what'd he *do*?" Eddie asked.

"He knows what he done," another man said. "Don'tcha?"

He kicked the colored man's legs out from under him, toppling him. Eddie jumped in, pushing the attacker away from the Negro. "Stop it!"

"Yankee Doodle's a nigger lover." The first man slugged Eddie in the jaw, staggering him. Then all three dogs were on him at once, hammering at his face, his stomach, and the coup de grâce, a boot-kick to the balls.

Eddie collapsed and blacked out.

When he awoke he found himself lying next to the colored man—face bruised, battered, and bleeding, like Eddie's—who was just coming around himself. Oddly, they were now on the opposite side of the street, as if dragged there. "You okay?" Eddie said, helping the man to his feet.

"Yeah. Thanks for tryin' to help. But it was my own damn fault."

"What was? What did you do?"

"I was in a hurry gettin' to the drugstore, and I went walkin' on the wrong side of the street. The white side."

Eddie was dumbstruck. He couldn't imagine this ever happening in the Ironbound.

He never used that word again, and couldn't hear it now, even from affable Lew, without seeing that young colored man's bloody, battered face.

When Eddie and Adele arrived in the Palisades ballroom they found the place packed with dancers—all white as the driven snow—stomping to a blend of swing, blues, and hot jazz tunes. Mrs. Armstrong was a handsome woman in her thirties wearing an elegant white gown and matching top hat, conducting the band with a baton when she wasn't herself performing at the piano. She attacked the keys with gusto, no daintiness about it, whether it was in the swing-flavored number "Hotter Than That" or the more down-tempo "Lonesome Blues," in which her forceful piano punctuated the mournful saxophone of George Clarke—the latter identified by Clem, who was standing at the back of the ballroom, beaming as he watched. "I just knew Palisades dancers would go for these colored bands in a big way," he told the Stopkas. "Never could convince the Schencks of it." Eddie and Adele even had time to do a little stomping of their own.

After half an hour they had to go back to work, and had been at it for less than an hour when Eddie, working the candy floss machine, heard a woman say, "I'll have a cotton candy, please, Eddie."

Something about the voice sent a jolt of adrenaline through him and he turned to find himself staring at a young woman in her early twenties, dark-haired, fair-skinned, with a nervous look on her pretty face.

Eddie said, "Viola?"

Whatever apprehension Eddie was feeling was quickly lost in the light of her smile. He jumped the counter and threw his arms around his sister.

"My God! Viola!" He took her in. "You're so beautiful!"

She laughed. "You look good too, Eddie. It's . . ." Her voice broke. "It's so good to see you again."

She began crying, and he embraced her again. "It's okay, Vi," he said. "I've missed you too."

But even as he held her, he couldn't help glancing up and around to see whether she was alone or not. From all appearances she was.

Adele, having seen all this from across the midway, wandered over to find out exactly who her husband was hugging, not once but twice.

"Honey," Eddie said, "this is my sister, Viola. Viola, I'd like you to meet my wife, Adele."

Adele, surprised, embraced her too. "It's so nice to meet you, Viola."

"Me too. You're even prettier than your picture in the paper."

"I like this girl, Eddie," Adele said with a wry grin.

As the crowd of customers at Eddie's stand grew larger he said, "Vi, I've got to work, but—can you stick around until the park closes, at midnight? Maybe we can go out and get some coffee . . . do you drink coffee?"

"I'd drink shoe polish if I could sit down and talk with you, Eddie," she said, which made him laugh and feel a stab of guilt at the same time.

"In some joints around here," Adele said, "shoe polish would be an improvement over the coffee."

Eddie said, "That's great, Vi, thanks. Let me get you that cotton candy too, all right? On the house."

At midnight Adele went to pick up the kids, allowing Eddie time alone with Viola: "You two have a lot to talk about, I'm sure."

Eddie and Viola walked over to Joe's Restaurant, ordered some hot coffee and slices of Boston cream pie, and Eddie said, "Jeez, it's good to see you again, Vi. I . . . I'm sorry it's been so long."

"Mama was glad to at least get those postcards you sent from the carnivals. At least she knew you were okay."

"You mentioned the picture in the paper—you saw it?"

She nodded. "I tore it out, though, before Mama and Sergei could see. It took me all this time to find the courage to come here. . . . I figured you had your reasons for staying away."

"It was never you, Vi. You saw how Sergei treated me. I was Jack Stopka's son, a constant reminder of the man Mom used to love, and he couldn't stand that." He looked at her. "You still living at home?"

"Not for much longer. I'm engaged. His name is Harold—Hal."

"That's great, Vi, I'm happy for you. And Mom and Grandma Lil? How are they?"

"Grandma passed away two years ago," Viola said.

"Oh, I'm sorry to hear it. She was a real character, wasn't she?"

She nodded. "For what it's worth she didn't think much of Sergei either. When Mom told her you'd run away, Grandma just looked at her, looked at Sergei, and said, 'What took him so long?'"

They both laughed heartily at that.

"Mama is fine but she misses you terribly. And I think she feels guilty, like she didn't stick up for you enough."

Eddie's eyes flashed with anger. "You mean, like she didn't lift a damn finger to stop Sergei from beating me."

"I know it's hard to forgive her that, I don't blame you for being angry. But I know it would mean a lot to her to see you. And her grandchildren."

Eddie considered that, then said quietly, "Vi . . . the day Sergei tore up my baseball cards, I went to bed but couldn't sleep. I heard him and Mom on the other side of the wall. I heard him say, 'I'm not doing anything my father didn't do to me, Rose. I'm doing him a favor.'

"Then I heard Mom say, 'Don't be so hard on him, Sergei. He can't help it that he's just an ordinary boy.'" Eddie winced, even in recollection. "I felt like I'd had a nail driven into my heart. That was the last straw. To hear my own mother call me *ordinary* . . . that was just too much to bear."

Tears welled in Viola's eyes. She put a hand on his.

"I'm so sorry, Eddie. You're not ordinary. You left home without a dime to your name and still managed to make a success of yourself here."

"I don't want my kids anywhere near that sadistic son of a bitch," he said. "I don't even want him to know where they are. And if Mom knows, he'll know." His tone softened. "But you're welcome in our home anytime. I'd be proud to introduce Antoinette and Jackie to their Aunt Vi."

She got to her feet. "I'll take you up on that. And I won't tell Mama where you are. It was good to see you, Eddie. I've missed my big brother."

Teary-eyed, they hugged again, for longer this time, then left the restaurant, Eddie walking her to the trolley that would take her down to the ferry. He kissed her on the cheek, then watched as the trolley, lit by the frosty yellow glow of a bare bulb hanging inside, rattled forward on its tracks and disappeared down the hill, along the stone gash cut into the face of the Palisades. Then he walked on, turning north on Marion Avenue toward Bergen Boulevard, and headed home to his family.

4

Palisades, New Jersey, 1938

IT DIDN'T TAKE LONG for the Rosenthals to turn around Palisades' fortunes—even before the 1935 season ended the brothers exercised their option to buy. Palisades Amusement Park would now become synonymous with their names, and they were not shy about promoting their kingdom in the clouds. Construction began on a new electric sign, a million-watt marquee perched on the edge of the cliffs: twenty-four feet high by two hundred forty feet long, its scrolling ballyhoo for Palisades became a familiar sight to motorists on New York's Riverside Drive. The Rosenthals claimed it was the largest moving sign in the world; this may even have been true.

New rides were introduced, including the Water Scooter—managed by an up-and-comer named Joe Rinaldi, who also ran the Dodgem cars—and a hair-raising new coaster, the Lake Placid Bobsled, whose steep drops and hairpin turns could hardly have been called "placid." The pool saw the inauguration of the new Sun & Surf Club: swimmers could enroll on a seasonal basis and enjoy use of the pool all summer, as well as their own personal lockers in the bathing pavilion (though patrons could also join the club on a daily basis). And the park's musical acts now included big-name bandleaders like Duke Ellington and Cab Calloway.

Arthur Holden finally retired from his long, storied diving career, but with Palisades a going concern again, old faces came back to the fold:

Dick "Lightning" Bennett returned from his nightclub ventures with several games of chance, including his wife Kate's balloon game (throw a dart, pop a balloon, win a prize). Dick also organized a baseball team to be played against one coached by Kid Fiddles on the first rainy day of the season. The Palisades baseball teams would meet for years to come, the rain-slicked parking lot reconfigured into a baseball diamond with sacks of sugar serving as bases. Eddie was a powerful batter who hit more than a few home runs for Dick's team, sending the balls hurtling into the stands—literally. If a ball went over the tops of the concession stands and onto the midway, it was considered a homer. But it was murder actually sliding into home, or any other base, on the parking lot's wet, gravelly surface.

Concessionaires who had stuck with Palisades through the hard times saw their perseverance finally paying off in dollars. Eddie began to see some real money from his two percent of the gross at the Chief's candy stand, and by the end of the '37 season he and Adele were able to move from their cramped apartment into larger quarters in Edgewater, renting the top floor of a two-story house on Undercliff Avenue for twenty dollars a month.

More important, when one of the French fry vendors—on the downhill side of sixty and weary of the smell of grease—decided the time had come to retire with a few shekels in his pocket, Eddie and Adele bought his entire stock—cutlery, cooking vats, fry baskets, fry cutter, and sundry containers of salt, vinegar, and Mazola corn oil—for twelve hundred dollars.

Thrilled by the prospect of owning their own concession, Eddie and Adele assumed that signing a lease at Palisades would be a routine matter, and arranged for a meeting with Irving Rosenthal.

Irving was a short, smiling, exacting man resembling either a leprechaun or "Little Caesar," as some concessionaires called him (but never to his face). He welcomed Eddie and Adele into his office, and though this was the first time they had met with him, he said at once, "You're the couple that got married on the merry-go-round, aren't you?"

"Yes, we are," Adele said, pleased.

"This will follow us to our graves," Eddie muttered.

"That was a sweet gag," Rosenthal said admiringly, *gag* being carny slang for stunt. "We may try it again next year, on the roller coaster this time. If you two ever decide to get divorced let us know, we may be able to work something out there too." They laughed. "So, what can I do for you?"

Eddie told him of their plans to open a French fry stand. Rosenthal listened quietly, then when Eddie was done he said, "Well, we're embarking on a new policy this season," and explained how he and his brother were expanding their personal ownership of concessions from twenty-five to fifty percent of those operating in the park. "This will mean, of course, fewer concessions available to outside operators," Irving said, "as we'll obviously be giving priority to concessionaires with a long history at Palisades."

Eddie's heart sank like a stone. Suddenly all he could think was that they had just foolishly blown twelve hundred bucks on a hundred gallons of corn oil and some old cooking equipment, with no place to set it up.

"But you know," Rosenthal went on, "history isn't always measured in years. I understand, Eddie, that you swallowed a great deal of smoke in the '35 fire, helping Chief McDermott get all those children out of the park."

"I wasn't the only one," Eddie said diffidently.

"You helped a lot of kids out yourself, didn't you, Mrs. Stopka?"

"Well . . . sure," Adele said. "Somebody had to."

Irving Rosenthal got up, looked out his window at the park spread out below him like his own personal Monopoly board. "If even one of those children had, God forbid, been killed or injured, it would've killed Palisades too. That early on, the publicity would have been fatal. We would have dropped our option like a hot coal." He turned, smiled. "But thanks to you and others, that didn't happen. That's what I mean by history."

He went back to his desk and unfurled a large map of the park that covered the entire desk. "I have a nice location available across from the pool, near the Carousel. Used to be a roast beef stand, I believe—has all the utilities you should need. I can offer you a two-year lease at a thousand dollars per season. How does that sound to you?"

A thousand bucks for five months' rent was far from cheap, but Eddie didn't hesitate. "It sounds great, Mr. Rosenthal."

"Irving. Mr. Rosenthal is my brother."

They all laughed at that. Eddie took out his checkbook and wrote a check payable to Rosecliff Realty Company. He and Adele then signed a standard lease agreement, and Irving smiled warmly and shook their hands.

"It's a pleasure," he said, "to welcome back people of your quality to Palisades Park."

The town of Edgewater was three miles long but only three blocks wide, a bootstrap of land that lay at the stone foot of the Palisades. Factories and refineries crowded the shoreline; rail line spurs from Weehawken serviced the manufacturing plants, bracketing Edgewater's waterfront with metal tracks. There were barely a handful of retail establishments, most near the ferry terminal: the Plaza Drug Store, Manufacturers Bank, a few taverns and lunchrooms. Between River Road and the base of the Palisades the streets were a rabbit warren of single-family homes, rooming houses, schools, and the odd commercial property like the Edgewater Loom Works. The houses had been built closely abreast of one another, but the ones on Undercliff backed up onto the slopes of the Palisades, with a whole forest in their backyards, as well as magnificent views of the Hudson and New York City.

The Stopkas were renting the top floor of one of these houses, at 670 Undercliff Avenue: the exterior walls of the first story had been laid with stone from the Palisades, while the second story, added later, was made more conventionally of wood. It had a kitchen separate from the landlord's downstairs, a back entrance of their own so they could enter and exit with some degree of privacy, and a living room whose windows at night framed the lights of Manhattan, glittering like sequins on an evening dress.

Antoinette loved Edgewater. She loved having a thickly wooded backyard that sloped up to meet a wall of granite taller and more awe-inspiring than any ride she had yet seen at Palisades Park. That fall she would tramp through a thick bed of oak, maple, and hickory leaves—bright red, orange, yellow, and green—her steps making a satisfying crunch all the way up to the foot of the cliffs, beyond which, at six years old, she didn't yet dare venture, contenting herself to merely gaze up at its beckoning summit.

But Antoinette would come to love Edgewater for another reason: Edgewater was where she ceased being Antoinette.

She and Jack attended George Washington School No. 2 on River Road, Jack in kindergarten, Antoinette in first grade, having transferred from Cliffside Park's School No. 1—where Antoinette had learned the many annoying ways her name could be mangled or mocked by fellow students:

"Antoi-*ne-e-e-tte*," one girl, who thought the name too highfalutin, would singsong.

"Aunty! Aunty Netta!" one boy would always greet her, knowing it annoyed any little girl to be called an aunt.

And then there was the classmate whose older sister was studying French history. "You know what happened to Marie Antoinette?" she asked. "She got her head chopped off!"

Enthusiastically, she mimed the falling blade with the flat of her hand.

By the end of her year of kindergarten at Cliffside, Antoinette was more than happy to transfer to Edgewater.

Since the school stood very nearly in the shadow of the George Washington Bridge, the first-grade teacher, Miss Kaplan, told her class, "You know, history and science are all around us. Just a few years ago, the men who blasted away the stone of the Palisades in order to build the George Washington Bridge found what we call a 'fossil' in the rock—a footprint of a dinosaur that existed two hundred million years ago! And years before that, in the same place, they found a skeleton of a prehistoric reptile called a phytosaur. This is what scientists believe it looked like."

She passed around a newspaper clipping, and when the picture came to Antoinette she gasped at the artist's rendering of what looked like a prehistoric crocodile with a long snout and sharp fangs—and next to it, an actual photograph of the creature's skull, with jaws like pincers and teeth like a saw blade. Antoinette couldn't stop staring at it, and the boy behind her had to give her chair a kick to remind her to pass it on.

At recess, she and her classmates spoke wonderingly of these pre-historic monsters, Antoinette voicing a thought that electrified them all: "If they found two dinosaurs here," she said, "maybe there are more!"

After classes ended that afternoon, Antoinette led an expeditionary force of half a dozen first-graders—all, but for her, boys—along with her brother, Jack, to the Edgewater shoreline, where they happily clambered over the mossy rocks in search of a brontosaurus, pterodactyl, or even just another run-of-the-mill phytosaur. They initially planned to hike all the way to the George Washington Bridge, but when that began to seem impractical they got as far as Van Dohln's Marina, a sleepy little boat basin at the northern tip of town. It was here that Antoinette's life changed forever, when—as they all busily searched the stones for dinosaur tracks—her classmate, Guy, called out, "Hey, Toni, I think I found something!"

She didn't know which was more thrilling, the idea of finding something prehistoric or the name Guy had just used. She climbed over the rocks between them and asked, "Why'd you call me Tony?"

"My aunt is named Antoinette. Everybody calls her Toni."

"They do?"

"It's spelled with an *i*. Look, you wanna see what I found or not?"

"Oh, sure, what is it?"

He reached into a crevice and pulled out a hard, triangular object about two inches long, wedged like a stone doorstop between two rocks. "It's a dinosaur bone," Guy declared excitedly, "it's gotta be!"

"If it is," Antoinette said dubiously, "it musta been a *small* dinosaur."

"That one Miss Kaplan showed us was only sixteen feet long."

Jack suggested, "Maybe it's part of its shoulder."

"Do dinosaurs *have* shoulders?" another boy noted skeptically.

"We'll ask Miss Kaplan," Antoinette decided. "She'll know."

They trekked excitedly back to school, where their teacher was working late. Though amused to learn of their archaeological dig, she regretfully informed them that what they had found was not, alas, a piece of dinosaur bone. "But it's almost as exciting as that," she said. "This appears to be an Indian arrowhead. It probably dates back to the mid-nineteenth century, when there were still a few Lenape Indians living here."

This was not anywhere near as exciting as finding a dinosaur bone and they all knew it. But along that slippery shore, Antoinette had found something far more exciting: a new identity.

Not only were she and Jack late coming home from school, it did not escape their mother's notice that their shoes were sopping wet and Antoinette's pretty floral dress—one Adele had spent many long hours sewing for her—was dirty and discolored, with swaths of green obliterating the pretty pink fabric. "Antoinette, what *is* this? Where on earth were you?"

"We were hunting dinosaurs," her daughter announced proudly.

"Are these moss stains? Were you by the river?"

"My teacher says that's where they find dinosaurs."

Adele sighed. "Both of you are too young to be playing by the river, until you learn to swim."

"We weren't playing, we were exploring. And Mama, my name isn't Antoinette anymore, it's Toni."

"What!" Adele was horrorstruck at the thought. "It most definitely is *not*. Tony is a boy's name, not a girl's."

"Guy's aunt is a girl and she spells it with an *i* and that makes it a girl's name," the newly christened Toni insisted.

"Well *your* name is Antoinette," Adele insisted right back. "Now go change your clothes and wash up for dinner."

"I need the potty first, Toni," Jack told his sister.

"Don't *call* her that!" Adele admonished him in a tone of voice usually reserved for warnings like, "Don't touch that plate, it's hot!" or "Didn't I *tell* you not to touch that plate?"

There the subject lay, better left alone, for the evening; but the next day at school, when Miss Kaplan called on her and asked, "Antoinette, can you spell 'horse'?" the teacher was promptly corrected: "H-O-R-S-E. And Miss Kaplan, everybody calls me Toni now."

"Do they? Well, that is something of a time-saver, I suppose." And she merely shrugged and corrected her seating chart.

The first report card bearing the name TONI STOPKA triggered a small earthquake on Undercliff Avenue, but though Adele was able to have this corrected on future report cards, it was not so easy to undo popular opinion. Whenever one of Toni's friends would visit they would invariably greet her, "Hi, Toni!" or "'Lo, Toni!" Adele was quick to correct them, but it was, Eddie pointed out, like trying to get Babe Ruth's fans to call him "George."

Adele was decrying this one Saturday morning as Eddie sat in his easy chair, vainly attempting to read the sports section of the paper. "We give her a pretty, distinctive, feminine name, and what does she do? She takes a boy's name, an ordinary one at that! *Toni,*" she finished with a shudder.

"She's just a tomboy, she'll grow out of it," Eddie said.

"I'd rather she didn't grow into it at all."

Their daughter trotted out of her bedroom with her friend Doris, announcing, "We're going to Doris's house, bye Mama, bye Daddy!"

"Bye, Toni," Eddie said reflexively.

The moment Toni was gone, Adele snatched the paper out of Eddie's hands and swatted him on the back of his head with the sports section.

"You're a big help," she snapped.

Eddie, displaying commendable patience, snatched back his paper. "And you're going overboard on this name business. She's a kid, kids have nicknames. Enough already, before they move you into a nice padded cell at Greystone."

She cracked a smile. "Somebody'd have to have me committed first."

"I've got the papers all filled out," Eddie said without looking up from the headlines.

Eddie's sister, Viola, and her new husband, Hal, became frequent visitors to the Edgewater house. On weekends Eddie would pick them up at the ferry terminal in the secondhand 1931 Studebaker he'd purchased when word spread that the public trolley lines would soon be eliminated. Adele would make a nice Sunday dinner. Both Toni and Jack loved their newfound Aunt Vi, who was always happy to play a game of checkers or Monopoly with them. On her second visit, Jack—who had been busily playing with crayons as the adults chatted—presented her with a drawing, a crayon portrait of her he had just made. "Why, thank you, Jack," she said, holding the picture up for Eddie to see: aside from the purple crayon he'd used for her hair, it was a fairly creditable, if cartoony, likeness of her.

"Looks like we have another artist in the family, Eddie," Viola said. "Just like Mom and—" She caught herself before Sergei's name escaped her.

"Hey, that's great, Jack," Eddie told his son with a smile—but in his heart, he wasn't really sure how he felt about this.

By the time Toni turned seven the following March, she had grown another inch in height—and feeling herself now more than a match for the Palisades, she began scaling it in the company of neighborhood friends. Along with Guy, Johnny Lamarr, and her next-door neighbor Davy, she made her way up the sloping hill, through patches of wild grapevines that smelled like purple Popsicles, as the ground became increasingly studded with impressively large boulders. One of the biggest was free-standing and about the size and shape of a large gray bear, a hump of stone just begging to be jumped on, which of course they all did. After that the rocks were joined together in more elaborate formations. Toni and her friends scurried up—and slid down—them as if they were playground rides.

One big stone had a donut hole in it, less than three feet in diameter; Toni narrowly squeezed into the tube and was disgorged like a pea from a pea-shooter. But on the way out, Toni felt a sharp tug on her dress, heard a loud, dismaying rip, and saw that her skirt had snagged on an outcropping of rock. She worked it free, knowing she would catch it from her mother when she got home, but there was nothing to be done about it.

Eventually they found themselves facing a straight vertical cliff with no way up. They realized with disappointment that they'd reached a dead end and began to descend the way they came.

As they slid off the last rock and onto the hill slope, they were startled by a hissing sound behind them—and turned to see a copper-colored snake slithering out of a crevice in the rock they had just slid down. It stuck out its tongue and hissed again before retreating into another crevice.

"Holy Toledo," Guy said, "that's a copperhead!"

"Are they dangerous?" Toni asked.

"Heck yes. Their bite can kill you."

"Kill you dead?" Toni said.

"Holy cow," Johnny noted.

"I'll say," Davy agreed.

They all contemplated that for a moment, then Toni said, "So how 'bout tomorrow we start a little ways down the street—behind the Looms? Maybe there's a better way up the cliff there."

They all agreed without a moment's hesitation. Intrepid explorers did not let little things like copperheads get in the way of expanding mankind's knowledge of the terra incognita men called Edgewater, New Jersey.

But when Toni returned home she was welcomed not with the huz-zahs that greeted Admiral Peary or Charles Lindbergh but a cry of hor-ror from her mother: "Antoinette, what in God's name happened to you?" Toni remembered now the torn dress, noticing for the first time that those parts of her dress that weren't torn were caked with dirt and moss.

"Oh. This? I tore it on a rock," Toni said.

"Oh, your beautiful dress," Adele said forlornly. "I spent so much time making that. Where were you? Down at the river again?"

"Oh, no, Mama. I was in Davy's backyard."

"Is that all?" Adele said. "Are you lying to me?"

"Mama, I swear, I never left his backyard!"

Technically this was true. Eddie, listening from his easy chair, said, "Are you hurt, hon?"

"No, Daddy, I'm fine."

"Well," Adele said with a sigh, "I may be able to fix the tear. But first I've got to wash all that dirt out of it. All right, young lady, off with it."

"Now?"

"Yes, now. Off."

Toni raised her dress over her head and her mother lifted it off as if she were shucking an ear of corn. Adele sighed again and headed for the downstairs laundry room. When his wife was out of earshot, Eddie glanced over at his daughter and said, "Toni?"

"Yes, Daddy?"

"Next time wear old clothes, okay?"

"Okay."

"And I want you to promise me something else."

"Sure."

"Never go higher than you think is safe. Never let anyone else goad you into going higher than you think is safe. Can you promise me that?"

Toni was surprised her father knew what she had been doing, but pleased that he was not forbidding her from doing it again. "Yes, Daddy."

"Good." Eddie smiled. "Was it fun?"

Toni grinned. "It was the mostest fun I've ever had in my whole life," she said, and ran gleefully, still in her knickers, into her bedroom.

In late April Eddie and Adele returned to Palisades Park to prepare their new stand for the May 14 opening. It was in an excellent location directly opposite the pool, where the enticing aroma of French fries would waft across to hungry bathers—as they had to Eddie on that long-ago day at the park. Since the stand had once been a roast beef joint, there was already a gas stove in the back; all Eddie needed to do was to test the gas, check out the electrical connections, and hook up the large cooking vats which would soon be filled with bubbling corn oil. Then he and Adele set about scrubbing the grease off the stove, mopping the floors, cleaning and repainting the walls, and constructing a new sign for the marquee that read:

10¢   *Saratoga*   10¢
French Fries

No one seemed to know why they were called "Saratoga" fries, but far be it for Eddie and Adele to mess with a good thing.

Adele always enjoyed these first few weeks before the opening, when she could renew old friendships and meet new neighbors—among which, it turned out, there was at least one familiar face.

She was returning from the ladies' room when she passed a new concession going up—a cigarette wheel. Similar in principle to ones used in roulette except hung vertically on a side wall, the wheel was already in place and someone was painting numbers and letters on the "layout," the betting counter. But the shelves that should have been on their way to being filled with prizes—in this case, cartons of cigarettes—were still bare. Out in front of the stand was a tall young woman—at least five foot eight and wearing heels, no less—with her blonde hair pulled back in a chignon. She was holding a carton of cigarettes from one of the many boxes around her, a steely tone in her voice—a familiar voice, that caught Adele's attention at once:

"Barking Dog Cigarettes?" the woman was saying to a sullen-looking fellow with a mustache, at least five years her senior. "Are you kidding me? Who smokes these things, cocker spaniels?"

"Lotsa people smoke 'em," the man protested.

Rummaging through another box, she read off the labels, "Smiles—Bright Star—Sensation—these are all discount brands! Is that it, you got some kind of deal on these cheap brands?"

"Ten-centers sell like hotcakes," the man said. "You got some Paul Jones in there too, that's a popular brand—"

"People buy discount brands because they can't afford the fifteen-centers. They don't want to win them as prizes at an amusement park." The woman dismissively dropped the cartons into the box. "Return 'em. All of them. If you can't return them, put one or two on the shelves as filler, but get me Luckies, Camels, Chesterfields, Old Golds—something that people *want* to smoke, not what they can *afford* to smoke."

She turned brusquely; the man grudgingly began picking up the cartons of rejected cigarettes. Now Adele put the face and voice together:

"Minette?" she said. "Minette Dobson?"

"Yes?" The woman turned. Even with her hair pulled back and only the barest amount of makeup adorning her face, she was absolutely beautiful, with high cheekbones and cupid's-bow lips. She eyed Adele with a flicker of recognition: "I know you. Where do I know you from?"

"Cumbermeade Road. I'm Adele Worth—well I was, now I'm Adele Stopka—Frank Worth's daughter?"

Minette smiled radiantly, seeming genuinely pleased to see her. "Oh my gosh—the movie star down the block!"

Adele laughed. "You were a much bigger star on that block. Even if you were hardly ever there."

"Are you kidding? I saw one of your old pictures in a movie house in Wichita, Kansas, when my dad and I were playing the Orpheum circuit. Oh, I was so envious—I wished *I* was back home in Fort Lee, making pictures, instead of dancing my fanny off in Wichita. It's been years, how have you been? Are you working at Palisades too?"

Adele nodded. "My husband and I have a French fry stand across from the pool. Is this your wheel?"

"I'm managing it for a friend," Minette said. "This is my first season."

"You must've got in just under the wire, the Rosenthals locked up half the concessions."

"They made room for my boss, he's a hotshot businessman around here. Your stand's by the pool? My little sister is applying for a job there as a locker girl, I was about to go over to see her . . . you want to walk with me?"

"Sure."

The two women struck up the midway together. "I really did envy you," Minette said frankly. "When I wasn't on the road with the Thirteen Sirens, my parents sent me to convent school in Massachusetts. I don't regret either one, but once in a while I did wish that I lived in one place, in a normal house, living a normal life."

Oh, sister, if you only knew. Adele kept the thought to herself. "Have you been in vaudeville with your dad all this time?"

"Oh no, I went out on my own a few years back. Started out as a cigarette girl, then a showgirl in a New York nightclub. After that I was a stand-up vocalist with a dance band—we toured all over the country."

"Wow," Adele said softly. "And you're, what, about twenty-four?"

"Twenty-three."

Minette was four years younger than Adele, yet had already done things Adele could only daydream about. She forced a smile. "So, you're finally back home in Fort Lee. You got your wish."

"Well, there's a fella I'm seeing who lives here, and I thought, why not stick close to home for a while? See how it goes. And I've never worked an amusement park before, it sounded like fun. You like working at Palisades?"

"It's all right," Adele said, though a minute ago she would have responded more enthusiastically.

Adele introduced Minette to Eddie, then they walked the short distance across the midway to the pool, presently being repainted in preparation for its opening on Decoration Day. After a few minutes Minette's sister, Georgiana Frances—Frannie—appeared with a big grin on her face. "Sis!" she called out excitedly, hurrying toward them.

"I got the job!" Frannie announced. "It's all pretty simple. I keep the ladies' locker rooms tidy, I hand them towels and bathing suits when they need them, take the used ones to the laundry . . ."

At sixteen years old, Frances was Minette's opposite in many ways: petite and dark-haired where Minette was tall and blonde, polite and sweetly timid where Minette was blunt and no-nonsense. But in one way they were similar: they were both absolutely gorgeous with apparently a minimum of effort, which depressed Adele more than she could say.

"Congratulations, hon," Minette said, giving her a hug. "You'll be the best locker girl Palisades has ever seen. Frannie, you remember Adele, Frank Worth's daughter—they lived on Cumbermeade too?"

"Oh, sure," Frannie said, "your dad directed movies. Nice to see you."

"Nice to see you too, Frannie."

"I'll take you home, sis," Minette offered. "Adele—see you on the midway. Don't be a stranger."

"Sure," Adele called after, more than a bit wistfully. "See you."

Once their concession stand was clean and shiny enough to pass muster with the Rosenthals, Eddie and Adele turned their attention to their product. Following instructions given them by their predecessor, they used an automatic peeler to peel enough potatoes for a test batch, then a stainless steel cutter that cut one or two potatoes at a time into large size pieces (so they retained more moisture). The cut fries were then stored in large containers filled with water and five ounces of Heinz malt vinegar.

Eddie filled the cooking vats with Mazola corn oil, heated one to medium temperature and one to high, and lowered a basket of fries into the medium-hot oil for two minutes—"blanching" them, cooking them most of the way through. After draining, the fries were immersed in the high-temperature vat—"flash-frying" them for a minute and ten seconds until they turned golden brown. Eddie sprinkled them with salt, scooped them into one of the white paper cones, and topped them off with malt vinegar.

His first bite took him back to 1922. But he felt even more transported on opening day, when the smell of the fries mingled with the smell of waffles and the nearby Carousel fired up its lilting calliope music. Crowds began making their way up the midways, the air filled with ballies from concessionaires—and two of the best were located near the Stopkas. Curly Clifford—Italian, handsome, black wavy hair—was a magnet for the ladies, who flocked to his canary stand as he strummed his ukulele and sang:

Canary Isle where birds are singing
A little while, and I'll be bringing
A song of love, to my lady fair (music will fill the air)
You'll hear my song, I'll see your smile
Then I'll belong in Canary Isle . . .

Few were the women visitors who, having heard this sung as if only to them, could resist spinning the wheel to win one of Curly's warblers.

His fiercest competition came from the stand next door: Helen's Radio Shop, run by longtime concessionaire Helen Cuny—as always dressed impeccably, with only a slight accent betraying her Viennese origins. With an amused glance at Curly she addressed the tip:

"Oh, ladies, don't listen to this one's promises of a fairyland romance! He's a charmer, but how many charming men have you met that you can trust? Fill your own air with music with one of these fine, dependable radios by Emerson—yes, that's right, Emerson—available here exclusively at Helen's Radio Shop! Step up, take a chance, win a brand-new radio!"

Eddie's grind was more simple: "Saratoga French fries, best in the world, only one thin dime!" His bally didn't need to be complex—the mouth-watering smell of the fries traveling down the midway did most of the selling. Very quickly there were long lines at the stand and within an hour they had sold out of their first batch of fries, sending Adele to the kitchen, peeling and chopping as fast as she could. She and Eddie alternated working the kitchen and working the bally, but even when she was at the front counter she was working harder than she ever had before— she did the grind, scooped up a cone full of fries for the customer, rang up the sale and made change, with barely a moment to catch a breath before the next customer had to be served.

At the end of the day the profits could almost make her forget all the hot, sweaty work that went into it. But as cool, rainy days at the start of the season grew hotter, so did the atmosphere inside the stand—the steam and the sizzling oil raising the temperature by a good ten to twenty degrees. On a day when the mercury outside topped ninety, in the back of the stand it climbed into triple digits and the oily steam made it feel like two hundred percent humidity. The first investment they made with their profits was the purchase of a large floor fan, which offered some relief.

At the end of the day they each also smelled like a giant walking French fry, a fact that was regularly noted by their children.

By this time Adele had gotten wise to the fact that her daughter was climbing like a monkey up the Palisades, and after yet another torn dress, Adele decided Antoinette needed some distraction. Ever since the "dinosaur hunt" at the Edgewater shoreline, she knew the children needed to learn how to swim—what better place to do it than in the Palisades pool? Marie would bring them to the park and watch over them, but Adele could keep half an eye on their progress from across the midway and visit them on her breaks.

The pool opened an hour and a half earlier than the rest of the park, so one morning Adele went over in search of someone to give her children swimming lessons. A breeze off the river carried a salt spray from the waterfalls, the memory of which still brought a small smile to Adele's face. She was looking for the manager, Phil Smith, but the first person she encountered was Fran Dobson, who was standing near the bathing pavilion where she worked, staring dreamily into the distance.

Adele came up beside her and saw that Frannie was watching one of the lifeguards as he walked away from his station and toward a ten-foot-high diving board, one of several on that side of the pool. He was in his mid-twenties and heart-stoppingly handsome, with wavy dark-blond hair, blue eyes, broad shoulders, muscular arms and legs; Frannie was eyeing him as if he were a Porterhouse steak. Before he started climbing the ladder he stripped off his white tank top emblazoned with the word LIFEGUARD, revealing an expansive chest that almost made Adele's knees buckle.

"Oh my Lord in Heaven," she said softly.

"Amen to that, sister," Fran agreed.

The lifeguard started climbing the ladder to the diving board.

"Who *is* he?" Adele asked.

Fran sighed. "Gus Lesnevich. He's a prizefighter. From Cliffside."

"Well he nearly floored *me*," Adele said.

"You're a married woman."

"I can dream, can't I?"

"Don't waste your time," Fran said airily. "I plan on marrying him someday."

Adele had to smile. "You may be a little young for him."

"I can wait."

"Yes, but can he?"

Fran gave her a sweet-sour look and said, "Party pooper."

Gus Lesnevich, standing at the rear of the diving board, took several quick steps forward, sprang off the tip of the board, then executed a flawless backward somersault, cleaving the water like a knife.

Fran said, "He's not just a boxer, he's a really good diver too."

Lesnevich's gorgeous blond head broke the surface and Adele said, "I imagine he's good at quite a lot of things."

"Zip your lip or I'm telling Eddie."

With a backward glance at the soaking-wet Lesnevich returning to his lifeguard station, Adele strolled over to the Casino Bar, where Phil

Smith was chatting with Harry Shepherd, the bar manager. "Phil," she said, "do any of your lifeguards give swimming lessons?"

"Sure, they're all certified by the Red Cross."

"Um, what about this Lesnevich guy?" Adele asked, feeling a twinge of guilt, but not so much that she didn't ask.

Phil just shook his head. "Naw, he's too busy training. He's got a fight coming up in two weeks. You want Bunty."

"Who?"

"He's a swim coach at the Hackensack Y. Trained some professional athletes, too." Phil went to the bar entrance and pointed to another one of the bronzed lifeguards overseeing the pool like minor Greek deities.

"That's the man you want. Bunty Hill."

5

His name may have sounded like a battle in the Revolutionary War, but even compared to Gus Lesnevich, Bunty Hill was hardly chopped liver: six feet tall, broad-shouldered, and ruggedly handsome, with crystal blue eyes that crinkled in the corners when he laughed. In his mid-thirties, he confirmed that he was indeed a professional swim coach for the Hackensack YMCA as well as the Women's Swimming Association of New York. He was happy to teach Adele's children to swim, and wouldn't brook any suggestion of payment: "Nah," he said, "I do it for all the kids here. Bring 'em over tomorrow morning and I'll have 'em swimming like guppies by afternoon."

He had a soft, soothing voice, carefully modulated from years of coaching swimmers indoors, where loud echoing voices could be a jarring distraction. Adele was tempted to ask for lessons herself, but her kids knew she could swim and would likely rat her out. Besides, she reminded herself, as good as Bunty looked in swimming trunks, Eddie looked even better.

The next morning, Toni and Jack were only too happy to be taken to the Palisades pool for the day. With Adele working her stand across the midway and Marie settled comfortably beneath the shade of a beach umbrella, Bunty told the youngsters, "You midgets ready to learn to swim?"

"Yeah!" Toni said.

"Sure," Jack agreed, following his established policy of concurring with anything his big sister said.

Bunty waded in with them into the shallow end. "Okay, first thing I want you to do is to bend down, cup your hands like this, scoop up a big handful of water, then take a gulp and gargle. You know what gargling is?"

Toni and Jack shook their heads.

"You keep the water in your throat and kinda blow bubbles with it. Here, watch me." Bunty sucked up some pool water, tipped his head back, and gargled with the salt water as if it were mouthwash—then spit it out over the side of the pool. "See? Easy as pissing in a jar. Your turn."

"Do we get to spit, too?" Jack asked eagerly.

"You bet. Live it up."

Toni and Jack obligingly scooped up water, took in a mouthful, tipped their heads back, and did their best to gargle. But they quickly gagged at the highly saline water, swallowing half of it, coughing out the rest.

"Ugh!" Jack cried out. "It's *salty*."

"Yep," Bunty said, "and that's good. You know why? 'Cause the more salt there is in the water, the more buoyant a swimmer is—it makes you float better. Every time I go for a swim in the Hudson, I gargle a mouthful of it first, to see how buoyant the water is that day."

"You swim in the river?" Toni asked.

"Every day. And on my birthday I swim across it—from Hazard's Dock in Fort Lee to the little red lighthouse on the New York side."

"Wow," Toni said. "All by yourself?"

"Sure. So can you, someday. But first you've gotta learn how the human body floats in water, and how you won't sink to the bottom, even if you're afraid you will."

"I'm not afraid," Toni told him.

"Sweetie, I can tell *you're* not afraid of anything. I was thinking more about your brother here."

"I'm not afraid either," Jack insisted.

"Great, we're all fearless fleagles. So let's start with floating." He had them curl up with their legs tucked to their chests—"Like a couple of cooked shrimp," he said, which made them giggle—then slowly straighten out until they were floating on their backs, the water pillowing their heads. "Good, now take a breath. Relax. You can't swim well if your muscles are all tensed up." He had them raise their hands above their heads to raise their center of gravity. "Keep your hips up, that's it—there ya go, you're floating."

Toni and Jack were grinning as they bobbed on the surface like untethered balloons. "Don't get cocky," Bunty cautioned, "so far all you're doing is a great imitation of a piece of driftwood. Kick your feet, just a little—it's called a flutter kick. Keep your knees bent and give a little kick." The kicks propelled them backward. Once they were comfortable moving through the water, he added a backstroke to the lesson: "One arm should always be in the water while the other is out. Elbows bent, one arm reaching down to your waist as the other comes up above your head—yeah, there you go, you got it."

When they had mastered a simple backstroke, Bunty had them flip over and moved on to the American crawl, or freestyle stroke. As with most kids learning to swim, their arms and legs were all over the place, and he had to show them how to keep their limbs extended in a straight but relaxed line from the rest of their bodies. Jack had a tendency to splay his fingers, and Bunty admonished, "That ain't gonna get you far, *kemosabe*. If you want to get any traction on the water, you've got to keep your hands loosely cupped—otherwise you're trying to row a boat without an oar."

After an hour of lessons they took a lemonade break at Bunty's lifeguard station, where he kept a stack of newspapers he read on breaks, and sometimes a book from the Everyman's Library. Bunty was a popular guy at the pool, especially among the ladies, with whom he flirted outrageously—and most of whom flirted right back.

"Is Bunty your real name?" Toni asked him.

"Nah, that's just a nickname I picked up in school. I was a great bunter in softball, soon everybody stopped calling me John and started calling me Bunty."

"So your name is John Hill?" Jack said.

"No, it's Hubschman. Hill was my mother's maiden name, I took it when I was doing a comic diving act with a friend named Dale. Hill and Dale, get it?" They stared blankly at that. "Besides, let's face it—if *your* name was John Hubschman, wouldn't you want to change it to Bunty Hill?"

Toni nodded. "My real name is Antoinette, but I like Toni better."

"See, that's the great thing about America," Bunty said. "Everybody can be whoever they want to be. When I was sixteen and the Great War started in Europe, I wanted to join the Navy and fight. So I just told the enlistment officer I was eighteen. Said I'd lost my birth certificate."

"You fought in a war?" Jack said. "Was it fun?"

Bunty shook his head. "No. And it's not gonna be fun this time around, either."

"What do you mean?"

"Nothin'," Bunty said quickly. "C'mon, no more goldbricking—let's get back to work."

True to his word, Bunty had them swimming like goldfish by afternoon. Toni loved swimming—loved being weightless in the water, soaring like an airplane across a liquid sky, imagining her arms as propellers. She'd never thought of water as anything other than something you drank or bathed in, but now she began to realize—as much as you can at seven years old—that it had other properties. It was thicker than air but not as hard as earth. It could be gripped, in a way, and that thing Bunty called "traction" allowed you to travel across its surface like a train on a track. You could submerge yourself in it, but only, Bunty warned, as long as you held your breath. Stop holding your breath—start taking in water the way you took in air—and you drowned, you died. Bunty was very clear on that: he loved the water, he wanted them to love it too, but you had to follow certain rules or the water would exact a price. Toni wasn't a hundred percent clear yet on exactly what dying meant, but she did understand that it would stop her from ever again scaling the cliffs or doing anything else she loved doing.

Her mother visited the pool in the afternoon and watched proudly as Toni and Jack demonstrated their swimming prowess. Bunty was pleased with the progress they'd made, but he also warned them, "Now don't go thinking you know all there is to know about swimming. I've been doing it for thirty years and *I* don't know everything. Johnny Weismuller, maybe he knows everything, but I've still got a thing or two to show you tadpoles." This excited Toni because it meant she'd be coming back to the pool, and she realized suddenly that she wanted to come back more than anything.

Just as thrilling was what happened shortly before they left. There were three diving boards projecting out over the side of the pool near the bathing pavilion: two were five feet high, the third twice that. Toni watched as Gus Lesnevich climbed up the ten-foot ladder to the tallest diving board, high above her head. Then he leaped into the air, diving like a seagull after its next meal, and plunged into the water. Dimly Toni remembered the silver-haired man, a long time ago, who had done this same thing—jumping off an even taller diving board into a much smaller pool. Up till now, she had thought that this was something only he could do—but here another man was doing it too. And if he could do it, she wondered . . . could anybody?

Toni quickly became a real waterbug, cajoling her grandmother into bringing her to the Palisades pool up to four times a week. "She's taken to it so fast, you'd think she was born in that pool," Marie said, puzzled by the stifled laughter this evoked from Eddie and Adele. They each took turns visiting their daughter as she swam, Eddie striking up friendships with both Lesnevich, with whom he talked endlessly about boxing, and Bunty—a huge baseball fan and one of the most well-read people at the park, even though, like Eddie, he had never graduated high school. Though Eddie wasn't a big book reader, he also enjoyed his morning paper, and he and Bunty shared their worries over the crisis in Europe and Germany's obvious designs on Czechoslovakia.

Sometimes Irving Rosenthal would drop by the pool, and Toni and Jack, as coached by their parents, would greet him, "Hello, Mr. Rosenthal."

"Call me Uncle Irving," he said warmly.

"Are you really our uncle?" Jack asked.

"No, but I'll give you a dollar to call me Uncle."

Their eyes popped like silver dollars.

"Hi, Uncle Irving!" they spoke in unison, and Rosenthal smiled and gave them each a dollar, which they stared at with astonished glee.

"Uncle Irving Uncle Irving Uncle Irving!" Toni added breathlessly.

"Nice try," Rosenthal said, "but it only works once a day."

No matter—Toni and Jack had two dollars, they were *rich*.

When they weren't at the pool, Grandma Marie took them on rides—as on one Saturday when the park was hosting an event that would become a thirty-year annual tradition. As they had for the first time in 1937, the NYPD's Police Anchor Club had transported thousands of orphaned and underprivileged children from New York, admitted free by the Rosenthals, who happily rode the coasters, ate hot dogs and cotton candy, and enjoyed the George Hamid Circus acts. Toni and Jack rode beside many of them on the Scenic Railway, laughed along with them in the Funhouse, and played games side by side in the Penny Arcade. But there was one thing about some of these children that puzzled Toni.

"What's the matter with your face?" she innocently asked a young boy in the arcade, whose face was a strange, dark brown.

"Ain't nothing wrong with it," he said. "I'm just colored."

"What do you mean?"

"Different people got different colored skin, that's all."

Toni was fascinated. "Can I touch it?"

"Sure."

Toni reached out and touched the skin of his arm. It felt just like her skin, warm and smooth. She was a little disappointed.

But before she could say anything, her arm was suddenly yanked away by Marie, who spun her around, saying, "Don't *do* that," and pulled her away from the young boy and his dark skin. "Come along. You too, Jack."

When they were outside the arcade, her grandmother explained, "He's not like us, Toni, and you shouldn't go touching him or others like him. It's better that people associate with their own kind, you understand?"

Since they had all been having a good time together, Toni didn't understand; but she didn't let on, just nodded and said, "Okay."

That night, when she casually recounted this to her parents, her father sat up straight in his chair and said, "That's just your grandmother's opinion, honey. People are people, you have to treat them all the same."

"You mean . . . Grandma's wrong?" Toni said, confused.

Eddie glanced at Adele, who turned to Toni. "Grandma is . . . mistaken," she told her. "Your father's right. People are people."

This would make a lasting impression, not least of all because it was the first time Toni realized that adults could be wrong about something.

For someone who grew up in the worldly realm of show business, Minette Dobson could be surprisingly parochial: she attended Mass every morning, and one Friday when they were having lunch together at the Grandview Restaurant, Adele ordered roast beef and Minette gave her a little grief over it.

"Eddie's the one who takes the kids to Mass on Sundays," Adele pointed out. "I'm Presbyterian."

"So? Would it kill you to have fish on Friday?"

Minette would sit smoking some of the discount cigarettes she'd been stuck with and didn't want to waste, as she recalled her experiences on the vaudeville circuit with her father. Her showbiz lineage extended to both sides of her family: her grandfather, Charles E. Dobson, was one of the all-time banjo greats of minstrelsy and he married Minnie Wallace of the singing Wallace Sisters, also headliners in vaudeville. Listening to Minette almost made Adele feel like she was still in show business and not just a hot, sweaty French fry vendor in an amusement park. But then she quickly told herself she was a damn fool and should thank God that she had a job—an increasingly lucrative one at that—in these hungry times.

"So what are you going to do," Adele asked, "after the season ends?"

"Choreography. I've got a gig lined up, producing chorus routines for theaters. Hey, do you dance?"

"Me?" The question took Adele by surprise. "I can rumba as well as the next girl, but—you mean line dancing?"

"Sure. You'd look great on a chorus line."

It killed her to say it, but Adele admitted, "I appreciate the thought, but . . . I really don't have enough experience."

"Too bad," Minette said. "I could've used a beautiful gal like you."

But Adele was flattered that Minette had even considered her. "So how are things going with this fella of yours? What's his name?"

Minette hesitated a moment—she was fairly close-lipped about her personal life—then said, "I call him Jay. No one else does." Reluctantly she admitted, "You've met him. He's . . . my boss."

"Really? That handsome businessman guy?"

"He's separated from his wife," Minette said. "We're trying to keep a low profile, you know? Until the divorce is final."

Adele said delicately, "So he's technically still married."

"Uh-huh."

"Pardon me for asking, but . . . how does that square with the Masses and the convent school and all that?"

Minette didn't bat an eye.

"That's what confession is for," she said. "None of us is perfect, so we admit our sins to the Lord and we ask His forgiveness."

"And then go back to being not perfect."

"Says the gal who orders roast beef on Friday," Minette shot back, and Adele could only laugh.

It wasn't long before Toni asked Bunty if he could teach her to dive like Gus Lesnevich. "Well, you *might* need to set your sights a little lower than that, at first," he laughed, but agreed to coach her. Gus himself even offered a few pointers, showing Toni proper body alignment by having her stand against the wall with her heels exactly one inch away: "Keep your arms straight, but not rigid. Relax." After she had mastered this, Bunty moved her to the edge of the pool, where he demonstrated the proper position of her arms and bend of her legs to propel herself into the water at the correct angle. Toni was getting very impatient with all this relaxing and bending and arm-raising—she wanted, literally, to dive into it—but eventually she made her first plunge. Her first few attempts were belly flops, but slowly she began to enter the water at the proper angle, diving off the side of the pool with acceptable enough form that Gus smiled: "Not bad, kid, not bad."

Toni now reckoned herself ready to begin diving off one of the tall diving boards jutting out over the pool. She was annoyed when Bunty told her she wasn't ready: "You're too small to be diving from that height, even the five-foot board. You've got to grow a little more first."

Grudgingly, Toni contented herself with side-of-the-pool dives and started making little pencil marks on her bedroom wall, noting her present height, then rechecking on a daily basis. But frustratingly, she didn't seem to get any taller in the next month and a half.

It was in late July that Toni noticed a very tall tower that had been set up, overnight, on the free-act stage. She recalled Arthur Holden plunging off a similar tower, and when Bunty confirmed there was in fact a high diver booked that weekend, she begged her mother to let her watch. Adele saw no harm in it, and at four o'clock that afternoon she took a break and brought Toni to the free-act stage. On closer inspection Toni could see that the tower was just a skinny ladder a hundred feet tall, secured to the ground by four thick wires and two heavy braces. At the base sat a round tank about twenty feet in diameter and five feet deep, with the words SOL SOLOMON'S DIVING ACT inscribed on its curved side.

After a short introduction by announcer Clem White, a fairly ordinary-looking man in swim trunks took to the stage: "Captain" Sol Solomon. He began ascending the tall ladder, Toni watching with excitement as he made the long climb to the top. He walked out onto the short diving platform—paused at the edge for dramatic effect—then sprang off the board, his body somersaulting as he fell. Toni's heart raced as Solomon's body flipped end over end, plummeting a hundred feet in just a few seconds . . . straightening just in time into a full gainer, feet pointed down at the shallow waters of the tank. He plunged in, creating a waterspout on impact. The crowd held its collective breath, waiting for him to surface.

A hand appeared above the rim of the tank, and Captain Solomon climbed out to the cheers and applause of the crowd.

Toni cheered longest and loudest. She thought it was grand.

Later, as she and her mother made their way back to the pool, Toni confided, "I really want to do that someday."

Adele looked at her and laughed. "I sincerely hope you don't."

"I do! I've never wanted to do anything so much in my whole *life*."

"Don't be silly," her mother said dismissively. "It's too dangerous. Women's bodies aren't built to withstand that kind of punishment. And besides, it just isn't ladylike."

Toni scowled. Anything that was fun, her mother said wasn't ladylike. "What if I don't *want* to be a lady?" she said stubbornly.

Adele fought back a flash of irritation: it seemed sometimes as if her daughter was deliberately rejecting everything Adele was trying to teach her. "Well you *are* one whether you want to be or not," she said in a tone that made Toni bite her lip and fall into sullen silence.

Two days later, when she and Jack returned to the pool with Marie, Toni splashed around on her back for a little while, gazing up at those diving boards high above—beckoning to her as the summit of the Palisades once did. She thought a moment, got out of the pool, told her grandmother she'd left something in the locker room, and headed for the bathing pavilion.

But instead of entering the locker rooms, she veered left, toward the tallest diving board—and without hesitation she began climbing the rungs of the ten-foot ladder. Her heart raced as it had when she was watching Captain Solomon, but this was even more thrilling: this was *her* adventure.

In moments she had reached the top. She hadn't bargained on the moment of dizziness she felt as she looked down, but that passed as she reminded herself it was no different from scaling the cliffs or riding a roller coaster. Slowly she inched her way to the end of the diving board.

Bunty Hill was turning in his seat at the lifeguard's station when he suddenly saw the figure of a little girl standing atop the ten-foot board. "Holy shit!" he cried, jumping to his feet, starting to run toward the ladder.

Toni saw Bunty below, tried to remember everything he had taught her—she wanted to make him proud—and dove off the board.

But the plunge down was a million times worse than her moment of vertigo and she panicked. She forgot her form, her arms akimbo, her body arching as if recoiling from the water that was hurtling up to meet her.

Her belly hit the water with such force that every bit of air in her lungs was squeezed out of her, along with a cry of shock and pain—and then, as they said in the movies, there was a brief intermission.

When she came to, she was being carried in Bunty's arms onto the sand, and as she glanced up she saw her father and mother running through the pool gate toward her, wearing their white aprons. Bunty turned and Toni's grandmother floated into her awareness, looking pale and stricken:

"Is she all right?" Marie asked, afraid.

"Don't die, Toni," Jack said tearfully, not helping matters.

"Nobody's dying, pal," Bunty said. "She's breathing okay."

He laid Toni down on a beach blanket as Eddie ran up and crouched down at her side: "Baby, are you okay? How do you feel?"

"My tummy hurts," she said plaintively.

"She took a real belly flop," Bunty explained, "from ten feet up. That's like getting whacked in the solar plexus by Max Schmeling. We'd better get her to the first-aid station so Doc Vita can take a look at her."

"Oh God, Toni, why did you *do* it?" Adele said in a small voice, and Toni was surprised to see she had tears in her eyes.

"I'll bring her over," Eddie said, then, to Adele: "Honey, you lock up the stand. Marie, maybe you should take Jack home."

Eddie tenderly took his daughter in his arms and carried her off. Adele ran across the midway to shutter and lock the stand, after which she went to join Eddie and Toni at the park's small but well-equipped first-aid station.

Dr. Frank Vita was a young physician who worked at a Cliffside Park medical clinic affiliated with Holy Name Hospital in Teaneck. In summer he was also the Palisades Park medic. When Eddie entered with Toni, Nurse Cooper prepared an exam table for her as Vita asked, "What happened?"

"She jumped off a ten-foot diving board and landed on her stomach."

"Did she lose consciousness?"

"I don't know," Eddie said. "Toni, honey, did you black out when you hit the water?"

"Uh. . . . just a little," she said sheepishly.

"Take a deep breath, Toni, okay?" Vita put his stethoscope to her chest, then her back. "Now cough." She complied. "I don't hear any fluid in her lungs. Look at me, Toni, and keep your eyes open." He shined a light in her eyes. "Normal dilation, that's good. What's your name again, honey?"

"Toni Stopka."

"Can you tell me your father's name?"

"Daddy."

Vita laughed. "What does your mother call him?"

"Eddie."

"Know what day it is today?"

"Thursday."

"Who's the favorite in the third race at Monmouth?"

"Huh?"

"Nurse," Vita said with a smile, "make a note: patient seems alert, awake, but useless at picking horses."

Eddie laughed, and that made Toni relax a little. Adele entered the aid station and hurried to her daughter's side as Vita said, "I'm going to feel your stomach now, Toni." He palpated her abdomen; she winced slightly. "Does that hurt? Do you feel sick, like you're going to throw up?"

"No, it's just sore."

"Okay, Toni, that's all." He turned to Eddie. "She'll be fine. She may have lost consciousness for a few seconds, but there are no other signs of concussion. None of her internal organs seem bruised—she's just going to wake up tomorrow with some very sore muscles. Apply liniment, give aspirin as needed for pain, and keep her out of the water for a while."

"Oh, I can guarantee you *that*," Adele assured him.

Toni found out what this meant when they got home, when after an ominous private consultation between her parents, her father told her, "We're glad you're all right, honey, but what you did was both wrong and dangerous. Dangerous because if Bunty hadn't rescued you, you could've drowned while you were out cold. And wrong because Bunty told you *not* to dive off those platforms and you did it anyway."

"I'm sorry," Toni said quietly. "I thought I could do it."

"We've decided," her mother said, "that as punishment you won't be allowed back in the pool for a month. Maybe that way you'll think before you do anything as foolish as this again."

Toni nodded, accepting her fate, but in truth, the average seven-year-old has at best an uncertain grasp on the notion of time—and it was only after she was denied a visit to Palisades for a whole week, and then another, that Toni began to understand that a month was *really a long time.*

What's more, Adele was taking no chances that her daughter would substitute rock climbing for swimming: Marie brought both children to her home in Fort Lee, where the most excitement to be had was a game of marbles with the neighborhood kids. Worse, Toni had to watch as several local boys returned from Palisades Park with their swimsuits still dripping—they, like most kids in Fort Lee and Cliffside Park, knew that there was a hole in the park fence behind the free-act stage, and behind the pool's waterfall was an opening through which you could swim into the pool without paying admission. What they didn't know was that Irving Rosenthal was well aware of this gap in security and made no attempt to fix it—on the theory that even if the kids sneaked into the park for free, they'd still part with some of their money on rides, games, and food, and everybody went away happy.

Everyone, that is, but Toni, who at the three-week mark began to chafe, asking her mother one morning, "Is it a month yet?"

"Nope," she was told, "not yet."

"How long before it's a month?"

"Try another week on for size."

"Another week?" Toni said in disbelief. "Mama, can't I *please* go to the pool? I won't try to dive, I'll just swim, I promise!"

"The deal wasn't three weeks with time off for good behavior, it was a month. Don't worry, you'll have about a week's worth of swimming left before the season ends."

"Only one week?" Toni was horrified. "That's not fair!"

"Neither was ignoring what Bunty told you not to do."

"You don't want me to have any fun at all," Toni insisted.

"You can have fun at Grandma's house. She still has my old dolls and dollhouse in the attic, you can play with those . . ."

"Who cares!" Toni yelled. "Dolls are stupid!"

"Lower your voice, Antoinette."

The name only stoked Toni's anger all the more.

"I hate dolls! I hate *you!*" she blurted.

Adele flinched, as if physically struck. Reflexively, her hand lashed out and slapped Toni across her left cheek. Not hard, but enough to sting.

"Don't you *ever* speak to me like that again, young lady," Adele said, though her voice nearly broke halfway through.

This was the first time either of her parents had ever struck her, and Toni sat there a moment, less hurt than shocked—then burst into tears. She jumped off the kitchen chair and ran into her room, wailing.

Adele looked down at her hand. It was trembling.

She stood, feeling wobbly and nauseous. Thank God Eddie had gotten up early to go to their wholesaler. Somehow she managed to propel herself into the bathroom, Toni's cries still ringing behind her.

Every awful memory of life with Franklin paled beside that of hearing your child tell you that she hated you. Adele turned on the faucet to drown out her sobs, then sat on the edge of the bathtub and cried her heart out.

She was a terrible mother; all this had been a terrible, terrible mistake. She'd thought having a daughter would be so joyous, being able to share with her all the things she had loved as a child—but at every turn Antoinette demonstrated her disdain for everything Adele loved, everything Adele *was.* Her own daughter's heart was a mystery to her. She sat and cried for five minutes—cried for letting her anger get the better of her, for being a bad mother, and most of all, for wanting more out of life than this.

Toni's hurt was forgotten almost as soon as she returned to the pool the next week—or most of it, anyway. She was still bothered by something her mother had said—not on the day she'd slapped Toni's face, but on the afternoon they had watched Captain Solomon's death-defying leap.

Now, as Bunty gave her some pointers on improving her form, Toni said hesitantly, "Bunty? Can I ask you something?"

"Sure, kiddo, what is it?"

"My mom says girls can't dive like boys. She says we're not strong enough. Is that true?"

Bunty snorted. "Aw, that business about women's bodies not holding up to the rigors of diving, that's just an old wives' tale—not that I'm calling your momma an old wife," he added with a wink. "Just 'cause you're too little now to dive off a ten-foot board, doesn't mean you won't be able to do it hands down in a couple of years."

"So could I"—she hesitated to even speak the words aloud—"could I dive like Captain Solomon when I grow up? Even if Mama says I can't?"

Bunty sighed.

"Listen, kid, at some point everybody gets told that they can't do something in life. Like this girl I knew at the Women's Swimming Association in New York. Her name was Trudy—Trudy Ederle. She had measles as a kid, so her hearing wasn't so good. But man, she was a torpedo in the water. She was fourteen, fifteen years old, and her dream was to swim the English Channel."

"What's that?"

"It's thirty-one miles of damn cold water between England and France," he said, "with strong tides and a helluva chop. The first time Trudy tried it, her trainer thought she was in trouble and pulled her out of the water only six and a half miles from shore—even though Trudy was sure she could have made it. On her second try, a year later, she wouldn't let anyone pull her out—and became the first woman to swim the English Channel."

"Wow," Toni said. "Really?"

"Yep. And there was another gal in New York—Millie Gade Corson— who I helped train, and she became the second woman and the first *mother* to swim the Channel.

"So look, honey—you're seven years old. When you grow up you may decide what you really want to be is a crocodile hunter, or an opera singer. You may *not* have what it takes to be a high diver. But don't take somebody else's word for that—give yourself the chance to find out for yourself."

Due to spotty weather, the '38 season didn't entirely live up to expectations, but Eddie and Adele, like most concessionaires, still made a profit, and that was nothing to sneeze at these days. On September 7, the last day of the season, the Rosenthals threw a big blowout, starting at midnight, in the park's Midway Restaurant. Staff and concessionaires toasted to each other's success, dined on roast chicken, listened to entertainers brought in—courtesy of "Lightning" Bennett—from local nightclubs like Ben Marden's Riviera, and a few even got up and serenaded the crowd themselves. (Frank Vita was a surprisingly good singer, for a doctor.) Bunty attended with a knockout blonde who could have been a model. Afterward, tables were moved aside as Palisadians joined in the dance craze that was sweeping the nation: the jitterbug.

This farewell party had become something of an annual tradition over the past four years, and Adele always looked forward to it; but tonight it just made her sad. She was going to miss these people, this place, for the next seven months. Increasingly it began to feel to her like these five months at Palisades were the only truly exciting part of her life. Toni and Jack were fast asleep at their grandparents' house so their parents could stay as long as they liked, but after jitterbugging to Duke Ellington's "It Don't Mean a Thing (If It Ain't Got That Swing)," Adele said she was tired and wanted to go home. They made their goodbyes to everyone, and were long gone by the time the party broke up in the wee hours of the morning, when the rumba contest finally ended in a draw, Minette Dobson among the winners.

In the parking lot, Adele blurted, "Eddie—can I take dance lessons?"

He looked at her in mild surprise. "You were doing just fine on the dance floor tonight."

"I mean professional dancing. You remember the Swift Sisters, from vaudeville? They've got a dance studio here in Cliffside Park. I thought I might take a few lessons—they say it helps an actor achieve grace and poise. Our bodies are our instruments, we need to keep them in tune."

Eddie had to smile at that. "How much do these lessons cost?"

"Five dollars a week."

"Well, I think we can swing that," he said. "Sure, why not?"

Adele smiled and gave him a kiss. She was careful not to let it show, but there was a big brass band in her soul, striking up a show tune.

Toni and Jack returned to school the following week, and one of the subjects that would be greatly discussed in the coming school year was the upcoming World's Fair in New York. There were already articles trumpeting its April opening in newspapers and magazines, and one of Miss Kaplan's assignments for Jack's first-grade class was to draw a picture of the fair's "theme center," the Trylon and Perisphere. The Perisphere was a white globe sitting next to a tall white obelisk reminiscent of the Washington Monument. This was, Miss Kaplan reasoned, a good opportunity for the first graders to learn the use of the compass (to draw the Perisphere) and the ruler (for the Trylon). Jack took the assignment very seriously, studying the newspaper pictures carefully, practicing with the compass to make a perfect circle.

When he came home that day, Jack proudly showed his artwork to his father. "Daddy, Miss Kaplan says we're gonna make a booklet about the fair and she'll use my picture for the *cover*!" he told him breathlessly.

Eddie looked at the drawing. He could see why Jack's teacher had singled it out: it had been drawn with a steady hand, no wobbles in the circumference of the sphere, and a little shading gave a real sense of solidity to the structures. "Where'd you learn to draw like this, pal?" Eddie asked.

"From reading the comic strips in the paper," Jack replied. "'Specially *Terry and the Pirates* and *Flash Gordon*. I copied 'em over and over."

His grandmother, Rose, would have been proud. Eddie felt a twinge of guilt that she wasn't here to see this, and a twinge of envy that *he* had never had a talent like this to display when he was a boy. He felt, in fact, a whole welter of emotions—but there was only one he intended to show his son. He'd be damned if he would do to Jack what Sergei had done to him.

"That's terrific, buddy," he said with a big grin. "You've got real talent. Maybe someday you'll have a comic strip of your own in the paper, huh?"

Jack beamed at that. "You think so?"

"Why not?" Eddie said. "You can be anything you want to be, Jack. And anything you want to be is okay by me."

6

Edgewater, New Jersey, 1941

EVENINGS AT THE STOPKA HOME, as in most homes in America, re-volved around the welcoming voice of the radio—a tall, mahogany-veneer Philco console, standing solemn as a church organ in the corner, the fam-ily gathered round in secular congregation. On weekdays services began at 5:00 P.M., when Toni and Jack rushed inside to hear "Uncle Don" Carney spin stories of inimitable characters like Susan Baduzen and Willipus Wallipus (both Sr. and Jr.) on Newark's WOR. Sundays at 5:30 P.M., Jack never missed an episode of that mysterious avenger of the airwaves, *The Shadow*; then after supper, the Stopkas all tuned in to *The Jack Benny Show*. Monday evenings brought Adele's favorites, vaudevillians Burns & Allen; Eddie enjoyed the new swing music of Glenn Miller on his three-day-a-week program; while Toni and Jack faithfully followed the *Adven-tures of Superman* on Mondays, Wednesdays, and Fridays, as well as those of an aviator of another sort, *Captain Midnight*. And as the family sat there in the living room—Adele working on the household budget as Jack and Toni read comic books and Glenn Miller's saxophone announced the stops of the "Chattanooga Choo-Choo"—Eddie thought of another train, of distant lights in passing homes, and it warmed him to know that one of those lights was now his, and his days of sleeping in side-door Pullmans were behind him.

But along with music, laughter, and adventure, the radio also carried the voices of newsmen like Edward R. Murrow and Gabriel Heatter, delivering grim bulletins as the lengthening shadow over Europe claimed one country after another: Czechoslovakia, Poland, Holland, Belgium, Norway, France, Hungary, Romania. Radio brought the whistle of German bombs above England, and their fatal concussion, straight into Eddie's living room. This presentiment of war could even be seen on the gaudy covers of his children's comic books, on which the red, white, and blue figure of Captain America slugged it out with Adolf Hitler, while the Human Torch and Sub-Mariner enthusiastically burned and sank Japanese submarines. America may not have been in this war yet, but its four-color heroes clearly already were.

Despite the cozy assurances by President Roosevelt in his "fireside chats" that the United States would remain neutral, defense spending ramped up, and in September of 1940, FDR instituted the nation's first peacetime draft. Like every other man in the country between the ages of eighteen and forty-five, Eddie had to register with the Selective Service. Inductees were chosen by lottery and so far, luckily, Eddie's number had not come up. Even if it did, as a father of two he was likely to get a deferment. Palisades Park had already lost its first employee to the military: Joe Gans, of the office staff, had been drafted even before the park opened for the 1941 season. The same people whose livings were often made on the spin of a wheel of fortune now found those livelihoods, and lives, determined by a similar game of chance. And there was nothing to be done about it but go about the business of daily life as if there were a future in it.

Certainly that was true for Johnny "Duke" DeNoia, who surprised many of his onetime associates by opening his own business—not at Palisades, but about as close to it as he could get. Johnny had become the proprietor of Duke's Clam Bar, a restaurant specializing in fine Italian cuisine and fresh seafood; Dick Bennett, with his nightclub experience, also had a hand in the operation. Fittingly, Duke's was located at 783 Palisade Avenue, directly opposite the main entrance to Palisades Amusement Park. It was hardly the only restaurant on that block: right next door was the 785 Club, a restaurant and cocktail bar that advertised a complete meal and dinner show for three bucks a head. Other close neighbors were the Palisades Bar & Restaurant and the popular Joe's Restaurant, aka Joe's Elbow Room. Duke's exterior wasn't very prepossessing—just a drab red-brick facade—and Eddie was skeptical that it would be able to compete shoulder-to-shoulder with three more established eateries.

But inside it was luxuriously appointed in Italian Provincial, with red leather booths lining the left-hand side of the restaurant and a long, well-stocked bar on the right. And the food was excellent: clams casino, veal marsala, shrimp linguine, and spaghetti and meatballs that would have done credit to Duke's old favorite, Tarantino's. Duke's Clam Bar—later known simply as Duke's Restaurant—quickly became a thriving business.

Eddie's first visit was a lunch in the company of Bunty Hill, both working an off-season construction job in Fort Lee. As they walked into Duke's—eyes adjusting to the subdued lighting as if they were divers descending into a grotto—they were greeted by a smiling Dick Bennett: "Two for lunch, gentlemen? Frankly you look like a pair of unsavory characters to me, but if you grease my palm sufficiently I *may* be able to find you a seat."

Bunty dug into his pocket and planted a dime in Dick's hand. "Here you go, my boy, show us to your best table."

"You amusement people are cheap sons of bitches, aren't you?" Dick said. They laughed as he escorted them to a very nice, secluded booth in the corner—en route pausing to say hello to Chief Borrell, sitting at another booth and tucking into a plate of manicotti in a rich tomato cream sauce.

Eddie and Bunty ordered lasagna and a steak, respectively, and two beers that came in tall, slender, conical glasses with a large head of foam, European style. Eddie excused himself to go to the men's room, heading to the rear of the bar and a big steel door along the back wall. But a heavy-set guy in a sharp suit slid off a barstool like a lizard off a rock, positioned himself between Eddie and the door, and said, "The john's over there, pal," helpfully pointing out the men's room, a little farther down.

"Oh. Sure. Thanks."

When Eddie returned to the booth, Bunty, nursing his beer, said quietly, "Take a look across the room. But make it casual, okay? Third booth on the left. And keep your voice low."

Eddie followed Bunty's gaze and saw two men in business suits, neither of whom made any particular impression on him.

"Yeah?" he said, drawing a blank. "So what? Who are they?"

Bunty said in that soft tone of his, "Shame on you, Eddie—I thought you were a man who liked to read his newspapers. You don't recognize the infamous Moretti brothers—Salvatore and Willie?"

The second name sounded a faint alarm in Eddie's memory. "Willie Moretti . . . isn't he the guy—"

"Voice low. 1931. He was booked for the murder of a stoolie named William Brady. Somehow the charges never stuck, even though before he died Brady ID'd Moretti as one of the men who gunned him down."

"Jesus. He doesn't look like much."

"He could kill you with a spoon. And if that's not enough to make you piss your pants, check out the booth next to him."

Eddie followed his gaze and saw a beefy but bland-looking man, also in his forties, chatting with Dick Bennett, who had stopped by his table.

"Tommy Lucchese," Bunty said. "Underboss of the Gagliano crime family. He's supposed to be in charge of the family's interests in Jersey."

Eddie noted, "He and Dick are sure jawboning like old friends."

"No shit. Dick's a bookmaker, didn't you know that?"

"No. But I knew he liked the ponies." Eddie glanced over at Chief Borrell, calmly eating his manicotti while sitting ten feet away from three of the most notorious mobsters in New Jersey. "What the hell is the Chief doing here? He doesn't seem bothered by the company he's keeping."

Bunty snorted. "Borrell's bought and paid for. He might as well still have a price tag on him."

Eddie felt disappointed, and embarrassed that he hadn't figured this out for himself.

Bunty took a bite of steak, chewing before speaking. "The food here's good—this is an excellent cut of beef," he said finally. "But I think, in the long view, eating here could be bad for your health."

They talked baseball for the rest of their meal, but when they asked for their check they received instead a visit from the proprietor himself, Johnny Duke. "Hey, Ten Foot," he said warmly, "good to see you. Bunty, how's the pool? You gettin' any pussy?"

"I get my share," Bunty said with a smile.

"He gets my share too," Eddie said, "me being married."

"Hey, that's never stopped me," Duke said. "Listen, lunch is on the house, okay? I just want to ask one favor of my pal Bunty here."

Eddie felt a chill. Bunty didn't show any of the distress he must have been feeling, just asked, "Sure, what is it?"

Duke leaned in and said, "Send me over some of your leftover pussy—for old times' sake." He laughed, slapping Bunty on the back, and Bunty and Eddie laughed, with some relief, along with him.

They could not get out of the restaurant fast enough for Eddie. Once they were in his car, he keyed the ignition and turned onto Palisade Avenue.

"I feel like such a goddamn idiot," Eddie said. "Here I thought the Chief was such a nice guy."

"He is, mostly. Hell, I met Albert Anastasia once—seemed like the nicest fella you could ever meet. He didn't have a business card that read 'Murder, Incorporated.' These mooks are all charming as hell—right up until they stick a muzzle in your mouth and provide you with some nice air-conditioning in your head."

Eddie winced. "So who else at the park is with the mob?"

"I hear Borrell's cousin Patsy, who runs the miniature golf game, rents offices to some bookie, but that's all I know of. Palisades is a pretty clean operation. Borrell got his concessions as payment for services done, but nothing shady, just helping out with traffic, zoning laws, stuff like that."

"And Borrell brought in Bennett." Eddie's jaw clenched at the thought. "I played on that guy's baseball team, for Chrissake."

"And you will again," Bunty said pointedly. "You don't want to be his pal, Eddie, but I wouldn't give him the cold shoulder, either. Guys like him are a fact of life around here—but you can be friendly around 'em without being friends. That's where Borrell crossed the line . . . if he even knew the line existed in the first place.

"Me, I'd rather just eat a good honest hot dog at Hiram's," Bunty declared, "than go back to *that* cozy little establishment."

In early May the park opened to good business, announced by the dazzle of new searchlights positioned on the edge of the cliffs: crisscrossing beams of light raking the clouds, their reflections casting a series of shifting, luminous ripples, like a moire pattern, on the surface of the Hudson River.

But there was a far different light show being presented in the skies above London, as word came that on May 10, the latest Nazi bombing raid had reduced Parliament's House of Commons to a pile of rubble.

On June 20, "Uncle Don" Carney began twice-weekly broadcasts of his radio show from Palisades, urging his listeners (among them Toni and Jack, thrilled to be in his audience at the park) to sing along to his theme song:

> *Hibbity gits, hot-sah ring bo ree! Skibonia skippity hi lo dee!*
> *Hony ko doatz with an ala ka zon! Sing this song with your*
>   *Uncle Don!*

Two days later, on June 22, Nazi Germany treacherously broke its nonaggression treaty with Russia and invaded the Soviet Union.

Public relations stunts staged by the always-inventive Bert Nevins included a beauty contest devoted to women who wore glasses (covered by all the newsreels) and a Diaper Derby that saw batteries of babies racing (well, crawling, anyway) to be the first to cross the finish line.

And on August 26, in Madison Square Garden, Palisades' own Gus Lesnevich battled Tami Mauriello to win the title of World Light Heavyweight Champion. There to cheer him on was his new wife, nineteen-year-old Georgiana Frances Dobson, whom he had wed on June 8.

It was disquieting to Eddie, this jarring contrast between the bright, cheery atmosphere inside Palisades and the slowly darkening world outside it. As calliope music played and diapered babies crawled in derbies, bombs fell on the other side of the world, which no longer seemed so comfortably distant.

For ten-year-old Toni, though, the war in Europe was about as real as that invasion from Mars on the radio a few years ago. The only thing that mattered was that it was summer and she was at Palisades and back at the pool she loved. Even more thrillingly—as August brought Gus Lesnev-ich a world championship, it would also bring Toni her own champion.

Adele was feeling pretty chipper these days herself. After her talk with Eddie in the parking lot, the next day she enrolled in the Swift Sisters School of Dance in Cliffside Park. Helen and Mae Swift had been danc-ers in vaudeville, often sharing a bill with Ginger Rogers (whom Helen resembled a bit), Burns & Allen, and Milton Berle. They retired and opened their dance studio in 1931, teaching "Toe, Tap, and Acrobatic" dancing.

Adele knew she was a little old to be studying dance, but all she as-pired to learn was some tap dancing and a good soft shoe, something that might land her a part in one of Minette's shows. It took a year of lessons before Adele was brave enough to try out for her, and she was surprised to discover how thrilling it was, just going out on an audition again. Slip-ping into her black dance leotard and stockings, she was pleased, when she surveyed herself in the mirror, at the way they accentuated her curves—hell, pleased that the curves were still *there*. She took the train into Manhattan, her heart pumping as she entered the theater on Forty-second Street. She stripped off her outer clothing and stood waiting in the wings with other girls—most of whom, she noted grimly, were truly *girls,* and not an old lady of thirty.

Minette sat in the audience with the show's producer as Adele, nearly dizzy with fear and exhilaration, went on. Somehow she managed to get through her tap routine without incident, though not without discom-fort: dancing in high heels was murder on your feet. She was no Ginger Rogers, she knew, but she didn't miss a beat either, and if her movements weren't quite as fluid and assured as some of the other dancers, at the end she was pleased that she'd managed to acquit herself honorably and not embarrass Minette—whose parting smile at her seemed warm and genu-ine.

After the auditions, she and Minette met for coffee at the Horn & Hardart Automat, where Minette told her, "I'm sorry, honey. They liked you, but they went with some other girl instead."

"Oh, that's all right," Adele said, unsurprised. "Honestly, I was just happy to be up there on the stage. I know how young and beautiful those girls are, and here I am, an old married woman."

At that, Minette inexplicably burst into tears.

"Minette, I— It's okay, really, I appreciate the chance you gave—"

Minette shook her head, tried to compose herself. "It's not that. It . . . it's Jay. He finally divorced his wife."

"Well, that's wonderful!"

"For somebody else it's wonderful. He married another girl." Minette dissolved again into tears.

"What? You mean he was two-timing you?"

Minette could only nod.

"That son of a bitch!" Adele cupped a hand over her mouth. "I'm so sorry, hon. But you're young and gorgeous—there are plenty of fish in the sea, and you're better off without a barracuda like him."

"Yeah, I keep telling myself that," Minette said, dabbing at her eyes with a handkerchief. "But when the hell do I stop loving the bastard?"

Adele had no answer for that, just put a consoling hand on Minette's.

Minette seemed to get over her heartbreak within a few months, but surprisingly, as the park season approached, she told Adele she was returning to manage Jay's stands for him: "No hanky-panky, strictly professional. I'm just doing it for the money."

Adele wasn't sure how wise a move that was, but she smiled and said, "Well, good. I'd miss you," and let it go at that.

Adele went back to the Swift Sisters to perfect her craft. At least it made her feel like she was a part of show business again, and not just a mother and maidservant to two precocious, often exhausting, children. And as Adele felt more fulfilled, she was less bothered by Toni's—God help her, she had actually begun calling her that—whims and occasional willfulness.

So when, one morning in mid-August—as she and Marie brought the kids to the pool while Eddie got the stand ready for opening—Toni cried out, "Oh my gosh, look at *that*!" Adele didn't especially mind.

Toni was electrified to see—rising high above the kiddie pool—a tall tower crowned by a tiny platform, braced by guy wires running diagonally on either side. She knew there was only one possible use for such a tower.

"It's for a high diver!" she announced, beside herself. "Mama, can I go take a look at it? Can I, please?"

It was 10:30 A.M. and only the Palisades pool was open; the rest of the park was populated solely by staff, all of whom knew Toni.

"Promise me," Adele said, "that you will *not* try to jump off it." Toni giggled at that. "I'm not kidding."

"I promise."

"Okay. And get back in ten minutes, tops."

"Thanks, Mama!"—and Toni took off like a rocket up the midway, toward the free-act stage. The Eiffel Tower could not have been a more thrilling sight to Toni than this narrow ladder standing more than a hundred feet tall. At the tower's foot was a tank about fifteen feet across—currently being fed water from a hose draped over the side—with the words BEE KYLE on it, though what bees had to do with a diving act Toni couldn't imagine. A woman was tightening one of the guy wires to the axle stakes that had been driven into the ground. Toni raced up to her and asked breathlessly, though she already knew the answer, "Is this for a high diver?"

The woman—about forty years old but with an ageless, pixyish face and tousled brown hair—stood up. She wasn't much taller than Toni—a little over five feet. "That's right," she said. "First show this afternoon."

"Where is he?"

The woman smiled impishly. "You're looking at her."

Toni was stunned. The woman laughed heartily, and Toni could see she had a charming little gap between two of her front teeth. "I'm Bee Kyle."

"But . . ." Toni's heart pumped with excitement and disbelief. "My mother says girls can't be high divers."

"Well," Bee said tactfully, "tell her to come around at four o'clock today and I'll clear up that little misconception for her."

A huge grin spread across Toni's face. "Boy, will I! How long have you been a diver?"

"Oh, I was jumping off sea cliffs as soon as I learned to swim. In Maine there's no shortage of big rocks along the coast to dive off. But professionally, I made my first real high dive when I was fourteen years old."

Had she heard right? Fourteen?

"I'm ten!" Toni declared. "I can dive off the five-foot boards at the pool. My friend Bunty says maybe next year I can try the ten-foot one!"

"That's the way to do it. My first dive was from thirty-five feet. I worked my way up, ten feet a year, until I got to a hundred and ten—any higher, I figure, is a job for a steeplejack." Plainly seeing Toni's excitement, Bee offered, "I was about to do a practice dive—would you like to watch?"

"Yeah, sure!"

"Okay, sit tight and let me finish checking my equipment. What's your name, by the way?"

"Toni. Toni Stopka."

"Nice to meet you, Toni." She gave her a wink. "I'll be right down."

Bee made sure the tank was full—all six feet of water—then she and a man Toni would learn was her husband checked the bracing of the guy wires supporting the tower. It was a little windy today and the tower trembled nervously at the wind's touch, but Bee Kyle showed no concern as she stripped down to her bathing suit, then began climbing the ladder. She ascended more rapidly than Toni expected, walked to the edge of the tiny platform, looked down—then, to Toni's surprise, she *turned around,* standing with her back to the empty bleachers facing the stage.

She gave herself a slight push off the platform, then fell backward into space.

In barely the time it took Toni to gasp, Bee's plummeting body began to somersault—tumbling end over end, not once but *twice*—ending upright just in time for her to plunge, feetfirst, into the water. Upon impact, a tidal wave of water lapped over the side of the tank and Bee was lost to sight. But in moments, a hand popped out of the water, and soon Bee was clambering down the tank's side ladder, a big smile on her face.

Toni had never seen anyone looking happier in her life.

"That's my girl," Bee's husband, Will, said proudly. "She's something, ain't she?"

"I'll say!" Toni replied.

"So how'd you like it?" Bee asked as she approached.

"That was great!" Toni was filled with a thousand questions. "But how could you see the tank if you were jumping backwards?"

Will handed Bee a towel; she began drying off her hair. "Before I turn around, I look down and gauge the distance," she told Toni. "There was a little wind, so I had to take that into account too. The trick is in straightening up so you're perpendicular to the water when you hit. That soft water can be a mighty hard landing field if you hit it wrong."

"But there's six feet of water and only five feet of *you*," Toni noted, not inaccurately, which made Bee laugh. "Do you hit the bottom?"

"Not if I can help it," Bee said cheerfully. "I wait till I'm waist deep in the water, then I pull up my legs to my chest to break my fall. It has to be done just so—too soon and my neck would snap back and break, too late and my back would be broken."

"Boy," Toni said, "I think you're the greatest diver in the whole world!"

"Well, thank you. Come see me tomorrow—at night I do a fire dive."

"What's that?"

"We spread gasoline on the surface of the water and ignite it, and I do the same to myself before jumping."

Toni was incredulous. "G'wan!"

"It's true. I wear a special asbestos suit, soak it in gasoline, then turn myself into a human torch."

Now *this* sounded scary to Toni, but also thrilling. Toni promised she would come, thanked Bee for letting her watch, and went racing to her parents' French fry stand, where she barely paused to catch her breath:

"Mama there's a lady high diver and she does a fire dive and she invited me to come tomorrow night and can I go see her, can I go?"

"Lady high diver?" Adele said. Oh, this didn't sound good.

Eddie told Toni, "We'll talk about it tomorrow, honey, we've got to open the stand. Go join your grandma at the pool."

Toni went skipping excitedly across the midway to the pool. Adele turned to Eddie: "Fire dive? What the hell is that?"

Eddie said, "You're not gonna like the answer."

Indeed, neither Adele nor Eddie were overjoyed at the prospect of their adventurous daughter watching a woman douse herself in gasoline, light a match, then fall flaming into a burning tank of gas and water. The unwelcome image of Toni standing on the roof of the house, clothes soaked in gasoline, a matchbook in one hand, came all too easily to both of them, and they were prepared to tell her, at breakfast the next morning, no fire dive.

But of course Toni told Jack all about Bee Kyle and her act, and by morning Jack's imagination was equally captivated, though for different reasons: "I want to see the Human Torch! I thought it was just a comic character, I didn't know it was real, *please,* can't we go see the Human Torch?"

He proudly presented his parents with the latest issue of *Marvel Mystery Comics,* whose cover depicted a flaming man—accompanied by what appeared to be a flaming *child,* no less—throwing fireballs at monsters. On the cover of another issue, the Torch—who could also fly—was dive-bombing oil tanks apparently marked for his convenience with swastikas on their roofs, his fireballs causing them to explode.

Eddie thumbed through the comic and told Adele, "If this is what they've been reading, it's a wonder they haven't already set the house on fire. Maybe the lady diver isn't such a big deal."

Adele examined the magazine—though she barely thought it deserving of the name—and winced, the acrid memory of the '35 fire still fresh. But Eddie had a point. And both kids seemed so excited. She hated always being the bad guy, the one to provoke that pall of disappointment in her daughter's eyes. She glanced at Eddie and shrugged.

As Eddie flipped through the magazines, his eye caught something that sparked an idea. He turned to the kids. "*If* we agree to let you come see this tonight, you have to promise me that neither one of you will *ever*—not until you're at least *eighteen* years old—so much as touch a matchbook," he said, then, adding the coup de grâce: "And you have to give your solemn pledge as members of Captain America's Sentinels of Liberty."

He held up the pertinent page, which depicted the good captain swearing in a group of youngsters to his club.

Sobered, the kids sat up a little straighter. Jack immediately raised his hand, as the children in the ad with Captain America were doing. "I pledge!"

Toni's hand shot up next. "I pledge too!"

"Good. It's one thing letting your mother and me down—it's another thing to let down Captain America."

Adele just rolled her eyes.

That evening, she manned the stand on her own as Eddie took the kids to the free-act stage, where Bee's husband introduced his famous wife: *"Voted the number-one favorite performer in outdoor show business by* Billboard *magazine, she's thrilled audiences across the country and around the world—in far-off China, in mysterious Japan, and just back from a ten-week engagement in the beautiful Hawaiian Islands! You will not see a more sensational act in your lifetime than the one presented here tonight! Ladies and gentlemen, I give you the incomparable* Bee Kyle!"

When Bee appeared, she was wearing a padded, fireproof costume—not as colorful, perhaps, as the ones Jack's comic book heroes wore, but it still excited his youthful imagination. Toni and Jack watched as the lady daredevil doused herself in gasoline—you could feel the sting of it in your nostrils even back in the tenth row—and then began climbing the ladder. After she'd reached the top, her husband announced to the crowd, *"And now, the ring of fire!"* He struck a match, tossing it into the gasoline-laced tank—which burst into a ring of flames, leaving only a donut hole of open water, no more than five feet across, in the middle of the fiery corona.

On the diving platform, Bee now did the same—igniting her gas-soaked costume and setting herself ablaze, indeed a veritable human torch.

Jack and Toni gasped along with the rest of the audience.

She turned her back on the crowd, the flames writhing around her body as if she commanded them to do so. She milked the suspense for all it was worth, the spectators squirming in their seats, wondering if they were bearing witness to a woman being burned alive.

And then she pushed herself backward off the platform, as Toni had seen her do yesterday. But this was even more remarkable, as Bee's flaming body tumbled end over end in a somersault—her fiery tail looking like pinwheeling fireworks as she fell like a burning meteor to the earth.

She righted herself seconds before plunging into the tank. A geyser of water and steam erupted inside the ring of flames, extinguishing the fire.

Toni held her breath. Then a padded hand broke the surface and Bee Kyle clambered out and down the side ladder, to the thunderous approval of the audience. The ovation thrilled Toni as much as the performance, the applause resonating deep inside her. She knew now why Bee did what she did for a living—and knew that someday, she was going to do it too.

While Beatrice Kyle was performing at Palisades, the indefatigable Bert Nevins came up with another inspired bit of press agentry: he had Bee write (or at least sign her name to) a letter addressed to Secretary of the Interior Harold Ickes, who administered the country's fuel and petroleum reserves for defense purposes. After describing her unusual livelihood, she explained her quandary to the secretary and sought his advice:

Over the summer season I use more than 300 gallons of gasoline, and if you feel that such use is wasteful I will be glad to change my act.

No response from Ickes was ever noted, though somehow the letter found its way into the hands of newspapers across the country.

It was, as Irving Rosenthal would have said, "a sweet gag." But in only three months' time, such a proposition would be no laughing matter.

7

EDDIE WAS LISTENING, that Sunday afternoon, to a football game on WOR—the New York Giants playing the Brooklyn Dodgers at the Polo Grounds. It was 2:25 P.M., midway through the first quarter, and the Dodgers' kickoff was caught at the three-yard line by running back Ward Cuff of the Giants. Assisted by some nice defense from teammate Tuffy Leemans, Cuff ran it up to the twenty-seven-yard line before he was taken down hard by Frank "Bruiser" Kinard of Brooklyn—at which point the game was interrupted by the crackle of an announcer cutting in with:

"We interrupt this broadcast to bring you this important bulletin from the United Press. Flash! Washington. The White House announces Japanese attack on Pearl Harbor. Stay tuned to WOR for further developments which will be broadcast as received."

Like many startled Americans that day, Eddie's first thought was: "Where the hell is Pearl Harbor?"

Taking the news in stride, WOR promptly returned to football, but Eddie immediately lost all interest in the game and switched over to CBS, where the news program *The World Today* was due to start at 2:30 P.M. It began with a bulletin from newsman John Charles Daly:

"The Japanese have attacked Pearl Harbor, Hawai'i, from the air, President Roosevelt just announced. The attack was also made on all naval and military activity on the principal island of O'ahu . . ."

Eddie knew where Hawai'i was, and he knew at once that the future he had been dreading had finally arrived.

On this unseasonably spring-like day in December, the kids were out roller-skating when normally they might have been lacing up their ice skates at Fettes Pond. Eddie quietly called Adele into the living room. Pulled by the shifting tide of news reports from CBS to NBC Red to Mutual to NBC Blue, they tried to piece together what was happening six thousand miles away in the middle of the Pacific Ocean. The news flashes were alarming but vague—until one reported grimly that it was believed hundreds of men had been killed at Hickam Air Field, adjacent to Pearl Harbor.

Adele's eyes filled with tears as she wordlessly gripped Eddie's hand.

At 4:05 P.M., NBC Blue announced that FDR would meet with his cabinet and congressional leaders that evening. This was followed by a live broadcast from the Pacific: *"Hello NBC, hello NBC, this is KGU Honolulu. I am speaking from the roof of the Advertiser Publishing Company building. We have witnessed this morning from a distance . . . a severe bombing of Pearl Harbor by enemy planes, undoubtedly Japanese . . . One of the bombs dropped within fifty feet of KGU tower. It is no joke, it is a real war."*

Adele said softly, "My God. Not again."

Each of them had been children during the First World War, and now it looked as though they were going to live to see the Second.

Eddie nodded soberly. "Yeah. My cousin Freddy came back from the first one with only one arm—and he was one of the lucky ones."

It would be another week before Secretary of the Navy Frank Knox, returning from the scene in Hawai'i, would reveal that casualties numbered not in the hundreds but the thousands, and that six warships had been lost in the attack: the battleship *Arizona*, three destroyers, and two smaller ships, crippled and sunk in their berths like men shot in their sleep.

Pearl Harbor shattered the American complacency that foreign wars would remain just that—fought on foreign soil, the United States existing in a permanent state of grace guaranteed by the vast bulwarks of the Atlantic and Pacific Oceans. Not within living memory—a hundred and twenty-five years—had the United States been attacked by a foreign power on its own territory. Eddie and Adele's reaction was, like that of most Americans, one of shock, rage, defiance—and an unaccustomed sense of vulnerability.

The Stopka children, however, were blessed with the invincibility of youth, and when they came in for Sunday supper, they greeted news of the attack enthusiastically: "Oh boy!" Jack whooped. "War!" "We'll show those Japs who's boss," Toni declared. They then went on to debate who would do more damage to the Axis war machine: the Human Torch, Captain Marvel, or Superman. And say, wasn't it almost time to listen to *The Shadow*?

The next day, after President Roosevelt asked for a declaration of war on Japan, Congress followed up with legislation expanding the draft call, requiring all men from eighteen to sixty-five years old to register. The Selective Service would also reexamine the status of the seventeen million men aged twenty-one to thirty-five who were already registered—like Eddie.

But this almost seemed unnecessary, at first. On December 9, the Army, Navy, and Marine recruiting centers in Newark were overflowing with men so eager to enlist that the offices had to remain open around the clock.

Eddie was not immune: his first, patriotic impulse was to join the stampede on the recruiting offices. Already friends from the lumberyard, all bachelors, had signed up for the fight. Eddie wanted to smash the Japs as much as they did—but if he did, who would provide for his family?

"Eddie, for God's sake, *don't enlist,*" Adele begged him. "I know how you feel, but we need you here, at home. How will I feed the kids?"

"I could send you all my service pay," Eddie offered.

"Which is what? Forty, fifty dollars a month? How far will that go?"

"I read in the papers, they're already talking about providing some kind of allowances for servicemen's wives," Eddie said.

"And what about our stand at Palisades? I can't run it by myself."

"You can hire somebody to help out."

"You can't trust an employee like you can family." Adele said pointedly, "How many carnivals have you worked where concession agents have been holding out on the owner from the day's take?"

Eddie frowned. "A lot," he had to admit.

"That's why the Mazzocchis and the Cunys are grooming their kids to take over their concessions."

She made a persuasive case, as did events later that day—when air-raid sirens blared raucously into life, all the way from Cape May to Boston.

The various municipalities in Bergen County hadn't agreed yet on a common air-raid signal; in Cliffside Park and Fort Lee, it was a siren wailing for two straight minutes. But in Edgewater it was four screeching blasts of a steam whistle, repeated four times—scaring the hell out of Adele when she first heard it, sending her laundry whites flying out of the basket and into the air like surrender flags. When she heard the rumble of planes overhead she raced to the windows—aware that this was the last thing she should be doing—and her heart pounded as she saw a squadron of planes bearing ominously down the Hudson River toward New York Harbor. But after a few moments she realized they were ours—Army Air Corps planes scrambling to meet enemy planes, thought to be coming in off the Atlantic.

Eddie rushed home from work in time to hear on the radio that there had been no enemy planes—it was just a case of jangled nerves. Adele hugged him as if there were real bombs falling all around them. "Thank God you're here, Eddie," she said in a shaky voice, then began sobbing. He held her, kissed her head, stroked her hair, and promised her everything would be all right, as empty a lie as he had ever told in his life.

Toni and Jack experienced the air raid at school and found it a good deal more exciting than did their parents. "Boy, that was fun!" Toni declared when she got home, and Eddie didn't contradict her: he'd rather they thought this all a lark than be frightened, as some of their classmates were, by the raid. And he had to admit, for the moment he was glad he was here at home, where he could comfort his children—and wife—if need be.

A meeting of the local Civil Defense Council drew fourteen hundred people to Cliffside Park High School, where officials noted that New Jersey's many defense plants—with more factories retooling for defense every day—represented prime targets for German bombers. "It is a certainty," one speaker said soberly, "that the New York metropolitan area will suffer at least a token bombing attack before the war is over." This inspired scores of volunteers for civil defense and Red Cross first-aid classes. Adele signed up for the latter.

But as it turned out it wasn't Nazi bombers that New Jerseyans had to fear—it was Nazi U-boats.

On the night of January 25, 1942, a German submarine torpedoed the Norwegian oil tanker *Varanger,* thirty-five miles off the coast of Sea Isle City, New Jersey. The concussion could be heard as far north as Atlantic City. Its forty crewmen survived the attack, but in March the American freighter *Lemuel Burrows* was sunk off Atlantic City, claiming twenty lives. A surviving officer said that the lights blazing along the Jersey shore "were like Coney Island. It was lit up like daylight along the beach" . . . perfectly silhouetting the *Burrows,* making it an easy target for the U-boat.

Prowling the waters from Newfoundland to the Florida Keys, Nazi submarines were soon sinking freighters with impunity. The government ordered street and boardwalk lights extinguished all along the Jersey coast and banned illuminated nighttime advertising. (Night baseball was also three strikes and out for the duration.) Now, in the evenings, families like the Stopkas sat within the violet nimbus of a blackout lamp, the only other light being the green gaze of the radio's tuning eye. Opaque blackout drapes were drawn across their windows, allowing no seepage of light to escape. Even Manhattan had lost some of its luster, its skyline dimmed with swaths of black where lights once burned all night long.

Across the Eastern Seaboard families gathered, each in their own private darkness—yet still laughing at Bob Hope and Jack Benny, still keeping rhythm with Glenn Miller and Paul Whiteman, and listening attentively to news of the war, *their* war, the one they were living and fighting even now, here in their own blacked-out living rooms.

With remarkable speed, America's economy shifted to a wartime footing. All civilian auto production was halted as car manufacturers—including the Ford Motor Assembly Plant in Edgewater—converted to the construction of tanks, tank destroyers, Jeeps, half-tracks, amphibious vehicles, aircraft engines, and munitions. Eddie, eager to contribute to the war effort, quit the lumberyard and applied for a job on the assembly line at Ford. Unemployment in America became, almost overnight, a thing of the past as the Federal government pumped billions of dollars into defense.

But money couldn't make ordnance out of thin air, and after the Japanese invaded the Dutch West Indies, rubber was instantly in short supply. Automobile tires became the first item to be rationed to the public, and to minimize wear, car owners were allotted four gallons of gas per week; the covers of the Gas Ration Books encouraged them to DRIVE UNDER 35.

Soon joining the list of rationed items would be bicycles, kerosene, sugar, coffee (one cup a day), butter, meats and canned fish, and shoes.

Conservation was the watchword of the day. Housewives like Adele were urged to save their beef drippings and bacon fat in a wide-mouthed can and take it to the local butcher in exchange for ration points. "Okay," Adele asked one morning as she dutifully began draining pork grease from the skillet, "can someone tell me what earthly use the U.S. Army has for *bacon* fat? Do they grease the battlefield and hope the Nazis slip on it?"

"They told us at school, Mama!" Jack piped up enthusiastically. "You make something called glycerin out of the fat—"

"And they turn the glycerin into *bombs!*" Toni finished with a flourish. "BOOM!"

"I've got to go blow up a few Nazis today myself," Eddie said, kissing his family goodbye to go to work—where for eight hours a day he inspected engine cowlings on tanks which, the minute they rolled off the line, were on their way to Moscow to resupply the besieged Red Army.

Toni and Jack did their bit for the war too, collecting all kinds of scrap—rubber, rags, tin cans, bedsprings, even foil wrappers from chewing gum and Hershey's Kisses—for salvage drives. Jack, in the ultimate show of patriotism, even turned in his old comic books for the paper drive. Like children all across the country, they prided themselves on being a part of the war effort. Even schoolyard play took on a different tone, as girls skipped rope to new lyrics to a song from Walt Disney's *Snow White and the Seven Dwarfs:*

Whistle while you work,
Hitler is a jerk.
Mussolini is a weenie,
And Tojo is a jerk!

Eddie, who closely followed the war news, found these mild epithets inadequate for an enemy capable of committing the kinds of atrocities that seemed to follow in their wake: In Hong Kong, on Christmas Day, Japanese troops invaded a hospital, shot the doctor in charge, and bayoneted fifty-six wounded soldiers. A month later, in Malaya, the Japanese ordered the mass execution of one hundred and sixty-one captured and wounded Australian, British, and Indian soldiers. Their bodies were heaped in the street and burned. And in February, after the British colony of Singapore surrendered to the Japanese, the occupying army began the systematic execution of thousands of ethnic Chinese believed "hostile" to the Japanese.

Reports like these made Eddie's blood boil, and for the first time in his life he started having trouble sleeping, haunted by the stories coming out of Europe and the Pacific. A safe stateside job on an assembly line, no matter how vital to defense, couldn't erase his nagging guilt at not being overseas, in the thick of it, doing his part for his country.

So in March, when Eddie's draft number finally came up and he was ordered to report to his local draft board, he was secretly happy to go. But if he was expecting a rousing, patriotic call to arms with an underscore of George M. Cohan songs, he was grotesquely disappointed. At the draft board he and a hundred other draftees were ordered to strip to their shorts, and even less, for a series of tests. Eddie found himself in one of many long lines of naked men doing their best to ignore their own sagging testicles—to say nothing of the fat ass cheeks and ripe body odor of the guys in line ahead of them. Eddie was fingerprinted, had blood and urine taken, underwent physical and psychiatric exams. There was nothing rousing about a proctologist's glove, though the mere suggestion otherwise would have been enough to keep a man out of the Army.

When Eddie was told to put his clothes on again, his hopes were dashed as his draft card was stamped 3-A: "Married, with dependent children." Neither the Army nor the Navy was yet drafting fathers—at least not fathers of children born before Pearl Harbor—and he was automatically given a deferment. Eddie felt a little sick to look at the paperwork he had been handed. He could've handed it back—demanded to enlist. But he told himself this was the way it had to be: he had a family to support. Nobody could fault him for that. Even so, as he walked out of the draft board, still a civilian, an increasingly large part of him couldn't help feeling like a coward.

Palisades Amusement Park, as it prepared to open in late April, had firmly committed itself to the war effort. No new rides were constructed in order to save building materials for the defense industry. Jack and Irving Rosenthal refitted all of the park's lighting to comply with the Federal dim-out regulations: all exterior lighting on rides and stands was to be extinguished, the neon spokes of the Ferris wheel going dark, and only interior lighting allowed to illuminate concessions. The huge scrolling electrical sign on the cliff would also go dark and the incandescent Palisades name would not be visible from New York City for the first time in decades.

The Rosenthals held War Bond rallies at the park and instructed head gardener Mike Corrado to plant a huge Victory Garden to help inspire visitors to grow their own produce at home. On Wednesdays ten percent of gate receipts were donated to the Army and Navy Relief Funds, and servicemen were admitted free of charge to the park. As Irving Rosenthal told the press, "We in the amusement business have a definite and important part to play in our country's war effort, and that is to provide wholesome outdoor recreation to bolster the morale of the people."

The park opened on April 25, accompanied by newspaper ads proclaiming MORE PLAY MAKES BETTER WORK. Despite the gas shortage, Palisades opened to big gate receipts and stayed there all summer.

Eddie took a leave of absence from Ford to honor his lease with the Rosenthals. Meat shortages limited hot dog vendors to one per customer, but fortunately potatoes weren't rationed and the stand's Saratoga fries were cooked in corn oil, not butter. (The leftover cooking grease, collected dutifully by Adele, was surely enough to blow up a Panzer division.) Eddie told himself that the more money he made, the more his family would have in the bank against the day when the Army began drafting fathers.

But he found it hard as hell to put on a jolly face when he knew men were fighting and dying outside the festive bubble of Palisades. He was reminded of this every day, with every soldier or sailor on leave—Hoboken was a major hub for servicemen shipping out to Europe and the Pacific—who came to the park for one last good time, an innocent taste of home and happiness before both became in very short supply.

Keeping a cheery tone was mandatory for the park's fortune-tellers, who each day had to read the palms of departing servicemen and reassure them, "All is not certain, but I believe things will turn out all right for you."

But after the park closed at midnight some of them, along with Adele and Eddie, went across the street to Joe's for a few stiff drinks. One "palmist," Opal, broke down crying: "Things *won't* turn out all right for some of them. I feel like a lying louse. But what else am I going to say?"

Adele said, "It's what they want to hear, hon. Just tell them what they want to hear and they'll go away happy."

"I know, I know," Opal said, drying her eyes with a napkin. "But I wouldn't blame them a bit if—God forbid—as they get hit by a Japanese mortar, they think, 'That bitch of a fortune-teller sure steered me wrong!'"

The departing servicemen weren't always strangers but familiar faces from Palisades. Jackie Morris, the son of Charlie "Doc" Morris—who with his father had booked group excursions for the park—had actually been inducted into the Army a month before Pearl Harbor. Hugh McKenna, chief lifeguard at the pool, was next to enter the service, followed by Jimmy Hannan of the Lake Placid Bobsled and Bill Gomez of the Casino Bar. Dr. Frank Vita soon said his goodbyes, too, as did Roscoe Schwartz's two sons, Roscoe Jr. and Laurent. Laurent was only nineteen when he joined the Marines.

It shamed Eddie to think that while nineteen-year-olds were putting their lives in harm's way, an old man of thirty-one like him was spending the summer risking nothing more than a hot splash of corn oil.

Nor was Eddie alone in feeling left behind—Bunty Hill had been turned down for military service due to his age. "I'm only forty years old, for Chrissake," he griped to Eddie on their lunch break. "I swim the goddamn Hudson every day. Do I look like I've got one foot in the grave?"

"Maybe you've got too many dependents, Bunty," Eddie said.

"What? I'm single! Never been married. And I haven't planted any seedlings along the way, either."

"I'm talking about all the lovely gals here at the pool who *depend* on you to take them out and show 'em a good time. Helen and Muriel and Edith and Rosalie—you're a one-man morale industry, Bunty."

"Aw, shaddup," Bunty said, but couldn't help laughing as he said it. He tossed a copy of *The New York Times* to Eddie. "And by the way, while we're cooling our heels on the homefront, here's the latest shit the land of my forefathers is visiting upon the land of *your* forefathers."

Eddie took the paper—yesterday's, dated June 27, 1942. He had read about the recent massacres in Poland—Jewish Poles slaughtered and stacked in mass graves in towns like Bydogszcz and Bialystok. He'd heard of the remark made by that pig Heinrich Himmler, head of the SS: "All Poles will disappear from the world." But he was still shocked by what he saw on the bottom of page five, two small paragraphs that read:

According to an announcement of the Polish Government in London, 700,000 Jews were slain by the Nazis in Poland. The report was broadcast by the British Broadcasting Corporation and was recorded by the Columbia Broadcasting System in New York yesterday.

"To accomplish this, probably the greatest mass slaughter in history, every death-dealing method was employed—machine-gun bullets, hand grenades, gas chambers, concentration camps, whipping, torture instruments and starvation," the Polish announcement said.

Eddie was stunned. Seven hundred *thousand* people? "Jesus Christ," he said softly. "Gas chambers? You think this is true?"

"I don't doubt it for a second. The sons of bitches are doing the same thing in Paris. Paris fucking *France,* for Chrissake! Rounding up French Jews and sending them to a 'labor camp' called Auschwitz."

Eddie reminded himself that these were the same monsters who had gone into mental hospitals in Bydogszcz and shot to death more than three thousand mental patients so their inferior genes could not contaminate the pure Aryan gene pool. Why should he be surprised that the Nazis would embrace the greatest horror of the First World War—poison gas—and "improve" upon it, turn it into a mass assembly line of death?

"God help us all," Bunty said, "if these bastards actually win. How many of us do you think'll be left once they start 'purifying' America? After they get rid of all the Jews, the Negroes, the queers . . ." He broke into a mordant laugh. "Christ, who'll be left in show business?"

Eddie laughed, but it was no joke.

Toni and Jack, of course, followed war news of their own—the Axis-smashing adventures of Captain America, the Human Torch, and others—and that meant a weekly trip to Pitkof's Candy Store on Palisade Avenue in Cliffside Park. Eddie drove them there in the morning before work. Pitkof's was a small store with a soda fountain, confectionary, and most important, a magazine rack which contained all the month's comic books. As Eddie pulled up to the curb he noted that one of the store windows was boarded up with plywood, but there was an OPEN sign on the front door. Inside, Jack Pitkof, wearing a gray service jacket, sat behind the counter reading a Yiddish newspaper. He was a quiet, mild-mannered man in his late forties who also served as a local Air Raid Warden. Eddie remembered him once telling him how he and his brothers had escaped Tsarist Russia "under cover of night, hidden under straw in wagons, and arrived in America with exactly nothing."

Eddie's kids made a beeline for the comics rack and began paging through the latest issues of *Sub-Mariner* and *Blackhawk.* Eddie warned, "This isn't a library, you two, it's Mr. Pitkof's livelihood. Pick out your favorites and I'll buy them for you."

"Eh, it's okay," Jack Pitkof said with a shrug, "all the kids do it. As long as they buy something, I don't care how much they read."

"You're too generous, Jack."

"No such thing" was his only response.

"So what happened to the front window?" Eddie asked.

"Eh, some hooligans broke it. It'll be fixed by tomorrow."

"This isn't the first time, is it? You have any idea who's doing it?"

"They didn't leave a calling card. Unless you count the words 'dirty kike' scrawled on the window," Pitkof said mildly.

He promptly changed the subject to baseball, the upcoming Yankees game, but Eddie wasn't listening. He was too shocked and angry.

Bunty was wrong. It wasn't that it *could* happen here. It already *was* happening here.

"All Poles will disappear from the world."

His sister was a Pole. His children were Poles. And he'd be damned if he'd let them disappear from the face of the earth.

Palisades Park finished the season well into the black: now that people had money to spend, they were happy to lavish it on a few hours of amusement, something to distract them from the otherwise omnipresent war. The Stopkas cleared a nice profit on their stand, a portion of which they invested in war bonds, the remainder going straight into the bank.

By summer's end the U-boat attacks along the East Coast dwindled as a combination of naval convoys and a more aggressive pursuit of Nazi subs began to pay off. There was also less talk of the possible bombing of cities like New York—perhaps because Hitler had his hands full in Russia and North Africa and couldn't squander his resources on targets across the Atlantic.

Adele continued to volunteer with the Red Cross, her dance lessons on hold for the duration—they felt frivolous now. It seemed as if everyone in the country had only one occupation—winning the war—and Adele fretted less over her career. Sure, she wished she could be like Minette, on a War Bond tour with her father, Frank, but for now she was content to roll bandages, help with blood drives, and be home in time to cook dinner for her family.

But when she got home on that last Thursday of September, she was surprised and puzzled to find Eddie already there.

"Hi," she said, giving him a kiss. "Your shift end early?"

"No." His eyes met hers and she saw immediately that something was wrong. "I quit Ford," he blurted out.

"You what?"

"I . . . took another job," he said. "I enlisted in the Naval Reserves."

She just stared at him. What kind of stupid joke was this? "Yeah, sure," she said, "and I just joined the WACs."

"I'm not kidding. Here."

He handed her a sheet of paper, which she took in with disbelief: a Certificate of Voluntary Induction into the United States Navy.

She felt a cold shiver of betrayal and looked up at him. "Eddie, how . . . how could you *do* this?"

"Honey, there's nothing to worry about," he said quickly. "Congress just passed a bill, the Servicemen's Dependent Allowance Act of 1942—"

He gave her another sheet of paper, some kind of government hand-out, but she didn't even give it a glance, just hurled it angrily aside.

"God *damn* it, Eddie!" she shouted, the chill of betrayal turning hot. "You promised we'd discuss this—"

"I know, but look, everything we talked about has been taken care of," he said with that big damn smile of his. "The government's going to pay a monthly allowance to the wife and children of every serviceman. They take twenty-two bucks a month out of my base pay, then they kick in another twenty-eight for you, twelve for Toni, and ten for Jack. Uncle Sam will send you seventy-two dollars a month, I can send you even more of my pay . . . and there's all the money we made at Palisades too. You won't have to worry about where the kids' food or clothing is going to come from, you see?"

He was looking at her as if he expected her to break into a relieved laugh. Or maybe throw her arms around his neck and give him a kiss.

"And what happens," she said in a flat tone, "if you're killed?"

"Well, that's covered too," he said without missing a beat. "I can purchase life insurance worth up to ten thousand dollars. And you and the kids will get free health benefits, too. It's a good deal."

His expectant eyes were still waiting for that laugh or kiss.

Instead he got a stinging slap across the face, connecting so hard it actually staggered him, rocked him on his heels.

"You son of a *bitch!*" she screamed at him. "Who gave you the right to decide whether your wife wants to be a widow, or your kids orphans? Did you give your children even *one* damn minute of consideration?"

He bristled at that. "I'm *doing* it for them—so they don't end up living in a country where they can be sent to a Nazi death camp."

"Oh, *you're* going to stop that?" she said, her voice a mocking razor. "Eisenhower and Patton can't swing that without your help?"

"Adele, it's my duty! I owe it to my country."

"You have a duty to us, too! You can serve your country by building tanks for Ford, why the hell do you want to *die* for your country?"

"I won't die," he insisted.

"Did Opal read your palm and tell you that?"

"Jesus, Adele, I just want to make a difference—to help!"

"Oh, you *always* want to help, don't you?" she said with cold fury. "Good old Eddie, always there to lend a hand, or a sawbuck, to anybody who needs it. Except your family. You going to walk out on me and the kids like you walked out on your mother and sister?"

He flinched at that, and Adele realized with a queasy regret that she had perhaps gone too far. Silence stretched painfully between them, until finally she said, "I'm sorry. That wasn't fair. Or true."

"No, you're right," he said quietly. "I did walk out on them. And I can't blame you for feeling like I'm doing the same to you." He took her hands in his; at least she didn't pull them back. "*I'm* sorry. You're right, I should have told you. But if I had, you know you'd have talked me out of it. Honey, I love you and the kids more than anything on earth, but . . . I can't just sit here while the whole world is going to hell on skates. There are six million other guys like me already out there, and if they'd all said, 'Let somebody else do it,' there'd be nobody to stop these bastards from burning down villages in China or gassing trains full of Jews. I'm nobody special, I know that—my mom once said I was 'just an ordinary boy.' Well, we're *all* ordinary boys, and if takes six million, seven million, *eight* million of us to stop these murdering sons of bitches, then that's what it takes. If we start thinking of ourselves as too important to serve—too important to die—then the Nazis will win, not because they're the supermen they say they are, but because *we're* no kind of men at all."

Adele wrapped her arms around him and cried, knowing there was nothing more she could say or do. There never had been.

When Toni and Jack got home from school, Eddie broke the news to them as gently as he could. They had seen enough of their classmates' fathers go away to understand what was happening, but now that it was their own father, they weren't so sure. "When will you be back, Daddy?" Toni asked, a quaver of fear in her voice.

Blinking back tears, Eddie said, "When the war's over, sweetie."

"How long will that be?" Jack asked.

"I don't know, honey," Eddie admitted. "I wish I did."

Toni would remember for the rest of her life the uncertainty in his voice. Daddy had always known *everything* before—the fact that he didn't know this was the first frightening chip in her childhood invincibility.

Two days later the family saw him off at Central Station in Newark, Eddie in his new white sailor's uniform and hat, along with hundreds of others boarding the train for Norfolk, Virginia. Eddie hugged Toni and Jack, told them he loved them very much, and promised he'd be back. He and Adele shared a long kiss, a passionate reminder of their lovemaking the night before. Now, as Adele looked into his face, she wondered fearfully if this would be the last time she would ever see him again. She tried not to think about it and yet could think of nothing else as she watched him board the train, then wave at them from a window as the train rattled down the tracks. Toni began to cry, and then Jack, and Adele squatted down and wrapped her arms around both of them at once. "It's all right, Daddy will be back," she said, even as tears were streaming down her own face, and by the time they had all stopped crying, the train and Eddie were both long gone.

8

Honolulu, Territory of Hawai'i, 1943

EDDIE STOOD IN THE BOW of the S.S. *Lurline*, once the queen of the
Matson Line's "white fleet" of luxury ocean liners, now a troop carrier—
its white hull grizzled to battleship gray, its ports smudged black, its
luxurious staterooms stripped of amenities and triple-tiered with bunks
for up to four thousand military personnel—as the ship cruised into
gentle trade winds. Their destination heralded itself before it even came
into view, the warm breezes balmy with the sweet smell of exotic flow-
ers, harbinger of land to come. He took in the scented air and thought of
Adele's perfume. Now a few shoots of green sprouted on the horizon,
which slowly grew into distant burls of brown and green. Soon there was
no mistaking them for what they were: islands. The Hawaiian Islands.

As more sailors gathered on deck, the bosun's mate told Eddie that
the ship was coming in on a due westerly heading and would be passing
between the islands of Moloka'i and O'ahu. Eddie's first close glimpse
of Hawai'i was dramatically different, yet more magnificent, than anything he had ever seen or heard in Hollywood movies or popular songs.
Off the port side he saw what he assumed to be Moloka'i, ringed with sea
cliffs—green rugged monuments taller even than the Jersey Palisades—
rising like sentinels thousands of feet above deserted beaches. Waterfalls
spilled down notches in the lush foliage, and it seemed there was barely
a dock or habitation visible anywhere along the shoreline.

Off the starboard side floated O'ahu, far less forbidding, its white beaches backed up by furrowed mountains bearded in soft greenery. The coastal waters were a brilliant turquoise, the island beatified by a halo of jade coral reefs. Within minutes *Lurline* was steaming past an instantly recognizable landmark: the caldera of the long-extinct volcano known the world over as Diamond Head. Its slopes were sere, drier and browner than Eddie had expected, but there was a stark beauty to them, like the granite face of the Palisades. As the ship rounded Diamond Head he saw the pale crescent moon of famous Waikīkī Beach, with several hotels situated at points along the crescent, one a white plantation-style building with a long pier jutting into the sea, another a coral-pink Moroccan-style palace.

Eddie was enchanted by what he saw, even the low-rise buildings of modern Honolulu that nestled at the foot of luxuriant green peaks and valleys. The *Lurline* steamed past Waikīkī and made its way toward Pearl Harbor, where small tugs drew apart the antisubmarine nets to admit the ship through the entrance channel and into the harbor's East Loch. Pearl was bustling with purpose and activity: destroyers, cruisers, battlewagons, and an aircraft carrier were in port; other ships were cradled in huge dry docks as their battle wounds were ministered to by Navy Yard personnel.

As *Lurline* passed the eastern flank of Ford Island—known as "Battleship Row" since December 7—Eddie was surprised to see remnants of that dark day still visible. The battleship *Oklahoma*, victim of a barrage of Japanese torpedoes, lay a few hundred yards offshore, listing to port and kept upright only by dozens of steel cables stretching to Ford Island, where they connected to a battery of enormous winches that had slowly and laboriously pulled and righted the capsized ship to its present position.

"Soon as she's floated again," the bosun's mate told Eddie, "they'll tow her to dry dock and try to repair her . . . or at least salvage whatever they can."

Farther along, that was exactly what was happening to the U.S.S. *Arizona*, her sunken hulk now a kind of steel cairn for eleven hundred sailors and Marines. Further recovery of bodies was impossible, and the decision had been made to let her rest where she had died, at the bottom of berth F-7. As *Lurline* passed, Eddie saw there was not much of *Arizona* left above the waterline—just gun tubs pointed helplessly into the air, from which workmen were now salvaging as much ammunition as they could. One of the turrets, emptied of its fourteen-inch shells, was in the process of being scrapped, amputated at the waterline so that eventually the sea would cover the remainder of *Arizona* and the souls who were entombed in her.

There was utter silence among the men on deck, and then one of them raised his hand in a salute to the crew of the *Arizona*. Eddie raised his hand as well, his eyes filling with tears of grief and anger, as the men of the *Lurline*, about to enter the war, offered a solemn salute to those who had already left it, and given their last full measure in doing so.

The majority of the troops aboard the *Lurline* would continue on to the South Pacific after a brief stopover on Oʻahu, but Eddie and a handful of others were assigned temporary quarters in the naval barracks at Pearl until they received orders to their final destination in a week or two. Where that might be, he had no idea—ship schedules were not published and sailors were usually the last to know where they were headed. But Eddie had trained for sixteen weeks at aviation metalsmith school and assumed he was headed for the front lines as a mechanic aboard, perhaps, an aircraft carrier.

Since there was a dusk-to-dawn curfew in the islands, all liberty took place during daylight hours—no bars and few restaurants were permitted to be open after dark. On his first day of liberty, Eddie and two swabbies he met in the barracks, Sal and Ernie, took the bus downtown to Hotel Street—or, as Sal described it, "the only action you'll find on this rock." They were not alone seeking action: the sidewalks were overflowing with servicemen, a swollen river of white and khaki uniforms jostling their way up the street or waiting in block-long queues to enter one of the many bars, tattoo parlors, arcades, and hotels that crowded each side of the street.

To Eddie it had the familiar look, sound, and rhythm of a carnival midway. Sidewalk photographers sold pictures of fresh-faced GIs smiling beside dime-store hula girls, posing against a cardboard background of phony palm trees on an island where real ones were scarcely in short supply. Other entrepreneurs shilled postcards, watches, and Hawaiian curios. The air was fragrant with the smell of prawns sizzling in coconut oil being sold by sidewalk vendors. As Eddie and his friends joined the surging tide of men, the buzzing of tattoo needles competed with the rat-a-tat of pellet guns from shooting galleries offering, in the words of one concessionaire, "the once-in-a-lifetime opportunity to shoot Hitler or Tojo right between the eyes! Here's your chance, gents, to demonstrate how well Uncle Sam has trained you—grab a rifle, set your sights, and show the Austrian paper-hanger what he's got to look forward to, eight shots for one thin dime!"

Other ballies were less familiar, if not almost incomprehensible, such as the barefoot young Hawaiian boy promising, "Numbah One shine heah! 'Ey, GI, you like da kine? Only nickel, yeah?"

But Eddie's friends weren't here for shoeshines. "C'mon, let's get some drinks," Sal said, joining a line to get into a tavern called the Just Step Inn. Belying its name, they waited for half an hour to belly up to the bar where a sign warned, "WE LIMIT our customers to 4 DRINKS PER PERSON." Eddie wanted a beer but they were out, part of a general alcohol shortage. Only a few cases of the real stuff found its way to Honolulu, so bars offered a brand called Five Islands—locally brewed gin and rum, fermented, it was rumored, for all of twenty-four hours and rushed to a thirsty, and necessarily undiscriminating, clientele. Sal and Ernie ordered gin, Eddie rum; the latter, as the barkeep poured it into one of four shot glasses he filled in advance, had roughly the same color as the real thing, but when Eddie chugged a shot he gagged at the bitter, medicinal taste.

"Shit," he said, wiping his mouth, "what's *in* this, iodine?"

The bartender showed him the bottle's label: "Says here it's brewed from 'sugar cane products,' and no, I don't know what they mean by 'products.' But it's all we got, and it does the job."

The label proudly announced, IT's 100 PROOF!!—and that was about all Eddie could say for the contents. He pushed aside his remaining three shots; if he wanted to drink turpentine he could get it at the base.

His friends downed their gins with a grimace, but they finished all four shots—the liquor, whatever it lacked in taste, did in fact "do the job," and they were thus fortified to face their main objective in coming to Hotel Street. "Okay," Sal said, "let's go climb the stairs."

"What stairs?" Eddie asked blankly.

In answer they led him half a block down to a nondescript building, The New Senator Hotel. As with everything here, there was a long line of servicemen coiled around the block, awaiting entry. Sal and Ernie joined their ranks, Eddie falling in line with them. "So what's in here?" he asked.

"Like I said—action," Sal said.

"What, like gambling?"

"Hell no! Girls."

Oh shit, thought Eddie.

"They got some great gals here," Ernie went on. "Mine's named Lucy. Cutest little blonde you ever saw."

"Jenny's my girl," Sal said. "Brunette. Sweet. But a real ball of fire."

"You two sound almost like you're married to these gals."

"Yeah—married for three minutes, twice a week. You can't beat that!"

Eddie's eyes widened. "You only get three minutes with them?"

"Hey, it's long enough to get your business taken care of," Ernie said.

Eddie stepped out of the slowly moving line.

"Well," he said, "last time I looked, I'm married twenty-four hours a day, seven days a week, so I'll give it a pass."

"So friggin' what?" Sal said. "Your wife's never gonna know."

"No, but I will."

"Don't be a pussy, Stopka, everybody here does it. For every woman on this goddamn rock there's at least five hundred horny, homesick men. The only way to get laid in this town is to pay for it."

"I'm *married*," Eddie repeated. "That means something to me, okay?"

"It just means you're a goddamn pussy," Sal shot back.

Eddie's temper finally flared.

"Fuck you," he snapped at them. "Go fuck your three-minute whores. Don't blink, you might miss it."

Eddie stalked off, rejoining the crowds thronging Hotel Street. It had been a long while since his last night with Adele, and he was as frustrated as any man in this war. But what else could he do? He loved her, he didn't want to go back home and have to live with a guilty secret forever separating them. He wasn't going to be like his mother, who took up with another man so soon after Pop's death—*he* was going to stay faithful to his wife, damn it.

He passed a pinball arcade and the dinging of its bells suddenly brought a smile to his face, bringing him back again to Palisades, Adele, and the kids, reminding him of what he had and what he didn't want to lose. And then, unexpectedly, he was brought up short by a sight quite unlike anything he had ever seen in a carnival showcase.

In front of a curio shop on the corner of Hotel and Maunakea Streets a huge wooden idol glowered down at him: a genuinely fearsome-looking face with big glaring eyes, a splayed nose, and an open, scowling mouth crowded with sharp teeth. Eddie stopped, fascinated by it—it was made of some dark wood, not mahogany but with a hint of red in it, and was polished to a fine gloss. The woodworking was impressive. It looked foreign, exotic, and despite its fierce ugliness, somehow alluring.

"You like buy?"

He turned to see a heavyset woman, dark-skinned, wearing one of those long, flowing Mother Hubbards so many women here seemed to wear. "What is it?" he asked.

"A *ki'i*," she said. "Sacred carving."

"Like from a church?"

"*Heiau*," she corrected him. "Temple. In old days, *kahunas* made 'em out of special trees—asked for a god's blessing, carved his face and prayed his *mana*, his power, would fill it. This one's Kū, god of war."

Eddie smiled and said, "If this is a good likeness, I wouldn't want to screw with this guy."

She laughed. "No screw with Kū. Good advice."

"What kind of wood is this?"

"Ah, that's *koa*. Very expensive. This one not for sale, but I have others.

Ovah heah." She showed him a gallery of similar carvings hanging on a wall. Some were no more than faces stacked atop a kind of totem pole; others had squat bodies and troll-like legs. Their wooden visages displayed a range of features, from long noses and big oval eyes to headdresses of elaborately carved ridges cascading down their backs. Unlike the idol outside the shop, these looked to have been carved out of palm trunks and stained a dark brown. "This one," the woman said, pointing to one with owlish eyes, grimacing mouth, and protruding tongue, "only five dollar."

"This may be a little big to take on my ship," he told her. "You got anything smaller?"

"Sure." She showed him to a table full of coral necklaces, shell bracelets, and small charms similar to the large *ki'i*. "You got wife? She might like, 'ey?"

Eddie took one of the necklaces in his hand. "Is this also Kū?"

"No, that one Lono. All different. These a buck and a half each," she said. "You buy t'ree, I t'row in fourth for fifty cent."

"It's a deal," Eddie said, and handed her a five-dollar bill.

Eddie left the shop with his souvenirs, telling himself that Adele and the kids might like them, but if not, the ugly little gremlins would look good above the French fry counter. He stood on the corner, wondering what else Honolulu had to offer other than trinkets and whorehouses. He still had at least five hours of daylight before curfew—where to go?

The answer came in a cloud of exhaust fumes, as a Honolulu Transit bus rolled to a stop a few yards away, a single word emblazoned on its metal brow—exotic yet familiar—entrancing him like some occult sigil of Kū's:

WAIKIKI.

Waikīkī Beach in 1943 was an uneasy alloy of prewar leisure and post–Pearl Harbor defenses: soldiers and sailors sunned themselves in lounge chairs or swam in the surf, as tourists did before the war, but now a tall fence of barbed concertina wire bisected the beach, separating loungers from swimmers, running from one end of the sandy scythe to the other.

Eddie bought a cheap pair of bathing trunks from a shop on Kalākaua Avenue, changed in one of the servicemen's dressing rooms on the beach, then headed for the water. One of the armed sentries standing guard checked Eddie's ID, then opened a gate in the barbed-wire fence so he could pass through. Eddie's feet were soon burning from the hot reflection of the tropical sun on the sand, and he quickly dove into the surf. It was warm as bathwater and as salty as the Palisades pool. But the waves here were real, though gentled enough by the encircling coral reefs that their lapping touch felt merely playful. Toni would have loved this. Eddie swam out near the first wave break and floated there a moment, looking back to shore at the hotels—the Royal Hawaiian, he'd heard, had been taken over by the military as an R&R center for returning troops, especially submariners—and, beyond them, the lush green mountains and valleys behind Honolulu and, farther down the coastline, the brown slopes of Diamond Head. The trade winds shuffled the waters like a deck of cards, carrying the scent of plumeria, jasmine, and coconut oil (wafted upwind from the sunbathers).

Eddie had not seen any place as beautiful, as soothing to his soul, since his first visit to Palisades Park. Hawai'i was beautiful in a wholly different way—a tranquil, natural beauty, though not without its carny charms—but the drone of patrol planes overhead and the presence of sentries with rifles provided an undercurrent of tension and urgency, like a somber sustained chord in an otherwise sunny song.

The only other thing that bothered Eddie was the surprising, and distressing, number of Japanese faces he saw around him, even more evident in Waikīkī than it had been on Hotel Street—not just vendors but pedestrians, hotel doormen, even policemen. He found himself recoiling a bit, each face reminding him of that grim day in December and of the Japanese atrocities he'd read about in the news. While waiting for the bus with another Navy man, Eddie noted quietly, "Lotta Japs here, aren't there?"

"Yeah," the sailor agreed, "too many for my lights. Hell, I'm sure some of 'em *are* loyal Americans, but—still gives me the willies, you know?"

The only Japanese person Eddie knew was Koma Komatsu, who operated the string game at Palisades, and Eddie had to remind himself that not every Japanese was the enemy. But he still couldn't help looking with a certain suspicion at the somehow sinister-looking faces around him.

Back at the base, Sal and Ernie staggered in shortly after Eddie. Sloppy with drunken camaraderie, Sal apologized for his "ribbing" of Eddie: "S'help me God, buddy, I wuz only kidding. Whatever you wanna do is okay by me. Uz swabbies gotta stick together, don't we? Huh?"

"He's juz sick about this," Ernie added helpfully, "honest t'God."

They were both so besottedly sentimental that Eddie couldn't hold a grudge and herded them over to the prophylaxis station—the "Clap Shack"—where he handed them a couple of Sanitubes and told them to apply liberally before their peckers fell off.

His next day off Eddie took alone, signing up—for two and a half bucks—with the Navy's Recreation office for one of their bus tours of the island, one of the many "wholesome activities" cooked up by the Navy to alleviate servicemen's "island fever." It carried Eddie and a couple dozen other sailors from Honolulu up the windward coast of O'ahu. Their tour guide was a big, affable Native Hawaiian named Oscar, who recounted the epic battle won by King Kamehameha's army at the Nu'uanu Pali, showed them the majestic fury of the waterspout known as the Hālona Blowhole, and related the history of the sugar plantation at Waimānalo.

Eddie thought it the most spectacular scenery he had ever seen, but the majority of men on the bus did not seem impressed—or wouldn't admit it if they were, since the received wisdom among soldiers and sailors alike was that Hawai'i, far from being Paradise, was a dull, hot, overcrowded Purgatory.

"Sure, it's all very pretty," one sullen GI said, "but what the hell do you people *do* on this rock?"

"We live," Oscar replied simply. "This is our home."

"And where," asked a sailor with a thick Bronx accent, "are all those little grass shacks and sexy hula dancers we see in the movies?"

"I dunno," Oscar said with a twinkle in his eye. "Same place all those Indians in New York wen go, maybe?"

Eddie was one of the few passengers who laughed at that, which earned him a smile from Oscar.

The price of the tour included a picnic lunch of sandwiches, Coca-Colas, and the local home-brewed beer, which, while not quite as bad as the gin and rum, still fell far short of Bunty's beloved Ballantine Ale. It was after seeing Eddie blanch after a few sips of beer that Oscar leaned in and advised him, "Listen, brah, you want real booze, forget Hotel Street—try go Trader Vic's ovah on Ward Avenue, I hear dey just get shipment of real Bacardi Rum from mainland."

"Thanks," Eddie said, surprised. "I will." Lowering his voice, he added, "Don't mind these jokers, this is a beautiful place. You're lucky to live here."

"T'anks. I grow up Maui, too bad you GIs can't go neighbor isles."

"Maybe I'll come back someday after the war," Eddie said hopefully.

But the pleasant day ended on a jarring note when, back at Pearl Harbor, a troop ship just returned from fighting in the Solomon Islands sent its passengers ashore in launches—and one of the soldiers, a haggard-looking GI, became suddenly unhinged at the sight of a Japanese-American MP standing guard at the dock. In an almost rabid rage he tore into the MP, screaming, "Goddamn fucking Nip! Fucking Jap bastard!" as he pummeled the man's face, splitting open his lip in a gusher of blood. The dazed MP finally slammed back with the butt of his rifle, but he looked pained to do it. Other MPs came running and pulled the GI away, still shrieking epithets.

Eddie must have looked stunned, as another onlooking sailor explained, "Some of these guys have come from places like Tarawa where they've seen the most brutal shit imaginable. Assigning that poor bastard to the guard post today was a major snafu on somebody's part—most of the time the Navy tries to keep these guys as far from the local *nisei* as possible."

The sight of an American serviceman, even one with Japanese features, being beaten and bloodied by another soldier, sobered Eddie, reminding him of the young colored man he had watched being beaten in the South for simply walking on the wrong side of the street. After this incident, Eddie found that the presence of so many Japanese-Americans on the streets of Honolulu was no longer quite so distressing to him.

Hunkered on the corner of King Street and Ward Avenue, Trader Vic's looked like something out of a Hollywood movie about Hawai'i: a low wooden structure with a grass-thatched roof spilling over the sides like a bad haircut, surrounded by tall palm trees and lush tropical foliage. Curiously, at least three of the thirty-foot Royal palms actually appeared to be poking through the roof of the building itself. A glowering *ki'i* idol greeted Eddie, Sal, and Ernie at the entrance. "That's Kū," Eddie said offhandedly. "Kū who?" Sal asked. "Kū's on first," Ernie joked. "He's a god," Eddie chided, opening the heavy wooden door. "Show some damn respect."

Stepping inside Trader Vic's was like crossing the Equator: the restaurant might well have been a South Seas trader's hut, decorated as it was with rattan chairs, bamboo dining tables, walls covered in tapa cloth, and net-covered lamps hanging from the ceiling like fishing floats. Most remarkable of all were the ringed trunks of palm trees that were, in fact, growing out of the floor and straight up through openings in the thatched roof, the building having apparently been constructed around them. Whoever built this place, Eddie decided, was a real showman.

At the door an affable host asked, *"Aloha,* gents, table for lunch?"

"Yeah, the liquid variety," Ernie told him.

He laughed. "I think that can be arranged. Heave to and follow me."

"Are you Trader Vic?" Eddie asked.

"No, I'm the manager, Waltah Clarke." He led them through the dining room, where pork chow mein and almond duck were being consumed by both civilian and military clientele—local residents and mainland war workers, NCOs and enlisted men, Army and Navy. Waitresses clad in the sort of colorful sarong that Dorothy Lamour wore in the movies weaved gracefully among tables, carrying an exotic array of drinks in fancy glasses.

Waltah showed them to an outdoor patio, or *lānai,* a tropical garden of hibiscus, orchids, plumeria, and other fragrant blooms. Eddie and his friends walked past the cozy tables shaded by palm-like umbrellas and eased up to the bar. "Are *you* Trader Vic?" Ernie asked the man behind the bar.

"Nope, I'm just the bartender. What's your pleasure, sailors?"

"We, uh, understand you just got in a shipment of Bacardi rum from the mainland," Eddie said, sotto voce.

"Yeah, and it's going fast too. Here, take a look at this and choose your poison." He handed them a drink menu listing "grog" with names like Skull and Bones, Kona Swizzle, Dr. Funk, Fog Cutter, and Singapore Sling. Eddie liked the sound of that last one, exotic and dangerous.

"What the hell are *they* drinking?" Ernie asked, nodding toward a table of non-coms sipping, through long straws, from a huge ceramic bowl decorated with images of palm trees and hula girls.

"Ah, that's a Scorpion. Got a nice little wallop. Serves four."

"Three enlisted men are the equal of four NCOs any day," Sal said. "We'll take one of those."

They watched as the bartender mixed together brandy, some kind of French liqueur, orange and lemon juices, mint, and, most important, a very liberal helping of Bacardi Superior White Rum. He blended it, poured it into one of the gigantic ceramic bowls, garnished it with a slice of orange, stuck three straws into it, and slid it over to the men.

"There you go, gents."

They each took custody of a straw and began sipping, as if they were sharing a milkshake. The Scorpion was delicious as well as potent— there was no mistaking the taste of real, honest-to-God rum. Within minutes the three had drained the bowl, which earned an admiring nod from the barkeep: "Well, you made short work of that."

"Man, oh, man," Sal said, "I can't remember the last time I had real booze. Set us up with another one."

Eddie, nicely buzzed, said, "I'll try one of these Singapore Slings."

"Those are usually made with gin," the bartender said. "I can substitute rum if you want, but I can't guarantee it'll taste the same."

"I'll take that risk," Eddie said.

"We are men of the United States Navy," Sal added. "We fear nothing."

The bartender obliged, mixing an ounce of rum and a shot of

grenadine in a cocktail shaker, shaking well, then straining the contents into a tall glass with a bas-relief of a hula girl on it. He filled it with club soda, then floated a dash of cherry brandy on top and handed it to Eddie.

It was smooth and sweet—almost like lemonade, or fruit punch. Didn't seem that potent, but it was damned tasty and went down real easy. Eddie ordered another, even as Sal and Ernie ordered a Zombie and something called a Pondo Snifter, allegedly from the North Coast of Borneo.

By the time Eddie had finished his third Singapore Sling it began to occur to him that either the earth had begun rotating differently or he was very, very drunk. Apparently Sal and Ernie's drinks were no less potent, because the two of them were as potted as the plants around them. When they tried to order a fifth round, however, the barkeep reminded them that all bars in Honolulu had a four-drink limit and they had reached it: "Sorry."

With a chorus of cheers for Trader Vic—*whoever* the hell he was—they lurched outside and onto a crowded city bus bound for Hotel Street. As they approached their destination, Ernie announced: "I wanna get laid!"

"*Grade* idea!" Sal said with enthusiasm. "Lez go!"

Eddie swore. "Jeez-us! Not this again!"

"Aw, stop bein' a pussy," Sal said.

"Stop *callin'* me a pussy," Eddie snapped.

"Chrissake, Eddie, thiz war might last years!" Ernie said. "What're you gonna do, be a friggin' monk for two, three, four friggin' *years?*"

"Stopka, I take it back. You ain't a pussy." Sal grinned. "You're pussy-*whipped*—scared of your wife!"

Despite feeling as if he'd been run over by a Mack truck, Eddie jumped to his feet, grabbed Sal by the collar of his shirt, and jerked him up off his seat.

"Bullshit!" he yelled.

"Talk's cheap, Stopka!"

"I'll show you!" Eddie said heatedly. "C'mon! I'll *show* you!"

He pushed Sal through the door of the bus and onto the carnival midway of Hotel Street.

Eddie woke with a headache the size of the island of Tortuga and a lancing pain in his right arm when he propped himself up on his bunk. He looked around him at the naval barracks, without the slightest memory of having come back here—with no memory, for that matter, of anything after he had grabbed Sal and shoved him off of the bus and onto . . .

Oh, shit.

His heart pounded, which only seemed to make his headache worse. He sat up on his bunk, panicky, and called out, "Sal! Ernie!"

Four bunks away, Sal groaned in response. Eddie propelled himself off the bunk and to Sal's side.

"Sal! Jesus! Wake up," he implored. When Sal didn't respond, Eddie slapped him once across the cheek. "Will you for Chrissakes *wake up*?"

Sal's eyes fluttered open. "*What?* Can't you just let me die?"

"Sal, what the hell did I do? After we left the bus, what did I do?"

"You threw up," Sal said. "We all did. Seemed like the thing to do."

"Is that all? Then what?"

"Then you showed us," Sal said, and lapsed back into unconsciousness.

Eddie shook him. "What? What did I show you?"

Sal made no response, but from the other end of the barracks came another voice:

"Jesus Christ, Stopka, stop shouting," Ernie said, wincing.

"Ernie, what the fuck happened?" Eddie demanded.

"You *showed* us," Ernie said, sighing, "how much you love your wife, okay? So shut the fuck up!"

And with that, he flopped back onto his bunk with a loud groan.

The lancing pain in Eddie's arm awoke a dim memory—a sound of buzzing, like a swarm of insects—and he slowly rolled up the sleeve of his undershirt, all the way up to the shoulder.

On his right bicep was the still-raw tattoo of a red Valentine's heart, and inside it, a single word: ADELE.

9

Edgewater, New Jersey, 1942–43

ADELE CRIED FOR TWO DAYS after Eddie left, though never again in front of the children. Resolutely dry-eyed, she woke them each morning, scrambled their eggs and fried their Spam (bacon being a casualty of wartime shortages), bundled them in the mummy wrappings of their winter clothes, and sent them shambling stiffly down Undercliff Avenue to school. Only then did she allow herself to sink into Eddie's easy chair and dissolve into tears. At night she curled up with her head on Eddie's pillow, still holding the pungent scent of his aftershave lotion; when she closed her eyes she could pretend he was still here, sleeping beside her. Then she would wake, alone, in the middle of the night, and weep tears of anger that he could leave her—alongside tears of fear that he might never return.

She thought she was doing it quietly enough that the children couldn't hear, but Toni, on the other side of the thin plaster wall, heard every sob. Toni was grieving too, though more for the loss of her father's everyday presence than concern that he might not come back. At eleven years old she knew what death was, but simply couldn't conceive of it happening to her father. He was like one of the tall, sturdy oak trees in her backyard, impervious to the storms and stresses of the world, and she assumed he would be there, roots firmly planted in her life, forever.

After the second day Adele regained some of her moxie, telling herself this was just the way things were and she would have to live with it as best she could. Many of the women she worked with in the Red Cross also had husbands in the service, and there was comfort in their shared loneliness. Driving up River Road to the Red Cross office, she passed house after house in whose windows hung a white ribbon bordered in red, with a blue five-pointed star—sometimes more than one—signifying a family member who was in the service. Occasionally one of the blue stars would be transmuted, by tragic alchemy, into a gold one, representing a man's life lost in service of his country. Adele flinched at these, and when she received her own blue-star ribbon she dutifully hung it in the front window, but far enough from the driveway that she couldn't see it when she left the house.

Being a housewife at war posed its own special challenges. Between what they had saved from Palisades, Eddie's Navy pay, and the military's dependents allowance, Adele had more than enough money to feed a family of three; but money was no longer all that was required to put food in her children's mouths. Each time she went to the market, she had to bring along her government-issued ration book with its perforated sheets of red and blue stamps, each one assigned a point value. So in addition to paying forty-nine cents for a pound of pork chops, she also had to give the grocer seven points in Red Stamps. Canned spinach cost only ten cents a can, but required seventeen points in Blue Stamps. Butter set you back twenty points; cookies, which Adele found hard to believe were vital to the war effort, were even more pricey at twenty-two points. Each household member was assigned forty-eight points per ration period; Adele had to plan meals weeks in advance in order to purchase everything she needed.

Supplementing their food budget was the Victory Garden that Toni and Jack planted in their backyard on the slopes of the Palisades, from which the family harvested a robust crop of carrots, celery, onions, and tomatoes, which Adele's mother showed her how to can for winter.

That first Christmas without Eddie wasn't an easy one, but Adele made sure Santa delivered everything on the kids' Christmas list—Jack got the watercolor paint set he craved, and Toni a Charlie McCarthy puppet. A holiday dinner at Marie and Franklin's made them feel more like an intact family: along with Adele's brothers, James and Ralph (who, as fathers, had so far avoided the draft), and their families, the Stopkas exchanged presents, sang carols, and gorged themselves on roasted turkey with all the trimmings, one of the few occasions they, like most Americans, were able to indulge themselves in these austere war years.

Her father was in good spirits, even managing to abstain *from* spirits for most of the day, but Adele noted with disquiet that his complexion was gray, he seemed easily fatigued and short of breath, and he had a bad cough. But he found enough voice to raise a glass of apple cider and toast, "Here's to our brave boys overseas . . . and one boy in particular," with a wink to Adele.

"Is Dad okay?" Adele asked her mother when they had a moment alone together, cleaning the dishes after dinner. "He doesn't look good."

"He's had that cough for a while," Marie admitted, "but whenever I ask him how he's feeling he just says, 'I'm fine.'"

"How much of the sauce is he putting away these days?"

"I don't like to think about that," Marie said, ill at ease. "There's nothing to be done about it anyway."

"Well, keep an eye on that cough, at least," Adele cautioned.

Even so, it came as a surprise when, a week later, Adele's mother called to tell her, in a strained tone obvious even over the telephone, that their family physician had checked Franklin into Holy Name Hospital in Teaneck. "That cough of his got worse," Marie explained, "and then he coughed up something pinkish brown, and I made him go to the doctor. They're running tests now, can you come over?"

Adele thought of cancer all the way there, an unexpected fear since she had worried for years about her father coming down with cirrhosis of the liver and had been alert to the telltale signs of it, girding herself against the day she noted a jaundiced cast to his skin. But instead she saw, as Franklin lay abed, that his legs and ankles were swollen and his neck appeared bloated in way she hadn't noticed when he was wearing a shirt collar. He looked tired and weak, but smiled when she entered the room. "Ah," he said, "everything will be all right now that my little star is here."

She kissed him on the cheek and forced some cheer into her voice. "That's right. Everything's going to be fine, Daddy."

Dr. Thomas DeCecio, a personable young internist in his early thirties, soon arrived with the test results and informed them soberly that Franklin was suffering from congestive heart failure.

"There's been considerable enlargement of the heart," he told them, adding pointedly, "due to excessive alcohol consumption. It's like a sponge oversaturated with water—the heart's been so weakened it's lost much of its pumping capacity. The blood is literally backing up into other organs, like the lungs, which is why we found traces of it in your sputum."

"Oh my Lord," Marie said, and began to weep.

"It's all right, honey," Franklin said, "don't cry."

Adele held her mother as the doctor went on, "The good news is, the damage is to some degree reversible. I can prescribe a diuretic to reduce fluid retention, and digitalis to regulate the heartbeat. But as I've been telling you for years, Franklin—you *must* stop drinking. If you don't, you'll die, sooner than later. Is that clear?"

"Yes." Franklin's voice trembled with palpable fear, striking a resonant chord of fear in Adele. "Abundantly."

"Good. Now, nobody's saying this will be easy. If you need help, there's this new organization, Alcoholics Anonymous, and I understand that Yale University is planning an outpatient program to treat alcoholism . . ."

"I don't need any help," Franklin insisted. "I'll lick this on my own."

That night, back home, Franklin went to bed without having had a single drink all day—for the first time in twenty years. Only hours before, Adele and Marie had searched every cabinet, cupboard, and closet for any bottles or flasks Franklin might have burrowed away. It took two hours to detoxify the house from basement to attic and pour all the booze down the drain—enough, Adele joked, "to sterilize the sewers for at least a day."

Franklin soon found himself running a torturous gauntlet of insomnia, tremors, sweats, chills, and deliriums. Marie was at his side and Adele visited whenever she could get away from the children, from whom all this was being carefully hidden. Finally, after ten long days, Franklin bottomed out and fell into a deep sleep, from which he did not stir for nearly twenty-four hours. When he at last opened his eyes it seemed to Adele as if he were truly awake, and alive, in a way she hadn't seen since she had watched him on the set of the last film he had directed, back in 1917. He had been drowsing, like a modern-day Rip Van Winkle, for twenty-six years.

Letters from Eddie to Adele, Toni, and Jack arrived at least once a week, and Adele made the reading of them an event to keep his voice alive in the household. In February, word came that another member of the Palisades Park family—Jackie Morris, son of Charles "Doc" Morris—had been awarded the Silver Star for heroism in the Battle of Guadalcanal. Toni and Jack were properly awed that they knew a genuine, real-life war hero, and were certain that their dad would distinguish himself in the same way.

As the park's opening day in April approached, Adele had to face the fact that she couldn't operate the concession by herself and reluctantly began looking for someone to help out. She asked for recommendations from friends and also placed an ad in the classified pages of *The Billboard*:

WANTED—Concession Agent and Cook, French Fry Stand. Experience Preferred. Salary plus Percentage. Contact A. Stopka, Palisades Amusement Park, NJ. Cliffside 6-1341.

The ad brought a dozen applicants, three of whom Adele invited to interview. They were all men, and all seemed startled upon learning that "A. Stopka" was a woman, but she bulldozed past their surprise and briskly inquired about their background and experience, even as she tried to draw some measure of their character. One was a grizzled old carny whose breath smelled of bourbon at ten A.M., which immediately eliminated him from consideration. The second was a middle-aged agent who had managed a pretzel concession at Rye Playland and who seemed to start every sentence with, "Listen, honey," which Adele decided might become quickly tiresome. The third was an experienced talker in his late thirties who had a slick bally and who seemed neither condescending nor crooked, though there was no way to be sure of the latter. His name was Jim Lubbock.

"And why did you leave your last job, Mr. Lubbock?" she asked.

"I came down with a bad case of hoof in mouth disease," he replied.

"Hoof in mouth?"

"I found out our meat supplier was stuffing ground horse meat into the hot-dog casings. The owner told me to keep my mouth shut. That night a lady asks me, 'Are these really Twelve-Inch Footlong Hot Dogs?' and I answer, 'Absolutely. That was the distance between the fetlock and the knee.'"

Adele laughed and hired him on the spot.

In the first warm weeks of spring, a number of local kids, taking advantage of the fact that Palisades didn't open until the end of April, commandeered its parking lot and converted it to a softball lot, even as the concessionaires did on rainy days. After school two teams of fourth, fifth, and sixth graders squared off on the asphalt, bases marked in chalk, for the championship of nothing in particular. The teams had a rotating lineup but Toni was always among them: at twelve years old she already stood five feet four and had inherited her father's batting prowess—she often sent the softball soaring off the edge of the Palisades, to fall like a canvas-covered meteor in somebody's backyard in Edgewater. She was also a pretty good outfielder, adept at catching pop flies.

Eleven-year-old Jack was on the same team, but his commitment to the game was questionable. Early on he had the bad luck to be sitting in the makeshift dugout just as a batter, connecting solidly with the pitch, tossed his bat aside and made for first base. The errant bat went flying into the dugout, where it connected with Jack's forehead, sending him toppling backward and, ultimately, into the Holy Name medical clinic in Cliffside Park. Jack suffered no concussion nor any ill effects other than a lump on his head, but it didn't exactly instill a love of the game in him.

Today he was playing third base when the batter on the other team hit a line drive toward right field. The ball bounced once, Toni snapped it up, and with a runner heading into third, she threw the ball to Jack.

Jack, however, seemed oblivious, the ball whizzing like a mortar round over his right shoulder, and the runner made it easily to third.

The team captain, a towheaded, pug-nosed twelve-year-old named Slim, stalked over. "Christ on a crutch, Stopka! How'd you *miss* that?"

"Oh," Jack said innocently, "sorry. I was thinking about a comic book I read yesterday."

Slim slapped the heel of his hand into his forehead.

"That's it!" he yelled. "I've had it. You're off the team, Stopka—go home and read your comic books!"

"Hey, wait a minute!" Toni came running up. "You can't kick my brother off the team!"

"He's lucky I don't kick him into the Hudson River!"

"Yeah? Well, if *he's* off the team," Toni told him, "then *I'm* off it too."

"What? Don't be nutty! You're our best batter."

"Is my brother on the team?"

"No!" Slim insisted.

"C'mon, Jack," Toni told Jack. "Let's go."

As Toni walked indignantly away from the playing field, Jack said to her, "Sis, you didn't have to do that."

"'Course I did. You're my brother."

"Yeah, but he's right," Jack admitted. "I *am* a rotten softball player."

"So what?" Toni said. "Are we playing for the National League pennant? Is it going to kill him to let you play?"

"Sis, it's no big deal. I don't even like the game all that much. I just like playing it with you."

Toni smiled and told her little brother, "Yeah, I like playing it with you too. But on our next team, let me cover third base, okay?"

Palisades opened on April 24 with a big War Bond rally headlined by "Uncle Don" Carney, an aerialist called The Sensational Marion, and a bevy of beautiful magazine cover girls from the Walter Thornton

Modeling Agency. The bond drive exceeded all expectations with $82,000 in bonds sold. A new ride, MacArthur's Bombers—named after General Douglas MacArthur's air defense corps in the South Pacific—was proving popular, and even Jackie Bloom's ball game got a wartime renovation, with Jackie replacing old targets with new ones that he'd watercolored himself, featuring the likenesses of Hitler, Hirohito, and Mussolini.

Business was brisk and Adele and the new man, Jim, were kept busy cooking and serving Saratoga fries for the crowds. On weekends, before the end of the school year, Adele had Toni help out with the stand—peeling potatoes, wiping the counter, making change for customers—which pleased Toni and made her feel very grown-up, like she was pulling her weight in Dad's absence. When school let out and the pool opened, she worked half a day at the stand and the rest she practiced swimming and diving with Bunty.

Bunty had finally okayed her to ascend to the ten-foot diving board: "Keep your head in line with your spine, remember to arch your back, keep your legs closely aligned and your toes pointed."

After a little work on her "approach," she was soon taking running jumps off the board, her momentum and the spring in the board launching her a good three feet up in the air. It was this moment, at the pinnacle of her flight, that thrilled Toni the most: for those few seconds of ascendancy and that split second before she began her downward plunge, she felt as though she were defying gravity, like a bird or a plane or—she could only admit this to one person—a strange visitor from another planet, with abilities far beyond those of mortal men (and women). In that moment of midair suspension, she felt free of the bonds of earth, capable of doing anything, going anywhere. And when her arched body, arms outstretched, began its descent to the water, she sometimes fantasized that she was on her way to rescue someone trapped in a raging river (no need to change the course of it with her bare hands, just pluck the poor devil out and fly him away) or diving into the ocean to foil some dastardly plan of Luthor's.

Headfirst she plunged in, and down here, too, her near-weightlessness in water felt like flying.

Sometimes Jack was at the pool too, though he didn't dive himself;

he would sit in a beach chair on the sand, his sketch pad in his lap, scribbling away with his colored pencils as Toni dove. One day she got out of the water and joined him to find that he had drawn a very flattering likeness of his sister in her blue bathing suit, back arched, head up, arms outstretched, floating in midair. It was very naturalistic, except for one detail: he had added a red cape, at the nape of her neck, to her blue bathing suit.

She laughed when she saw it, but he said, "Am I wrong, Sis?"

She shook her head. "No. That's exactly what it feels like."

"Like the start of an adventure?"

She sat next to him and nodded. "You should try it. See for yourself."

"I don't need to," Jack said. "That's what drawing's like for me too—an adventure. Most of the time I don't even know where it's going or how it'll turn out. It just comes out of my fingers and onto the paper."

"Now *that's* super," Toni said, impressed.

"Naw," Jack said modestly. "I'm more like Jimmy Olsen. Somebody's gotta get pictures of you mystery men."

They grinned at their shared adventure, their secret identities known only to each other.

The Sensational Marion had a good high-wire act, but Toni was flat-out astounded by the performer who followed her on the free-act stage. His name was Peejay Ringens, and word got around fast that he was booked at Palisades for an entire month—the longest deal the Rosenthals had made with one performer since they took over the park. Toni was baffled at first by the equipment and rigging that was being set up for him. There was a water tank, six feet in diameter and three feet deep, not unlike others she had seen; but instead of a single tall ladder there went up a series of ladders, the highest being a hundred feet tall and the lowest about forty feet, all of which supported a long sloping ramp. Between the tank and the ramp, workmen were stringing up a safety net, like the one used by trapeze artists. Was this an acrobatic act or a high dive? Toni couldn't figure it out.

She got her answer at his first performance. The audience was standing, not sitting, the benches having been moved to make way for all the equipment. The park announcer proclaimed, *"Ladies and gentlemen, Palisades Park is proud to bring you the most stupendous and thrilling act of all time by the premier high diver of the world today, Mr. Peejay Ringens!"* As the crowd applauded, a tall man—about six feet two, in his mid-fifties, wearing satin tights, diving cap, and a jacket with a red, white, and blue American shield on the chest—strode with a smile onto the stage and began climbing the hundred-foot tower to the recorded accompaniment of a brass band playing a stirring march. At the top of the ladder, Ringens walked onto a small platform. To Toni's amazement, he picked up a bicycle that was waiting for him there, and as the music swelled, he straddled the bike and pushed it to the lip of the platform. He looked down the long slope of the ramp, which at the forty-foot end had a little upturn, like a ski chute.

He pushed himself and the bicycle forward, drew up his feet and placed them on the pedals, and the bicycle began racing down the incline.

The crowd held a collective breath as the bike raced down the slope in what seemed like two heartbeats. Then it hit the upturn and was fired upward like a skeet shot—for a few moments bicycle and rider both soaring through space as though riding on air.

Until Ringens let go of the bike.

Toni gasped along with the rest of the crowd.

The bicycle fell away from him and into the safety net, but Ringens flew past the net, straightening his body and extending his arms like Superman in flight. He hurtled through the air another seventy-five feet until reaching the tank, where he made a perfect swan dive into the water, briefly disappearing from sight—then surfaced and climbed out to thunderous applause from the audience.

Toni applauded as loudly as anybody. She had never seen such a feat before—each part of it would have made a remarkable act by itself, but the two together were spectacular. How did he do it? How did he time it so that he knew just when to let go of the bike and allow his momentum to carry him into the tank? It seemed that a moment too soon would bring him crashing into the side of the tank, while a moment too late would have him sailing over the water and into a horrified audience.

She wanted to run up to him right now and ask him these things, but decided to come back for Ringens's evening performance, illuminated by spotlights. It was just as amazing the second time, though the bicycle overshot the net and came crashing to earth (Ringens later joked to the audience that he went through at least three Schwinns a week).

She watched his act another three times before she got up the nerve to approach him after an afternoon performance.

"Mr. Ringens, sir?" she said, coming up to him. "My name is Toni Stopka and I thought your act was really swell."

"Why, thank you, young lady," Ringens said, doffing his diving cap, revealing a receding fringe of graying hair.

"Can I ask you something?"

"Sure."

"Aren't you afraid you'll let go of the bicycle too soon? Or too late?"

He smiled at that. "Oh, I was afraid of that for a long time," he said, "and it nearly destroyed my career. The first time I ever tried to do this stunt, I set up the ramp on the edge of a pond in Kansas City, Missouri. But I let go too soon, I fell short of the deep water I'd intended to land in, and crashed into the shallows. Nearly broke my back."

"But you went right back and tried again?"

"Nope. I had the ramp set up beside a lake near my home in Florida, but I couldn't bring myself to make another attempt. Worse, I was so gun-shy I couldn't even make a regular dive. I thought my career was over."

"What did you do?" Toni asked breathlessly.

"I'll tell you what I did: every day I would climb to the top of the tower, and take an imaginary ride down. I did that every day for a month until the memory of that first terrible ride started to fade. Finally one day I called all my friends to come over to the lake, and I announced that they were here to either have the pleasure of seeing me perform a perfect dive or of attending my funeral." He laughed. "I've never missed a dive since. Fear has no place in this business—it'll kill you if you let it."

"I want to be a high diver someday too," Toni said in a rush.

Something shadowed his friendly eyes and Ringens's manner changed. "Well, that's all well and good," he said, more guardedly, "but you still have a long time to make up your mind what you want to be when you grow up."

"Oh, but I *know* this is what I want to do! Can you tell me how you—"

"Glad you enjoyed the show," Ringens interrupted, suddenly cooler, and brushed past her. "Thanks for coming."

As she watched him go, Toni puzzled at the sudden turnabout in his manner—had she said, done, something wrong? All she wanted was to ask his advice. But maybe he thought she was being too forward. Or he didn't think she was really serious about being a diver. Whatever it was, it didn't stop her from attending as many of his performances as she could over the course of the next month—but she didn't try to approach him again.

On a sweltering afternoon in July when the electric fans in the French fry stand were doing little more than churning the humid air, Adele lifted the frying basket out of the sizzling oil and was startled to see, through a cloud of greasy steam, the last person she expected to find standing on the other side of the counter.

"Dad?" She poured the just-finished fries into a bin, wiped her hands on her apron, and hurried up to the counter. She glanced around for her mother, but Marie was not in evidence. "What brings you to Palisades?"

He smiled, but it seemed like a nervous smile. "I went for a walk down Palisade Avenue, and next thing I knew, here I was. Anyway, do I really need a reason to stop by and say hello to my only daughter?"

"No, of course not." She tried to think of the last time Franklin had come to the park and realized it had been at her wedding on the Carousel, nearly thirteen years before. "Why don't we get a bite to eat together, it's almost time for my lunch break. Jim, cover for me, okay?"

"S'okay, boss," Jim agreed amiably.

Adele took Franklin to the Grandview Restaurant overlooking the Hudson, but he appeared disinterested in the breathtaking Manhattan skyline or the sailboats plying the river like gulls two hundred feet below. He was fidgety, restlessly drumming his fingers on the table as he studied the menu. They ordered roast beef sandwiches and a couple of Cokes. Franklin put the menu aside and his gaze seemed to bounce nervously around the room without really settling on anything.

"So you really walked all the way here?" Adele asked.

"Just needed to stretch my legs," he said. "A man can go crazy sitting on a couch all day. Say, the Schencks don't still own this place, do they?"

"No, they sold it to the Rosenthals years ago."

He nodded. "Thought so. Did you ever meet Eddie Mannix?"

Adele admitted she didn't know the name.

"I went to school with him in Fort Lee. Tough little guy. The Schencks hired him as a bouncer, eventually he became general manager."

"Is that so?"

"He asked me to come work for him. In the publicity department."

"I never knew that," Adele said, surprised.

"Oh, sure. This was 1914, 1915. I said no, of course. I was making movies." He stopped drumming his fingers and flexed them nervously. "The Schencks took him with them when they moved out to the Coast. Now he's general manager of MGM—can you beat that?"

Adele didn't know what to say to that.

"When I was looking for a job after the war, I gave Eddie a call." He glanced away. "He never returned it."

Their sandwiches and Cokes arrived. Franklin took a few bites of his, then lost interest in it, his agitation painfully clear.

"Toni's swimming in the pool," Adele said, trying to change the subject. "Why don't you stop by and say hi, I know she'd love to see you."

Franklin nodded, but his attention was elsewhere. After a long moment he said quietly:

"You make all these decisions in your life, and they all seem like the right decisions at the time. You think you're doing the right thing. And it's only later that you realize, no, they were exactly the wrong decisions, and instead of bringing you what you wanted, they only carried you even farther away from your dreams. And somehow you've got to live with that."

He was clenching and unclenching his right hand. Adele reached out and cupped his hand in hers.

"Daddy, you *did* do the right thing. You did right by your family. There's no use dwelling on what might have been."

He stared at her. "Tell me you don't," he said.

Adele flinched. She couldn't find the words to reply.

Franklin pushed aside his barely-eaten sandwich and said, "Guess I'm not hungry." He stood. "I'd best be getting home. Marie will worry."

He kissed her on the top of her head, like he used to do when she was a little girl. "Bye, honey." Before Adele could think of a way to keep him there, he was gone. She tried to finish her sandwich, but quickly found she had lost her appetite as well. She paid the check and left.

On her way back to the French fry stand, she glanced over at the pool across the midway, looking for Toni, who had worked her way up to the ten-foot diving board, much to Adele's distress. She didn't see her daughter, but to her surprise she did catch a glimpse of her father—as he was exiting the Casino Bar next to the pool, on his way to the Hudson gate.

She stood there, chilled to the quick on a hot sultry day, then hurried over to the Casino, where Harry Shepherd was filling in at the bar. "Harry," she said, disquieted, "that man who was just in here, did he order anything?"

"Just a beer," Harry replied. "Why?"

Adele blinked back tears, the pain in her father's heart filling her own.

More than once that day, Adele found the tears again welling up, but pretended it was the steam from the frying basket making her eyes water. This didn't seem to convince Jim, who, when the park closed at midnight, asked, "Adele, you okay? Something wrong with your dad?"

She locked up the cash register and forced a smile. "Not much gets past you, does it?"

"Hard to miss. All day you've looked so blue, I wanted to check to see if you were still breathing."

She laughed. "Thanks, but I'll be okay."

He still didn't look convinced.

"Look," he said, "once we're done here, why don't we go over to Joe's? Coffee's on me."

"That's sweet of you, Jim, but I've got to get home. My neighbor's been watching the kids."

"Okay. But if there's ever anything I can do . . ."

All at once his hand was touching her waist.

"I mean, I know it must be tough, running this stand on your own, and with two kids to boot . . ."

Adele found herself quick-frozen to the spot, but the touch of his hand felt warm—too warm. For a moment she welcomed it—then sense won out over sensation and she slapped his hand away.

"Don't you *ever* do that again," she said.

"Look, I was just trying to—"

"I know what you were trying to do," she told him, "and if you ever try it again, you're fired." She fought to keep herself, and her voice, from trembling. "You *got* that?"

"Yeah, sure," he said, backing off. "Sorry."

"Now drop the awnings and let's get out of here."

Jim did as he was told, she locked up the stand and hurried away toward the parking lot before he could say another word.

In her car she sat with her hands trembling on the steering wheel, jammed the key into the ignition, and went careening out of the lot, not sure who she was angrier with—Jim, for having exploited her trust, or herself, for wanting him, if only for a moment, to do just that.

10

ADELE AND MARIE WERE ABLE to keep liquor out of the Worth home, but Franklin easily circumvented this by doing his drinking outside the house, in one of the many taverns and roadhouses along Palisade Avenue. Marie kept the car keys in her possession at all times so Franklin would not commit vehicular suicide, but this meant he often staggered home dead drunk for all the neighbors to see, which added a new dimension of mortification for Marie. She and Adele, along with Dr. DeCecio, begged Franklin to stop, to go to Alcoholics Anonymous, but Franklin only withdrew further into himself, in final retreat from his battle with life.

After the incident with Jim, Adele contrived reasons for Toni to help out with the stand, and the buffer worked, keeping Jim at a safe distance. One morning in late July, as mother and daughter arrived as usual around 10:30 A.M., they were making their way across the main midway when Minette Dobson hurried up to them and asked, "Have you heard?"

"Heard what?"

"Laurent Schwarz," she said. "Roscoe's son. He's dead."

Toni lost her breath, like the time she had belly flopped and had it knocked out of her. "What!" she said when she could breathe again.

"How?" Adele said, equally stunned.

"Killed in action, I think. In the South Pacific."

"Oh, God," Adele whispered. "Is Roscoe here?"

"No, he's at home. Anna Halpin's covering for him."

Adele took Toni's hand and they reversed direction, out the front gate and down two blocks to 740 Palisade Avenue. Toni felt numbly unreal, as if she were dreaming something new and terrible. As the two of them walked up the steps to the Schwarz home, Adele saw in the front window a red-and-white ribbon emblazoned with two stars—one blue and one gold. Adele fought back tears as she rang the doorbell. It was answered by Roscoe, whose own eyes, Adele saw at once, were red from crying.

"Oh, Roscoe," she said, "I'm so sorry."

He nodded, as if unable to speak, and took them inside. Roscoe's wife, Hazel, was trying to comfort their four daughters, ranging in age from nineteen to twenty-six. They had all been crying, and looking at them, at the grief in their pretty faces, Toni felt anxious and afraid.

"Oh God, Hazel," Adele said as she embraced her friend, feeling Hazel's sob as she held her. "What happened to him?"

Toni remembered playing in this house, playing with toys belonging to Laurent, eight years older than her but amused by this little girl who rejected his sisters' dolls in favor of his toy trucks.

"He was stationed in American Samoa," Roscoe said quietly. "He wasn't even in combat. Some fellow fell off a landing barge and Laurent jumped into the water, trying to rescue him. But he . . . didn't make it."

Toni said in a small voice: "He died?"

Roscoe nodded. "Yes, honey. He did."

"But he died a hero," Adele said. "Trying to save someone's life."

"He was a good boy," Roscoe said, an almost unbearable sadness and pride in his voice. "He always tried to do the right thing."

He broke down into tears, unmanned by grief, his wife clinging to him. It was all too much for Toni. Terrified by the naked pain and loss all around her, she turned on her heel and ran out the front door.

She heard her mother cry out "Toni!" but she didn't stop, couldn't bear being in that house a moment longer. She raced down the street, unwilling to face the truth that Laurent was gone, that she would never see him again, and afraid to voice the fear that really drove her away from the Schwarzes and back through the bright welcoming gates of Palisades Park. In here she could find refuge, in here there was laughter and merriment and the roar of a roller coaster to drown out the sound of a grown man weeping.

But the park wasn't open yet, there were no roller coasters to occlude the sadness in her heart, and she didn't know where to run to. She stood there in the center of the midway, longing for the sound of a calliope.

"Toni?"

She turned to find her mother, winded from chasing her down.

Adele put a hand on Toni's shoulder. "Are you all right, honey?"

Toni grabbed her in a bear hug and clung to Adele as if she were a tree in a hurricane.

"Don't let Daddy die," Toni said as she burst into sobs. "Please, Mommy, I don't want him to die, I want him to come home!"

Tears welled in Adele's eyes as she held tight to her daughter. "Daddy won't die, sweetie," she assured her. "He'll come back to us."

Toni collapsed into helpless tears, terrified that what had happened to Laurent might happen to her father—knowing for the first time that it *could* happen to her father—as she wept into her mother's chest.

Espíritu Santo was a big island compared to the many tiny atolls, barely more substantial than a mirage, scattered like freckles across the face of the South Pacific: fifteen hundred square miles of volcanic rock and coral terraces, fringed by tall coconut palms and white horseshoe beaches. The climate was hot and humid, but the air was sweet, scented by frangipani. Eddie's barracks was one of dozens of Quonset huts clustered like mushrooms along the shore, amid palm trees bent by gentle trade winds.

Not so gentle was the clangor that awakened Eddie on his first night on Santo, around midnight—along with the cry of the watch officer, calling, "Condition Red! Air raid, everybody out!"

Eddie slipped on his britches and jumped to his feet, but the men around him just groaned their dismay and slowly, almost lackadaisically, rose from their cots. The guy next to Eddie's didn't even bother to get up, so Eddie poked him. "Hey! Fella. Air raid, get up!"

"Aw, hell," the man said, opening his eyes reluctantly, "it's just Piss Call Charlie, that's all."

"Who?"

"I was havin' such a nice *blonde* dream, too," he said in a soft Southern drawl. "Goddamn Japs."

Eddie and his bunkmates straggled out of the Quonset hut, where the watch officer was sounding the alarm by banging a length of pipe against an empty acetylene tank. From above came the drone of a plane circling overhead, its engine audibly different from the engines of American fighters.

In pitch darkness they stumbled to the ditches in which they were told to take shelter. "What is it up there," Eddie asked, "a Japanese Zero?"

Stifling a yawn, the Southerner nodded. "Ol' Charlie swings by 'bout once a week, drops a couple bombs in the bush—unless there's a full moon he can't see for shit, it's darker out here than the inside of a turd."

The men lay down, as ordered, in the ditches, as Eddie wondered aloud, "Shouldn't somebody be shooting back at him?"

"Waste of ammo. Charlie kills a cow from time to time, but that's all. By now he's probably got a whole herd of cattle stenciled onto his fuselage."

Sure enough, after half an hour of listening to the Japanese plane buzzing overhead—occasionally disgorging a bomb that scored a direct hit on a palm tree—the watch officer announced an all clear. Some men went grumbling back to the barracks as others headed for the latrines: hence the name "Piss Call Charlie." Eddie, somewhat disappointed in his first glimpse of combat, joined the men opting for the latrines.

The next morning, Eddie reported to the metal shop, part of the naval base's huge aviation repair facility. Carriers like the USS *Saratoga*, lacking the resources to repair planes damaged in sorties with the Japanese, off-loaded the aircraft here on Santo. Eddie was put to work cleaning out one of the torpedo bombers—shot up pretty good by Japanese pilots with far better aim than Piss Call Charlie—that had just come back aboard the *Saratoga*.

A Grumman TBF Avenger, its fore and aft had taken a lot of flak. Eddie and a machinist's mate named Wilkowski were told to "hose out" the cockpit cabin. Eddie wasn't fazed by the blood on the Plexiglas canopy, laced with bullet holes from the Zero's 7.7-millimeter machine guns; but he was puzzled by the gray lumpy substance, looking vaguely like dry cement, on the inside of the tailgunner's compartment. "Jesus," he said, "what the hell *is* this stuff?"

"What the hell do you think it is?" Wilkowski said. "Chopped liver?"

A light dawned, and Eddie realized that what he was hosing off the canopy was what remained of the tailgunner's brain matter.

He felt a wave of nausea, could taste bile rising in his throat.

"Oh, Christ," he said softly. All at once he was back in the foundry in Newark, the sight of his father's seared, mangled flesh causing him to vomit—as he feared he was going to do now.

"Hey. Stopka. You gonna be okay?"

Eddie fought back his gag reflex, nodded. "Yeah. Shit. Poor bastard."

"Get used to it. God hates tailgunners."

Eddie held it together for the next hour, purging the compartment of all human traces, making note of the equipment that had been shot up and the degree of repair necessary, then casually took a bathroom break.

Inside the latrine he threw up, thinking of his father, feeling tears welling up for him as well as for the dead gunner. He took a few deep breaths—not the smartest thing to do in a latrine, he quickly realized— then wiped his mouth off even as he wiped all trace of fear and revulsion from his face. He walked casually back into the repair hangar, wondering whether he could keep this up for the rest of the day—much less the rest of the war.

In November, Franklin Worth died of congestive heart failure, surrendering in his sleep to the armies of night and regret. He had been admitted to Holy Name Hospital a week before in critical condition and Marie had been dreading the phone call that finally came on a Monday morning. Adele found herself sleepwalking through those first few hours after Franklin's death, feeling—from the moment she saw her father's lifeless body in the hospital, swollen to three times its natural size—as if she were little more than a radio relaying messages from her conscious mind, which had sunk to the bottom of a deep well. Every comforting word she uttered to her mother, every careful question she asked the funeral director, seemed to come via wireless, or maybe ventriloquism, from a deep pit of conscious thought that animated her body as Edgar Bergen did Charlie McCarthy. She felt about as real as Charlie, and didn't begin to climb out of that pit until she went to pick up the children at school and had to tell them that their grandpa, the only one they had ever known, was dead.

"Him, too?" Toni said, voice breaking. Adele did her best to console her and Jack before they all shambled to bed, eager for the release of sleep.

But Adele couldn't sleep. She kept thinking of the afternoon Franklin had come to Palisades, the raw, aching regret in his voice as he confronted, clear and sober, what he had made of his life, and what might have been. Could she really blame him for quailing at it, for choosing to face it the only way he could—through the sweetly distorted prism of a glass bottle?

Tell me you don't.

"Mom, where's Grandpa being buried?" Jack asked the next morning.

"Hackensack Cemetery, honey. It's a very nice place where a lot of important people are buried."

"Shouldn't we tell Daddy what's happened?"

Adele agreed they should, sat down and wrote a short V-mail to him, and brought it to the post office after dropping the kids off at school.

The day before the funeral, Adele was pleased to find that Franklin's passing was noted in a single paragraph in *Variety*, which referred to him in flattering terms as one of the "pioneer filmmakers" of the one-time motion picture capital of Fort Lee, New Jersey. Adele bought three copies of that week's *Variety*. She sleepwalked through the service at the church, during the short funeral procession to Hackensack, and as she listened to James's and Ralph's graveside eulogies to their father. When her time came, she simply walked up to the temporary grave marker on Franklin's grave and taped a clipping of the *Variety* obituary onto the marker.

"Your last notice, Daddy," she said softly, "and it's a good one."

And then she finally wept, the emotions she had been bottling up spilling out in a torrent.

That night she yearned for Eddie's arms around her, the consoling warmth of his body enfolding hers as she was wracked with sobs. This was too much to bear alone. And where was Eddie? First in Hawai'i, where, according to his letters, he'd had a grand old time—sightseeing, frolicking in the surf, buying trinkets like those grotesque little shrunken heads he'd sent her. She wouldn't have wasted a dime trying to win those things if they'd been a prize in Jackie Bloom's cat game! And now he was on some tropical island with swaying palm trees, working on engines just like he could've been doing in Edgewater. But no, the stupid, big-hearted Polack, he had to *enlist*—had to leave his family, leave her, to face this alone. She cried into her pillow, wishing Eddie were here so she could hug him—and then slug him. And God help her, she didn't know which she wanted more.

On his first drive around Espíritu Santo, Eddie ran into a few old friends: stone and wooden idols guarding the entrance to shops or scowling at him from street corners. Here they were called *tiki*, not *ki'i*, and apparently represented different gods, but they looked similar to those he had seen in Hawai'i. He took a shine to one that resembled an anteater with a pig's nose, out of which sprouted two long dried palm leaves—either like a mustache or nostril hair gotten badly out of hand. Eddie bought it for five bucks and installed the *tiki*—dubbed Colonna after the mustachioed comedian Jerry Colonna—on the wall of the metal shop.

Life on Santo—notwithstanding Piss Call Charlie's weekly visits—was dull enough that to amuse himself, Eddie salvaged a piece of driftwood, sawed off the ragged ends, and took a socket chisel to it, trying to carve a likeness of Colonna. Today, sitting on the beach after his shift, he was trying to duplicate the ridges that fringed the shop's *tiki* mascot. Using a mallet to drive the chisel resulted in a choppy cut, so he switched to using his hand only, which worked slightly better.

He was interrupted by mail call, and was pleased—at first—to receive a V-mail from Adele. But after he opened it his mood quickly sobered:

Dear Eddie,
I'm sorry to have to tell you that my father passed away two days ago, of congestive heart failure . . .

She related it all, he thought, in a curiously calm, detached tone. She spoke of the funeral arrangements, selecting a casket as if she were inspecting the bumpers of a new car, comforting the children—but nothing of the loss she must have been feeling, as if she couldn't bear to express it. Her words were carefully chosen, emotionally weightless, except for a P.S.:

God how I wish you were here.

The words twisted like a knife inside him and tears sprang to his eyes. He would have given anything to be back home, helping to comfort the kids, trying to comfort his wife, instead of here on the other side of the world.

But there was another piece of news in the letter that shocked him even more, related almost offhandedly:

It wasn't entirely unexpected—he had been ill for some months—but it still came as a shock, especially to Toni, coming so soon after Laurent Schwarz's death (he was killed in an accident in American Samoa).

Eddie put the letter down, gazed into the blue vastness of the ocean, and said a prayer for Laurent Schwarz and his family. Only now did he truly understand the selfishness of what he had done by enlisting—and only now could he imagine the grief his own family would endure, should the war find him as it had found poor Laurent.

11

Palisades, New Jersey, 1944

DETERMINED TO AVOID a repeat of her difficulties with Jim Lubbock, Adele hired a longtime carny woman in her fifties named Goldie, who had experience at grab stands and fell comfortably into the routine of grease and grind at a fry joint. Adele also made it clear to Toni, now thirteen, that once school ended in June she was also expected to help out at the stand, working eight hours a day with only an hour off for swimming and diving at the pool, and the usual half hours for lunch and supper. When Toni balked, Adele stated flatly, "If those Mazzocchi girls can start at the Penny Arcade when they're twelve, *you* can start now." But at least the Mazzocchi girls got to wear those snazzy coin aprons that jangled with change for the arcade games—Toni's cooking apron was heavy, grease-stained, and made her feel like the neighborhood butcher.

Jack also helped out, but since he had a paper route too, he spent less time at Palisades than Toni. Marie no longer came as regularly as she once had. Adele's mother had surprised her by selling their old house—which without Franklin seemed vast and empty—and accepting an invitation to live with Ralph and Daisy in their home on Knickerbocker Road in Tenafly. Surrounded by her son, daughter-in-law, and three grandchildren, Marie was happy in her new situation, but Adele saw less of her these days and felt sometimes as if she had lost her husband, father, and now her mother's comforting presence, though she never let on to Marie that she felt that way.

The 1944 season saw Joe McKee taking over as park superintendent, with Joe Rinaldi as assistant superintendent. Palisades opened on April 29, the gates admitting some sixty thousand visitors. The pool opened on May 27, also to capacity crowds. The weather helped—the summer of '44 was the hottest on record since 1896, with every state east of the Mississippi roasting under a merciless sun.

The following week, on June 6, the long-awaited "second front" was opened up in Europe when Allied forces stormed the beaches of Normandy. But for Toni, the most eagerly anticipated event of June was the return to Palisades of "The Super Man," as he now billed himself—Peejay Ringens.

It was basically the same act as last year, but Toni never tired of it and took her supper breaks during Ringens's evening performance. She was in the audience night after night, eating hot dogs as the daredevil diver rode his bicycle down the slope, abandoned it in midair, and dove into the tank. Sometimes she was there long after the rest of the audience had left, watching Peejay dry off as his pretty wife recovered what was left of the bicycle and secured the gear for the next day's performance.

The temperature soared into the nineties, but if Ringens broke a sweat as he ascended the ladder, Toni couldn't tell: he always seemed cool and collected. The night of his final performance, Toni felt a pang of regret as she began to leave . . . then heard a familiar voice behind her:

"You there. Young lady."

She turned, surprised to see Mr. Ringens, still in his diving costume as he toweled his hair, looking right at her.

"Me?" she said.

"You're the little dynamo who wants to be a high diver, aren't you?"

She hesitated, then admitted, "Yes, sir."

"I've seen you here every night and I thought, 'This girl is either serious about wanting to dive or desperate for entertainment.'" He smiled.

"My wife and I were just going back to our trailer. Would you like to come along and ask me those questions you wanted to ask?"

Toni's supper break was almost over, she really had to get back to the stand—but she might never have this chance again. "Sure. Thanks!"

Ringens's lovely wife smiled at her and offered Toni her hand. "My name is Renie," she said in a melodic French accent.

Toni shook her hand. "I'm Toni."

"Short for Antoinette?" Renie gave her a wink. "Are you French too?"

Toni walked with them to the dozen-odd trailers clustered at the edge of the cliff, where some visiting performers lived while playing Palisades. Ringens and his wife led her to a trailer hooked up to a Packard station wagon, opening the door into a comfortably large mobile home with a living area, bedroom, and kitchen. "Would you like some soda pop?" Renie asked.

"Sure, thanks."

Renie took a Pepsi-Cola out of a small refrigerator and handed it to Toni. Peejay took one too, downing it quickly.

"I owe you an apology," he told Toni, sitting down opposite her. "I was rather brusque with you last year. Would you like to know why?"

"Sure."

"Because you reminded me of somebody. My daughter, Anne—well, more an adopted daughter, she took my name while she worked with me."

"Do I look like her?"

"Not in the slightest."

"Oh," Toni said, puzzled.

"Years ago, I worked with a troupe of divers: Swan Ringens and Her American Diving Girlies, as they were billed in Europe. Swan was my first wife. Anne was one of our Diving Girlies. Oh, she was a sensational diver," Peejay said with a fond light in his eyes. "Entered her first amateur competition in Florida at seventeen—won breaststroke, backstroke, high diving. Swan and I hired her for our act. Anne never knew her real father, he died before she was born, and she took my name as her stage name. But I couldn't have been more proud of her if she had been my real daughter. She wowed the audience with her double back-flips, jack-knives, and swan dives from a height of fifty feet.

"In the summer of '31 we played all across Europe—Berlin, Paris, Stockholm, Madrid, Barcelona. Anne was the most popular member of the troupe. In July we were performing in the Prater—the big amusement park in Vienna, Austria." There was a catch in his voice, like a phonograph record skipping over an old scar. "She tested the board, judged the distance to the tank, then leapt. Perfect leap. But halfway down a sudden gust of wind hit her and her body twisted at an awkward angle. She hit the water clean, but then . . ." Renie clasped his hand as he flinched at the memory. "She floated to the surface like a broken twig. We dove in after her and pulled her out. She'd struck bottom with her back and shoulders. The impact snapped her spine in two."

The color drained from Toni's face. She felt cold as an ice cube and could almost hear the crack of the poor girl's back being broken.

"The best surgeons in Europe worked on her but there was no hope she would ever walk—move—again. Finally we were able to raise enough money to get her back home to Miami, and her mother. She lived there for five months before dying of her injuries." He shook his head. "Later that year, in Paris, I nearly did the same thing—hit the water wrong, struck the bottom of the tank hard. Luckily it just shook me up a bit. I can't begin to explain why I should have survived and poor Anne didn't."

He saw the upset in Toni's face and leaned forward. "This is a dangerous line of work, Toni. Disaster can strike any one of us. Look at what just happened to Bee Kyle, and she's one of the best in the business."

"What about her?" Toni asked, alarmed.

"You haven't heard? She was doing her act down in Alabama, same act she's done all her life. Hit the tank coming down. She's in the hospital in Birmingham. She'll live, but they say her diving career may be over."

"I—I met her. Bee Kyle. She played here. I . . ."

Tears welled up in Toni's eyes. Renie put a consoling arm around her.

Ringens said, "Toni, I love doing what I do. It can be thrilling, exciting—especially when the music's playing and you're making your way up that ladder. But once you get to the top, your eyes have to be wide open. If this is your dream, then by God, pursue it, it can be a great life. And I'll be happy to help in any way I can. But you can't go into it oblivious to the fact that you could get hurt—or die—doing it. Are you willing to face that?"

"I—I don't know," she said honestly.

"Then you're not ready yet," Peejay said gently. "Maybe someday you will be. Talk to me then." He handed her a business card with his name, address, and phone number in Florida. "And if not—you'll find another dream. At your age they're never in short supply."

She thanked him, not knowing what else to say, surprised by her own uncertainty—she had cherished the dream of flying, of diving, for as long as she could remember, but how easily its foundations had been rattled! She thought of Bee, of Anne, their courage in pursuing their dream, and she wondered whether she had that kind of courage. She didn't know, and it bothered her that she didn't know.

When she finally got back to the stand she found her mother furiously trying to keep pace in the kitchen, and mad as a hornet to see her: "Where have you *been* all this time? You've been gone almost an hour!"

"I—I was talking with Mr. Ringens."

"Oh for heaven's sake, will you stop bothering that man?"

"He didn't mind, he's a nice—"

Adele steamrollered over her: "You have a *job*, Antoinette, and a responsibility to show up when you're supposed to and come back when you're told to. I wish you'd pay as much attention to that as you do some crazy old coot who jumps off a bicycle into a sponge."

"He's not crazy!" Toni snapped.

"Don't take that tone with me," Adele warned.

"You think everything I do is crazy, but you don't know a thing about it! You don't know *anything*!"

But neither, anymore, did Toni. In something of a hissy fit, she stalked over to the side door of the stand, lifted it up, and stormed out.

"Antoinette! Toni! Get back here!" Adele shouted. But Toni was already being swallowed up in the crowd thronging the midway. Goldie tossed Adele a sympathetic look.

"This is why I never had kids," she said.

Adele sighed. "Where were you when I got pregnant?"

"You want to go after her, I can cover for you."

Adele shook her head. "She can walk home. I don't need the aggravation."

The heat wave turned tragic in July, when a fire broke out in the main tent of the Ringling Brothers and Barnum & Bailey Circus as it was playing Hartford, Connecticut. One hundred and sixty-eight people died that day under the big top. Closer to home, on the evening of Friday, August 11, a series of resounding explosions split the hot stifling air at Palisades. It took a few minutes for Adele and others to realize that the sound came not from anywhere in the park, but from below the cliffs. People rushed to the edge of the Palisades, where fingers of thick black smoke groped the air above the Hoboken waterfront. It turned out the heat had violently ignited drums of highly flammable liquids that were among war supplies being loaded onto a ship at Pier 4. It took fire companies from Hoboken, Union City, Jersey City, and even New York to finally quench the blaze—but not before the smoke blotted out the view of Manhattan from Jersey.

That weekend the heat also sparked a record turnout for the Palisades pool: on Sunday, August 13, the turnstile would clock some four thousand bathers by midafternoon. Trying to smooth over the recent friction between them, Adele gave Toni the day off and told her to enjoy herself at the pool with Jack. It wasn't until Adele walked across the midway to her stand that she heard the other big news of the weekend.

"Luna Park," Goldie announced, "is *kaput.*"

She handed Adele a newspaper story telling of how, the day before, a short circuit in the Dragon's Gorge ride at Coney Island touched off a blaze that quickly consumed the dry tinder of the railway as well as the rest of Luna Park. There were no serious injuries, but the 125-foot

Coca-Cola tower in the center of the park was turned into a fiery torch and Luna Park was gutted—now just a charred shadow of its former glory.

"My God," Adele said, "it's a miracle everybody got out alive."

Coney Island was the grand dame of amusement parks and the destruction of Luna Park was pretty much all anyone at Palisades could talk about that morning. But by midafternoon the park was packed with visitors seeking relief and distraction from the torrid weather. It was all concessionaires like Adele could do to take care of business—and to turn up whatever fans they had in their stands, as the temperature neared a hundred degrees outside and considerably more than that inside.

A little after two P.M., Adele took a short break to buy a cone of vanilla custard from the vendor next to the Carousel. She was relishing its welcome chill when she happened to glance down the midway at the Scenic Railway.

What she saw chilled her far more than the ice cream: John Winkler, hurrying away from the Scenic, pushing a big fire extinguisher on wheels toward the main midway.

Only moments later, Adele could smell the smoke for herself.

She tossed away the cone and followed Winkler past the Carousel and the Bingo game. As he turned the corner, the big extinguisher tipped a little on its wheels, but he righted it, turning left up the midway. Adele followed in his wake, turning the corner—then stopped short, aghast at what she saw.

Less than fifty feet away, black smoke was pouring out of the Virginia Reel, a ride with a circular, concave base that today looked like a smoldering crater—amid screams from somewhere inside the ride.

Concession agents had rolled out a fire hose and were pouring water on the fire, and now Winkler raced up and began spraying it with fire retardant. Heat rippled the air around the ride like a shimmering corona.

The Virginia Reel carried passengers in spinning tubs along curved, twisting tracks and into dark tunnels—tunnels now hellishly transformed, with riders trapped inside flaming tubes. Several good Samaritans—two Merchant Marines, a priest, and John Albanese, operator of a nearby waffle stand—ventured into the smoking carnage, trying to pull out victims, most of them children whose terrified pleas for help were heartbreaking to hear.

Several teenage girls had managed to escape and were now running, in a panic, down the midway. At first glance, Adele thought they were Negroes—then realized in horror that the girls were charred black from the waist up, their hair burned off, their skin seared to a crisp. Tears streamed down their blistered faces. As they passed, Adele was assaulted by an acrid odor that she realized queasily could only be the smell of burning flesh.

"My God," Adele said to John Winkler, futilely spraying retardant onto the blaze, "all those *children*—"

"I might as well be pissing on it for all the good this is doing," he said. "And the water hose isn't doing much more."

They watched hot sparks flying off the Reel like dying fireworks, carried by a strong southerly wind onto the Skyrocket coaster next door.

"This isn't going to stop at the Reel," Winkler said. "I'm going back to try and save the Scenic. Is your daughter here today?"

"She and Jack are in the pool."

"Get them the hell out of here. This is only going to get worse."

Toni was just coming up from a dive when, as she broke surface, she noticed that her first taste of air was tinged with smoke. At first she thought it was a grease fire from the hot-dog stand or the Casino Bar; but then she saw the roiling clouds of white and black smoke rising up above the concessions across the midway, including her mother's, and she realized it was much more than that. But she didn't see her mother at the fry stand, and worse—she didn't know where her brother was, either.

When the call to evacuate came over the park's PA system, Bunty and his fellow lifeguards began calmly directing swimmers away from the pool, toward the nearby Hudson gate. "But what about my clothes?" one swimsuited woman asked. "They're in the bathhouse. I can't leave like this!"

"You ain't naked, lady," Bunty said. "You can get your clothes later."

"But my wallet is in there!" her husband objected. "With money in it!"

"Paper money?" Bunty said in that soft voice of his. "Hey, you know what they make paper from? Wood. See the coaster over there? See all these food stands around us? Ninety percent wood, plus maybe thirty or forty coats of paint. Get my drift?"

The man paled and wordlessly led his wife out of the pool area.

There were thirty thousand people at the park at the moment—four thousand at the pool alone—and the Hudson gate quickly became overwhelmed by the exodus of men, women, and children in bathing suits. Those forced to wait by the pool grew increasingly restless as columns of smoke loomed ever higher above the Carousel building, sirens keening in the distance—with the exception of one enterprising young woman who was standing atop the ten-foot diving board, snapping photos of the blaze.

"Hey," Toni called up to her, "are you nuts? Get down from there!"

"Are you kidding?" the girl said. "These are going to be great shots! And if the fire gets anywhere near, I'll just jump in the pool."

Burning cinders were drifting like clouds of deadly faerie dust across the park. Toni felt one alight on her shoulder with a pinprick of heat. She was getting more and more anxious when she finally heard, "Antoinette!"

Toni was never so happy to hear that clunky name in her life.

Adele ran up breathlessly and said, "Thank God! Are you all right?"

"Yeah, I'm okay."

"Where's Jack?"

Unable to keep the fear from her voice, Toni said, "He's not here."

"What do you mean? I thought he was with you!"

"He got dressed. He said he wanted to go on some rides."

Adele lost her breath. "Oh my God—not the Virginia Reel?"

"I don't know which one."

"Was it the Skyrocket?"

"I don't *know!*"

"All right," Adele said, struggling to stay calm. "You get out onto the street and I'll go look for your brother."

"I'm coming with you," Toni declared.

Adele snapped, "No! This is no place for a little girl to—"

"I'm thirteen years old! And it's *my fault* I let Jack go! *Please.*"

Adele heard the tremor of guilt and fear in her daughter's voice and decided not to fight her on this. "All right, but—stay *right* with me, you understand? I don't want to lose you too!"

The midway was jammed with panicky people trying to exit. Adele took Toni in hand and pushed their way through the crowd to their French fry stand. "Take out the money and get the hell out of here," Adele told Goldie, who replied, "Already done," handed Adele a wad of cash, then vaulted the counter with surprising ease for a fifty-year-old woman. "Good luck!"

Adele and Toni ran across to the Scenic Railway, where motormen were evacuating riders even as John Winkler was trying to sweep the sparks off the tracks with a broom. But Jack was nowhere to be seen.

The narrow artery connecting the two main midways was too congested to pass through, so Adele and Toni took the long way around the Scenic, alongside thousands of frightened visitors escaping through the main gate on Palisade Avenue. Frantically, Adele and Toni checked out the Lindy Loop, the Flying Scooter, the Whip, and the U-Drive Boats, but there wasn't a glimpse of Jack anywhere.

"Shit!" Adele snapped.

Toni was used to hearing her dad use this word, but coming from her mother it alarmed her.

As they made their way up the midway, Adele saw that the front of the Skyrocket was now engulfed in flames, dense smoke pouring across the midway as they approached. Adele handed a handkerchief to Toni— "Put this over your mouth and nose"—covering her own mouth with her hand.

Toni had never seen anything like this, had never felt anything as hot as the wall of shimmering heat surrounding the blaze, preventing them from getting within twenty feet of it. There were now firefighters trying to contain the flames, and one of them told Adele that no one had been injured on the Skyrocket, that everyone had gotten away safely.

Adele looked with dread at the furnace that used to be the Virginia

Reel. *Oh God,* she prayed, *please, please don't let him be in there!* She recognized one of the motormen on the Reel—she remembered that he'd just been discharged from the service after being wounded in action. He looked shell-shocked, as if he were still at war, staring into the hellish heart of what had been, just half an hour ago, a children's ride.

"Have they gotten everybody out?" Adele asked him.

"Everyone they can," he said, his voice flat. "Just before it started, I—I heard a boy say, 'It's smoking,' as his car headed into the tunnels, and I told him"—his voice cracked—"'Don't worry, there's nothing wrong.' I—I didn't think there was." He turned, and Adele saw the tears in his eyes. "Jesus, Jesus, forgive me—I didn't think there was anything wrong!"

Adele didn't know what to say to him. She took Toni by the hand and pulled her away. "C'mon, let's try the Bobsleds."

"But what if Jack's in *there*?" Toni said, eyes fixated on the Reel.

"He's not."

"But what if he *is*?"

"He's not!" Adele snapped. "Come on!"

They ran up the midway, past the Penny Arcade where "Fat George" Mazzocchi and his family were clearing out. From behind them they heard someone shout, "Look out!"—followed by a thunderous roar, like a wounded elephant trumpeting its pain. They spun round to see the wooden bones of the Skyrocket give way, fire dragging the tracks and timbers down to earth. Bystanders ran for their lives. As the coaster came crashing down, it sent up a cyclone of hot cinders that immediately jumped the midway, igniting the Penny Arcade.

Toni's heart was pounding, and yet she stood frozen to the spot, hypnotized by the fiery spectacle of the Skyrocket disintegrating like paper.

Adele grabbed her by the arm, turned her around, and pushed her forward. "Keep going!" she yelled. They raced on up the midway. The Lake Placid Bobsled was just ahead, so far untouched by the flames. The motormen were evacuating the last of the riders, bringing the "bobsleds" down the twisting, looping tracks and the chute to the bottom. Terrified riders jumped off and started running toward the free-act stage and the Hudson gate.

"Mom! Toni!"

Jack jumped out of the second car and began running toward his mother and sister.

"Jack! Thank God!"

With tears in her eyes, Adele hugged him, and Toni was about to do the same when another thunderclap—smaller than the collapse of the Skyrocket—came from their right. They all jumped as the first blast was quickly followed by another, and another—a whole series of explosions, coming from the parking lot on the other side of the Bobsled.

Moments later, shards of hot metal began raining down on the midway. Toni screamed, her relief at finding Jack turning quickly to terror.

Adele hurried her and Jack across the midway and sought refuge under the mushroom-like Chair-o-Plane ride.

"What *is* all that!" Jack shouted over the continuing explosions.

"The fire must've reached the cars in the parking lot!" Adele shouted back. Their gas tanks were exploding like a string of firecrackers.

The shrapnel of exploded automobiles continued to fall around them. "Isn't *our* car in that parking lot?" Toni asked nervously.

Adele looked up and saw that the fire was consuming most of the main midway. Columns of mottled gray smoke, like a line of thunderclouds, obscured passage to the main gate on Palisade Avenue. The only way out was now through the Hudson gate.

"Forget the car," she said. "Let's go!"

They ran across a short connecting midway, past the free-act stage.

A fire engine had been backed up to the edge of the pool so the salt water could be siphoned out to combat the flames; firemen, standing up to their chests in the pool, trained their hoses on the adjacent bathhouses, keeping them wet enough to dampen any sparks alighting on the roof. There were still dozens of people in the pool area waiting to get out, growing increasingly anxious as the fire consumed the Carousel building just across the midway. It would be a short jump from there to Adele's stand, but that wasn't what alarmed her. The Scenic Railway was also in flames, and the strong wind from the south was like a blowtorch spewing cinders across the midway to the Jigsaw and the Funhouse, next to the pool. The fire department was pouring as much water on the buildings as they could, but it was barely slowing the flames' advance.

Bunty Hill was standing next to the bathhouse, talking intently with a fire captain and George Kellinger, the short, curly-haired young man who maintained the pool's machinery. Not far away, the girl who had been taking photos from the diving board was back on the ground, still snapping pictures of the blaze. Toni ran up to her and asked, "You okay?"

"Yeah," the girl, whose name was Agnes, said, her voice shaky. "You should've seen it. The Scenic Railway went up like a pile of straw."

Adele walked past them to Bunty and the other men. "Bunty, what in God's name are all these people still doing here?"

"We can't risk taking them out through the Hudson gate," the fire captain told her. "Any minute now those buildings are going to blow and there'll be a solid wall of flame blocking that midway."

"And it's already started to spread to the Casino Bar," Bunty added, "so we can't get to the gate through there."

"Unless you've got experience in fire dancing," George added wryly.

Adele usually found George's jokes funny, but not today. "And how in the *hell* am I supposed to get my children *out of this firetrap?*"

"We'll get 'em out, dollface," Bunty said reassuringly. "George, you sure it's safe to bring 'em all down there?"

"Safer than staying here," George said. "Just tell people to take it slow and easy and everybody'll get out okay." He turned to Adele. "Just follow me, Mrs. Stopka, and your kids will be fine."

The blithe confidence with which he stated this startled Adele. She hoped to God he was right.

Bunty and the other lifeguards had the remaining beachgoers form an orderly line, and with Adele, Toni, and Jack in front, George Kellinger led them onto the wooden sundeck on the eastern edge of the pool. Between the lemonade stand and the pool's waterfalls there was a narrow gangway. George cautioned everyone, "Okay, take it nice and easy going down," and to Adele's amazement he led them down the gangway and into a cellar with a wooden floor hidden behind the waterfalls. The roar of the falls grew muted, the cavernous space humming with machinery.

"This is the filter room," George explained. "Takes eight of 'em to keep the pool water clean."

"Wow," Jack said. He and Toni were entranced by this underground world they never knew existed, as George led them past eight coal-burning filtration machines the size of apartment house boilers. There was also a pair of huge valves—like something out of a Flash Gordon serial—that George said released the pool water when it had to be drained, and five-foot-high gauges almost as tall as George himself.

"Keep looking up, you don't want to hit your head on one of these," he said, rapping his knuckles on one of the big wooden ceiling beams.

"My God," Adele said, "it's like a catacomb down here."

"Yeah, Lon Chaney lives here during the off-season," George said with a smile. He motioned to the right and said, "This leads under the bathhouses, it lets out near the old trolley tracks. We'll be out in no time."

He led them past the enormous motors powering the artificial wave machine, the floor vibrating a little as they walked. Behind them Toni could see the rest of the pool patrons, all in their swimsuits and most of them barefoot, being shepherded along by Bunty and his fellow lifeguards. They were looking around them as if they had, indeed, wandered onto the set of *The Phantom of the Opera*, but Toni and Jack exchanged delighted grins.

"This place is the greatest," Toni declared.

"Can we come back after the fire's over?" Jack asked.

"Sure, but let's get out first," George replied. "We're right below the bathhouse now. Just a little bit farther."

He was right. Within a few minutes they were ascending another gangway and out into hazy sunlight tinted a Martian orange by the fire—finding themselves on the park's northern border on Route 5, where a dozen fire engines were lined up along the park fence.

"Hallelujah, we have reached the promised land," Adele whooped, giving their rescuer a big hug. "You're a regular Moses, George, thanks!"

George blushed, then made sure all the remaining pool patrons were safely out of the park. Joining earlier escapees in a line that ran uphill to Palisade Avenue, most people wore only bathing suits, clutching no more than a towel. So they fell into line in varying states of undress, looking embarrassed but relieved that they had made it out.

Adele herded the kids past the line and onto Palisade Avenue, where twenty fire companies from all over Bergen and Hudson Counties were battling the blaze. Water from dozens of fire hoses fountained above the roped-off entrance to the park, cascading down onto the flames; other hoses snaked inside the park itself as firemen bravely fought the fire close up.

Ambulances were parked on both sides of the street as medics tended to the injured, treating civilians and firemen alike for heat exhaustion and smoke inhalation. One man sat on the ground breathing gratefully into an oxygen mask. Onlookers gaped at the sight of flames shooting a hundred feet into the air as smoke wreathed the collapsed Skyrocket in the distance.

Adele was puzzled to see Anna Halpin sitting on the curb, rubbing salve from a huge jar onto John Albanese's hands.

"That should hold you until you get to the hospital," she told him.

Adele and the kids came up to them. "John, that was very brave of you, going after those girls in the Virginia Reel. Are you okay?"

"Aw, hell, this is nothing," he said, "compared to what those poor kids in the Reel went through."

Anna nodded. "Some of them, their whole bodies were nearly burnt to a crisp. I covered them from head to toe with salve, then flagged down every passing car and told the drivers to take them to Englewood Hospital."

Into the sober silence that followed, Jack said innocently, "That's a *big* jar, where'd you get it?"

Anna had to smile. "Funny thing, Jack. I'd ordered a smaller jar for the first-aid station, but last week the medical supply company sent me a gallon jar by mistake. I was going to return it, but then the fire broke out and this salve turned out to be a godsend."

The fire burned for two hours, at the end of which Palisades Park was a smoking ruin. This was not the 1935 fire, where only a small portion of the park had been destroyed and the rest reopened that evening. This time the fire had gutted the main midway, the very heart of the park—

three-quarters of it lay in cinders. The Skyrocket was little more than a pile of burnt bones. The Scenic Railway had gone up, in John Winkler's words, "in a single blast." The grand old Dentzel Carousel on which Adele had taken her wedding vows had also been ravaged; all that remained of the painted ponies were charred stumps of wood clinging to brass poles. The administration building, the Funhouse, Penny Arcade, Casino Bar—all gone. The only attractions left untouched were the pool and bathhouse, Bobsled coaster, and free-act stage. It was speculated that the fire began when sparks off a hoisting cable ignited oily rags in a storage room below the Virginia Reel.

Worse, one hundred and fifty people had been injured, twenty-four requiring hospital care, seven critically—and all of these between the ages of twelve and twenty-one.

That could have been any of us, Adele thought numbly.

Irving Rosenthal went consolingly from person to person, reassuring them that he and his brother would rebuild Palisades. Adele almost snapped at him, *Who gives a shit, Irving?*

When the embers had cooled, Adele and the children went into the parking lot and found what remained of their old Studebaker: a blackened chassis squatting in four pools of melted rubber. Two cars down, a woman stood weeping over the burnt-out shell of her sedan. "I don't care about the car," she explained tearfully to Adele. "But there was a photo in the glove compartment of my boy. He's with the invasion in France. I don't know if I'll ever see him again, and now I've lost the only photo I have of him."

Adele put her arms around the woman as she wept, and she shed no tears for the Studebaker. She used a telephone at Johnny Duke's to call her brother James, asking if he could take her and the kids back to Edgewater.

There the children fell asleep quickly, exhausted, but Adele remained awake for hours, the heat outside still oppressive even late into the night. The courage she had mustered to get her through the cataclysm dissolved and she lay in bed sobbing and alone. The thought of how close to death she and her children had come made her sick. The thought of returning to Palisades, even in the distant future, made her even sicker.

Over the course of the next two weeks, all seven of the most severely burned youngsters would die at Englewood Hospital.

Even after writing its brutal signature on so many lives, the heat wave would not loosen its grip on the Northeast. Thunderstorms bellowed and raged, turning daytime skies as black as the soot and smoke that had shrouded Palisades Park. Driving rain, gusting wind, and lightning strikes raked the New York metropolitan area. Even so, it was gentle compared to the storm that was raging in Adele's heart.

12

THE ROSENTHALS ESTIMATED DAMAGES to Palisades at a million dollars and wasted no time in fulfilling Irving's promise to rebuild. Within a week the U.S. government had granted them priority in acquiring the necessary building materials, strictly regulated due to the war, judging Palisades vital to morale by providing recreation to servicemen. Perhaps, too, the government could now begin to see an end to that war, since that same week Allied forces liberated Paris. Irving Rosenthal put the sunniest face on the disaster that he could, announcing that he would create "a bigger, better and safer playground than ever dreamed of by park owners before" and that the new Palisades would open on Easter Sunday, 1945.

The true tragedy of the fire was the loss of seven young lives and the injuries suffered by many more, but it also exacted an economic toll on the concessionaires whose livelihoods had been wiped out in the blaze. They lost everything—their stands, their stock, a full season's income. Those who could quickly replace the tools of their trade jumped onto the carnival circuit. Hardest hit was Helen Cuny, who just that season had elected not to renew the insurance on her stands: "I thought, 'I haven't had anything happen in thirty-five years, I'm not going to worry about it,'" she told Adele. "In hindsight my timing might have been better." She lost eighteen thousand dollars in merchandise, including stock purchased for the next season, yet never considered folding her tent, vowing to return in '45.

Adele had insurance, but it would take months before she saw a dime of it. Of more immediate concern was the loss of income for that season: without it they had only Eddie's servicemen's allowance of seventy-two dollars a month. Fighting back panic, Adele decided the only thing to do was to get a job.

Jobs were plentiful these days, but not necessarily ones to her liking. She had done some waitressing before going to Palisades, but the pay was low—as little as twenty cents an hour, plus tips. The real money to be made was in the defense industry, factory jobs that had, with the advent of the war, been opened up to women in greater numbers than ever before. Women could earn between forty and sixty dollars a month on the assembly line, and in most cases required only minimal training. There was no shortage of defense factories in Edgewater, and Adele had no trouble securing employment at the Ford Motor Plant where Eddie had worked before gallivanting off to the South Pacific in pursuit of guts and glory. She was given a position on the line, assembling and installing light switches in Jeeps being made for our Russian allies.

She had thought the atmosphere inside the French fry stand was greasy, but inside the assembly building the air was thick with the smell of motor oil, and the ventilation system merely stirred the viscous grease in the air like chicken fat congealing in soup. The building was a high-ceilinged barn illuminated with dead white fluorescent light that would have done justice to a police interrogation cell. The ambient noise around her was loud and constant, a clanging racket of gears shifting inside conveyor belts, the triphammer stutter of rivets being driven into metal, the gunning of engines being tested, the hiss of blowtorches spitting fire.

But for Adele the worst part was being forced to wear slacks—dresses presented too much risk of getting your skirt caught in a gear or motor or wheel base—and, even worse, having to cover her long blonde hair with a snood, a ghastly fabric hairnet that covered the back of her head and made her feel like a frumpy, middle-aged fishwife from Vladivostok. Some women at the plant actually wore these things out on the street as a proud badge of service to their country, but Adele tore hers off the instant she went off-duty. She knew she should feel *some* kind of pride in what she was doing, but she didn't. She hated this place. She hated looking like a man, doing a man's job. *Eddie* should have been here doing this, goddamn it, not her.

The day after the fire, Adele had sent a postal telegram to Eddie, care of the Armed Forces APO in San Francisco:

PARK DESTROYED BY FIRE. STAND LOST. CHILDREN OK. WHERE WERE YOU. ADELE.

She knew it was needlessly cruel when she sent it—but found she no longer cared.

Toni stood atop the pool's ten-foot diving platform, watching the flames across the midway consume her parents' concession as if it were no more than an appetizer before a really good meal. WHOOSH, and it was gone! Sparks flew like spittle across the midway and ignited the Funhouse, the exterior walls gobbled up like a snack, exposing bones of dry tinder, which were then devoured in turn. The bathhouse behind her was next for the fire to feast upon, and Toni on her high perch found herself nearly surrounded by the hungry flames. Her body was covered in sweat, she shook with fear and called for help, but there was no one to come to her aid. Where was the Human Torch? Where was Bee Kyle? She could command these flames to retreat, couldn't she? The skies above her glowed red and the air all around her was choked with acrid smoke, making her cough up black soot. There was only one safe place to go, and that was the water below her. She stood at the edge of the diving board, telling herself to jump, but fear paralyzed her—fear of falling, of hitting the water the wrong way, her body snapping like a twig. She looked up and saw the flames converging on the pool like a blazing army battalion, eating up what little air she was able to take into her lungs. Finally her fear of the fire won out, she pushed off from the diving platform and dove into the air, a perfect swan dive, her body arcing gracefully down toward the water . . .

But on her way down the water ignited and burst into flame, and she found herself diving headlong into a sea of fire.

She screamed, waking herself but not really—the flames were still all around her, licking at the walls of her bedroom. Her shrieks brought Adele racing in to comfort her: "Honey, it's okay, you're home, you're safe—"

The flames were quenched more easily than Toni's fears. She hugged her mother and collapsed into sobs.

Jack came running in from his room, joining them in bed. Adele cradled them both, stroking her daughter's back and comforting her as best she could: "Everything's okay, you're safe. It won't happen again . . ."

She was wrong. It happened again the next night. And the night after that. And every night for weeks to come.

Eddie opened the small envelope addressed to "Seaman First Class Edward Stopka, APO 708" to find a telegram from Adele, which alarmed him even before he'd read it: why would she send a telegram if not bad news? Her terse, carefully chosen words had the desired effect upon him: shock, confusion, fear, shame. Palisades burned down? *All* of it? Thank God the kids were okay, but were they there when it happened, were they *really* okay? Finally, there was no mistaking her intent in that mocking, angry last line:

WHERE WERE YOU.

Now he asked himself the same question.

I'm on an island in the middle of the fucking Pacific Ocean, he answered, instead of being with my family when they were in danger.

He balled the telegram up in his hand but couldn't bring himself to toss it, even with that barb in its tail, and stuffed it in his trouser pocket.

Adele would surely have known that news was slow to reach the South Pacific and that the telegram would arrive well before any newspaper accounts—and that between the time he wired back and she responded, Eddie would spend several days agonizing over just how close to harm's way his wife and children had come and what the full extent of damage to the park and their business had been. It was her punishment for his leaving them, and he understood that, understood the hurt and sense of abandonment that motivated it. If her feelings of anger and betrayal were as painful as the helpless disgrace he felt now, he could hardly blame her.

He wired back:

```
SO SORRY NOT THERE WISH ANYTHING I COULD
HAVE BEEN. PLEASE CLARIFY WHETHER
TONI AND JACK AT FIRE. HOW MUCH DAMAGE
TO PARK. LOVE TO ALL WILL WIRE
MORE MONEY. EDDIE.
```

He wired her all that remained of his Navy pay for that month.

In his quarters, Eddie sat down and wrote a long letter to Toni and Jack, telling them how much he missed them and how much he wished he were there, but that their mother was a strong woman and would take care of them until the day he came back. The only bright spot for him was that that day seemed to be getting closer. In addition to the good news out of Europe, the United States in June had begun bombing the Japanese home islands, starting with the island of Kyushu. A month later, the Americans wrested Saipan away from the enemy, and in August, Guam fell to U.S. forces. The slow tide of history was finally turning in the direction of the Allies.

To calm himself, he went back to working on another *tiki*, his fifth so far this year. This time Eddie was using his chisel to sculpt a wide-mouthed, jagged-eyed Kū out of a six-inch palm log, lopped off clean and straight at the bottom, which he would hollow out from the top. His idea was to create a *tiki* mug, in the vein of the ceramic glasses he had seen at Trader Vic's. After he hollowed it out, he would burnish it with a fine sandpaper and varnish it with shellac from the paint shop. He tried to lose himself in his carving, telling himself there was nothing else he could do for Adele and the kids until he knew more about what had happened.

He turned the mug-to-be over in his hand, appraising the hollow eye sockets that seemed suddenly to be staring into his soul.

They were saying: WHERE WERE YOU?

With their mother working the day shift at Ford, Toni and Jack were left to their own devices—reading comic books, scaling the cliffs, roaming Edgewater on their bicycles, and longing for Palisades Park, especially the pool. One morning, as Jack was occupied elsewhere—swapping issues of *Blue Beetle* and *All-Winners Comics* with friends before they were given up to the paper drive—Toni biked up River Road, then turned right onto Henry Hudson Drive, which forked north toward the George Washington Bridge. She was looking up at the curved, yellow-and-blue facade of the famous Riviera nightclub—jutting like a ship's prow beached atop the summit of the Palisades, though closed for the duration of the war—when she noticed a familiar figure making his way down through the bramble of the cliff's slope, carrying a rucksack and holding a walking stick.

"Bunty!" Toni yelled joyously.

She pedaled furiously to meet her friend as he reached the road and waved to her. "Hey, toots, what're you up to?"

She braked and jumped off the bike. "Not much. Summer's pretty dull without the park." She could see now that the walking stick he was holding had what looked like a can opener taped to its side. "What's that for?"

"My shillelagh? I carry it in case I run into any copperheads as I come down the cliffs. I use it to chase 'em away. And this," he said of the can opener, "comes in handy for tapping the occasional can of ale."

He crossed the road to an old boat dock on this pebbled river frontage beneath the G.W. Bridge tower. "You been to Hazard's before?" he asked.

"What's that?" She abandoned her bike on the side of the road and followed him toward shore.

"Hazard's Beach. I was a lifeguard here for six summers in the twenties—this was all white sand back then, though we had to have it shipped in by barge. It was a popular place—there was a ferry that came over from 157ᵗʰ Street and New Yorkers just swarmed over here. Three boats daily, five on Sunday, when there must've been five thousand people on this beach. They'd give the lifeguards box lunches and whenever we pulled somebody in trouble out of the water, we'd get a quarter tip. Man, those were the days.

"Up there"—he pointed north—"was Bloomers Beach, where I got my first lifeguard job when I was eighteen. Worked there three years. Today it's an oil slick. There was a dance pavilion here too—lots of dancing, laughing, cold beer, wonderful music, and beautiful girls." He smiled at old ghosts, adding quietly, "But the bridge put the ferry out of business, and eventually, all the beaches too."

At water's edge he took off his T-shirt with its tiny crucifix pinned on, kicked off his shoes, and shucked off his pants, revealing his red bathing trunks.

"You really swim here every day?" Toni asked.

"Weather permitting, yeah. I've been swimming in the Hudson since my brothers threw me in when I was five." He laughed. "Swam across it for the first time when I was twelve. This river is my life—I was born within sight of it, grew up along its banks, worked here when I was young. And I still do, kind of, since this is where the Palisades pool's water comes from."

"Don't you ever get tired of coming here?"

"Hell no. Who could get tired of this?" He gazed fondly into the distance. "See how calm it is now? In an hour, it could kick up and the big waves'll roll in. Unpredictable—I like that. I follow the river. The river never has plans either. It's cold one day, hot the next.

"See, the Hudson's a tidal river—the tide rolls in from the sea, pushing all the way up to Albany. Before it even gets there we get an ebb tide here, going in the opposite direction. The Indians called it Mahicantuck—'the river that flows both ways.'" He pointed to the mile-wide gulf between bridge towers. "See how it narrows here? As the waters squeeze through, the currents run faster. You gotta be damn careful."

"Sounds like fun," Toni said wistfully.

Bunty put on his little red diving cap. "So give it a try sometime. Not on your own, mind you—I can't tell you how many kids I've had to pull out of these waters before they drowned. But I can show you the ropes, how to swim in the river and stay safe."

Suddenly Toni wanted to do nothing else. "Okay!" she said brightly. "How about tomorrow?"

"I'll be here. Same time." He gave her a two-fingered salute, then dove off the dock and into the Hudson, his powerful breaststroke and kicks propelling him through the water like a motorboat.

Toni jumped on her bike and excitedly pedaled home. She couldn't wait to come back the following morning.

The next day she brought Jack along too, and Bunty instructed them in river swimming, considerably different from swimming either in the Palisades pool or in the ocean. Bunty had them gargle with the water, as always, to determine buoyancy. Toni blanched a little at this—the water wasn't nearly as clean as it became when it reached the pool. He had them stick close to shore at first: "These currents can run as fast as two and a half knots—three miles an hour. That may not sound like much, but take it from me, it is." When they came up against a swift current, he showed them how to use eddies—currents that formed in the lee of outcroppings of rock, and which flowed in the opposite direction from the main current—to their advantage.

Toni was surprised how choppy the water could be—the result of heavy water traffic in the Hudson—and how navigating in the chop was like swimming inside a washing machine. She spent most of her time just trying to keep her head above water to take in enough air before the next wave buffeted her. It was nothing like swimming in the pool with its tame artificial waves—this was *real*. But that made it even more exciting.

Over the next few weeks, more of Toni and Jack's friends from Edgewater and Fort Lee joined Bunty on his morning swim, the river taking the place of their beloved pool in this summer without Palisades. He was happy to instruct them all in swimming—though never admitting that any of them ever *really* knew how to swim—and afterward they would sit on Hazard's Beach as Bunty shared slices of liverwurst on Saltine crackers (and occasionally a sip from his can of Ballantine Ale) and he would read the comics section of the newspaper aloud to them. He would tell stories about the river, or show them how to catch blue claw crabs, or sometimes Toni and her friends would assist him as he scanned his daily racing form:

"Okay," he'd say, "in tomorrow's fourth race at Monmouth we've got Frisky Filly, Six of One, Dreamboat, Full Moon, Champion . . ."

"I like Dreamboat," Toni said.

"Aw, that's sappy," Dave objected. "Champion's a winner!"

"I think there's a full moon tonight," Jack said.

"That's a good omen! Full Moon, it is," Bunty decided.

The horse placed, and the next day Bunty bought lunch all around.

After a few weeks of swimming and watching Bunty cross over one day to the little red lighthouse at Jeffrey's Hook and back, Toni decided she wanted to try to cross the Hudson, too. "If that's what you want," Bunty said, pleased, "I'll coach you like I did Millie Corson." They spent a week working on her stroke, her kicks, her breathing, building up her stamina for the mile-wide crossing. The plan was to swim across to Jeffrey's Light, then swim back, but if the tides were against her she would climb up the New York side and walk back across the George Washington Bridge.

When Bunty decided she was ready, he dove into the water and shadowed her as she headed for open water. At first she cleaved the water like a fish, until Bunty called out a caution: "Don't use up all your energy at the start! Pace yourself." But her enthusiasm got the better of her and she slowed down only a little. By the time she was a quarter way across she began to tire and now slowed down out of necessity. Then a ferry crossing the river fifty yards south of them kicked up some heavy chop, the waves slapping her sideways, obscuring her sight of land. She fought back a surge of panic by reminding herself that Bunty was right beside her, but the fear had taken root. As she fought the waves, trying to move forward, she thought of Anne Ringens lying at the bottom of the water tank, and suddenly it seemed that much harder to swim. She gritted her teeth and kept going, but the currents were starting to pull her northward. "Keep on course!" Bunty called, but it took more of Toni's strength to do it.

Finally, only halfway across, Toni came to a dead, weary stop. Treading water, she called, "Bunty!"

He was alongside her in a moment. "Yeah? You okay?"

"I—I can't do it," she told him.

"Sure you can. Don't panic."

"I can't!"

"You're halfway there, kiddo. You gotta swim the same distance to get home. But if you keep going, you can say you swam across the Hudson."

"I can't *do* it!" she yelled, pivoting in the water and starting back.

Bunty heard the fear in her voice, said, "Okay, then, let's go back," and turned in the water to follow her.

She made it back safely, but was ashamed as she touched the coarse pebbles of Hazard's Beach. She quickly threw her clothes on over her wet swimsuit and she and Jack headed back to Edgewater.

"You okay, Sis?" he asked as they biked home side by side.

"Yeah, sure I am," she said, but knew she wasn't.

This would be the end of river swimming for her that summer.

A few days later, she faced another arduous task: the annual shopping trip for school clothes at Schweitzer's Department Store in Fort Lee. This would be Toni's first year of high school, but since there wasn't one in Edgewater, she would be bussed up the hill to Cliffside Park High School. Toni would have to abandon her summer wardrobe of blue jeans or shorts and revert to dresses for the school year. Adele enthusiastically pointed out some lovely floral prints by Carole King, a darling ruffled blouse from Joan Kenley, and a smart Vicky Vaughn peplum dress; but as usual Toni resisted any kind of frilly petticoats, pinafores, or embroidered eyelets in favor of simple (and to Adele's mind, simply boring) Tattersall checked dresses.

"Why can't I wear these?" Toni asked, pointing out a "playsuit"—a pair of cotton slacks and a blouse that looked like a man's striped shirt.

Adele was appalled. "It's one thing to wear overalls and jeans when you're scrambling up those cliffs, but you can't wear pants to school."

"*You* wear pants when you go to work," Toni pointed out.

"You go to work on an assembly line like me, I'll buy you slacks. You go to school, you're wearing dresses."

Toni acquiesced, but her mother's torture did not end when they got home from the store. Toni was told to sit down at her mother's makeup table, something she had never done nor ever wanted to do.

"Now that you're entering high school," Adele said, picking up a small brush, "you're going to need to know how to apply makeup."

"Why would I want to know that?"

"Because all the other girls are going to be wearing it and you'll stand out like a sore thumb if you don't." She opened a tin of face powder and lightly touched the brush to its surface. "Now this doesn't *quite* match your skin tone but we'll get you one that does . . ."

She brushed the powder onto Toni's face as meticulously as a painter laying down strokes on a canvas, then evened it up with a sponge. Toni crinkled her nose. "It smells like perfume."

"Yes, isn't that nice? Now, after you've applied an even base of powder, you apply a little blush on the cheekbones . . ."

She applied a light swath of blush to Toni's cheeks.

"It's *pink*," Toni said in alarm.

"It just puts a rosy glow in your cheeks."

"Take it off!"

"Stop being a baby. We're almost done. You're too young for mascara and eye shadow anyway. Now this is the most important part: your lips." Adele picked up a tube of lipstick, unsheathing a crimson fingertip which she liberally applied to Toni's lips.

"Is it supposed to be so *red*?" Toni asked.

"Yes, that's the style. Stop talking, I can't apply it with you jabbering."

Within a minute Toni's mouth, which had hardly even commanded her own attention before, now shouted back at her from the mirror, shrill and scarlet as a circus clown's mouth.

"Jeez-us!" Toni gasped.

"Watch your mouth, young lady."

"I can't watch anything else!"

"You look lovely."

"I look like Emmett Kelly!"

Toni grabbed the nearest handkerchief and began furiously rubbing off the lip rouge as if it were blood from a wound.

"Antoinette, for heaven's sake," Adele sighed, "you're going to have to wear makeup someday!"

"Give me one good reason," Toni replied, going to work on the blush.

"Well, for one thing, a girl who doesn't care about her appearance isn't going to attract much attention from boys."

"I know lots of boys and I don't have to wear this stuff."

"You may be just one of the guys now, honey, but one day you're going to start looking at them differently. Don't you want to get married someday, like me?"

"No!" Toni snapped. "I don't want to *be* like you! Your life is *boring!*"

Scraping off the last of the powder, Toni jumped to her feet and stomped out of the room. Adele looked after her, feeling—what *did* she feel? There was a time this would have infuriated and depressed her, might have made her collapse sobbing onto the bed, devastated that her daughter was rejecting everything Adele was, everything she loved.

But not now. Now she had to admit: Toni was right. Her life *was* boring. Even she hated it—how could she expect her daughter to want to follow in her footsteps when Adele herself didn't want to be in them?

Reconstruction of Palisades proceeded throughout the winter: the sinking of power lines underground was completed before a blast of icy weather blew in, and a new water main was installed with an eye toward future fires. Joe McKee designed a new coaster, the Cyclone, similar to the one the Rosenthals had built at Coney Island, as well as a novel dome-shaped building to house the new Philadelphia Tobbagan Company Carousel; surrounding it was a block of food and candy concessions, quickly dubbed Candyland and largely owned by Chief Borrell. All the old wooden buildings were replaced by brick, concrete, and other fireproof materials.

The park was the last place Adele wanted to return to, but she and Eddie had a lease and she knew that one good summer could net more than her annual salary at the Ford plant. So as the park was resurrected out of its own ashes, Adele collected the insurance money, reluctantly ordered new cooking equipment and supplies, and tendered her resignation from Ford.

On April 12, 1945, President Roosevelt died, just one month short of Germany's surrender. All Bergen County schools and courthouses closed for a day out of respect. On May 8—V-E Day—two hundred thousand New Yorkers flocked to Times Square, which fully blazed with light for the first time since dim-out regulations went into effect.

Four days later, Palisades Amusement Park just as triumphantly reopened with a gala party attended by invited members of the National Association of Showmen. Forty thousand patrons filled the park that day; no sooner had Adele and Goldie cooked one batch of fries when they had to start on another. As the cash register rang up a merry tune, Adele thought less and less of the inferno of last summer and more about her deliverance from slacks, snoods, and the assembly line. The stand could also be something of an assembly line, but at least she could wear a dress under her apron.

On May 28 the Palisades pool opened for the season, a welcome reward at the end of Toni's freshman year of high school. She grudgingly admitted to herself that her mother had been right, high school *was* different from grade school—bigger, for one thing, with students from three neighboring boroughs attending. The kids seemed to band together in little cliques—gym rats, eggheads, bobby-soxers—none of which Toni comfortably fit into. She was also frustrated by the fact that outside of Phys Ed, there were few varsity sports for girls, and she chose gymnastics only because Bunty had once advised her it would prove useful in her diving.

She still played sandlot baseball with the boys, but in Edgewater she had been on more of an equal footing—able to climb, swim, or play ball with the best of them. Now, as the boys entered puberty, getting bigger and stronger—eliciting new and disturbing feelings in Toni—she found herself no longer on an equal par. And she was too much of a tomboy to fit in with most of the girls. She felt confused, isolated, and missed the comforting presence of her brother, still in junior high in Edgewater.

So she was relieved when classes ended and she once more became a full-time employee at Palisades, with her usual hour off for the pool.

She hadn't seen Bunty since her failure to cross the Hudson, but he quickly put her at ease: "People do things in their own time. You'll tackle it again when you're ready. I've got faith in you, kiddo."

Toni beamed. That faith was as warming to her as the summer sun.

Jack worked his paper route and helped out some at the stand, but through a chance encounter at Woolworth's five-and-dime he had acquired a new enthusiasm: magic. Standing in line behind a dapper man with a familiar voice, Jack found himself face-to-face with Joseph Dunninger, a Cliffside Park resident and professional magician and mentalist whose national radio program went out over NBC Blue. Dunninger was warm and friendly to the starstruck boy, and when Jack asked, "Can anybody learn to do what you do?" Dunninger smiled and said, "Absolutely. Why, a three-year-old could do it—with thirty years' practice," and winked a goodbye.

The "three-year-old" part got Jack's attention—the "thirty years" barely registered—and he immediately set out to learn everything he could about the magic business. He listened religiously to Dunninger's Wednesday-night radio show and borrowed from the library a copy of *Blackstone's Secrets of Magic* by the world-famous magician Harry Blackstone.

So when a banner went up at the Palisades sideshow announcing the engagement of MASTER MAGICIAN—LORENZO THE MAGNIFICENT! Jack wasted no time catching his performance. And after he did, he quickly corralled Toni into seeing the act, too: "This guy is aces! Ya gotta see him!"

Happy to be back on familiar ground with her brother, Toni agreed.

Lorenzo, a dark-haired, good-looking fellow in his thirties, was impressively debonair in tuxedo and tails and did some fancy tricks with cards and coins—he made a fan of playing cards magically appear in his hands, then shuffled them up the length of his arm; made coins vanish, then reappear under the hat of a man standing in the front of the audience; tore a card into shreds, rolled the shreds into some cigarette paper, then lit the cigarette and produced the intact card out of the smoke. "Just like the Vision appears out of smoke!" Jack whispered, referring to the green-faced, other-dimensional hero from *Marvel Mystery Comics*.

But the high point came when from behind a curtain a young woman—Toni recognized her as one of the "bally girls" out front—wheeled in a black wooden box on four legs that looked uncomfortably like a coffin.

"Ah, isn't she lovely?" Lorenzo said. His accent was unfamiliar to Toni but had a pleasantly exotic ring to it. "Courageous, too, because she has agreed to be part of one of the most dangerous feats a magician can perform. Take a good look, ladies and gentlemen—you may never see her again as she is now, beautiful and vibrant with life!"

He removed the coffin's lid, then held out a hand and helped the girl up onto a footstool and into the box. It barely accommodated her, as the crowd could plainly see. Then he closed the lid and said gravely, "Let's hope this does not turn out to be her funeral casket."

From off the floor he picked up a long metal blade that glinted menacingly under the sideshow lights.

"Now, should any of you be thinking these might be stage blades, made of rubber . . ." He invited audience members up to examine the blades. One middle-aged man couldn't resist running his finger along the edge of the blade, then yelped as the steel drew blood.

"Thank you, sir," Lorenzo said. "After the performance, management will present you with your Purple Heart."

The audience laughed, but this quickly turned to gasps as Lorenzo vigorously plunged the first blade through a slot in the lid of the box. It sank clean through, the tip emerging out the bottom. He repeated it with another blade, this one close to where the girl's head must have been; a woman in the audience cried out in alarm, which rattled the rest of the crowd, who thought the cry might have come from the girl in the box. Again and again Lorenzo plunged the blades in with gusto, until there were at least ten protruding from top and bottom. The crowd murmured its unease.

"That ought to do it, don't you think?" Lorenzo asked rhetorically, whereupon he began withdrawing the blades one by one. When the last of them clattered into a pile of metal on the floor, Lorenzo gazed out at the expectant audience—slowly lifted the lid of the box—

The bally girl sat up, smiling, like a jack-in-the-box. Lorenzo helped her up and out, where everyone could see that she was completely unharmed.

Amid enthusiastic applause from the crowd, Lorenzo took his bows.

Toni and Jack clapped as loudly as anyone else. "C'mon!" Jack told his sister. "Let's go try and meet him!"

Often, between performances, the sideshow headliners would go outside for a break, to smoke a cigarette or quench their thirst with potables. Toni and Jack ran behind the sideshow and waited. Within a minute Lorenzo exited, lighting up a Lucky Strike.

"Mr. Lorenzo, you were great!" Jack told him.

"Yeah, that was tops," Toni agreed.

Lorenzo looked at them, blew out a plume of smoke, and smiled warmly. "Well, thank you. I am honored you enjoyed the show."

"I want to be a magician," Jack said, "can you give me any hints?"

"Well, I'm going off to have some supper now," Lorenzo said, "but if you come back when the show closes, at midnight, I will be happy to give you some advice." He smiled, and Toni knew he was thinking that these two kids would be long gone by the time the park closed at midnight.

"Thanks!" Jack told him. Lorenzo turned and walked away as Jack and Toni hurried back to their mother's French fry stand.

"I thought you wanted to be a comic strip artist," Toni said along the way. "Now you want to be a magician?"

"Who says I can't be both? I can draw about them too, like Zatara the Magician in *Action* and Ibis the Invincible in *Whiz*."

Bursting into the French fry stand, Jack announced, "Mom, Lorenzo the Magnificent says he'll tell me how to be a magician if I come back when the park closes!"

Adele rolled her eyes. "Oh God, not you too. Are you going to make your sister disappear before she dives into a teacup?"

"Please, Mom, can I stay?" His eyes were limpid with longing.

She sighed. "Okay. I'll take you over to see him, but after five minutes we've got to go home, all right?"

When they got to the sideshow at midnight, the magician was just leaving and Jack called out, "Mr. Lorenzo!" He turned, clearly surprised to see them here so late; but he smiled charmingly and said, "Ah, the aspiring prestidigitator! Just the boy I wanted to see," as if he actually meant it.

"This is my mom, Mr. Lorenzo," Jack said. "She runs the French fry stand by the pool."

Lorenzo looked at the boy's willowy blonde mother and his smile became more genuine.

"Hi. Adele Stopka." She held out a hand for him to shake, but instead, to her surprise, he bowed low and kissed it.

"Lorenzo Marques. A pleasure, Mrs. Stopka." He straightened.

Adele said, "Marques? Are you from Spain?"

"Cuba. I got my start playing nightclubs in Havana." He ruffled Jack's hair. "Say, young man . . . I'm on my way to a party with some of the other performers. Why don't you and your family join me? And I'll be happy to answer all of your questions."

Adele hadn't been to an after-hours party in years—not since Toni was born. "Sure," she said. "Why not?"

"Excellent. Come, it's over here by the cliffs, where my trailer is parked." As they walked, Lorenzo fell into step beside Jack and asked, "And how long have you wanted to be a magician, my boy?"

"At least a month," Jack replied enthusiastically.

"So, a lifelong dream," Lorenzo said wryly, and Adele had to smile.

At the cliff's edge, behind the towering PALISADES AMUSEMENT PARK—SURF BATHING sign, several sideshow performers—many of whom were also living in the trailers perched atop the bluff—were gathered around a portable barbecue, steaks and hamburgers sizzling on the grill. Against the glittering cyclorama of the Manhattan skyline, a midget was standing on a stepstool grilling the steaks, a tattooed lady was mixing drinks in a tumbler, and the show's fire-eater was plucking foil-wrapped potatoes out of a roaring fire with his bare bands. Adele smiled, feeling as though she had stepped back in time to that night she and Eddie had sat and chatted with Jolly Irene—who, according to her obituary in *Billboard*, had died in 1940 at the age of sixty—and Susi the Elephant Skin Girl. The last Adele had heard of Susi—Charlotte—she was in New York working for the Gorman Brothers Circus, where her act now included a real elephant as a partner.

The performers warmly welcomed Adele and her family and soon they were all sitting in beach chairs, the kids wolfing down hamburgers as their mother cut into a perfect medium-rare steak. Chewing around his own steak, Lorenzo asked the children, "So what was your favorite part of the act?"

"The lady in the box!" Jack replied immediately. "How'd you *do* that?"

"Very carefully," Lorenzo said soberly, and all three Stopkas laughed.

"I'm quite serious," he said, smiling. "You see, the blades really do go through the box and out the bottom. The girl really is inside the box. She has to contort her body every which way to avoid the blades, which of course we have rehearsed well beforehand. I must admit, though, that today she came perilously close to being—what do they say?—*shish-ka-bobbed.*" More laughter. "The girl was a bit nervous and had a few drinks at the Casino Bar to shore up her courage. When she showed up for the first show, she was so gloriously drunk that she could barely squirm into the box. I was terrified I might turn her into a pincushion—and I did nick her ankle once. After the first performance I poured hot coffee into her until she was sober enough to do the next show." He shook his head. "This is the danger in relying on local talent instead of having a traveling assistant."

"So why don't you get one?" Toni asked.

Lorenzo admitted, "My last assistant was my wife, Inez, and since our divorce, I have not been able to bear the thought of another partner. That's what a properly trained assistant is, you see—a partner. She does much more than look pretty or curl up in a blade box—she is part of the illusion, she misdirects the audience and knows how to improvise if something goes awry." He seemed to look past his listeners. "Inez was irreplaceable."

Into the sad silence that followed this, Adele sought to change the subject: "How long will you be performing at Palisades, Mr. Marques?"

"Two weeks, Mrs. Stopka. Then I'm off to the Steel Pier in Atlantic City. A nightclub manager there has agreed to come see my show . . . this might be my ticket back into the sort of larger venues I played in Cuba."

Finally, after an hour of good food and congenial conversation—far longer than the five minutes Jack had originally been promised—Adele thanked the performers and Mr. Marques for their hospitality, invited them all to her stand for free French fries whenever they liked, then gathered up her children and drove them home to Edgewater.

Jack could not talk about anything but Lorenzo for the next several days and must have gone to see his show a half-dozen more times. Sometimes, if Lorenzo had a few minutes between shows, he would show how to do a simple card trick, and Jack was thrilled when he mastered it.

About a week later, Toni was working her mother's shift in the kitchen while Adele took her dinner break with Minette Dobson at the Grandview. But as Toni lifted a frying vat off the burner, her wrist twisted, the vat tilted, and a hot teardrop of grease spilled onto the open flame.

The flame promptly flared into a gout of fire two feet high, the heat nearly singeing off Toni's eyebrows. Startled, she dropped the vat onto the stove, and now more hot oil flew up and out, feeding the grease fire. She froze as the flame flared larger, nearly reaching the ceiling.

"Goldie!" Toni shouted. "Fire!"

Toni turned off the burner, but the grease on the stove was still feeding the flames. Within seconds Goldie ran into the back wielding a fire extinguisher. In one smooth unbroken movement she pulled the pin, aimed the hose, and sprayed fire retardant onto the fire, damping the flames.

"Wow," Toni said with a sigh of relief, "thanks."

"Better get your mom. Don't know if we should use that burner yet."

Toni ran over to the Grandview Restaurant, but her mother was nowhere to be seen. Puzzled, she went up to the manager, Flo Lyons, and asked, "Has my mom been in here? With Minette Dobson?"

"She was here, but not with Minette," Flo replied. "She ordered some food for takeout. I saw her head off that way."

She nodded off to the left, toward the giant PALISADES sign—or, seen from this side, ƨƎb∀ƧI⅃∀ꟼ—on the brow of the cliffs.

"Thanks," Toni said. Maybe the sideshow was having their dinner break there too, and Mom had gone to join them—she did seem more interested in the performers these days. But when she got to the brink of the Palisades, there was no portable barbecue, no party, no one around at all except for the fire-eater, smoking a cigarette on the stoop of his trailer.

"'Scuse me," she said, "have you seen my mom? Adele Stopka?"

He looked up and drawled, "Blonde gal? Kinda weird eyes?"

"Yeah, that's her. Where is she?"

He hesitated a moment, then pointed to a trailer three doors down. "She's in there. But I'd knock first if I were you."

Toni hurried over to a modest Gulfstream trailer. But she didn't knock on the door. She heard a woman's laugh from inside and recognized it instantly as her mother's. Ignoring her own better judgment, she went to the side window, raised herself up on tiptoes, and peeked inside.

Her eyes popped wider than Barney Google's. Her mother was inside, all right—and so was Lorenzo. They were lying side by side on a foldout bed, they were naked, and Lorenzo, as even Toni could see, *was* magnificent.

13

Toni jerked back from the window, traced the sign of the cross across her chest, then fled like holy hell, certain she was about to be struck blind by what she had seen. As she barreled past the fire-eater he said, "Toldja you shoulda knocked," but aside from a couple of fast glances behind her to see if her snooping had been detected (it hadn't) she didn't slow until she was safely back on the main midway. There she collapsed onto a bench barely shaded by a newly planted poplar tree, and once safely behind a veil of hundreds of park visitors, tears rolled down her face. She felt sick to her stomach, sad, and angry, all at the same time. How could her mother have *done* that to her dad? And how could Toni ever look her in the eye again? The question was not rhetorical—she had to find an answer pretty fast, since it wouldn't be long before her mother was back at the stand.

Taking a last deep breath, Toni hurried back to their concession, where Goldie asked, "What did your mom say about the burner?"

"Couldn't find her," Toni lied, brushing past her to the kitchen. "I'll clean it up but we won't use it till she's fin— until she gets back."

Toni scrubbed the burner, still faintly warm from the fire, then deep-fried another batch of fries on the second burner. Fifteen minutes later, Adele strolled breezily into the stand, hair and makeup impeccable as usual.

Toni refused to meet her gaze as she entered.

"What happened here?" Adele asked, spotting flecks of foam on the side of the stove.

"Grease fire," Toni said tersely, eyes still downcast.

"Are you okay?"

Yeah, I'm just swell, Toni thought. "Goldie put it out. I cleaned the burner—is it okay to use it again?"

Adele walked up to Toni's side and gave the burner a once-over. "Looks fine to me. You did a good job cleaning it up."

Standing this close, Toni could smell Lorenzo's cologne on her mother's skin. Her stomach began to turn cartwheels.

"I—I gotta go pee." She jumped the counter, racing up the midway to the nearest ladies' room. She locked herself into a stall and vomited into the toilet as if she had eaten a month-old hot dog with a side of rancid butter.

When she was finished she flushed the toilet, then closed the lid and sat there for several minutes, her body trembling with rage and disgust.

Somehow she made it through the rest of the evening, still avoiding her mother's gaze. If Adele noticed her coldness toward her, it wasn't so far out of the ordinary that she bothered to comment on it. When the time came for her swim break, Toni gratefully dove into the cleansing waters of the pool, taking refuge in the sheltering silence beneath the surface. She desperately wanted to tell someone what she had seen—her father; Jack—but how could she? If she wrote her father it would just make him angry and miserable, helpless to do anything about it. She couldn't tell Jack—he might not tell anyone else, but his face was an open book and she couldn't take the chance he might somehow betray what he knew to their mother.

She could confront her mother with what she knew—tell her how horrible and traitorous she was—but then what? She and Jack still had to live, and work, with her until Dad came home. Yeah, that sounded like fun.

No—she had to keep this secret, *top* secret, until her father returned. And besides—Lorenzo would be leaving the park at the end of the week, off to his engagement at the Steel Pier, and that would be the end of that.

Leaving the pool at the end of the hour, Toni slapped on the closest thing she could manage to a smile and went back to work.

Only days later, Toni discovered she would not have to keep the secret much longer: on August 6 came the news that the United States had dropped some kind of super-bomb that "harnessed the power of the sun itself" on the city of Hiroshima, Japan. The world waited for Japan to surrender, and when it didn't, three days later a second bomb was dropped on the city of Nagasaki, the furnaces of the sun incinerating it in an instant.

On August 14, 1945, the Japanese Empire surrendered to the Allied forces. V-J Day was here.

Her father would finally be coming home.

Eddie, as a member of the Naval Reserves, didn't have to wait for his two-year tour of duty to be completed—he had enlisted for the duration of the war and would be discharged upon its end, though his status as a reservist would continue in the event of another war. But from what Eddie had heard about this so-called "atomic bomb," it sounded as if any future wars would be pretty damn short.

It took a few weeks for a troopship, the *Willard A. Holdbrook,* to arrive at Espíritu Santo and begin redeployment. Eddie was disappointed when he learned the ship wouldn't pass through Hawai'i this time, but soon he would be back home in New Jersey with his family—that was all that mattered.

Meanwhile, at Palisades, the Rosenthals threw a closing bash to celebrate the park's successful rebirth that season; and quickly thereafter, Toni found herself starting her sophomore year of high school, even as Jack now entered Cliffside Park High as a freshman.

The first pickup softball game of the school year was held on the athletic field on a day when the varsity teams weren't playing. It was September, the weather was still warm, and Toni's excitement upon the first game of the school year was given a new, and unexpected, dimension.

One of the regular players was "Slim" Welker, on whose team Toni and Jack used to play, years ago, in the Palisades parking lot. Toni was startled to see that over the summer Slim had gone through a growth spurt, gaining about two inches in height and—though he still lived up to his nickname—packing on a good twenty pounds of muscle. This was plainly evident through the undershirt he wore while playing, his newly toned biceps flexing as he swung at the ball. The bat connected with a loud crack, sending the ball arcing into space. He was a good runner, too, and made it to third before Toni caught the ball and threw it to the third baseman; by which time Slim was safe. Even from the outfield Toni could see the sweat glistening on Slim's face—still a boyish face, nicely contrasting with the man's body he was developing. She had never paid much attention to Slim Welker before, but now it was all she could do to tear her eyes away from his sandy hair and pug nose and force her attention to the next pitch.

In the next inning, on her turn at bat, Toni hit the ball squarely and strongly, and its impressive trajectory got her all the way to second base. She glanced over at Slim, playing infield, but his attention wasn't on her but on one of the pretty girls sitting in the bleachers watching the game.

The next pickup game assembled in the parking lot of the Trinity Episcopal Church across from the high school. As the players formed teams Toni casually moseyed over to Slim and said, "Just like those games we used to play in the Palisades parking lot, huh?"

His smile felt like a kind of victory to Toni. "Yeah, those were good. Just tell me your brother isn't playing on my team today, okay?"

Toni laughed. The laugh felt like a betrayal of Jack, but when Slim joined in, all she cared about was that Slim Welker had not only noticed her but was sharing a joke with her. The fact that the joke in question was her brother bothered her only a little.

But after the last inning, it was the pretty bobby-soxer Maria De-Castro who Slim walked home. Toni was left feeling empty and guilty.

On a Sunday afternoon in late September, Eddie, in his Navy whites, stepped off the *Champion*, the Atlantic Coast Line's passenger train from Florida to New York's Pennsylvania Station, and into the arms of his children, who sped toward him like torpedoes cleaving through the water.

"Dad Dad Dad!" they both were yelling simultaneously. He was startled to see how much they'd grown in not quite two years—Jack was at least five feet six though still gangly, and Toni was taller too, growing into a lovely young woman. Then the human torpedoes hit and he was hugging them both at once, tears streaming down all their faces, and it felt just as good as it had every time he had imagined this moment for the past two years.

But when he looked up at Adele, standing about ten feet away and watching the scene with a tight smile, Eddie felt the autumn chill in the air.

Despite this, he took her in his arms and kissed her. She returned it briefly—then gently pushed back from him as soon as she feasibly could. "Welcome back, Eddie," she said, almost making it sound sad.

"It's great to be back. You look beautiful, Adele."

"You've been stuck on a desert island for two years," she said lightly. "Your standards are low."

It was only a pale flicker of her usual wry wit, but Eddie smiled, happy to have it. "No, I mean it, you look great. Just great."

She looked uncomfortable, but all at once the kids were at their side, Jack helping Eddie with his duffel bag. "Wow, this is heavy, what's *in* here?"

"Open it up and see."

Jack's eyes popped as he extracted a carved *tiki* head, the best of the lot Eddie had made: a fierce Kū, nostrils flaring, mouth a scowling gash of jagged teeth. "Wow! This is swell!" Jack said. "Where'd you get it?"

"I made it," Eddie said proudly.

"You did?"

Toni said, "Dad, this is good. Whatever it is."

"It's called a *tiki*. Like the little ones I sent you from Hawai'i."

"So this is how you won the war for us," Adele said caustically.

The barb stung, but Eddie ignored it. To the kids he said, "C'mon, let's go home," and they followed in his wake out of Penn Station.

Toni and Jack chattered nonstop all the way across the George Washington Bridge and back to Edgewater, but Adele—at the wheel of the '39 Chrysler she'd bought with the fire insurance money—was unusually quiet. When they finally got home, Eddie breathed in the familiar smell of the house as if it were one of the exotic floral scents he had encountered in Hawai'i. But none had ever smelled as good as this.

As Adele cooked a pot roast for dinner, the hearty aroma of meat and spices only added to the sweet, rich flavor of home.

After dinner they listened to Jack Benny on the radio, as if no time at all had passed since the last time they had gathered to laugh at Jack, Rochester, Mary Livingston, and Dennis Day. But there were no blackout curtains on the windows now; a warm light filled the room and spilled out onto the street. Afterward, Eddie played ball with the kids in the backyard while Adele did the dishes, then Eddie packed the kids off to bed.

Finally alone together in their bedroom, Eddie went up to his wife, cupped her arms in his big hands, and said, "I'm sorry, honey. For not being here. For the fire, for—for all of it. I should never have left."

Adele's voice trembled as she said, "But you did."

"I'll make it up you, Adele, somehow. I promise."

He tried to draw her toward him but she pulled back. "I'm not in the mood to be made up to, Eddie. I'm tired. Let's just go to sleep."

She slipped out of his grasp, kicked off her heels. As she unbuttoned her blouse she kept her eyes averted, avoiding Eddie's hurt and hapless gaze.

"I'm sorry about your dad. I should've been here for that too."

She turned to hide her tears. "I survived."

She wriggled out of her skirt and threw it in the laundry hamper, then got into bed. Eddie, seeing she wasn't ready to give him an inch, sighed and began undressing. He tossed his Navy whites into the hamper and slid into bed beside Adele, who lay on her side facing the wall, her eyes shut.

He reached out and touched her on the shoulder, felt her body go rigid at his caress, then drew back.

"G'night, honey," he said, surrendering, at least for the moment, to the situation as it was.

"Good night, Eddie," she said quietly.

Eddie switched off the light and rolled onto his side, facing her back.

Adele waited until his breathing became regular and shallow, then waited longer for the sound of his faint snore, so familiar to her and yet so strange to hear again after such a long time. After twenty minutes she finally slipped out of bed, went to the closet, pulled out a dress, picked up her high heels from the floor, then padded barefoot out of the bedroom.

She dressed quickly in the hallway, all but her shoes, which she carried with her, then moved down the corridor to the children's rooms. Peering through the open doorway into Jack's room, she saw her son asleep in bed, the floor surrounding him piled high with comic books, magic manuals, and open drawing pads with colored sketches of top-hatted magicians and costumed heroes on their pages. She made her way through the four-color clutter to his bedside—then bent down and kissed him, lightly, on the forehead. Jack stirred in his sleep but didn't wake. She smiled and blinked back tears. He was a good boy, a sweet boy—she could take some measure of pride in that.

The window in Toni's room was half-open, a billowing shade creating a ripple of moonlight in which Adele saw her daughter illuminated in flickering light and shadow. Her daughter, whose heart was an abiding mystery to her, and the signal failure of her life. Adele stood on the threshold of Toni's world and peered into it without seeing, as always. But Toni, she knew, would not miss her. Toni had her father, her brother, and her dreams—as unfathomable as they may have been to Adele.

She lingered only a moment at the door to her own bedroom. Despite everything that had come between them, when she looked at Eddie she still could see the young man, hungry for a family, who had rescued her from her parents' house, and a part of her would always love him for that.

She put on her shoes and opened the hall closet. Behind the woolly camouflage of the family's winter coats, her suitcase had been carefully hidden from view. She lifted it out, quietly closed the closet door, dropped an envelope addressed *Eddie* on the kitchen table, and left the house.

She walked down the back steps, into the driveway, and past the new

Chrysler, her heels clicking on the sidewalk like the tapping of impatient fingernails. Two houses down, a '42 Chevy with a small Gulfstream trailer attached to it was parked at the curb, its engine idling.

Lorenzo got out of the Chevy, took Adele's suitcase, and swung it into the back as she slid onto the front passenger seat. When he settled behind the wheel again, she leaned in and kissed him gratefully.

As Eddie had once done, he was rescuing her.

Toni woke the next morning to the knocking of the half-drawn shade against the window frame. When her eyes focused on the clock she saw it was almost 6:30—half an hour past when her mother usually woke her for school. But this morning all was quiet. Puzzled, she got up and went to her parents' bedroom, where her father lay sleeping—alone. Her mother *had* to be up—why hadn't she awakened Toni and Jack? "Mom?" she called down the hallway, getting no response. And weirdly, there were no sounds or cooking smells coming from the kitchen, either.

This was because the kitchen was empty. "Mom!" she called again, moving into the living room: no one there either. Had her mother gone out, gone grocery shopping? But no—Toni looked out the window and saw their car still parked in the driveway. What the heck?

Returning to the kitchen, she now noticed an envelope on the kitchen table—an envelope with her father's name written on it.

A shiver of intuition ran down her spine. She knew she should wake her father, give this to him to open—but *she* was the one with this terrible foreknowledge, and somehow she felt as if she should be the one to open it.

Her hands trembled as she undid the flap and pulled out a single page of notepaper, the message written in her mother's flowing cursive:

Dear Eddie,

I wish I had the courage to tell you this to your face, but I don't.

For fifteen years I've put family first and career second. But I'm thirty-four years old and running out of time. I have an opportunity on the stage and I'm going to take a chance I should've taken a long time ago.

You followed your heart when you went to war and left me to pick up the pieces at home. Well, it's your turn now.

Tell Jack and Toni that I love them and that I'm sorry.

Adele

"Toni?"

She jumped, as if she'd been caught stealing. She turned to find her father standing behind her in his bare feet, wearing only boxers and an undershirt, innocent of the words that would shortly make his heart bleed.

"Where's your mother? Why aren't you getting ready for school?"

Wordlessly Toni handed him the letter and the opened envelope. Unable to bear seeing his face as he read it, she ran past him, tears pooling in her eyes, to Jack's room down the hall.

"Get up!" she said, shaking her brother awake. "Now!"

"What?" he said, shrugging off sleep. "What's goin' on?"

"Just get *up!*" she snapped. "It's important!"

She ran back to the kitchen, where her father was staring almost uncomprehendingly at the letter, as if it were written in Sanskrit, or Greek.

He looked up at Toni. "She's . . . gone?"

Toni nodded. "But the car's still in the driveway."

Eddie shook his head and, to Toni's amazement, he laughed.

"She's just got some wild hair again about getting back into the movies," he said. "She'll be back home in a week, don't worry."

"No. Dad. She won't." Toni hesitated to say more, but who else could? "You don't know the whole story."

Jack padded bleary-eyed and pajama'd into the kitchen.

"What do you mean?" Eddie said.

"Mom hasn't . . . I mean, she's been . . . there's this man—"

Her father looked as if he'd been gut-punched. "What man?"

"His name is Lorenzo."

"What about Lorenzo?" Jack asked sleepily.

"He's run off with Mom," Toni told him.

"*What?*" Jack yelped. "No! That's not true!"

Eddie sank into a kitchen chair. "Lorenzo who?"

"His last name's Marques," Toni explained. "He's a stage magician who played the park last month. I . . . saw them together. In his trailer."

"So? Big deal," Jack countered. "So they were talking in his trailer, so what? Maybe they were talking about magic."

"Jack, they were in . . . in bed. Together." He was dumbstruck.

"Are you sure of what you saw, Toni?" her father asked quietly.

She nodded. "I'm sorry, Dad. They were in the . . . altogether." She saw the hope die in her father's eyes. "I was waiting until you got back to tell you. I didn't think she'd just . . ."

"Why didn't you tell *me*?" Jack snapped. "Didn't you trust me?"

"Jack, I hardly trusted myself!"

"What else do you know about this . . . Lorenzo?" Eddie asked.

Toni recounted everything she could think of, up to and including the fact that he had left Palisades to play the Steel Pier in Atlantic City. She described his car and trailer. When she was done, Eddie stood and sighed.

"Shit," he said. "I should've seen this coming. But I always thought you got 'Dear John' letters while you were away, not after you got back."

"But how—" Jack broke into a sob. "How could she just *leave* us?"

He started crying, and then Toni found herself weeping too. Eddie put his arms around them both and drew them close.

"Ssh. Shh. It's okay. We'll be okay. It's my fault she left, not yours. You understand that? Not your fault."

"We don't need her," Toni said, her grief transforming to anger. "She lied to us. She cheated on you. To hell with her, who needs her anyway?"

Jack suddenly said, "Dad? Where'd *that* come from?"

He was pointing at his father's right bicep and the tattooed red heart with the name ADELE inside it.

"Oh. This." Eddie smiled sheepishly. "It, uh, seemed like a good idea at the time."

Toni and Jack couldn't help but crack rueful smiles.

"I'll find her," Eddie promised. "I'll try to convince her to come back. Meanwhile, you two need to get ready for school."

"We have to go to school?" Jack said incredulously. "Shouldn't this be like a snow day?"

"What are you gonna do, mope around here all day? Life goes on."

"Dad, are you okay?" Toni asked nervously.

"Yeah, sure I'm okay," Eddie said. Toni wasn't sure she believed him. "We'll all be okay. C'mon, let's get you some breakfast."

He poured them bowls of cereal and glasses of orange juice, had them shower and dress, and by 7:25 they were on their way down Undercliff Avenue toward the bus stop.

On the way, Toni turned to her brother and said, "Jack, whatever you do, *don't tell* anybody about this! Nobody needs to know what's going on. Who knows, she may come back tomorrow and it'll all have blown over."

"You really think so? She might come back?"

"Sure. Maybe Dad'll talk her out of it. Just don't tell anybody."

In truth, Toni wasn't sure that her mother would be returning anytime soon. But she was embarrassed beyond words that Adele had skipped town like one of those cheap floozies you saw in the movies, and she knew that if the kids at school found out, she and Jack would know no end of shame. And so she carried the shame bottled up inside her all day, revealing it to no one, smiling blandly at classmates and teachers when what she really wanted was to shout and curse out her mother in front of the whole world. Jack was right—how the hell could she just *leave* them all?

And then she heard again every unkind word—and they were considerable—she had ever said to her mother, every bit of childish scorn and cruelty she had heaped upon Adele.

"I hate you! I hate you!"

"I don't want to be *like you. Your life is* boring!*"*

In the middle of gym class she fought back tears, ran to the bathroom, locked herself in a stall, and wept.

Dad was wrong. This was all *her* fault.

The minute the kids were safely off to school, Eddie jumped into action—any action he could think of—to keep the hurt at bay. He showered, shaved, dressed, and within twenty minutes was driving up the hill to Fort Lee and into Palisades' employee parking lot. The park was closed but hardly empty: in the off-season there was always a steady staff of about twenty-eight workers who kept the park in shape during the winter months. And of course the office staff was at work too. Eddie hiked over to the new administration building, an impressive redbrick structure that any fire would think twice about attacking, where he greeted Margie Cadien, wife of the Bobsled manager, as he entered. "Eddie! You're back!" she cried out, and soon he was being welcomed by other staff members. When she heard the commotion from her office, Anna Halpin came out to add her well wishes. "You just missed the season, Ten Foot," Anna said. "It was a good one, too."

"So I hear from Adele." He answered their questions about where he'd been stationed during the war, spent an appropriate amount of time catching up with park gossip, then casually mentioned, "Hey, I understand you had a magic act here last month—Lorenzo the Magnificent?"

This brought a chorus of whistles from the women in the office. "He can plunge a sword into me any day of the week," Margie said, to catcalls all around. "And if you tell Bill I said that I'll deny it to my death."

Eddie laughed. "My son kinda took a shine to him, wants to write him a letter—can anybody dig up some contact information for this guy?"

One of the booking staff promptly looked up the entertainer's file and found the name and address of his agent: Bernard Goldschein, 630 Tenth Avenue, New York 19, NY. Phone: Circle 6-9750.

Eddie bid goodbye to the staff and headed for the nearest newsstand to pick up the latest issue of *The Billboard*. Then he stopped at the bank, where he was surprised to find a total of some five thousand dollars in their savings account, deposited in weekly increments this past summer— the season profits from Palisades. The most recent withdrawal, dated three days ago, was a mere hundred and fifty dollars. Adele could have taken a lot more than that and Eddie would not have blamed her, but she apparently only took as much as she felt she needed to start her new life. He thought of what that new life entailed—the handsome Latin magician who had all the girls at Palisades swooning—and he felt a stab of jealousy, anger, and loss.

He beat back the grief and drove to his onetime employer, Grantwood

Lumber Yard. Five thousand bucks in the bank was more than enough to meet the family's needs until next summer, but Eddie wasn't taking any chances—and he needed something to keep himself occupied. His old boss, Bill Holahan, was happy to offer the returning vet a part-time job.

At home, Eddie opened *The Billboard* to the "Magic" column by Bill Sachs, which reported on the comings, goings, and bookings of performers in the magic biz. There were items about magicians both renowned and not-so-renowned—Harry Blackstone, Prince Samara, Jack Gwynne, Paul Rosini—but no mention of any Lorenzo, not even a classified ad.

So Eddie simply picked up the phone and called Lorenzo's agent, Bernard Goldschein, in New York. "Hi," he said, in the hard-sell tone of one of his park ballies, "this is Ed Worth of Worth Amusements in Ocean City, New Jersey. I operate a small sideshow on the boardwalk and I'm looking for a magician to play a week's engagement later this month."

"Well," the agent replied enthusiastically, "we have several available. There's the Great Rudolpho, he does a swell variation on the vanishing trunk gag—we've got Ron LeRon, his specialty's the Ten Card Trick à la Leipzig—"

"I was up at Palisades this summer and saw one of your acts, does a great Blade Box—Lawrence something?"

"Lorenzo. Lorenzo the Magnificent."

"Yeah, that's it, what's his availability?"

"He's playing state fairs in Maryland and Virginia through early October. Sorry. Now, Rudolpho, though, he's—"

"I really liked this Lawrence guy," Eddie said, laying it on thick. "When's the next time he'll be in the Jersey area?"

"Well . . ." The sound of pages in a booking calendar being flipped. "He's playing the Traymore Hotel in Atlantic City in late October. But won't your show be closed by then, for winter?"

"Yeah, afraid so." Eddie feigned disappointment. "Well, thanks anyway, buddy, I appreciate it."

"But Rudolpho or LeRon are avail—"

Eddie hung up with a smile. He could, of course, take the train down to the Maryland State Fair and confront Adele there. But that meant leaving the kids with Ralph and Daisy in Tenafly, and he wasn't yet ready to publicly acknowledge Adele's departure. He harbored hopes of talking some sense into her, winning her back—and that might even be a little easier to do once Adele had been on the road for a few weeks, living out of a suitcase, playing every sawdust-covered stage between here and Virginia.

He could wait until the Traymore Hotel in late October. It would also give him time to figure out what the hell to say to her.

When the kids got home from school that afternoon, Eddie consoled them as best he could. Toni seemed shaken but unwilling to talk about her mother's absence, while Jack responded by throwing out every magic book, deck of cards, and silk handkerchief in his possession. From that moment forward his passion for magic turned into a bitter aversion.

For dinner Eddie cooked fried chicken and French fries, which delighted the kids. They were nearly as delighted the next day when dinner turned out to be fish and chips. The night after that—when it was chicken-fried steak and a side of, you guessed it, French fries—Toni took her father aside and asked, "Dad? Is this all you know how to cook?"

Chagrined, Eddie admitted that it was.

"Okay," Toni said, "I'm taking over the cooking."

"Since when do you know how to cook?"

"I'm taking Home Ec. We have a cookbook. I can skip ahead."

"Maybe I should ask your Aunt Viola for her help—"

"No!" Toni said vehemently. "Nobody needs to know about this, Dad, okay? You're gonna get her back, so until then, *maintain radio silence*."

He smiled at that. "I don't disagree with you. But what happens when your grandma calls for your mom?"

Toni thought for a moment and said, "She got a job as a line dancer. Working for Aunt Minette. In Chicago."

"Minette's spending the off-season right here in Fort Lee."

"Jeez, Dad! Do I have to think of everything? Make something up. Ad lib it!"

Eddie smiled and said he would try to improvise something.

That Sunday, while dressing her first roasted chicken, Toni was appalled when her father reached into the bird's chest cavity, pulled out its heart and something called a "gizzard," and announced he was going to cook them "like they do in the South." He could not be dissuaded from first parboiling, then deep-frying the creepy things and serving them with a hot sauce made of Worcestershire sauce and horseradish. Toni took one nibble and nearly retched, but Jack ate it up enthusiastically along with his father.

But the chicken itself was delicious, and Toni, emboldened, moved on to other recipes in her cookbook. Even Eddie began picking up the book, educating himself on cuisine not requiring hot grease of any kind.

Eddie and Adele's honeymoon in Atlantic City in 1930 had taken place over Labor Day weekend, the traditional end of summer and beginning of the off-season that saw the city on the sand shrink from a boom town to a virtual ghost town. At least that was the case until '42, when the U.S. Army leased the city arena for use as a training facility for the Army Air Force, and a sudden influx of soldiers swelled the off-season ranks. Many were still there in October when Eddie drove down to the Traymore Hotel, a grand old edifice whose tan-bricked facade crowned by yellow-tiled domes had earned it the nickname "the Taj Mahal of Atlantic City." Walking into the airy lobby, Eddie couldn't help but think of the Hotel Rudolf, in which he and Adele had spent three blissful days. Atlantic City was where their marriage began; Eddie hoped it would also be where he would rescue it.

Carrying an empty envelope addressed to Lorenzo Marques, he walked up to the front desk and told the clerk he had an urgent delivery for Mr. Marques, and could he be directed to the magician's suite? "We'll see to it that he gets it," the man said, taking the envelope, and Eddie, prepared for this, handed him the envelope, thanked him, and walked away.

He went no farther than one of the thick columns supporting the lobby ceiling, behind which he hid until the desk clerk rang for a bellboy to take the envelope to Mr. Marques's room. When the bellboy headed for the elevators, Eddie followed, slipping inside the car just before the door clanged shut. The bellboy got off on the fifth floor and so did Eddie, though he turned in the opposite direction . . . then doubled back and followed him to room 532. Eddie watched from around a corner as the door was opened by—Adele, her hair still in curlers. "For Mr. Marques," the bellboy said.

"He's not here right now. I'll see to it he gets it."

Adele closed the door.

Eddie had considered the possibility that Lorenzo might be in the hotel room, and was prepared for an ugly scene if it came to that. But this was much better. He walked up to the room, knocked twice on the door, and was rewarded with the gratifying sight of Adele standing in the doorway, staring goggle-eyed at the husband she had abandoned.

"Eddie!" she said. "How did you—"

"The Shadow knows," Eddie said lightly. "Can I . . . come in? And talk?"

She balked. "Not a good idea, Eddie. Lorenzo's downstairs checking out the equipment for the first show. He could be back at any minute."

Hearing her speak that name, Eddie flushed with jealous anger.

"And what'll he do?" he asked, his tone no longer light. "Call the management and tell them his assistant—who's sharing his room and bed—is in talking with her husband? Contracts have morals clauses, don't they?"

Surrendering, Adele stepped back to admit him. It wasn't a sumptuous suite, just a bedroom and sitting room, nicely appointed; the afternoon sun bounced off the white sand outside and its light dazzled the windows. Adele led Eddie to a couch, on which were draped parts of a costume, including a ruffled green skirt. "'Scuse the mess, I was doing some repairs on my costume," she said, making room for him.

"That's pretty, what is it?"

"It's called a ruffle-tiered train. It's made of silk taffeta, I just love it. I wear it with this." She held up a sequined leotard. "Snazzy, huh? And these shoes are three-inch peep-toe heels." The shoes glittered silver in the sun.

"Nice." His gaze softened as he watched her sit in a chair opposite the couch. "You're looking—"

"Don't tell me I'm looking good in my rollers," she quipped.

"Okay, I won't. But you do. How's life been on the road?"

"It's been great. Exciting. We've played two state fairs and a half-dozen smaller venues." She sighed. "Why did you come here, Eddie?"

"Because I love you," he said. "And the kids love you and need you."

She shook her head. "They don't need me anymore. They're teenagers—almost adults."

"Toni misses you. She still needs a mother."

Adele laughed shortly. "Does she miss the way she used to scream at me and tell me she hated me? Oh yes, those were good days, weren't they?"

Eddie looked at her and said quietly, "Don't you even miss them?"

That hit her square between the eyes; her face hardened.

"Of *course* I miss my children," she said, raising her voice. "I never said I never wanted to see them again, did I? Because I do. Someday. When they've stopped being angry at me for leaving, and I can explain—"

"Isn't this really about you being angry at *me* for leaving?" Eddie said. "Look, I admit it—I was an idiot. Me and my stupid male pride. I spent two years as a grease monkey in the South Pacific, never saw a minute of combat—I might just as well have stayed in Edgewater at the Ford plant. I was wrong to leave you. Wrong to enlist without asking you." He leaned forward earnestly. "I swear, honey, it killed me being so far away when I knew you were hurting—when I should have been by your side. I'm sorry, Adele. I really am. I am so, so *sorry*."

His voice caught and Adele could see him fighting back tears. She'd always loved that about him, the way his feelings showed in his eyes like light through frost, and seeing it, she could forgive him almost anything.

"I . . . know you are," she said softly. "But that's not all of it, Eddie. Like I said in the note—I'm not getting any younger, I've only got a few years left to make my mark in show business."

"What, by getting sawed in half three times a night?"

"Yes! It's a start."

"Only if you're a two-by-four, for Chrissake!"

She wouldn't let that rankle her. "I'm onstage. I'm performing. And I *love* it, Eddie, I love hearing the audience gasp or cheer or applaud . . .

I haven't felt this alive since I was a kid acting in my father's two-reelers."

Eddie sighed.

"That's just it, Adele. This isn't your dream, it's your father's. He's the one who drummed it into you that you had to be a star."

She calmly took that in, then said, not unkindly, "You mean like your father took you to Palisades Park just before he died . . . and now by working there, there's a part of you who's still a kid, and who'll always have a father?"

Eddie looked away, embarrassed, at a loss how to respond to that.

Adele sat down next to him, touched him gently on the arm. "There's nothing wrong with that, Eddie. Maybe my father did fill me with his unrealized dreams. But they're my dreams now, and I want to live them. They make me happy. Happier than I was as a . . . wife and mother."

He nodded. "Okay. I get it. But we . . ." A last, desperate try: "We could live them together, Adele. Travel the carny circuit, like you wanted. Come up with an act for you—"

She shook her head. "It's too late for us, Eddie. I'm sorry."

Eddie had run out of things to say.

"Lorenzo really will be here any minute," Adele said. "You better go."

Lorenzo. It reignited the fever in him. He felt hot, angry, helpless. He turned away and headed for the door.

"Eddie?"

He looked back. There was a melancholy smile on her face. "Tell the kids I miss them and I do want to see them again. I just can't say when."

Eddie nodded wordlessly and left.

He took the elevator down to the lobby and headed straight for the hotel bar. Sliding onto a stool, he asked the bartender, "I don't suppose you know how to make a Singapore Sling?"

The guy stared blankly at him. "A what?"

"Make it a Scotch and soda."

The Scotch, as potent as it was, did nothing to alleviate the grim realization that Eddie's marriage was over, that the woman he loved was with—if not actually in love with—another man. He didn't want to go home, didn't want to have to face the kids and tell them their mom wasn't coming back. So he nursed his drink and felt sorry for himself until he finally roused himself off the stool and out of the bar.

On the way out he passed the hotel's main dining room, outside which was a framed poster heralding the appearance there that evening of LORENZO THE MAGNIFICENT and FEATURING THE ALLURING ADELE.

Eddie stared at the poster. FIRST SHOW 6:30 P.M. Eddie's watch said it was a little past five.

He couldn't let go of her just yet.

He made a reservation for six with the hostess, then found a pay phone and called home, telling Toni he would be a little later than he had expected—careful not to give her any false hope for her mother's return.

He returned to the bar for another Scotch, listened to a Giants game on the radio, then left at six for the dining room. The tables were fanned out around a raised stage in the shape of a seashell, backed by coral-pink stage curtains. Eddie asked for a table toward the back, then ordered a steak in mushroom sauce—the food, and the prices, sobering him up a bit before the six thirty curtain, when an announcer came up to the big floor microphone:

"Ladies and gentlemen, the Traymore is proud to present that phenomenal prestidigitator, Lorenzo the Magnificent!"

The crowd, all but Eddie, applauded the entrance of the dapper magician, looking elegant in his black tux and tails. Eddie took in the guy's pencil-thin mustache and slicked-back hair and thought he looked like an oily prick. But then, maybe he was a little biased.

Lorenzo started out with his usual card tricks, magically making a fan of playing cards appear in his hands, then shuffling them up his arm before making them disappear. As the audience applauded, the stage curtains parted slightly and out of them appeared "the Alluring Adele."

And so she was. She wore the costume he had seen in the room, filling it out more breathtakingly than Eddie could have imagined: a strapless, dark green hourglass of a leotard with sparkling silver brocading; black silk stockings and silver heels showing off her shapely legs; and the ruffled taffeta train, a lighter shade of sea-green, fanning out behind her like a peacock's plumage. Her blonde hair, set in a permanent wave, fell in soft curls down to her shoulders.

She looked beautiful. More beautiful than Eddie had ever seen her.

Smiling, she walked gracefully to Lorenzo's side, then stood there with one foot slightly in front of the other, one knee slightly bent, looking supremely poised. She assisted the magician both passively—taking one silk handkerchief after another as Lorenzo produced them out of thin air—and then more actively as she mingled with audience members to assure them that the steel rings she was displaying to them were, in fact, completely solid. "Take a look," she said, wearing them around her wrist like bracelets, then handing them to the people seated at the nearest table. "Go on. Look for a seam; you won't find one." The audience members agreed they were solid steel . . . and then, of course, minutes later, Lorenzo miraculously linked those seemingly solid rings to loud applause, as Adele watched with a smile. She seemed totally at ease on stage—as if she were born to be there.

Then, midway through the act, Adele wheeled out from behind the curtain a black wooden box on four legs that looked like a coffin. Eddie remembered the kids telling him about this, and his stomach tightened as Lorenzo gestured to his lovely assistant and said, "The alluring Adele has agreed to brave one of the most dangerous feats a magician can perform. You may never see her again as she is now, beautiful and vibrant with life!"

As Adele climbed gracefully into the box, Lorenzo winked at the audience: "If this trick goes wrong, at least she already has a funeral casket!"

The audience laughed. Eddie didn't. Lorenzo picked up the first of his many long metal blades and plunged it into the box. Eddie flinched. He plunged in another, and Eddie found himself growing unaccountably angry. Again and again Lorenzo pierced the box with blades, as if the woman inside were his property to do with as he wished. Eddie bristled at every penetration, until there were at least ten blades perforating the box.

"That ought to do it!" Lorenzo proceeded to withdraw the blades, then paused dramatically before opening the coffin lid.

Adele sat up, smiling as if she had just spent a few minutes in a good hot bath; Lorenzo helped her up and out of the box. The audience clapped and cheered, and Eddie could see Adele basking in the applause.

After the reaction had died down, Lorenzo told the audience, "For my next trick I will need a volunteer from your ranks. Would anyone care to—"

Before the magician could even finish, Eddie's hand shot up, he bolted to his feet, and within seconds was making his way toward the stage.

Eddie could see the queasy recognition in Adele's eyes, but it was too late for her to get Lorenzo's attention. With a few quick strides, Eddie was up and on the stage at Lorenzo's side.

"Ah, thank you, my good man," Lorenzo said, oblivious to the frozen smile and fearful eyes of his assistant behind him. "And what is your name?"

"Eddie. Eddie Stopka."

"Stopka?" Lorenzo said, only now realizing something was not kosher.

"Yeah. That's right."

Eddie's fist came up like a piston, cold-cocking the magician with a right cross to his jaw.

Lorenzo the Magnificent folded like a pair of deuces.

Adele put her hand to her head and muttered, "Shit."

The audience erupted in shock and confusion. Eddie took a long, satisfied look at his fallen adversary and said, "Prick."

He turned, and on a whim, took a bow to the audience—then jumped offstage and strode back up the aisle to the exit.

He smiled. It may not have actually accomplished anything, but it sure made him *feel* a hell of a lot better.

14

As Eddie drove homeward down Palisade Avenue, he couldn't help but notice the long line of cars—black sedans and flashy limousines—parked on the street opposite the park entrance, in front of Johnny Duke's restaurant. During Eddie's time overseas, mobster Joseph Doto, aka Joe Adonis, had moved his gambling operations from Brooklyn—increasingly in danger from the New York District Attorney's office—to the more hospitable business environment of Bergen County, where Adonis took control of the rackets and purchased a fortress-like home near the Palisades. Duke's became his base of operations, and according to Eddie's friends from work, the "store" next door with its soaped-up display windows was a front for one of Adonis's casinos and bookmaking operations. It purported to be a record shop dispensing 78 RPM records from vending machines, but at least one curiosity-seeker found that the records it dispensed were worn smooth, worthless, as phony as the storefront itself.

More disturbingly, Eddie had been told by Bunty that Dick Bennett was now serving as one of Adonis's top lieutenants, and that Chief Borrell continued to lunch regularly there, as did mob chieftains like Willie Moretti and his brother Solly, Thomas Lucchese, and Cliffside Park–based Frank Erickson, the biggest bookmaker on the East Coast.

Not my business, Eddie told himself, and turned right onto Route 5 and down the winding hill to Edgewater.

When he got home, he sat the kids down and soberly told them that their mother wasn't coming home, but assured them that she did want to see them again—someday. Jack seemed shaken but Toni immediately snapped, "Fine. Who *needs* her, anyway? We'll do fine without her, won't we, Jack?" To which Jack replied, "When will we be able to see her?"

"She doesn't know," Eddie said with a sigh. "She figures you're angry at her and wants to give you time to get over it."

"I don't care if I ever see her face again," Toni insisted.

"You may feel different about that someday, honey." He went on to explain about Adele's childhood and their grandfather's failed dreams for his daughter. But while Jack seemed interested, Toni just got up from the sofa, said, "I've got to do my homework," and huffed out of the room.

The holidays were soon upon them like an onrushing car, and when he received the annual invitation to Ralph and Daisy's house for Thanksgiving, Eddie was forced to level with them. Marie was shocked that her daughter had abandoned her family, and though she understood better than anyone the dreams and demons that had driven Adele to do it, she became consumed with the idea that she might have somehow prevented it—should have left Franklin when he started drinking and taken Adele with her.

As a result her guilt and grief led to an excruciatingly uncomfortable Thanksgiving, as Marie, trying too hard to be solicitous and sympathetic, smothered her grandchildren with attention and a cloying pity that made Toni, Jack, and Eddie cringe. "My poor babies," she cooed to them as if they were just that—words no teenagers, no matter how bereaved and abandoned, wanted to hear, and certainly not on average of twice an hour.

At the end of a long, trying day, the Stopkas bundled up in their winter coats and scarves and quickly fled, though not before Marie's parting invitation of "See you all on Christmas Day!"

On the way home in the car, Jack was the one to break the exhausted silence. "Dad," he said, "I think I'd rather hang myself with my Christmas stocking than go back there next month."

"I second that." Toni bunched her scarf up into a noose and mimed strangulation, her eyes bugging out. "Oh, the poor babies!" she choked out.

Eddie laughed. "Okay, a quiet Christmas at home. But what'll I tell your grandmother?"

What he eventually told Marie was that they were going to spend Christmas with Eddie's sister and her family in New York, which was half true since Viola's family did come over to spend the holiday in Edgewater. Eddie and Toni cooked the turkey, with Viola handling stuffing, sweet potatoes, and dessert. Eddie, who loved to eat, found he was enjoying cooking; he and Toni had begun alternating making dinners, and for Christmas she gave him a copy of *The Good Housekeeping Cookbook*.

Adele's departure was now known among family, but Toni still kept it secret from her classmates at school—certain that to reveal it would mean social banishment and dashed hopes for any chance at all that Slim Welker might actually notice her again now that softball season was over.

So it was a mark of her desperation that Toni now, during Christmas break, chose to reveal her secret to someone outside her extended family.

That week, as drifts of snow were banked high on Edgewater's narrow streets, making the town look like a frozen topiary, Toni, alone in the house, slipped into her parents' bedroom—and sat down at her mother's old makeup table. She gazed into the mirror at what had seemed to her, only a few months ago, to be a perfectly good face— maybe not beautiful like her mother's, but not hideous either. Now all she saw was the way her straight brown hair hung limply almost to her shoulders, the freckles that blemished her nose, and how pale and thin her lips looked. Why, she asked herself with disdain, would Slim Welker ever notice a face like *this*?

She opened the table drawer, but it was empty—her mother had taken her cosmetics with her, of course. And anyway, Toni could scarcely remember what her mother had tried to teach her about applying makeup.

There was only one person she could think to ask for help, but she didn't know her phone number.

Twenty minutes later, bundled up in her wool coat and scarf, Toni ascended the twisting switchback curves of Route 5 and made her way to Cumbermeade Road in Fort Lee—not to her grandparents' old house, but to another one a bit farther up the street, and knocked on the front door.

It was answered by just the beautiful blonde Toni was looking for. Toni blurted out, "Aunt Minette, I need your help!"

And with that, she burst into tears.

"Oh my gosh, Toni honey, what *is* it?" Minette Dobson asked as she led Toni inside the modest home she shared with her mother, Sarah. As they settled down in the living room, Toni told her about her mother skipping town with Lorenzo, and it sounded just as tawdry and embarrassing as she was afraid it would. But though Minette's eyes widened in surprise at first, there was nothing judgmental in her face or her tone.

"Oh, honey, I'm so sorry," she said. "I knew your mom wanted to get back into show business in the worst way, but this really *is* the worst way. None of us are saints, God knows, but . . ."

"She tried teaching me about how to look pretty," Toni said, a bit breathlessly, "but I didn't listen to her and now there's a boy at school and I don't know how to look pretty like you—Aunt Minette, can you help me?"

Minette seemed touched that Toni had come to her. She smiled.

"You *are* pretty, Toni. But a girl can always stand to look prettier when she's trying to get a boy's attention."

Minette took her upstairs to her bedroom, sat her down in front of her vanity, pulled Toni's hair back behind her ears, and fixed it in place with a bobby pin or two. "There, that gives us a better idea of the shape of your face. It's oval, that's good—we don't need to highlight your cheekbones.

"I don't put on a lot of war paint myself unless I'm onstage or out on a big date, and at your age you don't want to overdo it. Your eyebrows are nicely shaped, but they could use a little more definition." She picked up a pair of tweezers and plucked a few stray hairs from below Toni's brow line, making her yelp. "Sorry. Always seems to hurt more when you tweeze below the brow line." Minette finished plucking, picked up a brown eyebrow pencil, and began lightly filling in Toni's brows: "You want to use a pencil shade that's slightly darker than your hair, like this. At fifteen you're not ready for Bette Davis eyebrows, just the hint of an arch—the way your body itself is hinting at what's to come." Toni blushed at this.

Within minutes, Minette had subtly shaped Toni's brows into neat crescents arching, as if surprised by their own elegance, above her blue eyes.

She brushed some matte powder onto Toni's face, "just enough to even up your skin tone," in the process concealing her troublesome freckles. Minette then set to work on her lips. She opened a bullet of Revlon lipstick, redder than a fire engine, but Toni balked at it.

"Ah," Minette said, "I think what you want is monotone—a slightly more natural look. Let's see . . ." She pulled open a drawer to reveal a standing armory of cartridge-like tubes—dozens of live rounds, each color a different caliber, poised and ready for action. "There's Tangee, an orangish red . . . but with dark hair like yours, a darker red is usually better. How about . . . raspberry?"

"They make lipstick that tastes like raspberries?"

Minette laughed. "No, that's just what they call the color. But lipstick has a fresh taste all its own, you'll come to like it." She popped open a tube and expertly applied a coat to Toni's lips, adding a thin border of red to her top lip "to make your lips looks fuller and softer."

When she was done she stepped back and allowed Toni to survey herself in the mirror. She was relieved to see that she didn't look as though she had just graduated from clown college—the raspberry was less garish than the ruby red her mother had tried on her. Her eyebrows looked natural, but more feminine than they had before. And the face powder had given her face a smooth matte finish—again, not shiny or clownish.

"It looks . . . nice," Toni said with a smile. "And I still look like me."

"When you're a little older I can teach you about mascara and eye shadow. For now this should do fine."

"Can you—" Toni hesitated. "Can you do anything with my hair?"

"Depends on what you want done."

Sheepishly: "Can you make it look more like what the girls at school are wearing?"

Minette fingered a few strands of Toni's hair. "You've got beautiful hair, hon, nice and thick. You usually wear it shorter than this, don't you?"

"Yeah, I haven't been for a haircut since before Mom left."

"This is almost a perfect Middy length. We can do things with this."

"We can?" Toni said with relief so naked and poignant it made Minette's heart almost break.

Minette smiled. "Sure. But we're going to have to set it before you go to bed tonight, then I'll style it tomorrow morning. So call your dad and ask him if it's okay if you have a sleepover tonight at Aunt Minette's, all right?"

Minette's mother made a delicious dinner of chicken croquettes, mashed potatoes, and succotash; over supper, she and Minette regaled Toni with stories from the career of Frank W. Dobson and the Seven Sirens. After supper, Minette proudly showed Toni a new dress she had just bought at Bamberger's Department Store in Montclair—a beautiful blue silk evening gown, like something a goddess would wear. "My boyfriend's taking me to the Stork Club in Manhattan on New Year's Eve," Minette said with a smile.

"You'll look beautiful, Aunt Minette," Toni said. "What's his name?"

"Jay," Minette said brightly. "So—you ready to have your hair styled?"

Toni washed her hair, then dried it with a towel until just damp. "You need more volume," Minette said, "and the easiest way to achieve that is with pincurls. All you need are a few bobby pins and a lot of patience."

Minette lifted up an inch-wide section of Toni's hair and began twisting it around her index finger. "You wind the strands of hair around your finger, like so—each loop *outside* of the last loop—until you have a curl. Then you slide your finger out and pin it in place, like this." She laid the loop of hair flat against the side of Toni's head, then clipped a couple of bobby pins, crossing each other like an X, through it. "Now you try it."

Cautiously Toni began wrapping strands of hair around her index finger, but Minette stopped her: "No, you're twisting the curl in the opposite direction of the last one. You want them all curling in the same direction." Toni undid what she had done and wound the hair in the proper direction. When she had finished, she slid out her finger and Minette handed her a bobby pin. Toni awkwardly opened the pin, slid one half of it through the inside of the loop and the other half outside— repeated the process with a second pin that crossed the first—and the curl hung neatly in place.

"Good," said Minette. "Now you repeat this until you have about an inch-square section of curls, and you repeat that for your entire head."

"My *whole* head?" Toni gasped.

"I said you'd need a lot of patience, didn't I?"

Toni found this more tedious than cutting potatoes into fries, but Minette made it fun by joking or gossiping about people at the park, and before she knew it Toni had a head full of curls—and bobby pins.

"Now you cover it with a scarf, like this"—Minette tied one of her silk scarves around Toni's head—"and then go to bed."

Toni was horrified. "With all this shrapnel on me?"

"It's worth it in the end," Minette promised.

Toni went to bed in Fran's old room and gingerly laid her head onto the pillow. It felt like she was resting on a porcupine. She turned over on her side, and now the porcupine was pricking the whole left side of her head. She saw a sideshow act once called the Human Pincushion—this must be what he felt like. Was being popular worth all this? Was Slim Welker worth all this?

Well, okay—Slim, maybe.

She turned over onto her stomach, her face pressed into the pillow. The prickling was gone, but after twenty seconds she found she couldn't breathe and turned, gasping like a fish on a hook, back onto her side.

She finally managed to drift to sleep—but it was a light, fitful sleep. Around three in the morning, waking for the hundredth time that night, she decided that this beauty stuff was a *colossal* pain in the ass. Even for Slim.

The next morning, after breakfast, she finally shucked off the scarf and Minette set to work, making a "V" part in Toni's hair, then starting to comb out the curls. "This is why you want them all twisting in the same direction," she explained, "so they all form a wave . . . like this."

Toni looked in wonder as a thick roll of hair bounced off the side of her head. "I get it now," she said. "Like an ocean wave."

"Watch me again as I do the next one. The simpler a line is, the easier it is to comb, at least for someone just getting started, like you."

Minette combed the curls on the top of Toni's head into a "roll bang" curling elegantly toward her forehead. Then she combed back the left- and right-side hair and held them in place with small barrettes. And finally she teased the curls over her ears and below into a mass of soft, fluffy waves.

"And *voíla*," Minette said, "a Victory Roll—the latest style!"

"Omigosh," Toni whispered. "I can't believe it, it's so pretty! *Thank you, Aunt Minette!*"

"You are most welcome. Now get dressed," Minette ordered, "and we'll go get you your own makeup kit, all right?"

Toni showered and dressed, all the while casting disbelieving glances into the nearest mirror: was that really *her*? The memory of being pin-pricked all night by a porcupine faded like the evening star. Why hadn't she listened to her mother when she tried to teach her about all this?

At Schweitzer's Department Store on Main Street they went straight to the cosmetics department and found a more exact match of face powder for Toni's skin tone. Minette also picked out Toni's first cosmetics kit: a primrose case by Max Factor complete with powder, rouge, face cream, eyebrow pencil, and a lovely white cameo hairbrush and hand mirror made of Bakelite, which Toni thought were beautiful. When she tried to pay for it, Minette waved her aside and pulled her wallet from her purse. "No, no, this is on me," she said. "Merry Christmas."

"Gee, thanks!"

On their way out they passed through the "Misses" department, and though Toni showed no interest in the frilly dresses by Jane Holly, Miss

Deb, or Judy Kent, she did slow, then stop in front of a display of manne-quins wearing Shetland sweaters, pleated skirts, white socks, and saddle oxford shoes—the now-standard uniform of the ubiquitous "bobby-soxer."

"Maria DeCastro has a sweater like that," Toni said wistfully.

Minette saw in her face something she could only describe to herself as "confused longing."

"You want to try one on, hon?" she asked.

"No, I—well, maybe," Toni replied uncertainly.

Minette put a hand on Toni's shoulder and said gently, "What do you want, hon? Whatever it is, it's okay."

Toni said, very softly, "I . . . I just want to fit in. I don't want kids looking at me, thinking, 'There's that poor strange girl whose tramp of a mother ran off with a sideshow magician.' I just want to . . . blend in."

Minette smiled gently. "Then let's put together a few things you can try on, and see if you like the look." She helped Toni pick out a matching ensemble consisting of a white blouse with Peter Pan collar, a wool "Sloppy Joe" sweater in a color called Sunset Rose, and a red-and-white plaid skirt.

Toni took the clothes into the dressing room with a mix of excite-ment and embarrassment. She slipped into the blouse, then the skirt, and then shrugged on the Shetland sweater that hung loosely just down past her waist. She straightened out the folds without looking into the dressing mirror; she was terrified to look at her reflection lest she hated what she saw. So without a single backward glance at the mirror, she left the dressing room and found Aunt Minette standing just outside.

When Minette's face lit with a smile, Toni felt a rush of relief and finally turned to look into the nearest mirror.

She saw a bobby-soxer dressed in the latest fashions, her red lips slightly parted in amazement, face framed by bouncing curls of brown hair.

"Oh, Aunt Minette," she said softly. "*Thank* you . . ."

Tears sprang to her eyes, and she hugged Minette as hard as she had hugged her mother on the day the park burned down.

———

Eddie spent that morning cleaning house and performing other domestic duties. The Navy had fortunately taught him how to make up a bunk, or bed, how to swab floors, even how to iron clothes. But washing the laundry had been somebody else's department until now, and today's hard lesson learned was the discovery that somewhere in the load of whites he had thrown into the washer was one of Adele's newer red handkerchiefs. Result: a dozen pink boxer shorts, pink undershirts, and some lovely pink cotton socks in Men's Size 10. Sighing, he put them aside and made a mental note to rewash them later in bleach.

"Hey! What's all the noise out there!" That was Jack, bellowing from the depths of his bedroom. "I'm trying to sleep."

Eddie pushed open Jack's door and said, "It's ten thirty. Get the hell out of bed and *do* something."

Jack sat up groggily in bed. "Like what?"

Eddie tossed a heap of clothes at him. "Try a load of colors, to start."

Eddie went outside to lay the foundation for a small workshop the Murphys had graciously allowed him to build on the adjacent lot they owned, when an unfamiliar car pulled up to the curb. The passenger door opened and out stepped a teenage girl wearing a too-large sweater, plaid skirt, and white socks. He almost called out, *Hey, miss, you interested in a nice pair of pink socks?*—then she turned, tossing her fluffy brown hair away from her face, and with a shock Eddie saw it was Toni.

"Hi, Dad!"

As Minette Dobson got out of the driver's side, Eddie's brain quickly tried to formulate an equation that made some sense of this:

TONI + MINETTE + SLEEPOVER = NEW HAIRDO + MAKEUP + NEW CLOTHES = FOR GOD'S SAKE, STOPKA, *SMILE*!

He had learned this much, at least, from fifteen years of marriage.

He smiled a big smile and said, "Toni! You look beautiful!"

It wasn't a lie. It may have been a shock, but as Toni hurried up the driveway toward the house, he marveled at the change in his daughter, no longer looking like a girl but like a lovely young woman.

She beamed at the compliment. "Thanks. Aunt Minette did it all, she's a miracle worker."

Minette demurred: "I didn't raise the dead, honey, I just styled your hair and took you shopping."

"Well, seeing as how you're both here, why don't I fix us all some lunch?" Eddie suggested.

"Sounds swell," Toni said.

Inside, Jack had finally gotten dressed. He took one look at his sister and said, "Holy Toledo! What happened to *you*? You look like a girl!"

Toni felt a flush of embarrassment.

"She *is* a girl, Jack," Eddie noted. "But she's still the same old Toni."

Jack looked at his sister's long waves of hair as if they were some exotic vegetation. "Where'd you get all that hair? Is there a naked poodle somewhere in the neighborhood?"

Toni punched him, not too hard, in the shoulder. Jack yelped.

"One more crack," she warned, "and you're going to be using a girl's bicycle seat for a while."

"Okay, okay." Jack was actually grinning. "You're right, Dad. Same old Sis. Hey," he told her excitedly, "the Astor in North Bergen is playing Chapter 1 of *Secret Agent X-9* next week, you wanna go?"

"Is that based on that comic strip you like?"

"Yeah, Alex Raymond. Starts next Friday. We can catch the second matinee after school."

"Sure, swell. We can meet at the bus stop in front of the school."

"Now that you two have reached a peace accord," Eddie said, "you can help me make lunch for your aunt. C'mon, hop to it."

The kids hurried into the kitchen, but before Eddie could join them Minette said, "Eddie, I'm so sorry about Adele. And that Lorenzo character . . . yuck, he looked like he'd crawled out of a tube of Brylcreem."

Eddie shrugged. "I've got to admit, it hurts, but . . . mainly I'm just scared. I've got two kids to take care of. What am I supposed to do, be both father and mother to them? How the hell do I do that? I was barely able to figure out how to work the frigging washing machine."

"Just be what you are, a good father. That's all they need. I'll help out however I can. They're good kids, they'll get through this okay."

It didn't take long for Toni's new look to be noticed at school. On her way into Miss Carleton's history class, she was spotted by a surprised classmate, a bobby-soxer named Celia Dolinski, who addressed Toni for the first time all year: "That V-roll is simply delish, who did your hair?"

"Oh, my mom did it." Toni reasoned that if her mother could lie about Lorenzo, *she* could lie to preserve her reputation. "You really like it?"

"Yeah, it's slick. That's a smart sweater too—is it Bonnie Lassie?"

"No, Hi-Girl. The color's Sunset Rose. I also got one in Sunset Pink." She had committed the brands and colors to memory as if in preparation for an algebra exam. "They were Christmas presents. From my mom."

She got several more compliments in home room and Mr. Bandino's English class, and at lunch time, as she carried her tray of milk, fruit, and a grilled cheese sandwich away from the cashier and into the cafeteria, she saw Celia waving to her from a table where she was seated alongside a phalanx of bobby-soxers with teased hair, ruby lips, Shetland sweaters, and saddle shoes—including Maria DeCastro. "Toni, come over and join us," Celia beckoned, and Toni tried not to betray her thrill at the invitation.

Toni was acutely aware that she was still a couple months shy of her fifteenth birthday; these girls may only have been fifteen, but they seemed far more mature and worldly than Toni. A few were even wearing mascara.

Bridget Cullen, peering suspiciously at Toni from beneath bangs of bright red hair, said, "You're on the girls' gymnastic team, aren't you?"

Toni poked a straw into her carton of milk. "Yeah."

Maria DeCastro said, "You play softball, too, right? I've seen you."

Arlene Bratton raised an impeccably penciled eyebrow. "You used to wear your hair so short, I had you figured for one of those girls who—you know—don't like boys."

Shocked, Toni protested, "Me? No, no, I like boys fine—as a matter of fact, there's one who I—"

She hit the brakes when she remembered who was sitting across from her, but Arlene leaned in: "Oh, so you've got your eye on some hunk of heartbreak, huh? C'mon, spill it, who is he?"

"Uh, nobody special," Toni said quickly. "I mean, there are scads of boys I could go for. Just *scads,*" she emphasized.

"Is that why you play softball?" Maria said, closer to the mark than she knew. "The better to check out the, uh, athletic equipment?"

The other girls laughed merrily and Toni thought it best to join in.

"Look, she's *blushing,*" Bridget noted cheerfully. "I can't remember the last time somebody in this group blushed!"

"Relax, hon, we're all boy-crazy," Maria said. "Take my boyfriend."

Toni nearly coughed up her milk.

"Every time I look into his eyes," Maria continued dreamily, "I still get vertigo. And we've been dating forever—since June!"

From that point on, Toni seemed to have passed muster with the group. At the end of the day, so elated that she had to tell the one person who could understand what it meant to her, she took the bus to the Dobson home.

"Aunt Minette, it worked!" she told her in wonderment. "I think the girls at school like me now!"

Minette smiled. "That's great, honey, I'm happy for you."

"I'm going to use my savings to buy another skirt at Schweitzer's. Will you help me pick it out?"

"Sure. Let me get my car keys."

"Oh! How was New Year's Eve? Did you have a good time at the Stork Club?"

Minette's expression, usually so bright, clouded over.

"Not exactly," she said quietly. "I . . . didn't go."

"What? Why not?"

"Because the miserable SOB never showed," Minette said bitterly.

Toni was stunned. "He . . . stood you up?"

"Yeah. I 'cried in' the New Year." But she was clearly more pissed off than sad now. "I was an idiot for starting up with him again in the first place. He's done this for the last time—I'm through with the louse." She snapped up her car keys, grinned. "C'mon—let's go do some *shopping.*"

To her delight, Toni was invited back to the bobby-soxers' table the next day, and the day after that, and then, on Friday, they asked her to join them after school at Bischoff's Confectionery and Ice Cream Store on Anderson Avenue. At a quarter past three that afternoon Toni, Celia, Arlene, and Maria sat down at the counter and ordered ice-cream sodas and malteds as Bridget popped nickel after nickel into the jukebox, ordering up the first in a succession of Frank Sinatra tunes:

> All or nothin' at all
> Half a love never appealed to me . . .

Bridget swooned her way over to the counter, exclaiming, "*Ohhh* God, doesn't he just *send* you? Doesn't he?"

There followed a spirited debate over whether "You'll Never Know" was superior to "Saturday Night (Is the Loneliest Night of the Week)" and could either of them ever compare to "Embraceable You"?

"What's your favorite, Toni?" Celia asked.

Toni had heard Sinatra on the radio but could not for the life of her think of a song title. But taking her cue from the first song on the jukebox she ventured, "I like 'All or Nothing at All.'"

"Oh yeah, that's strictly delish," Celia agreed.

By the time their sodas arrived they were going into graphic detail as to what made the pride of Hoboken such a "drooly"—it was clearly not just his voice that caused them to swoon. Toni found him a bit stringy and bony for her taste, but the girls talked about him as if he were a thick, juicy steak.

Toni managed to hold her own in the conversation, but it was a boy's voice, heard from behind her, that struck Toni temporarily dumb:

"Hey, doll, you ready?"

A delicious chill ran down Toni's spine—it was Slim Welker.

She turned automatically, but of course it was Maria he was addressing—who immediately got up, hugged him, and was the lucky recipient of a kiss from those full, sexy, absolutely mag*nif* lips of his.

"Sure," Maria said. "Let me just pay for my soda." She explained to the girls that she and Slim had a "study date" at the library. Toni was reasonably certain that the only studying Slim was interested in involved baseball, specifically first and second bases. And boy, would she ever be happy to help him with *those* studies . . .

Then, as Maria fished in her purse for coins, Slim Welker turned and looked directly at Toni.

His cute little pug nose wrinkled in puzzlement as he squinted at her. "Do I know you?"

Before a thunderstruck Toni could reply, Maria laughed. "Ha! Know her? She struck you out."

Toni winced. It was true. She had pitched against him once, and he had missed three easy slow balls. "Toni Stopka," she told Slim. "We used to play softball in the parking lot at Palisades Park?"

He looked stunned. "That was *you*?" And then the most wonderful thing happened: his astonishment turned into a simply perfect smile. "Wow. You've grown up. And then some."

Maria, not liking the direction this conversation was taking, slapped her quarter down on the counter and quickly looped arms with her boyfriend. "Study time, Slim, remember?"

"Right, right." He turned—but not before his gaze lingered, for the briefest yet longest of moments, on Toni. Her entire body tingled, as if Slim were training his X-ray vision on her. And then he and Maria were gone.

Bridget and Celia went back to chattering about Frank Sinatra and Vaughn Monroe, but Arlene—holding her soda straw like a cigarette holder—leaned over to Toni and said quietly but knowingly, "I'd take that one nice and slow if I were you, honey."

Toni blushed. "What do you mean?"

In a low voice, Arlene counseled, "You know what I mean. Maria's a sprinter, not a long-distance runner. Bide your time."

"Why are you telling me this? Isn't Maria your friend?"

Arlene smiled slyly and shrugged. "What can I say? I find it more entertaining than radio serials."

The word *serials* stirred a vague unease at the back of Toni's mind, but was forgotten amid her elation that Slim Welker had finally noticed her.

She practically ran all the way home, where her buoyant spirits were abruptly punctured by the sight of a glowering Jack.

"Oh my God!" she said. "The movie!"

"Yeah, it was pretty good, thanks. Where the hell were *you?*"

"Jack, I'm so sorry! Some girls invited me to Bischoff's for ice cream, we were talking, listening to music, I lost track of time, and I—I *forgot.*"

Jack said, "Yeah? What was so important that you forgot about me?"

"Well, these girls, they're really nice, they're my friends . . . and there was this boy there, well technically he's Maria's boyfriend, but I've been trying to get him to notice me for the longes—"

Jack looked at her in disgust. "I've got a news flash for you, Sis," he said caustically. "You can't bring Mom back by *becoming* her."

Toni felt as if he'd just slapped her. Anger boiled up inside her.

"That—that's just stupid!" she yelled at him. "You don't know anything about anything!"

"I'm going out to look for Dad," Jack called over his shoulder. "You want to be Mom so bad, why don't you go fix us all some dinner?"

"Go to hell!"

Jack stormed out, and Toni's elation melted suddenly into tears.

Eddie, bundled up in his old Navy sea jacket, walked along wintry Hazard's Beach, surveying the flotsam and jetsam that lapped out of the Hudson and onto the shore: gnarled tree limbs, splintered pieces of a packing crate, the occasional rubber tire tread. He walked for ten minutes before he found what he was looking for: a piece of driftwood about two feet long and six inches in diameter. It looked like part of the trunk of a white birch tree, the kind that studded the hillside below the Palisades. He picked it up, turning it over in his hands; it was smooth, and free of blemishes. He took a pocketknife out of his jacket and made a small cut in the wood near the top. The bark was soft but not too soft, and came away clean with one stroke. This would do just fine. Already he was envisioning the face he would uncover with his chisel: a beetled brow of ridges, deep sunken cat's eyes, and a scowl that was almost a smile. A good face: the face of Kū.

15

Palisades, New Jersey, 1946–47

THE SUMMER OF '46 saw the return of old faces to Palisades: not just Eddie but Dr. Frank Vita, back on duty at the first-aid station, as well as PR man and hero of Guadalcanal Jack Morris, and a dozen more ride operators and concessionaires. Only Laurent Schwarz would not be coming home—the one fatality in the park "family"—even as his father prepared to mark his fortieth season with Palisades.

Despite frigid weather on its April 20 opening, the park was packed with twenty-eight thousand patrons in heavy overcoats, intent on having fun. All across the nation returning GIs and their wives or girlfriends were flocking to the parks they frequented before the war. This season there would be more entrants than ever in Palisades' annual Baby Crawling Contest as America's "baby boom" got under way. Eddie raked in bigger profits than ever before, and working alongside Toni and Jack in the family business helped to mitigate the grief he'd felt upon receipt of Adele's divorce petition earlier that spring. He didn't contest the divorce. His marriage was over; he had to accept that.

Jack took the news badly, becoming moody and withdrawn, deflecting Eddie's one attempt to console him: "You okay, pal?"

"Yeah, sure," Jack lied.

"Good. Sometimes you just have to roll with the punches in life."

In truth, Eddie didn't want to discuss this with Jack or anyone; it hurt too much. Jack's namesake, Eddie's father, would never have discussed such things with him—he would have expected his son to follow his example and "roll with the punches"—and so that became Eddie's example as well.

"We don't need her" was Toni's only comment. She had found the maternal guidance she needed in Minette, and her attitude toward Adele only hardened. But equally distressing to her was the return to Palisades of Peejay Ringens, whose bicycle act was as popular as ever. Though tempted to watch at least one of his dives, Toni couldn't quite bring herself to do it.

She had weightier issues on her mind, after all. Her friend Arlene had been right about Maria DeCastro: Slim and Maria broke up that summer. Toni wasted no time buying several stylish new fashions at Helene's Dress Shoppe on Anderson Avenue, and Minette instructed her in more sophisticated "war paint"—mascara and eye shadow. Suitably armed, Toni marched into her junior year. She shared no classes with Slim, unfortunately, but when word got out of the semester's first afterschool softball game, Toni hurried to the athletic field—not to participate, but to sit in the bleachers and watch the teams compete. She thrilled to the sight of Slim, who'd grown even more strapping over the summer. At his first turn at bat, he hit a home run and she cheered for him— loudly enough, she hoped, that he could hear her. Watching the game, part of her longed to be out there on the field too, running the bases or playing outfield; but she told herself that she was out to catch something bigger than just a pop fly.

Her cheers did catch Slim's attention, and now he glanced over to the bleachers and looked straight at her. She put two fingers between her ruby lips and whistled. He smiled, waved, then went back to the game.

After Slim's team won 7-2, he came over to the stands, stood with one foot on the bench in front of Toni, and smiled. "Hi. Missed you out there."

"Oh, you did fine without me," she said. "You were super."

"Would've been a shame, I guess, getting that pretty hair of yours mussed up," he said, sitting down beside her.

"Can't have that," Toni said, fluffing her curls. Sweat was dripping down Slim's forehead and into his eyes; she took out a handkerchief. "Here, let me get that for you," she said, standing up to mop his brow.

"Thanks."

The handkerchief had his scent on it, and she resolved right there and then to never, ever wash it again.

"Hey," he said, "you want to go to Bischoff's and get some ice cream?"

Toni beamed. "I'd love to."

The rest of the afternoon was strictly a dream, the two of them talking and drinking malteds as Tommy Dorsey and Sinatra played on the jukebox. They chatted at first about baseball, and Slim seemed impressed with this girl who not only enjoyed the game but knew who Ted Williams and Snuffy Stirnweiss were; she could even rattle off their batting averages and RBIs.

"I really like baseball," Slim told her, "but I'm thinking about going out for football."

"You should! You're so big and strong, you'd make a great quarterback. Or wide receiver."

Slim grinned. "Are you an expert in *every* kind of sport?"

That flustered her—was she being unfeminine? "Oh, no . . . not—"

"It's okay. I like sports. I've never known a girl who liked them as much as me . . . especially not a girl who's a knockout like you." She blushed at the compliment. "So what's your favorite sport?"

"Oh, that's easy. Swimming and diving. For a long time I thought about being a high diver, but . . ."

"A high diver? Like those guys who dive into tiny tanks of water?" He laughed. "Girls don't do that, do they? Doesn't seem very . . . ladylike."

Her worst fear realized, Toni said quickly, "Oh, that was when I was a little girl. Like little boys wanting to be cowboys when they grow up." Slim looked relieved. "But I do like swimming . . . my family owns a French fry concession at Palisades, I practically grew up in that pool."

"French fries? With that malt vinegar? Those are the tops."

"I know how to make them," Toni said, "if you ever want some."

He looked at her as no boy had ever looked at her before and said, "Oh, man. She cooks, she's beautiful, and she knows who Spud Chandler is. You *are* a rare dish."

Slim moved fast—he was "active duty," as Arlene would say—wasting no time in asking her out again. The next afternoon, he took her bowling at Taylor's Bowlarium. Toni had never tried this game before, but being a good softball pitcher she had a fair sense of aim, and did well in her first few frames—a little too well compared to Slim, who left more than a few spares. Afraid of showing him up, Toni pulled back, allowed herself a couple of gutter balls, and finished just a few points behind Slim.

Afterward they walked down to Miller's Ice Cream Parlor, ordered milkshakes, and Slim held her hand as they drank. Despite the cold shake, Toni felt herself overheating like a car radiator on a hot, sultry day.

That weekend they had their first formal date, Slim picking her up in his pre-war jalopy, a '39 Oldsmobile. Slim passed inspection from Eddie, who told him with a smile, "You seem like a nice guy, Slim. But that won't stop me from gutting you like a trout if you don't have her back by eleven. Enjoy yourselves, but not too much."

Slim didn't let it faze him. "Yes, sir. Understood."

Eddie shook his hand and settled in to make dinner and prepare to listen to Harry Owens's *Hawaii Calls* radio show at eight o'clock.

They had dinner at the Fairmount Diner in Hackensack and then walked down to the Oritani Theater, showing Edward G. Robinson, Loretta Young, and Orson Welles in *The Stranger*. As they sat under the lush fabric dome of the theater auditorium, Slim looped an arm around Toni's shoulders and she felt as if she was going to pass out right there. Somehow she managed to retain consciousness, if not the plot of the movie, which vanished from her memory within minutes of leaving the theater.

It was almost eleven and all the way home to Edgewater, all Toni could think about was whether Slim would try to kiss her goodnight and whether she should let him. This wasn't technically their first date, after all—Bischoff's and bowling counted for something, didn't they? If this wasn't their third date it certainly wasn't their first, either.

Lights were on in the second floor of Toni's house as Slim walked her round back and up the stairs to her door. When he leaned in and kissed her, she shut her eyes and welcomed the soft but firm press of his lips against hers. It was a brief, polite kiss—the kind a boy gives when he's standing on a girl's doorstep with her father lurking nearby—but it thrilled her more than anything had since she had seen Bee Kyle dive that first time.

"See you again?" Slim asked when they broke the clinch.

"You bet," Toni replied, which may not have sounded "ladylike" but it made him laugh.

She watched him walk back to his car and drive off, excited and amazed that she was actually dating Slim Welker.

Inside, Eddie was waiting up. "Have a good time?" he asked casually.

"Oh yes," Toni said dreamily.

"Do I have to kill him?"

"Oh, trust me, Daddy, that would be *such* a waste," she said, and her father laughed. "G'night."

"G'night, honey."

Before she went to bed she washed her hair, painstakingly rolled and pinned her curls into place, and didn't complain to herself for a moment about the discomfort. She marveled at how much better life was when you were pretty, something her mother had tried in vain to tell her.

Whether it was buying the latest Sinatra records at Taliferro's Record Shop with Arlene, Celia, Bridget, and Maria—who tried not to show her annoyance that Toni was now dating her former boyfriend—or sitting in the bleachers watching Slim, nicely filling out his crimson and black uniform, quarterbacking for Cliffside as they trounced Tenafly 8-0 and Hackensack 35-6—everything about her life *was* better than she could have imagined six months ago. She and Slim grew closer over the winter months, ice-skating together at Sunny Park Rink or necking—and a little petting—in Slim's car as they parked in a quiet turnout on River Road along the waterfront.

When Slim had picked her up at her house a half-dozen times without meeting Toni's mother, Toni finally admitted the truth, though couching it more casually than anyone in the family really felt about it: "Oh, my mom and dad are divorced," she said, and when Slim displayed no shock, only sympathy, she gradually told her friends at school—leaving out any mention of magicians. They found it only mildly scandalous: this was 1947, after all.

Toni's relief at this was tempered by increasing tensions with her brother, once he found out who she was dating: "Slim Welker?" he said incredulously. "The guy who kicked me off his softball team?"

"For Pete's sake, Jack," Toni said as she painted her nails at her mother's old vanity table, "that was four years ago! He was just a kid."

"So?"

"So, people change."

Jack said pointedly, "Yeah. They sure do."

Stung, Toni snapped, "Will you grow *up*? You're just jealous because I'm popular and you're not!"

Jack snorted. "Like hell!"

"Ever since Mom left you've been sulky and moody. I don't think you've made a single friend at school this year, have you?"

"That's none of your beeswax," Jack snapped, walking away. And he pretty much stayed out of her way for the rest of the school year. Toni felt bad, wishing there was some way to convince him that just because she was making friends—and dating Slim—it wasn't a personal betrayal of him.

She wished that he could see Slim as she saw him—never more so than on one chill night in February, after a snowstorm. The roads were cleared by evening, and as Slim drove Toni down Palisade Avenue she looked out and saw the slopes of the Cyclone padded with two feet of snow. "Oh, wow," she said. "The coaster looks like a map of the Himalayas."

The park gates and the towers behind them were also draped in snow. "Yeah," he said, and then, with a grin: "You want to take a closer look?"

"What do you mean?"

"That hole in the fence is still there, isn't it?"

He parked off Route 5, and in winter coats they sneaked through the hole behind the free-act stage. Hand in hand they stole into the empty park, giggling. The midways had been plowed by the steady staff that maintained the park in winter, but the rides and concessions were blanketed in white. The pool was a sloping valley filled with fresh snow, the diving boards standing like bare birch trees around it. The Funhouse was an ice fortress, its two snow-covered towers standing sentinel like wintry paladins. Toni and Slim walked over to the Cyclone, which did resemble a mountain range with snowy peaks. Toni had practically grown up in Palisades Park, but she had never seen it like this—and the fact that she was seeing it with Slim made it all the more special. They walked down the main midway toward the cliffs, past shuttered concessions whose marquees were studded not with hot lights but icicles, toward the Ferris wheel looking like elaborately spun white cobwebs against the night sky.

When they approached the edge of the cliff, Toni's stomach tightened as she recalled the last time she had been here. But the performers' trailers were all gone, leaving only the towering letters of the Palisades sign crowned with snow and ice. If Palisades in winter was like an abandoned faerie kingdom, across the river the kingdom of Manhattan was the exact opposite, its castles and parapets of light glittering eternally in the cold, clear air.

Still holding her hand, Slim turned and kissed her. It was the deepest, longest, most passionate kiss they had shared; and even though they were bundled up like store manikins, it was more intimate contact than any of the petting and groping they had done in Slim's car. Toni believed it was because, at that moment, she realized how much she truly loved him.

"So, kiddo," Bunty said, digging into the steak Eddie had just grilled, "how'd you like to become a lifeguard?"

Even though he was staring straight at her, Toni couldn't grasp at first that he was addressing her. "What?" she said.

Bunty took his first bite of steak, told Eddie, "Excellent cut of meat, Ten Foot. When you're grilling steak, never buy low-grade meat." Then he repeated to Toni, "I said, how'd you like to be a lifeguard at Palisades?"

They were sitting at the Stopkas' kitchen table for what Toni had thought was just a friendly Sunday dinner, but appeared to be about more.

"But I'm a girl," she said.

Bunty rolled his eyes. "Jeez-us. What's got into you? How far across the English Channel do you think Trudy Ederle or Millie Corson would've gotten if they'd said, 'But I'm a girl'? For your information, plenty of beaches these days have lady lifeguards on duty."

"They do?"

"Sure. Manhattan Beach in Brooklyn, for one. Irving Rosenthal thinks having a pretty young girl as a lifeguard at Palisades might boost attendance at the pool. I told him pretty is nice, but what counts is getting the strongest swimmer for the job. So I suggested you."

Toni beamed. "I'm the strongest girl swimmer you know?"

"Don't let it go to your head, you're still just a tadpole in the grand scheme of things. Yeah, you've got the strongest stroke, the most stamina, and you ain't bad to look at either. But it's no cakewalk. Before you can be hired you've got to be trained and certified by the Red Cross. I'm a trainer at the Hackensack Y and I can fit you into my afternoon class, after you get out of school—two hours a day, five days a week, for three weeks. You game?"

Toni looked to Eddie. "But—don't you need me at the stand, Dad?"

"Jack can take up the slack, honey. And I can always hire a third hand. This is a good opportunity for you."

Jack, listening to this with incredulity, asked Toni sarcastically, "Aren't you afraid diving in and rescuing someone will ruin your hairdo?"

"Ha, ha. You're a panic, Jack, really you are." But he wasn't far wrong. She *was* excited by what Bunty was offering her, but she worried what Slim would think. Would he find it—unfeminine? She wanted to say yes, but checked the impulse: "Can I think about it and let you know tomorrow?"

"Sure, kiddo," Bunty said. "Whatever you want to do."

The next day at school, Toni sat down to lunch with Slim, took a deep breath, and told him about the job offer. "My dad says it's a really great opportunity," she said. "Lifeguards work all day, seven days a week, but just like at my dad's stand I'd get time off for lunch and dinner and we could see each other then and"—breathlessly and nervously—"what do you think?"

Slim considered a moment, then said with a smile, "I've been wondering what you'd look like in a swimsuit. Guess now I'll find out."

Happy and relieved, she threw her arms around him and kissed him, ignoring the catcalls of "Hubba hubba!" from surrounding tables. After school she hurried home, phoned Bunty, and told him she wanted the job.

She was fairly bursting with excitement. To think—her, a lifeguard at Palisades! What could be more delish? Other than Slim, of course?

That week she began training with Bunty, the only girl in a class with a dozen young men. Bunty gave each of them a copy of the American Red Cross's book *Life Saving & Water Safety*. "This is your Bible," he told them, "and that's how you treat it—like the Gospel, you got that?"

Bunty hadn't exaggerated: this was no cakewalk. Toni went home each night bone-tired, every muscle aching. The worst came when they practiced the "fireman's carry," the rescuer emerging from the water with the victim draped across his shoulders. Since the male students outweighed Toni by a good thirty or forty pounds, she felt like she was carrying a hundred-and-fifty-pound bag of cement on her shoulders, and though she managed it without complaint, her back ached for hours.

This was followed by intensive training in artificial respiration, kneeling astride a "victim" and pumping air back into his lungs.

She was working harder than she ever had in her life, but she was holding her own with full-grown men bigger and stronger than she was, and she could sense Bunty's satisfaction in her performance—expressed more in his twinkling blue eyes than his words, which were usually on the order of, "Okay, kid, not too terrible. Try not to screw up this next one."

At the end of the course, when Bunty handed her a certificate in senior lifesaving, he finally awarded her a smile: "Congratulations, you're a lifeguard. Now for God's sake try not to let anyone die in your first week."

She was given a patch on which her LIFE SAVING—SENIOR rank was embroidered in a circle around the Red Cross insignia. Toni proudly sewed it onto the new bathing suit Eddie had bought her. Palisades issued her a whistle, a kind of white pith helmet to shield her from the relentless summer sun, and her very own lifeguarding station—a red enameled chair sitting on a raised platform, the same as Bunty, the head lifeguard, sat on.

There were four lifeguards on duty this season—Bunty, Toni, the deceptively slim Hugh O'Neill, and a big, tanned side of beef named Al Soyaty—stationed around the pool like the points of a compass. They all had their individual "zones" of responsibility; when on duty they had to scan those zones at all times for possible hazards or bathers in distress. It did not escape Toni's notice that she was given a station in the southeast corner, overlooking the shallow end of the pool—but she chose to interpret that not as a comment on her gender as much as her experience.

The pool opened on Decoration Day, May 30, and as the ticket booth opened, Toni climbed onto her lifeguard station and took a deep breath of the briny air. The roar of the waterfalls nearly drowned out the calliope from the Carousel across the midway as well as the light popular music piped in from WGYN, New York's first full-time FM radio station, that issued from the park loudspeakers. Despite somewhat cool weather, hordes of bathers swept through the gate, onto the beach, and into the pool.

She had never felt as proud. She was a lifeguard at Palisades Park—for now, at least, her soul could not possibly aspire to anything better.

Making her day even sweeter was seeing her father watching proudly from the other side of the fence—and a few minutes later, when Slim unexpectedly showed up with his family. He looked up at Toni on her lifeguard station . . . and his jaw dropped. The gape turned quickly to a smile, and as he wandered over he said, "Damn, you sure fill out that suit nicely."

Toni blushed to the same deep red as her chair, or so she feared. "Thanks. I'll see you on my break, okay?" And she blew him a kiss.

She took her job seriously, scanning her zone of responsibility constantly—taking in the toddlers wading in as they held their parents' hands; the grade-school kids leaping into the water as if they had been waiting all their lives for this day; the show-offy teenager who cannonballed off the lowest diving board, hitting the water like a depth charge. But the minute they moved out of her zone into Bunty's or Hugh's or Al's, her gaze swept back to her own zone, as uneventful as it was.

All at once the smell of maple syrup from the waffle stand made her mouth water, and the sharp tang of lemonade made her thirsty. She even caught a whiff of French fries, carried across the midway from her dad's stand. These were all familiar smells she had grown up with at the pool; but they seemed somehow different at this altitude, just three or four feet above the provinces of her youth. The whole pool looked different, as though she were seeing everything at once, all charged with the urgency of her attention to every detail. Just three or four feet, that's all it was—but it was the difference, thrillingly, between being a child and being an adult.

Jack and Irving Rosenthal, determined to surpass even last season's record take, increased the park's promotion budget, opened a day nursery where parents could "park" their youngsters for a time, and geared prices for volume business. Adding to attendance that summer were two thousand children—white, Negro, Puerto Rican—from tenements in New York City, who on July 2 were brought to Palisades by the *New York Tribune*'s Fresh Air Fund and given full run of all the rides as well as free refreshments.

Thousands visited the Palisades pool each day, and in her first month on the job Toni was witness to the usual run of accidents and near-accidents: kids running, tripping, and taking a header on the sundeck; swimmers with stomach cramps, usually from a greasy lunch of hot dogs, French fries, and ice cream; and both children and adults who, having exhausted themselves on a dozen rides, jumped into the pool and wore themselves out faster than they had anticipated. There was only one serious rescue: a man in his forties who belly flopped off a diving board, the shock of hitting the water triggering a heart attack. Bunty saw him sinking, leapt in, and dragged him to shore, where he performed artificial respiration while Toni ran to the phone and called for an ambulance to take him to Englewood Hospital.

But Toni's most satisfying moment came when the young mother of a six-year-old boy came up to her asked, "Could you teach my son how to swim?" Toni was flattered and pleased, instructing the boy in the basics of swimming even as Bunty had done for her . . . and for the rest of that day she sat a little straighter in her lifeguard's chair, feeling on top of the world.

She was still happily sitting there—the only deficiency in her life being the absence of Slim, who was on vacation in the Poconos with his family for the week—on the morning of Sunday, July 13, when shortly after opening she heard some raised voices coming from the nearby ticket booth. It was only 9:30 A.M. and there were relatively few people in the pool, so Toni wandered over to the main gate of the pool to see what was going on.

What she found was a young, pretty Negro woman in her twenties, holding a pool ticket and saying to one of the ticket takers, "I don't understand. This is a perfectly good ticket, it was just purchased—"

"Did *you* purchase this ticket?" the man asked.

"No, a friend bought it for me."

"Are you a member of the Palisades Sun and Surf Club?"

"I—no, I've never heard of it."

"Well, that's the problem," the man explained. "The pool is operated as a private club, you have to be a member to use it. A ticket's not enough."

The young woman sighed and said, "So how do I become a member?"

"Just go to the administration office, they'll give you an application to fill out." He gave her directions to the administration building, and the woman nodded, thanked him, and headed down the midway.

Thinking that was the end of it, Toni headed back to her chair.

Twenty minutes later, the same young Negro woman was once again standing outside the pool grounds, waiting patiently in the rising heat.

And waiting. And waiting. Another twenty minutes crept by, and occasionally a ticket taker would come up to her, saying something like, "Why don't you just go enjoy some of the other rides?"—but the woman just smiled politely, shook her head, and said, "I'll wait here, thanks."

Toni told Bunty she was taking her morning break, walked to the lemonade stand and bought two lemonades, then walked back to the pool and up to the Negro woman.

"Hi, I'm Toni," she said. The woman looked up at her, puzzled. "It's pretty hot, I thought you might like something to drink."

The woman smiled, surprised. "Why, thank you. That's very thoughtful." She took the lemonade. "My name is Melba. Melba Valle."

"Nice to meet you. Are you still having trouble getting into the pool?"

Melba took a sip of lemonade and nodded. "Oh, yes. They had me go to the administration office and fill out an application to join their 'Sun and Surf Club,' then when I did that they said, 'We'll notify you by mail.' I said, 'I came all the way from New York City. I want to swim in the pool *today*.' They told me, 'We'll notify you by mail. Why don't you enjoy some of the other rides in the meantime?' I said, 'I'll save you the cost of a stamp. I'll go wait by the pool.' So here I am."

"Well, I'm sure they'll be along any minute with your membership," Toni assured her. "You live in the city?"

"Yes. I'm a model at the Manhattan Art Students League."

"A model? I should've known, you're pretty enough to be one."

"Well, thank you," the woman said, disarmed by Toni's earnestness.

"Did you always know you wanted to be a model?"

Melba laughed—a warm, open laugh. "Oh, I'm not sure *now* I want to be one. I just sort of fell into it. I also study ballet and flamenco. What about you? Did you always want to be a lifeguard?"

Toni laughed. "Not hardly. But I've always loved the water. I practically grew up in this pool. For a while I thought I'd like to . . ." She paused. "Oh, that doesn't matter. People tell me it's a silly dream—"

Soberly, Melba said, "Don't do that—don't let anyone tell you that. If you want to do something new, there are always people who'll take that as, 'Oh, she wants to be different. She thinks she's better than us.' When I talk about wanting to dance, some people in my neighborhood say, Oh, that Melba, she doesn't want to be 'just another Negro.' But that's not it. I just want to be Melba. Like you want to be Toni. Don't you ever let go of that."

Toni felt a sudden kinship with this woman she barely knew. But before she could say "Thanks," a park security guard came up to the young woman and in a stern voice told her, "I'm sorry, miss, but you're going to have to move along, people need to get through here. Why don't you—"

"Go enjoy one of the other rides?" Melba finished for him.

Toni said to the guard, "Listen, maybe I can do something to help hurry along her application . . ."

Melba told the guard, "Fine. I'll leave. Just give me a minute." After he turned and walked away—though lingering at a distance to make sure she followed through on her promise—Melba turned back to Toni and put a hand, gently, on her arm. "Hon, don't get yourself in any trouble on my account. They're not going to give me any membership card. This whole 'private club' thing is just an old dodge to exclude Negroes."

Toni was shocked at the suggestion. "Oh, but that, that's not true— Palisades lets anyone in. Why, just a couple weeks ago there was a group of kids from the Fresh Air Fund . . ."

"Did any of them get into the pool?"

"Well, I . . . I didn't notice. But when I was little, I rode on rides with Negro and Puerto Rican children all the time—"

"You ever swim with any?" Melba asked.

Toni started to reply, then thought about it—and realized to her dismay that she couldn't automatically say yes.

"Thank you for the lemonade, Toni," Melba said warmly. "It was very kind of you. I enjoyed meeting you."

"Nice meeting you too," Toni said, still baffled. Melba Valle turned and walked away from the pool, and Toni watched her figure retreat down the midway until she turned a corner and was gone.

Toni went back to her station and looked out across the pool—really *looked* for the first time.

She saw people sunning themselves on the boards of the sundeck— their backs white, occasionally pink. She looked across the beach at families sprawled on towels or huddled under beach umbrellas—but not a brown or black face among them. The waters of the pool were packed with hundreds of bodies—pale bodies. A sea of white.

My God, she thought, blushing with her own shame and naïveté. How had she never noticed before?

16

SHORTLY AFTER NOON, Melba Valle returned, and she brought company: eleven men and women, both white and black, an uncommon enough sight in and of itself. When she tried once more to gain entry to the pool and was again denied, the members of the group lined up in front of the ticket booth in what they referred to among themselves as a "stand-in"—refusing to move until Miss Valle was admitted, even as they chanted in unison:

"Don't get cool at Palisades Pool! Get your relaxation where there's no discrimination!"

Upon hearing this catchy refrain, ticket sellers burst out of the booth in a panic and ran like startled chickens toward the administration building.

Toni saw a little of this, but first and foremost she had to keep her eyes on her zone of responsibility; so mostly she just heard the chants, as did almost everyone in the pool area.

"Don't get cool at Palisades Pool! Get your relaxation where there's no discrimination!"

After several minutes of this, a number of pool patrons, annoyed that their "relaxation" was being spoiled, began jeering at the demonstrators. One woman leaned over the gate and summed up the general feeling: "Why don't you all go away and let us enjoy ourselves!"

The protestors did not stop chanting.

Toni decided to take her lunch break, getting to the ticket booth in time to see the arrival of a flying wedge of park security guards, headed by Irving Rosenthal, striding onto the scene like the potentate he was. "Who's in charge here?" he demanded. A slightly built white man around thirty identified himself as James Robinson and informed him that they were members of an organization called the Congress of Racial Equality, or CORE.

"You can't just stand here and chant your Bolshevik slogans, disrupting my business," Rosenthal told him. "You need to leave."

"We'll leave when Miss Valle is admitted to the pool," Robinson said.

"The pool is a private club, and Miss Valle's application for membership has been taken. We'll notify her by mail of our decision."

"We'd rather wait here until she's been accepted."

Toni could see Rosenthal's jaw clench, his avuncular manner turning steely. He strode over to the pool gate, cast a perfunctory glance inside, then went to the ticket booth and announced in a loud voice, "The pool is crowded to capacity. Suspend all ticket sales for the rest of the day."

Toni knew damn well the pool wasn't anywhere near capacity.

Ticket window shutters came crashing down like a theater curtain in mid-performance—distressing not just the demonstrators but the many paying customers waiting to get into the pool.

"Hey! What gives?" one heavyset man shouted. "We came all the way from Parsippany for this!"

"There—no one else is getting in today," Rosenthal told Robinson. "Now why don't you all just leave?"

"We won't leave until Negroes are admitted to this pool."

Rosenthal's face flushed with anger; he obviously wasn't used to being contradicted here in his own dominion.

"In that case," he warned, "I'll have to have you forcibly removed."

The CORE members were not intimidated and did not budge.

Rosenthal ordered his security guards to eject the demonstrators.

One burly guard, stepping forward eagerly, went straight to the heart of the ruckus: Melba Valle. He grabbed her roughly by the arm, yanking her out of line. "C'mon, lady, move it!"

"Hey!" Toni found herself calling out. "Leave her—"

Suddenly Bunty was at Toni's side, laying a hand gently on her arm. "Don't," he said quietly. "It stinks, kiddo, but he's the boss."

Toni watched helplessly as the demonstrators appeared to let their bodies go limp as soon as they were seized, forcing the security guards to literally drag them like dead weights away from the pool. As he was hauled past Rosenthal, one CORE member promised him, "We'll be back!"

Rosenthal, nearly popping a vein, shouted at the guards, "Put these Communist agitators on the next ferry back to New York!"

Toni wasn't the only one watching this scene play out with astonishment and dismay. At the first sounds of confrontation, Eddie had left Jack in charge of the stand and hurried over to his daughter's workplace. Now he stared at the park guards manhandling women, dragging Negroes away as if they were trash to be thrown out—and felt, uncannily, as if he had been transported to the Deep South he had traveled in his carny days.

He couldn't believe this wasn't Alabama, but New Jersey.

Things returned to normal at the pool though no one else was admitted for the rest of the day, doubtless damaging the park's bottom line.

On the way home late that night, Toni and Jack peppered their father with questions: "How could they do that to people?" "Mr. Rosenthal always seemed so nice—" "Did you know colored people couldn't use the pool?"

"I never thought about it," Eddie said in answer to the last question, ashamed at his own ignorance. "I saw coloreds in the park, on the rides, in the restaurants, and I never thought about the pool."

"There was a big brouhaha last year about Negroes in the dance pavilion," Jack said, "but I thought it all blew over."

"Really?" Toni said. "I hadn't heard about that."

"You were too busy scheming your way into Slim Welker's—"

"Your next word better be 'heart,'" Eddie warned.

"Melba's such a nice girl," Toni said. "It's not fair she can't get in."

"Life isn't fair. Especially if you're born with the wrong color skin."

"Can't you talk to Mr. Rosenthal and convince him to let her in?"

Eddie reminded himself this *wasn't* Alabama, it was Jersey, and even if cities like Trenton were segregated, others, like Newark, weren't.

"I can give it a try," he said. "But don't get your hopes up."

The next morning, Eddie found Irving Rosenthal patrolling the midways, as usual, at the moment dressing down a hot-dog vendor over his wares: "These dogs are stale and tasteless," he told the man. "How many days have they been sitting there? Redo the whole batch with fresh franks."

"*All* of 'em?" There were thirty frankfurters revolving on his rotisserie.

Rosenthal said, "In thirty years I've learned that when a hot dog sours a youngster's stomach, you'll lose him as a customer no matter how many stupendous thrill acts and exciting rides you offer. I take no chances."

Eddie had never worked for anyone more conscientious than Irving—he liked and respected him. But he sure didn't like the side of him he'd seen yesterday.

"Mr. R.," Eddie said, approaching, "can you spare a minute?"

"Sure, Eddie, what's on your mind?"

Walking alongside him, Eddie said, "I wanted to talk to you about what happened yesterday. At the pool."

Rosenthal winced. "That was uncomfortable for everyone, wasn't it?"

"Look, I don't get it. If Negroes are allowed in the park, why not let them into the pool? What's the big deal?"

Irving sighed. "Some white people—and I'm not one of them, Eddie, you know me better than that—have this idea that Negroes are . . . unclean."

"What, they're afraid the black is going to rub off on them?"

"Bathing is an intimate thing, Eddie. Whites are simply not ready to get that intimate with colored people. If I let Negroes into my pool, business would dry up. I can't afford that. It's strictly business."

Eddie measured his words. "Y'know, I spent a lot of time in the South when I was a carny. One town we were playing, they hung a colored boy because he dared *speak* to a white woman. They just strung him up and lynched him—no trial, no lawyers, no waiting."

"We're not lynching anybody here," Rosenthal said testily. "It's our right to admit whoever we want to our pool."

"It's dangerous. You never know what this kind of thing can lead to."

Irving thanked him, rather frostily, for his opinion, then reminded Eddie that he had a French fry stand to open.

Eddie swallowed his annoyance, thanked Irving for hearing him out, and went off to the stand.

The following Sunday, July 20, was a hot day that held the prospect of good pool attendance. The CORE demonstrators returned as promised, picketing the main gate on Palisade Avenue with signs reading PROTEST JIM CROW—FIGHT FOR CIVIL RIGHTS and DON'T GET COOL AT PALISADES POOL! GET YOUR RELAXATION WHERE THERE'S NO DISCRIMINATION!

But it was a peaceful protest, with the picketers scaring off few, if any, paying customers. Nevertheless park security guards watched them like circling hawks, as did the small contingent of officers that made up the Cliffside Park Police Department, including Chief Frank Borrell.

His family back from the Poconos the night before, Slim met Toni on her lunch break at the Grandview Restaurant overlooking the Hudson. It was a warm, sunny day, made more idyllic for Toni by Slim's presence after what had seemed an eternity apart. After a welcoming kiss they sat down, ordered sandwiches and a couple of Pepsi-Colas, and Slim remarked, "So what the hell's going on outside? All those picket signs?"

"Oh, you missed all the excitement," Toni told him. "A young Negro woman tried to get into the pool but they wouldn't let her in. So this group is protesting until the park agrees to let colored people into the pool."

"What? That's ridiculous."

She nodded. "I know, I think it's terrible that they—"

"The whole idea's ridiculous," Slim repeated. "Everybody knows coloreds don't have the same standards of cleanliness we do."

Toni felt a chill in the eighty-degree heat. Was he kidding her? She looked into his eyes—they were the same eyes she had spent hours gazing into dreamily, but now they seemed suddenly opaque to her.

Her reply to this pronouncement was a feeble, "What?"

"I've got a cousin goes to high school in East Orange," Slim said, "and they've got the right idea. They only allow coloreds to swim in the pool on Fridays, so over the weekend they can clean it and change all the water."

Toni managed to eke out a protest: "But this girl, Melba . . . she's a very pretty, very clean-cut girl . . ."

"Well, I guess some of them are," Slim allowed, "but most of 'em come from farms in the South and they don't know squat about hygiene. How do you know they won't just shit and pee in the water, right next to you?"

No, Toni thought, this couldn't be happening, these words couldn't be coming from this boy she adored.

"My dad says if the races aren't kept separate," Slim went on, "the next thing you know, you'll have coloreds living right next door to you."

"I—I wouldn't mind having Melba live next door to me," Toni said, though her voice quavered as she said it.

Slim looked uneasy. "Look, honey, I'm sure she's nice, for a colored girl, but . . ." He leaned forward, his brow knitting in concern, lowering his voice a notch: "Watch what you say, Toni, okay? You don't want people thinking you're some kind of nigger lover, do you?"

Stunned and sickened, Toni stared desperately into his eyes, hoping they would twinkle with amusement and let her know this was all a joke. But no—his eyes were dead serious. He was waiting for her to say something, she knew what he wanted her to say, so she said—albeit weakly:

"No . . . no, of course not." The words burned in her throat, but she hated even more the guilty blossom of gladness she felt when Slim smiled in relief. That smile could make her forgive anything. Or it used to.

"All of this will . . . blow over, I'm sure," she said, then quickly changed the subject: "So, how were the Poconos?"

He began telling her about his vacation, but though she nodded and responded with all the right words in all the right places, at the end of lunch Toni could not recall a single thing he had said after the words *nigger lover.*

His kiss goodbye was too sweet to enjoy without guilt.

She went back to the pool and concentrated on her work, eyes tracking back and forth across her zone of responsibility, trying to ignore the distant, angry consonance from the street:

"Don't get cool at Palisades Pool . . ."

After work she said nothing about any of this to either Eddie or Jack, instead going straight to her room, where she quietly cried herself to sleep. Cried for the boy she thought she knew, the boy she thought she loved. No, worse, the boy she *still* loved—but how could she, after what he'd said? And loving a boy who felt that way—what did that make *her*?

That week, word spread throughout Palisades that Melba Valle and others had filed suit in district court against the Rosenthals' Rosecliff Realty Company for denying her admission to the pool and bathhouse "because of her race and color." They were seeking damages in the amount of $270,000. By Sunday, the battle lines had hardened on the Rosenthals' side as well.

Ticket sellers at the pool were braced for another demonstration, but did not recognize anyone waiting in line that morning as any CORE members who had previously protested. So when a small party of white men and women purchased tickets, they were routinely admitted.

But soon after, a group of Negroes appeared, tried to buy tickets, and were given the standard, "I'm sorry, you have to be a member of the Sun and Surf Club. You can apply for membership at the administration building."

"Well, my friends there just purchased tickets," one of the Negro men said, nodding to the whites who had just been admitted to the pool. "They weren't members either, but you let them in."

Security guards were hastily summoned.

Toni watched anxiously from her lifeguard station as the whites returned to the ticket booth to "stand in" with their black compatriots, and park guards arrived shortly thereafter.

Suddenly, like a storm sweeping in on a previously sunny day, the guards charged at CORE's standing line. The mildest action they took was to violently push the demonstrators out of line. Other guards, more enthusiastically, hauled off and slugged protestors. One CORE member, a white man, was shoved face-first onto the concrete pavement, a spray of blood marking the place where he fell. When the protestors—refusing to fight back in kind—got up and simply tried to return to the ticket window, they were again punched and shoved with what seemed like personal animosity.

"Stop it!" Toni cried out, abandoning her station and running up to the gate. "Stop hitting them!"

Eddie, hearing the sounds of violence, jumped the counter of his stand and hurried toward the pool.

Irving Rosenthal arrived in the company of a squad of police officers from Fort Lee under the command of Police Chief Fred Stengel. But he and his men just stood by as the guards—many of them moonlighting police officers themselves—attacked the protestors with relish.

Rosenthal told Chief Stengel, "Get these people out of my park."

Stengel nodded and gave the word to his men.

If the guards had been zealous in executing their duties, the police were even more so. They seized the protestors, slugging them repeatedly as if they were punching bags—which, since the nonviolent demonstrators would not fight back, they effectively were. When one man fell, the police kicked viciously at him. One Negro man was blackjacked from behind.

This shocked even Irving Rosenthal, who told Stengel, "Now wait a minute—tell your men to take it easy—"

Chief Stengel snapped back, "We're handling this."

By now a number of white pool patrons had joined Toni at the park gate, sharing her horror at the scene playing out in front of them:

"Hey! There's no call for that!"

"Leave 'em alone!"

But Stengel's men continued to beat at the demonstrators, then dragged them roughly away from the pool area.

Eddie came up behind Rosenthal and said, "I tried to tell you, Irving."

When all the demonstrators were finally rounded up, Chief Stengel generously offered them a little advice:

"Negroes are not allowed in this pool. No Negro will *ever* be admitted to this pool. They *are* allowed in the park—*if* they behave themselves."

Then he had them dragged off and herded onto an empty bus. Stengel told the bus driver, "Edgewater Ferry Terminal."

A protestor smiled through bruised lips: "See you next week, Chief."

Clearly, it was going to be a long summer.

When Rosenthal tried to scurry back to his office, Eddie blocked his path. "Where the hell are we, Irving? Biloxi?"

"Things got a little out of hand. It won't happen again."

"I won't have anything to do with a place that continues to allow this."

Irving pegged him appraisingly. "That's up to you, Eddie. Let's see, if memory serves, you have a three-year lease at $10,250 a season. If you want to break that lease, just write me a check for $30,750 and we'll call it square."

He brushed past Eddie, who had no response—and nowhere near enough money, of course, to break the lease.

Eddie went over to the pool to see if Toni was all right. She looked shaken and angry but said, "I'll be okay."

"You don't look okay."

"Neither do you."

"I got put in my place by Uncle Irving. Tell you at home."

They arrived in Edgewater exhausted but too keyed-up to sleep—except for Jack, who hadn't seen the worst of the violence and went straight to bed—so Eddie put on a pot of coffee. "If you're old enough to see what you saw today," he told Toni, "you're old enough for a cup of joe."

"The police and the guards just kept hitting and hitting them and the protestors wouldn't fight back—why not?"

"It's what Mahatma Gandhi did in India. Passive resistance, I think it's called. Not sure I'd be able to turn the other cheek like that."

"I wanted to run out there and help them," she said. "But I didn't."

"And a good thing, too—you saw how those cops were laying into them, you could've been seriously injured. Besides, you've got a job."

"It's—not just the job." Her voice broke along with her heart as she told him about her lunch with Slim. Eddie winced as he listened, then as her words turned to sobs he went and held her. "Ssh. It's okay, honey . . ."

"He'll hate me if I take their side. And not only will I lose Slim, but my job too. I love that pool. I love being a lifeguard there. It's not *fair*."

Eddie nodded. "I know what you mean. I've loved Palisades ever since I was a kid. I've loved working there all these years. But I don't much love it right at this moment."

"So what do I do if it happens again next Sunday?"

Her father's answer surprised her.

"Nothing," Eddie said firmly. "Not if there's a chance you'll get hurt. And judging by what I saw today, I'd say there's a helluva good chance."

"But how can I just—"

"I've never run from a fight in my life," Eddie said, hating this, "but I can't watch you get beaten up by goons, and I won't go bankrupt getting out of Rosenthal's lease—how would I pay the rent here? You and Jack are all I've got—I won't lose you a home like I lost you your mother."

The guilt and shame in his voice nearly brought tears to Toni's eyes.

"So I'm supposed to just . . . look the other way?"

Eddie suggested, "Call in sick on Sunday. And the Sunday after that, and the one after that. Bunty will cover for you."

"I can't do that. I'd feel like a coward." She sighed, frowned. "Everything about this is shitty."

"Watch your language. And yes, it is."

On Saturday Toni reluctantly told Bunty she would not be coming in the next day, and Bunty gave her a sympathetic look and said, "I understand, toots. I wish to hell *I* didn't have to come in."

But she slept badly that night, waking with the same feeling she'd had after failing to swim across the Hudson. So when Eddie started up the car that morning, he was startled when the rear passenger door opened and Toni slid in beside Jack. "I thought you were staying home sick," Jack said.

"Do I look sick?"

Eddie briefly considered trying to talk her out of it, but knew it was pointless—she could be just as stubborn as her mother.

Once the pool opened, Toni watched nervously as a squadron of park guards and Fort Lee police—overseen by Chief Stengel and Irving Rosenthal—stood by as seven CORE members began a stand-in at the ticket window. But there was barely enough time for them to chant their now-familiar refrain before guards and police swooped in and attacked.

Toni looked to Bunty, who nodded his okay, and she ran to the gate.

A Fort Lee police officer grabbed one white man, pinning his arms behind his back while a fat security guard repeatedly punched him in the face, then in his side. The man's ribs snapped with a sound like walnut shells being cracked open. Another police officer inflicted similar punches on several other demonstrators, who as usual refused to fight back.

Eddie arrived on the scene in time to see the protestors being arrested, handcuffed, and dragged away like sacks of cement.

When Toni saw blackjacks being whipped out of policemen's pockets, she couldn't take any more. She pushed through the pool gate and made her way through the brutal melee, toward the police lines.

Eddie saw the fury in her face—it was equal to what he was feeling—and steeled himself to do whatever was necessary to protect her.

Wordlessly, Toni walked right up to Irving Rosenthal, tore off her Palisades ID badge, and hurled it in his face. He looked stunned.

Luckily he didn't notice her hand trembling as she did it.

Toni turned on her heel, got in line at the ticket window, and began chanting: "Don't get cool at the Palisades pool! Get your relaxation where there's no discrimination! Don't get cool at the Palisades—"

Stengel started toward her, but Rosenthal stopped him: "No, you idiot, leave her alone! Can you imagine what that would look like in the press—arresting one of our own lifeguards for picketing us?"

Eddie breathed a sigh of relief, at least for the moment.

One by one, Stengel's men dragged the beaten CORE members away, leaving Toni alone and chanting.

Finally, Irving Rosenthal went up to her and said, "Miss Stopka—"

She kept chanting, "Don't get cool at Palisades Pool! Get your—"

"*Miss Stopka!*" This startled her into silence, and he continued: "I understand your feelings. You got caught up in the emotions of the moment. Here, take your badge—and don't do this again."

He held out her employee badge, but Toni made no move to take it.

"I'll see you next Sunday," she said, and brushed past him.

Eddie couldn't help but give his daughter an admiring smile as she approached him. She smiled back and said, "Sorry."

"Ah, you've always been a troublemaker," he said with muted pride. "Take the bus home. I'll see you after we close." He caught Irving Rosenthal giving him the eye and added, "Who knows, maybe sooner."

Once Toni had left, Rosenthal came up to Eddie, a chill in his voice. "Eddie—tell your daughter that she is *not* picketing this park again."

"I can't do that, Irving. If you want to break my lease, go ahead."

"Oh, you'd like that, wouldn't you? No three years' rent to pay. I'm almost tempted. But if I do . . ." He looked Eddie straight in the eye. "I have a feeling I'll be seeing *you* on the picket line next Sunday, too."

Eddie shrugged. "You never know about these things."

If there was one thing Irving Rosenthal understood, it was the power of publicity—good *or* bad—as he now seemed to be computing the public relations calculus of father *and* daughter ex-employees picketing the park.

He finally shook his head in exasperation. "God help me, Stopka. Your whole family is *meshugga*, isn't it?"

"No, sir. Jack's fairly sane."

"I stand corrected. Now get the hell back to work."

Up till now, the Rosenthals' influence had kept accounts of the CORE demonstrations out of the local newspapers (only *The New York Times* had reported on the previous protests). But this Sunday's incident had been big enough, with eleven arrests, that the *Bergen Evening Record* finally had to print something about it. But when she saw the front-page story in the paper, Toni was incensed:

"Listen to this!" She was sitting at the kitchen table when Eddie and

Jack came home that night. "'Patrolman Arthur Bruns of Fort Lee and Special Patrolman Chester Zaneski of Cliffside Park were standing near the swimming pool in the amusement park when the trouble started. The five men, they said, began pushing them around. Bruns said he thought it was a joke at first until he felt his uniform being ripped . . .'"

"So that's what the whole thing was all about," Jack said dryly. "Torn apparel. You know how picky cops can be about their uniforms."

"They make out like this 'rumpus' was all the demonstrators' fault! And don't even mention why they were there until the end of the story."

"The Rosenthals have a lot of clout in this area. You saw the way the police kowtow to him," Eddie said. He sat down beside his daughter, his tone sober: "Toni, you got lucky. Irving didn't want a picture in the papers of you in your lifeguard's uniform being hauled to the pokey. But if you go on that picket line next Sunday, what happened to those poor bastards from CORE may happen to you . . . and so help me, if one of those goose-stepping cops lays a hand on you, I'll split his goddamned head open like a melon."

Jack spoke up: "She's only standing up for what you always told us, Dad. People are people."

Toni, surprised, said, "Thank you, Jack."

"You're welcome," Jack said grudgingly.

Eddie had never been prouder of her—or more frustrated with her, either.

"I'll ask Mr. Robinson if I can picket at the main gate," Toni told her father, "so you won't be tempted to split any melons."

Eddie wasn't happy at her decision, but realized it was *her* decision. God knows at her age he had already left home and done even more reckless things.

The next morning, after Eddie and Jack left for work, Toni was at loose ends—her summers had always revolved around Palisades. Worse, from Undercliff Avenue she could hear the distant rattle and creak of the roller coaster as the cars ascended, then the falsetto shrieks of passengers as they plunged earthward. This sound, oddly, used to lull her to sleep at night with the comforting proximity of a place she loved; but now the scales of the music it made sounded remote, lost, forbidden. For the first time she began to wonder what would happen if the desegregation didn't succeed—could she ever show her face at Palisades again? Would she ever want to?

She jumped on her bike and rode as far north as she could, up Henry Hudson Drive and past Hazard's Dock, pedaling under the western tower of the bridge before finally stopping at the old Alpine Beach, its sand long ago stripped away by the wind. For several hours she shared the waterfront with a flock of gulls pecking the ground for food, calming herself by watching the Hudson, only a light wind riffling its surface today.

Around noon she started getting hungry—and then it hit her: It was Tuesday. She was supposed to have lunch today with Slim.

At the *park*!

Oh God, she thought in a panic, jumping back on her bicycle. She pedaled in a frenzy, racing as fast as she could with her heart keeping pace. She knew that by now Slim might have already gotten to the park, gone inside—gone to the pool, where he expected to see his girlfriend sitting there in her white lifeguard's outfit, perched on a red lacquered chair . . .

She biked madly up the snaking horseshoe curves of Route 5, huffing and puffing by the time she reached Palisade Avenue. She biked to the visitors' parking lot, weaving amid hundreds of cars until she spied the familiar '39 Oldsmobile—and Slim walking out of the park, toward it.

She braked, jumped off the bike. "Slim! I'm sorry, I forgot—"

Forgot what? Forgot to tell him she had quit her job, and why? But she didn't need to finish the sentence—the disappointment she saw in Slim's eyes as he drew closer told her he knew everything.

"Toni," he said, "what the hell is *wrong* with you?"

His judgmental tone wasn't unexpected, but it still hurt. "There's nothing wrong with *me*," she replied stubbornly. "What's wrong is what they're doing at the *park*."

"Go back in there right now and tell them you're sorry and you want your job back," he said in a tone she had never heard from him before. Those beautiful blue eyes of his had turned hard and disapproving.

"I . . . can't do that," Toni said.

"You mean you won't do it." He shook his head. "Christ on a crutch,

Toni, what are you thinking? Giving up your job so some dirty coloreds can take their bath in a pool meant for white people?"

She felt her stomach cramp, tasted bile at the back of her throat.

"They're people, Slim. Just like you and me."

"They're not like us, Toni, can't you *see* that? Just look at them!"

All Toni saw was the memory of the boy she had loved, ghosted over, like a double exposure, the face of this stranger.

"I thought I knew you," she said softly.

"I thought I knew *you*." His tone was edged in resentment and contempt. "I guess you are a nigger lover, after all."

She saw red at that. He turned away, and she wanted to lash out and hit him for his words, for not being what she wanted him to be.

Instead she jumped back on her bike as his car engine coughed into life, and she careened out of the lot, down Palisade Avenue and Route 5—keeping her tears at bay all the way home to Edgewater, where in the privacy of her own room she finally let them flow.

Sunday morning, Toni met the group from CORE at the Edgewater Ferry Terminal and asked if she could picket with them. An unassuming man with several cuts on his face—the one Patrolman Bruns pinned from behind while a park guard slugged him—introduced himself as Jim Peck.

"If you do," he told her, "you have to play by our rules. That means that no matter how you're provoked—verbally or physically—you *do not* fight back. If they punch someone next to you, just keep on picketing. You yield the moral high ground when you engage in the same violence they do. If they grab you and start dragging you away, let your body go limp. Don't fight, but don't make it easy for them to get rid of you, either. Is that clear?"

Toni agreed, and Peck gave her a brief demonstration of what he meant, how to let your body fold up when seized. Later, when their bus reached the summit of the Palisades, she was stationed along with six others, men and women, at the park's main gate. There they were to picket as well as to distribute leaflets, which urged people to boycott the park.

The Cliffside Park Police Department was positioned menacingly on both sides of the street, standing or watching from cars. Chief Borrell stood in front of Duke's restaurant, drinking a cup of coffee. The seriousness of what she was doing sank in—she could go to *jail*—and her hands trembled a little as they picked up a handful of leaflets and her picket sign.

The young woman next to her, who looked to be about twenty-five, noticed Toni's nervousness and asked, "You okay, honey?"

"Oh, sure." She tried to sound casual and grown-up. "I've . . . just never been arrested before, that's all."

"I was scared too, my first time. I was marching in an Easter Sunday Peace Walk down Fifth Avenue—protesting the bomb. I was arrested along with my friend Marion. Believe me, I was terrified when they marched us into the Women's House of Detention."

Toni had a horrifying presentiment of her future self: haggard, drawn, dressed in drab prison coveralls, scrubbing clothes on an old washboard in the prison laundry. And her life had held such promise!

"We were out in three days. It was no big deal. I'll be right there alongside you, like Marion was for me, okay?"

Toni felt, if not exactly relieved, then at least not so alone. "Thanks. My name's Toni, by the way."

"Vivien Roodenko."

"How long ago did this happen?"

"About four months back," Vivien said. Toni's eyes popped. Vivien laughed. "See? You'll be an old pro at this in no time."

Toni laughed nervously. As the Palisades gate prepared to open, the man in charge of the group told them all to take up their positions. Toni proudly held up her picket sign, prepared to distribute the leaflets in her other hand, and began marching in step with her CORE compatriots.

They hadn't even made a full circuit of the block before Chief Borrell walked up to one of the men in the group and announced, "Your group is engaged in disorderly conduct. You are ordered to disperse immediately."

"What?" the man said. "What's disorderly about it?"

"You're causing a nuisance—obstructing passage on a heavily trafficked street."

"We're not obstructing anybody. And may I remind you, the Supreme Court has upheld the right to peacefully picket and distribute leaflets?"

"Not in my town," Borrell said cheerfully. "I refuse to recognize your so-called rights, and if you insist on asserting them, my men *will* arrest you."

"We stand by our legal rights," Vivien said doggedly. "We're not going anywhere."

"Wrong again. You're going to jail." He signaled his men and they moved in, seizing the demonstrators, snatching away their signs and leaflets.

"Hey! That's our property!" someone objected.

"Didn't think you folks believed in personal property, comrade," Borrell said with a chuckle.

Toni's right arm was being held in a vise grip by a patrolman and her first instinct was to pop him in the nose with her free hand. But she saw the other picketers go limp as the cops tried to lead them away, and Toni forced her body to relax into something like a 120-pound bag of concrete.

"Not her!" Borrell called to the cop holding Toni. "Let her go."

The patrolman obeyed, letting go of Toni's arm, which only infuriated her. "Why *not* me?" she demanded, stepping toe-to-toe with Borrell.

"You're not a member of this pinko organization, are you, Toni?"

"That's bull. Uncle Irving doesn't want me arrested and making bad publicity for him."

"I just follow the law. You're free to go."

"What if I decide to stay here and picket?"

"With what?" Borrell asked with a grin.

She saw a patrolman loading the signs and leaflets into a police car.

Stubbornly, Toni marched up and down in front of the burgeoning line of customers queued up at the ticket booth.

"Don't get cool at the Palisades pool!" she exhorted them, her voice trembling a little. "Get your relaxation where there's no discrimination!" But the customers were looking at her in amusement, not enlightenment. Clearly, you needed props for this sort of thing—and company helped too.

As her friends were herded into squad cars, Toni—feeling guilty and angry at her freedom—skulked away to the nearest bus stop.

Picketing continued for the next two Sundays, with Chiefs Borrell and Stengel quickly and violently rounding up the demonstrators in flagrant violation of their constitutional rights. On the second Sunday, as the arrests began, Toni watched Vivien boldly go up to Irving Rosenthal and begin talking to him in a language she didn't recognize. They actually had quite an extended, almost cordial conversation; after which Vivien returned to Toni's side. "What language was that?" Toni asked.

"Yiddish. Turns out the Rosenthal family comes from the same part of the Ukraine my family does. We talked about the war. He tells me, 'Look, I know what persecution is—I have relatives who were put in concentration camps, even killed, by the Nazis. I'm not like them, I'm not doing this because I hate anyone, it's just business. Now won't you please go get your friends and try to persuade them to get out of here?'"

"What did you tell him?"

"I told him there were probably some German businessmen who didn't hate Jews but only thought they were bad for business, too."

Minutes later, the whole group, minus Toni, was led off to jail.

Feeling solidarity with her friends, Toni attended their trials in the Cliffside Park courthouse, though "kangaroo courthouse" might have been more apt. The prosecution labeled the protests "a Communist-inspired attempt to force admission of minority groups" to the pool. Chief Borrell paced back and forth in front of Recorder Valentine C. Franke and every time CORE's lawyer brought up the issue of Jim Crow, Borrell objected as if he were an attorney: "This is just a plain case of disorderly conduct!"

Unsurprisingly, Recorder Franke found the CORE members guilty and fined them each twelve dollars. CORE's lawyers immediately filed appeals.

The next Sunday, August 31, nineteen demonstrators from CORE showed up at Palisades, splitting into two groups, and this time Toni insisted on being part of the stand-in at the pool. They found themselves

264 | ALAN BRENNERT

ringed by both park guards and Fort Lee police, with Irving Rosenthal the glowering ringmaster. When he saw Toni, he told Chief Stengel, "Get them out of here, *now*. No arrests, just put them all on a ferry back to New York!"

"What about the Stopka girl?"

"Send her too. Maybe it'll scare her into giving up this nonsense."

As the arrests and beatings began, Eddie ran over from his stand in time to see Toni, her body limp as a rag doll, being dragged off to one side, though not being abused in any way. This was more than could be said for the other CORE members, who were being manhandled roughly as usual.

One of them, a Negro named Albert Morris, tried to take a photo of the scene. To Morris's astonishment, Irving Rosenthal stalked up and grabbed the camera away from him. When Morris tried to snatch it back, Rosenthal told Stengel, "Arrest this man for assault!" Stengel did so.

As long as Toni wasn't being mistreated, Eddie held back from action, as she had asked him. But it wasn't easy for him.

Now she and the other protestors were taken out of the park and onto a bus destined for the ferry terminal. Defiantly, CORE members leaned out the open windows, shouting "Stop Jim Crow!" and other slogans.

One of the police officers walked up to where Jim Peck was leaning out of the bus, spat in his face, then walked away.

The police made sure they were on the next ferry to 125th Street in New York, and Toni at least felt a perverse satisfaction that she was being treated like her fellow demonstrators. She came up to Jim Peck, leaning over the ferry's railing as the salt spray of the Hudson washed away the blood from the cuts he had incurred, and asked, "So what do we do now?"

He looked at her and smiled. "Go right back, of course! What else?"

When they reached Manhattan they got more signs and leaflets from their offices, then eighteen CORE members, plus Toni, marched onto the next ferry bound for Edgewater. In less than an hour they were back on the picket line in front of the main gate on Palisade Avenue.

This momentarily flummoxed the ticket takers and security guards at the park entrance, who were hardly expecting a second wave of protest.

Chief Borrell and his men were quickly summoned and they just as quickly began arresting the eighteen CORE members.

Word of the second protest outside the gates flashed across the park within minutes. When he heard, Eddie tore off his apron and jumped the counter of his stand. "Stay here!" he ordered Jack, but Jack snapped, "Hell if I will!" He dropped the awnings and locked up the stand, even though there was a line of customers waiting to order French fries. He raced after his dad, running toward the Palisade gate.

When the last CORE member was arrested, Toni, as usual, was the only one not being lined up at the curb to await the arrival of more police cars to take them to the station.

"Dammit, arrest me too!" Toni snapped at Borrell, but he ignored her.

At the curb, a park guard suddenly approached Jim Peck, his eyes blazing with hatred. "I'd like to kill you!" the guard declared—but he settled for delivering a haymaker to Peck's jaw. Toni could hear the snap of Jim's jawbone, and watched in horror as, knocked unconscious, he collapsed in a heap onto the sidewalk. His fellow CORE members rushed to his aid.

Eddie arrived in time to see his daughter, enraged, heading for the guard who'd clocked Peck, now turning away with a bloody-minded smile of satisfaction. Toni took several quick steps, standing toe-to-toe with the guard. He was at least a foot taller than she was, but she had her way of equalizing that. Without a word she jerked up her right knee and buried it in the man's groin. He howled like a cat being gelded.

Eddie thought, *Oh, Christ!*

Toni turned and taunted Borrell: *"Now* will you arrest me?"

Angrily, Borrell came up and grabbed her wrist, intending to slap a handcuff around it. Eddie started forward—

But Jack rocketed past him. "Leave my sister alone!" He propelled himself, clumsily but forcefully, into Borrell, knocking him off balance.

Borrell snapped, "Jesus Christ! No wonder your mother left you two!"

Furious, Jack took a swing at him, but missed. Two patrolmen seized him as well as Toni, slapping them into handcuffs before they could blink.

Borrell barked, "Book both of them for assault and fuck Irving Rosenthal!"

Jack looked at the cops and said with a grin, "Uh-oh. Which one of you has to fuck Irving Rosenthal?"

Toni laughed. The cop holding Jack, not finding it as funny, raised his hand to give Jack a good slap in the head—but the blow was intercepted by Eddie Stopka's strong right arm.

"There's been enough violence here today, don't you think?" he said.

The cop backed off and Toni and Jack were herded, but not violently, into the next squad car that pulled up to the curb.

"Toni, Jack—keep your cool from here on, okay?" Eddie said. "I'll be at the station to get you out soon as I can."

In the car Toni turned to Jack and said, "Thanks. For lending a hand."

"Anytime." He gave her a lopsided smile. "Who'da thought they'd send mystery men like us to jail?"

Toni smiled as the squad car pulled away from the curb.

Eddie watched it go, then stalked over to Chief Borrell.

"Eddie, I'm sorry," the chief said, holding his hands palm out, "I didn't want to arrest them, but they gave me no choice."

"Funny, the choices you make, Chief." Eddie looked him straight in the eye. "You sit in Duke's, rubbing shoulders with Joe Adonis and Willie Moretti, and you don't arrest *them*. How many households in Cliffside Park have a telephone line put in for use by a bookmaker—fifty bucks a week, found cash—but you never arrest any of them, do you? But Negroes who want only to be treated like any other human being, and the people who take their side? Them you arrest, and worse. You goddamned hypocrite."

Borrell looked stunned that anyone in "his" town would dare confront him like this. "God damn it, Eddie, I brought you into this park . . . you've got an interest in keeping out the wrong kind of elements, too—"

"You did bring me in. And you treated me fairly and kindly. But as much as I owe you, Frank, I promise—you will not charge my son and daughter with assault or anything else. Because if you do, I will not hesitate one fucking *second* to go the Feds and tell them everything that goes on across the street at Duke's, and the company you keep in there. You understand?"

"I got nothing to say about who chooses to have lunch in Duke's! I don't even know half those guys."

"Bullshit. I'm not the only one who's seen you with them, Frank. Anything happens to me or my kids, people will know who's responsible."

"Eddie, c'mon, this is ridiculous! Nothing's happening to anybody." He forced a laugh, but the color had drained from his face and he started to back off: "Look—that guard who slugged the guy from New York, that was uncalled for, agreed? So was what Toni did to him—but I guess she's just like her dad, always looking out for somebody else." He placed a paternal hand on Eddie's shoulder. "I'll talk the guard out of pressing charges, and I'll forget about that swing Jack took at me. All right, Ten Foot?"

"All right," Eddie said guardedly.

Borrell smiled, a bit sadly. He brushed a piece of lint off Eddie's shoulder, then fingered the lapel of Eddie's jacket. "Nice cut. I remember a time when you didn't have a clean shirt to your name."

"Yeah," Eddie said, tone softening. "You took a chance on a pretty raw-looking kid, didn't you?"

"Ah, you had an honest face. Dopey but honest." Borrell smiled again. "Guess I'm still taking a chance on you, eh, Eddie?"

Neither Toni nor Jack were charged, which somehow disappointed them; but their shared combat—and Toni's disaffection from Slim— had healed some old wounds. Together they listened to radio shows for the rest of the day, both so exhausted they went to bed before Jack Benny was over.

The next morning, Toni woke early, refreshed in a way she hadn't felt in a long while. She wolfed down some milk and cereal, then, on a sudden impulse, slipped on her bathing suit beneath a pair of shorts and a T-shirt, grabbed her bike, and started pedaling toward Henry Hudson Drive.

When she got to Hazard's Dock she waited, and at precisely nine A.M., Bunty Hill came ambling down the cliff's side with his walking stick, breaking into a wide smile when he saw her. "Hey, Joe Palooka," he said, "I hear you broke some goon's balls. Sorry I missed it."

"Thanks," she said proudly. "Mind some company on your swim?"

"Be my guest."

"I was—thinking of going over to the New York side," she said casually.

"Yeah?" Bunty seemed pleased. "Looks like a good day for it."

Toni shucked off her shirt and shorts as Bunty stripped down to his bathing suit, then snapped on his red bathing cap. He walked to the water's edge, scooped up a handful of water and gargled it, then spit it out and gave her a thumbs-up. Then he walked onto the dock and smiled back at her: "Ready, kiddo?"

"Ready."

Bunty dove off Hazard's Dock and into the steel-blue Hudson. Without hesitation, Toni dove in behind him, cleaving the waters with renewed joy and confidence. Above them roared hundreds of automobiles rolling across the span of the George Washington Bridge, but here in the water the only sounds Toni was mindful of were the slap of the salty waves and the excited pulse of her own heart—and the only thing that mattered, in the distance, was that little red lighthouse at Jeffrey's Hook.

17

St. Petersburg, Florida, 1949

TONI GAZED OUT EAGERLY from her window seat as the Atlantic Coast Line's *Florida Special* rolled into St. Petersburg, past a colonnade of tall palm trees lined up behind a chalk-white depot building with a red gabled roof. As the brakes screeched and sighed, the train's vibrations sent a shiver of excitement through her. At the age of eighteen she was away from home, alone, for the first time in her life, arriving in a place as different from what she was used to as—well, as different as she felt in her blue rayon-gabardine suit dress and jacket from the people at the station, all of them dressed in summer whites and short sleeves even though it was well past Labor Day.

Summer apparently never ended here, a point driven home by the bright sunlight and a sticky wave of heat that assaulted her as she got off the train, waiting for her baggage to be unloaded. The air was so humid she found herself sweating like a bricklayer as she picked up her suitcase. She had packed lighter clothes, of course, but had wanted to make a good impression with a more formal outfit. What kind of impression was she going to make now, with her dress shields working overtime?

She enjoyed a brief respite from the heat as she passed through the air-conditioned depot, only to hit another wall of hot, moist air as she exited. She scanned the row of cars parked outside and had little trouble picking out the one belonging to the person she was meeting. Dwarfing all the sedate sedans was a one-and-a-half-ton panel truck hooked up to a twenty-two-foot house trailer. On the side of the truck was a brightly colored illustration of a woman wearing a cape of orange fire, diving from a ninety-foot ladder (it said so right on the side) toward a tank of writhing flame. Alongside this were the words:

ELLA CARVER
Internationally Known
As the Only High Swan Diver in the World
On Fire Into Fire
The Greatest Diving Act
"THE ONE THAT NEVER FAILS
THE PUBLIC"

Standing beside the truck was a woman in her late fifties, a square-jawed face framed by a curly wreath of brown hair slowly being silvered by time. She stood about five feet four, maybe a hundred and twenty pounds, and looked just like the photograph Toni had seen in *The Bill-board*. Toni approached the woman, said, "Hi, I'm Toni Stopka," and held out her hand.

Ella Carver's grip was the firmest Toni had ever felt from a woman; a broad smile softened the square face. "Hello, Toni Stopka, I'm Ella Carver. Welcome to Florida. Hot enough for you?"

"Oh yeah. I feel like an idiot in this suit."

"Feel free to eighty-six the jacket. We've got a little ride ahead of us and there's no point in being uncomfortable." She spoke with a faint trace of an accent from her native West Virginia.

"Thanks." Toni gratefully stripped off her jacket as Ella lifted her suit-case as if it were a paperweight and hoisted it into the truck. "Climb in."

Toni did just that. Ella slid into the driver's seat, keyed the ignition, and shifted gear into reverse. Backing up a truck *and* a trailer seemed like a dicey proposition to Toni, but Ella effortlessly angled the whole rig out of the parking space and up Central Avenue, past City Hall, the police station, and the other civic pillars of downtown St. Petersburg.

"Peejay thinks you're a very bright, talented girl." Ella rolled down the side window and a warm breeze carried the scent of jasmine into the car. "But he didn't say why he wasn't training you himself."

"Peejay told me, 'If anybody's going to teach you to be a world-class lady high diver, it ought to *be* a world-class lady high diver, and Ella's the best in the world.'"

Ella laughed. "Best 'lady' diver—old Peejay sure knows how to parse a phrase. We haggled for years over which one of us could be billed the world's highest swan diver. He starts from a height of a hundred feet and me from ninety, but I pointed out he rides a bicycle down to fifty feet and only then goes into a swan dive. He was forced to concede the point."

Toni was only half listening, fascinated by the stands of palm trees adorning almost every street, the quality of the sunlight, the homes and storefronts with facades white as coral. Was this the glorious tropics her father was always raving about?

"So is Peejay right? *Do* you want to be a world-class lady high diver?"

Toni shook off her reverie and said, "I just want to be a high diver, as good as you and Bee Kyle. If that's world-class, then I guess I want that."

"Ah, poor Bee," Ella said sadly. "Last I heard, she and her husband were selling popcorn and souvenirs at a railroad circus in Mississippi."

"My dad owns a food concession at Palisades Park," Toni said, a bit defensively.

"No offense meant, honey. At least she's still in the business. It gets in your blood—been in mine for fifty years, ever since my mama took me to the circus and I saw a woman dive off a high tower. As soon as I saw her flying through the air, I knew that was what I was going to be."

"That's how I felt when I saw Bee Kyle and Arthur Holden."

"You have any prior training, Toni?"

"My friend Bunty coached me in diving at the Y. He had me practicing off their ten-foot springboard: backward and forward somersaults, both piked and tucked, jack-knives, half gainers . . ."

"You want to learn the high swan dive or come down feet first, like most high divers?"

"If a full gainer was good enough for Bee Kyle, it's good enough for me."

"Fine by me," Ella said. "I can do without the competition." She laughed warmly and Toni joined in. "All right, you want to apprentice with me, we start right now. I've got a short gig at a county fair in Savannah, Georgia, last one for a couple of months. You can help me set up my rigging, check the equipment, fill the tank—the grunt work behind the glamour. We spend days doing grunt work, including driving— all so we can have those three seconds in which we launch ourselves into space and fly."

She looked at Toni and said with absolute conviction, "But I promise you this—they're the best damn three seconds you'll ever have in your life."

Four months earlier, toward the end of her freshman year at Fairleigh Dickinson College, Toni had worked up her nerve and knocked on the door of her father's workshop. "Come on in," he called. Entering, Toni glanced up at the dozens of *tikis*—carved from driftwood, pine, oak, and a special wood he ordered from Hawai'i called *koa*—that crowded the shelving on the walls. They looked down at her with jeweled eyes, bared teeth, shaggy headdresses, and scowling mouths. Her father had assured her there was a purpose to these, but so far he hadn't shared it and right now she had a purpose of her own.

"Dad? Can I talk to you about something?"

He barely glanced up from the *tiki* he was carving. "Sure, what's up?"

Toni blurted out, "I'm leaving college after this year."

That got his attention. His head snapped up. "What? Why?"

"I've been trying to tell you all year, this isn't for me. I've just been . . . going through the motions, to please you. What I *want* is to be a high diver."

He winced. "I thought you'd grown out of that. Honey, it's a dangerous way of making a living."

"As dangerous as riding on top of moving trains?"

"I knew I should never have told you about that," Eddie muttered.

"Bunty's been coaching me. He says I'm pretty slick. And I wrote to

Peejay Ringens, he wants to put me in touch with a lady named Ella Carver."

That sounded familiar to Eddie. "She related to the Carvers who high dive on horseback in Atlantic City? I read where one of them lost her sight when she hit the water with her eyes open."

"I'm not planning on diving on the backs of any horses."

Eddie tried to avoid his daughter's gaze by looking around his workshop at the carved wooden idols squatting on their shelves like a parliament of household gods weighing these too-human concerns.

"Have you written your mother about this?" Eddie said finally.

"Yeah, and she sent me a letter begging me to give up diving before I got myself killed. What else is new?"

"She and the Great Lozenge are playing the Steel Pier and she'd really like to see you and Jack. He's agreed to have lunch with her."

"Great. He can eat my lunch too," Toni said dismissively.

"Well," Eddie said with a sigh, "I can't say I'd be overjoyed to see her myself. Either my heart would break or Lorenzo's nose would . . . again."

"Dad," Toni said gently, "you've really got to start seeing—"

"I suppose you've been wondering why I've been making all these *tikis*," he said suddenly, deflecting the imminent advice on his social life.

"It has crossed my mind."

"I spent only a couple of weeks in Hawai'i, but I can still see it, smell it: the warm trade winds, the scent of plumeria and jasmine in the air, the sweet ukulele music . . . and Espíritu Santo had its own beauty, too."

"So why don't you go back to Hawai'i for a vacation?"

"I will, someday. But for now I was thinking more along the lines of"—his eyes twinkled with amusement—"bringing the islands *here*. To New Jersey."

Off her look of bafflement he explained, "In Honolulu there's a place called Trader Vic's. South Seas decor, waitresses dressed in sarongs, a whole menu of tropical drinks in the damnedest colors. Some of 'em even bubbled and smoked. There's a Trader Vic's in California, too, but I read where the granddaddy of 'em all was a place in Beverly Hills started by a guy who calls himself Don the Beachcomber. But now—what with all the GIs who passed through the Pacific during the war—these South Seas restaurants are popping up all over. There's even one in Paterson. It's called Martin's Hawaiian Paradise, and get this—their ad says, '*Italian Food Our Specialty.*'"

They both laughed. "I want to open a place like that, only better," Eddie said. "Outside there'd be a *tiki* idol guarding the door, and inside, palm trees, coconut shells, bamboo wallpaper. I'd have Hawaiian music piped in, Harry Owen and his band playing 'Sweet Leilani.' There'd be no windows, see, so after you came in, there'd be nothing to say you weren't really *there*, in Rarotonga or Tahiti or Honolulu. Outside it may be freezing, the middle of winter, but inside it's always warm. Inside it's always paradise.

"That's what Palisades used to be for me—a place where you could forget the mess that's going on in the world, or the heartaches you've got in your life. Come in, sip a mai tai, listen to some ukulele music, and be transported to a faraway isle that knows no trouble."

There was something so wistfully poignant in this that Toni found herself wanting the same thing for him.

"I'm thinking maybe I can start small—rent an old tavern, refurbish it, do all of the woodworking myself . . ."

"It sounds absolutely magnif, Dad," Toni said. "*I'd* go to that place."

"The hell you would, you're not old enough." They laughed together, and then Eddie said, "Look, you love diving, you're good at it—I understand that. Why don't you start training and competing nationally? I'll pay Bunty or any other trainer you want—maybe you'll even qualify for the '52 Olympics. You could bring home a gold or silver medal, like Vicki Draves or Zoe Ann Olsen. Whatever it takes, however much it costs, I'll pay for it."

Toni was touched—and a little bit tempted—by his offer, but she countered, "It's not the same thing, Dad. All I need is enough money for a train ticket, training, and room and board for four months in Florida."

Eddie considered a long moment, then reluctantly shook his head.

"Honey—even your friend Peejay admitted, people *die* doing this. Or they can be crippled for life. If I gave you the money to do this and something went wrong, I . . . I'd never forgive myself. I love you too much to risk your life like that. Can you understand that?"

Toni saw the tears he was trying to hold back and she couldn't bring herself to be angry at him.

"Yeah," she said, "I can. But I'm still gonna do it—you know that?"

"Since you were two years old," Eddie said with a sigh.

All right, Toni told herself as she left the workshop, she could still manage this—she just had to be a little more creative about it. She had just over eight hundred dollars in savings from her salary at the French fry stand and her aborted lifeguard position. Ella Carver had said she would train Toni and provide room and board for two hundred dollars a month. She had that covered—but no money for a train ticket.

But then, neither did her dad when he was her age . . . did he?

She spent a day or two planning things out, then one morning after her father had gone to work she packed as many clothes as she could fit into one suitcase, including her nice new blue gabardine suit, along with a couple of peanut-butter-and-jelly sandwiches and a thermos of water. She put on an old shirt and pair of dungarees, sneakers, and one of Jack's old corduroy jackets. She wrote Jack an IOU for the jacket and her father a note telling him she loved him and not to worry, she'd see him in a few months. She caught a bus to Jersey City and the Jersey Central Railroad Station, where she consulted the posted schedules—finding a Baltimore & Ohio train leaving in fifteen minutes for Washington, D.C., on Track Five.

She left the terminal through the front entrance, then sneaked around back to the railyards. She put on a cap, stuffing as much of her hair under it as she could. Recalling her father's tales of riding the rails, she kept an eye peeled for railroad cops and hurried over to Track Five, where a long line of freight cars was idling. Most were fully loaded, but she spied one of what her dad called "one-eyed Pullmans"—an empty boxcar, one door open—and after checking twice to make sure no one was around to see, she ran to the car, threw her suitcase up and into the compartment, then put her hands up onto the floor of the car and hoisted first her leg, then her whole body, into the car, exactly as her father had recounted to her a zillion times.

Thanks, Dad. She smiled and hid herself in a corner of the empty car. Fifteen minutes later she was "catching out" of Jersey for points south.

In Washington she caught a freight that took her to Richmond, Virginia, then she picked up the Atlantic Coast Line bound for Savannah, Georgia. It took a while to get used to the rattle and roar of the train, much less to get any sleep, but she was too excited to sleep anyway. She wished she'd packed a third peanut-butter-and-jelly sandwich—she was starving by the time the train slowed for its approach into Savannah. She jumped off before it reached the station and caught a bus to the nearest YWCA, where she rented a room, took a hot shower, and enjoyed a cheap meal and a good night's sleep. The next morning she put on her blue gabardine suit, went back to the train station, and purchased a passenger ticket for the *Florida Special*—which a few hours later pulled into St. Petersburg.

Now, ironically, she found herself headed back to Savannah—a six-hour drive, straight up U.S. Route 301 to Highway 17 and into Georgia—and Ella seemed determined to do it in one jump. Finally, in the fifth hour, Toni asked meekly, "Can we stop to get something to eat?"

"Oh, heck, honey, I'm sorry, of course. Sometimes I go all day long without a meal—I believe in lettin' the stomach rest."

"Mine's gotten plenty of rest since breakfast. I could use a sandwich."

Ella pulled over at the next truck stop, a diner called Molly's Place.

En route, Toni had learned from Ella that she was born on a farm in Bluefield, West Virginia, into a family of seven boys and four girls. Their father left early in Ella's life, leaving her mother alone to rear the children. It sounded like a hardscrabble life, and Toni wondered how much practice in "letting the stomach rest" Ella had had, growing up as a child.

"After seeing that lady high diver at the circus, I must've climbed every tree in the county . . . I even remember climbing a windmill. My mother's never stopped worrying about me. She used to say, after I left, that I'd be the first of her children to die. Every time a wire came, she'd say, 'Ella's gone.' But it's starting to look like I might be the last to go!"

Now, between bites of her roast beef sandwich, Toni asked, "How did you become a professional diver?"

"Pure serendipity. When I was ten, a Wild West show passed through town—The Great Carver Wild West Show. It was run by 'Doc' Carver, a former buffalo hunter and sharpshooter. Six foot four, two hundred pounds, flaming red hair—my sister-in-law Sonora said he was like a giant redwood, nothing could knock him down. He was called Doc 'cause he'd studied to be a dentist in California, before he thought better of it."

"Irving Rosenthal at Palisades used to be a dentist, too."

"Something about the profession just sends men into the outdoor amusement business, I guess," Ella mused. "Anyway, when he saw what a good climber and jumper I was, he asked my mother if he could adopt me, and train me for a diving act he was planning. She said sure."

"She did?" Toni said in amazement.

"Of course she did. She was struggling to raise eleven kids on her own, and here was somebody offering to give one of them a better life than she ever could. And I was rarin' to go and be a diver, just like you. So she signed some papers making Doc Carver my guardian.

"He taught me to swim, dive, and ride horses. That was the act he'd come up with—diving horses. You'd ride the horse up a long ramp to the top of a forty-foot tower, then dive headfirst together into a tank of water."

Toni was amazed—her father hadn't just made that up to scare her!

"Doc had another daughter named Lorena, and the two of us rode five different horses—Lightning and King Klatowah were my favorites—all over the world. We even made a tour of China. But eventually I knew I wanted to go out on my own as a swan diver," Ella said, "and I made good at it."

Nursing her cup of coffee, she added, "Doc was wonderful to me, but I had one thing against him. When Gertrude Ederle swam the English Channel in 1926, I knew I could do it faster than her. He wouldn't let me."

"My friend Bunty helped train Amelia Gade Corson, the second woman to swim the Channel."

"There you go. That could've been me. I may give it a try yet." She looked impatient. "You about finished? We should get back on the road."

They pulled into Savannah a little after sundown and slept the night in Ella's comfortable house trailer with its two-bunk bedroom and kitchenette with a small gas range, on which Ella cooked breakfast the next morning before they began the "grunt work"—and Toni found herself doing a lot of grunting—of unloading Ella's equipment from the truck. The water tank, twelve feet in diameter, came out first in eight pieces, and Ella put it together with the skill of a trained mechanic. The ninety-foot ladder followed, in nine ten-foot sections, each with its own platform. Toni marveled as she watched Ella wield a ten-pound sledgehammer to pound axle stakes into the hot asphalt pavement; Toni was young and strong but for every stake she drove into the ground, Ella managed to do two.

The stakes secured guy wires from the ground to the ladder sections; once the wires were tied off to the first ten-foot section, Ella climbed up and used a pulley called a gin pole to raise the next section of ladder, attach it, then tie off four more guy wires until that section was secure. Toni did most of the toting and Ella most of the rigging, but Ella had Toni tie off a few wires herself so she knew how to do it—and Toni watched Ella's every move, sensing that at some point she could be called upon to do any or all of this.

By Friday morning tank and tower were ready, standing nine feet apart. Toni gazed up at the small diving platform jutting out a few rungs down from the top; from down here it looked as substantial as a postage stamp. But Ella, wearing a dark one-piece bathing suit for her practice dive, was hardly cowed, though she did take a precaution that puzzled Toni: she tore off a piece of duct tape. "What's that for?" Toni asked.

"Honey," Ella explained, "I take about three and a half feet of water when I hit—pressure's equal to five hundred pounds per square inch. Once I reach the top, I tape my mouth and nose shut to withstand the shock."

She began climbing up the ladder. When she reached the top she taped her mouth and nose. On that tiny platform, she looked about as big as a bird perched on the topmost branch of a bare, wintry, ninety-foot tree.

The little bird inched forward to the edge of the platform, pausing only a moment before she dove into space.

It was a perfect swan dive, Ella's body arcing out and down as if sliding down a rainbow. Her head was nestled between her outstretched arms, to cushion the impact. When she hit the water, her body was rigid and she created a geyser that erupted over Toni as she stood on the catwalk surrounding the tank. Through the spray she was able to see that as soon as Ella entered the water, her rigid body went supple, curving like a smile, turning the steep dive into a shallow one; had she not, Toni knew, she would have slammed headfirst into the bottom of the five-foot tank. Instead her arched body sank only three or four feet, easily skirting the bottom, before surfacing on the other side of the tank.

"That was *magnif*!" Toni told Ella as she climbed up the side ladder.

Ella stripped off the tape covering her nose and mouth, smiled, and said, "Ah, that's nothing. Wait'll you see me do it when I'm on fire."

Toni had assumed that Ella would perform in the kind of heavily padded outfit that Bee Kyle had worn when she was doing the same act. So she was shocked when Ella, just before showtime, suited up in nothing more than some woolen tights and a shirt, under a canvas jacket.

"Are those made of asbestos?" Toni asked hopefully.

"Asbestos is for sissies," Ella said with a grin.

"But don't you get burned?"

"Sometimes. The trick is, the motion of my body as I fall pushes the flames away from me, and the splash when I enter the water extinguishes the fire in the tank—most of it, anyway."

Over the canvas jacket she now strapped on a pair of gasoline packs.

"You look like Rocketman," Toni said in awe, "from the serials."

"Ha! I'd like to see Rocketman try this," Ella said, picking up a can of gasoline. She began pouring it into the water, along the rim of the tank.

Ella handed Toni a box of matches and said, "Go ahead, light it."

Ever since '44, Toni was terrified of fire, but she wasn't about to show it as she took a match, struck it against the side of the box, then tossed it into the tank. Immediately the gas ignited, five-foot flames shooting up like lava out of a caldera, causing the audience to gasp and Toni to wince; in seconds the fire sped all along the rim of the tank, creating a flaming hoop of fire with barely five feet of open water in the middle.

"And now, ladies and gentlemen," an announcer boomed from the loudspeakers, *"the amazing Ella Carver will climb to the top of this ninety-foot ladder, set herself ablaze, and dive into the inferno you see before you!"*

The air pungent with the smell of burning gasoline, Ella said, "That's my cue," and began climbing the tower. Now from the loudspeakers came a piece of music familiar to many circus-goers: Khachaturian's "Sabre Dance," punctuating Ella's ascent with its pulsing rhythms and dramatic percussion. It took a few minutes to climb ninety feet, and with every rung the tension increased. When Ella finally reached the top, Toni couldn't see her actually striking the match to the gas packs— but she saw the fireball that flared on Ella's back as her jacket burst into flame, and shared the crowd's collective gasp when she hurled herself off the platform and into the air.

Trailing flame like a falling star, she plummeted as the fire seemed to consume more and more of her pathetically inadequate clothing, before plunging into the middle of the tank, threading the eye of the flaming needle. As she predicted, the huge waterspout extinguished most of the flames—and within seconds Ella broke surface, climbed up the side ladder, and stood, uninjured, on the catwalk, as the crowd cheered.

Toni looked at her and thought, How on God's green earth can I *ever* live up to that?

Ella said she was usually paid fifty dollars per dive, one dive nightly, or three hundred dollars a week: good money even by the standards of the booming postwar economy. "The real challenge in this business can be in getting paid," she told Toni on the drive home. "Couple years ago I had to sue some fly-by-night operator to get the four hundred and twenty-five bucks he owed me. I've gotten burned plenty—and not from fire diving!"

Taking that as her cue, Toni presented Ella with the first of her monthly training fees of two hundred dollars.

Back in St. Petersburg, Ella entered a trailer park on Fourth Street between Fifty-first and Fifty-second Avenues. Young palm trees did their best to shade the clusters of low-roofed trailer homes. Ella pulled into one of three adjacent lots she owned, unhitched the trailer from the truck, and reconnected the gas, sewer, power, and water lines. On the other two lots bloomed a patchwork of flower and vegetable gardens that Ella had begun when she first bought the lots, which often went untended while she was on the road.

After a quick lunch, Ella and Toni began unloading the diving equipment from the truck and reassembling it again, this time on one of Ella's adjacent lots. "I don't have anything booked for the next few months," she explained, "so I can start whipping you into shape before the next round of fairs and festivals starts up in February."

By the next day the tank was set up and filled with water, and the first section of ladder was erected nine feet away and secured to the ground with guy wires. But that was as high as it would rise for the moment: "You say you're used to diving from a height of ten feet, so that's where we'll start."

Toni was thrilled to begin training and even the short climb up to the ten-foot summit of the ladder seemed exciting. She stepped onto the small platform, which was much shorter than the diving boards she was used to at the Y, and called down to Ella, standing on the narrow walkway surrounding the tank: "So what should I try first? A tuck-and-roll somersault?"

"Hold your horses," Ella told her. "For now I just want you to look down. Even from only ten feet up, diving into a tank twelve feet in diameter is a different kettle of fish from diving into an Olympic-size swimming pool. For one thing, you're not standing on a board hanging out over the pool but aiming for the middle of a tank of water nine feet away. Go on, take a good long look and gauge the distance you've got to cover."

Toni went to the edge of the platform and looked down.

"And you're not standing on a springboard," Ella added, "but a little wooden pedestal. So the spring you'll need to cover those nine feet—"

"Has to come from my legs, not the board," Toni said with a nod.

"Exactly. Now, you want to make your entry into the tank at a ninety-degree angle, *precisely*. From ten feet it doesn't matter much, but when you're dropping from ninety feet up and traveling about fifty miles an hour, even an entry just ten degrees off the beam can break a rib, or worse. The minute you enter the water, relax your body, extend your legs like you're sitting down, and throw back your head and arms—to cushion your impact, slow your descent, and stop you from hitting bottom with all that velocity."

"Okay," Toni said, a bit chagrined to learn how easy it was for things to go terribly wrong. She gazed soberly down at the tank, silently judging the amount of spring she would need to bridge the gap, plus another three feet to land in the center of the tank.

"Take your time, if you need to."

"I'm ready." Toni gripped the edge of the platform with her toes, bent her legs—and jumped.

She sprang up, putting as much oomph into the jump as she could to cover the nine feet of ground. It was an exhilarating leap, but scary too, at least until she had cleared the side of the tank and was plummeting safely down toward the water. She kept her body straight, perpendicular to the water, and as soon as she entered it she extended her legs and threw back her head and arms, as Ella had said. Her curved body only lightly brushed the bottom of the tank and she floated to the surface, feeling triumphant.

As she climbed up the side ladder, Ella stood on the catwalk and said, "Well, you missed hitting the ground, which is always a good thing, but I saw your rear end kiss the bottom of the tank. If you'd done that from ninety feet up your tailbone would be halfway up your rectum by now."

Toni's triumph was quickly punctured, though Ella's colorful description made it quite clear that worse things could be punctured.

Once Toni was sufficiently practiced in takeoff and landing, Ella judged her ready to move on to a simple forward somersault. At the pinnacle of her jump she would start a tuck-and-roll, coming out of it perpendicular to the water.

"You've got to gauge two things now, distance and time," Ella said, "and whether you've got enough time to do the somersault while still landing in the water at the right angle."

"I got it." Toni had done this a hundred times before. Confidently, she gauged her time and distance, then jumped. At the pinnacle of her jump she started to tuck her body, the world spinning around her—

But she was used to her pinnacle being higher off the springboard, and just as she was starting to untuck herself, she hit the water on her back—the impact knocking the breath out of her lungs and sending a huge waterspout splashing over the sides of the tank.

She sank like a stone to the bottom. As she surfaced, her embarrassment was compounded by the sight of Ella standing on the catwalk, dripping wet.

"Well, that's just fine," Ella said, shaking off the water, "if you're of a mind to do a cannonball act in a clown show. And again, from a height of ninety feet, you would now be unconscious, with a broken back."

Toni worked the rest of the day on improving her spring off the platform, finally gaining the necessary height to complete a perfect somersault and entry into the water at the proper angle.

And when she did, Ella surprised her by applauding.

"Good work. You're a fast learner. And watching you has whetted my appetite. Take a shower while I go fix us some supper."

Ella cooked a delicious dinner of fried chicken, parboiled potatoes, and collard greens in her small but serviceable kitchen.

"I bought this place," she told Toni, "when I tried retiring from the diving game in '43. I'd had a bad fall that required some emergency surgery, and my son Lewis, who's in the Navy, was flown all the way back from hell and gone by the Red Cross to be by my side. He told me, 'Mom, I don't worry about the war, but I worry every night when I think of you setting yourself afire and then jumping into space. Promise me you'll stop it.'

"Well, what else can you do when your son asks you that? And I had a gentleman friend who wanted to settle down with me, too. So I retired, and got married for the second time, to boot. Inside of a year I was itching to get back on the road, diving. My retirement didn't last any longer than my marriage. I'm happy to see my son and daughter when they visit, but now I know—I wouldn't be happy settling down anywhere permanently."

"Did you and your first husband get divorced too?" Toni asked.

Ella's eyes softened. "No, God love him, I would've stayed married to Fred Grabbe forever. But God had other plans for him, I guess." She smiled tenderly. "I still use his name—I'm Ella Carver-Grabbe on everything except the stage billing. It's like keeping a little bit of him for myself."

Moved, Toni didn't know what to say, and Ella, seeming a bit uncomfortable to have shared this, cleared away the dinner dishes and said, "Well, young lady, you get a good night's sleep. We're back at it tomorrow."

Toni advanced up the ladder at a rate of ten feet every five days, quickly learning to gauge the increases in height and adjusting her jumps and somersaults accordingly. This was how all high divers learned their trade, with incrementally greater ascents to make them gradually more comfortable with the height. At forty feet, the climb up the ladder began to seem more formidable to Toni. But it was offset by the exhilaration as she leapt into the air and reached her pinnacle—a timeless moment in which she seemed to be defying gravity itself—tucked herself into a ball, spun end-over-end, then straightened out, feet flat in order to "punch a hole" in the surface tension of the water big enough to squeeze her body through. Then she curved her body, dissipating her velocity so she wouldn't strike bottom.

It felt fantastic!

Frustratingly, even as she ascended higher on the ladder, there was one stunt she couldn't seem to master: a double somersault, like the ones Bee Kyle had done so beautifully. It should have been easy—just a matter of continuing to tuck her body for one more revolution—but at the start of the second spin she would panic, afraid she wouldn't be able to come out of the tuck at the right angle to enter the water. She made two abortive attempts in which she came out of the second tuck halfway through, turning it into a clumsy one-and-a-half somersault. The third time she hit the water with feet splayed, the impact sending an excruciating jolt through her right ankle. She cried out in pain as she went under, taking in a mouthful of water.

Ella dived in and grabbed her, got her up the ladder and onto the catwalk. "Can you stand?" she asked Toni.

"Sure," Toni said, letting go of Ella. Her foot buckled under her and Ella grabbed her before she collapsed.

One hospital visit later, it was apparent that Toni had torn a ligament in her ankle. The doctor bandaged it, told her to ice it for twenty-four hours, and keep the foot elevated. "You'll be fine in three to four weeks," he assured her, "but no diving. Not even from the side of a pool."

As if that wasn't bad enough, the hospital bill took a twenty-dollar bite out of Toni's cash reserves.

"Well, there's no law says you have to do a double somersault," Ella said philosophically as they drove back to her trailer. "Once that ankle's healed, we'll pick up where we left off and stick to single somersaults."

Toni was angry at herself for botching the stunt, and frustrated at being sidelined for possibly an entire month. Ella tried to relieve the tedium by taking her to Tampa Bay Beach, or across town to a barrier island called Long Key, where they fished, caught dinner, and barbecued it on the beach.

Toni's ankle slowly healed, but she grew increasingly anxious as she realized the training would now take five months, not four. And when, after three weeks, the doctor pronounced her fit and whole—a day on which she should have been jubilant—she instead burst into tears in Ella's car on the way back.

"Ella, I'm so sorry," she said, "but I—I can't go on. I can't stay."

Ella looked at her, dumbfounded. "What! Why not?"

Her shame, anxiety, and guilt all came out in a rush: "Because I only had enough money for four months' training and room and board and I wasted a whole *month* on this stupid ankle and I'm sorry, I'm sorry I wasted your time, I'll *never* be a high diver!"

And then she collapsed into sobs. Ella pulled the car over to the side of the road, parked, and put a hand on Toni's shoulder.

"Honey, calm down," she said gently. "First off, accidents happen to all of us, it comes with the territory. Second, you don't have to pay me another red cent. Third: you *will* be a high diver. I personally guarantee it."

One month later, Toni was standing on the diving platform, a few rungs below the top of the ladder—the ninety-foot mark—savoring the view. The tower faced east, and at nine stories was taller than many of the buildings in St. Petersburg. She looked northeast and saw the green sprawl of two golf courses enclosed by the waters of Placido and Coffee Pot Bayous, and beyond that, Tampa Bay. She looked southeast and saw the gables and cupolas on the rooftops of the Old Northeast neighborhood.

But looking straight down, she was seized by an unexpected vertigo. The tank—which hadn't seemed that much larger at eighty feet, had it?—looked about the size of a Dixie cup. She was going to jump into *that*?

"I feel like I'm standing on the top of the Empire State Building!"

A seagull glided on an air current about twenty feet below her, only heightening the surrealism of the moment.

"It's just psychological!" Ella called up. "You're only ten feet higher than you were yesterday. We all felt the same way the first time we did it!"

Toni gauged the distance, time, wind direction—her usual pre-jump checklist. Ella was right—it was only ten feet higher, she could do this.

No fancy somersault on the first try—she just launched herself into space, soaring briefly higher than the diving platform, then began to drop.

And *what* a drop! She was falling at thirty-seven feet per second, as the buildings, trees, sky, everything seemed to be falling upward, away from her. Her heart trip-hammered with excitement and terror as the Dixie cup turned into a water dish, then a dinner plate, a wading pool—

Her feet struck the water, which at fifty miles an hour felt like hitting concrete. As she penetrated the water, she extended her legs, tipped back her head, raised her arms . . . and then she was underwater, slowing, drifting toward the bottom like a leaf. She smiled, mirroring the attitude of her body. She felt both calm and exhilarated, safely cocooned in water.

When she surfaced, Ella was standing on the catwalk, grinning.

"Where's your tailbone? Has it migrated up your rectum?"

"Nope," Toni said. "It's right where it should be."

"Congratulations. You are now, officially, a high diver."

18

Largo, Florida, 1950

TONI'S MIND WAS SPINNING with excitement, like the Ferris wheel re-volving gaily behind Ella's diving tower. It was the first day of the Pinel-las County Fair, the first performance of the day—and the first day of the life she had previously only dreamed of. She stood behind the tank, adjusting the straps of her colorful, one-piece bathing suit—an arched rainbow of red, orange, yellow, and green splashed across her chest and a sky-blue background. She felt a bit uncomfortable with the amount of décolletage on display, but Ella had assured her, "You're an attractive young lady and crowds always like to see attractive young ladies doing unexpected things—like jumping off a forty-foot tower into five feet of water. I used to trade on the same lack of convention, but now that the last blush of spring has left my cheeks I'll soon be the sweet little old grandma who sets herself on fire and dives into a flaming tank. That's what makes for a good act, the tension between what the performer ap-pears to be and what she *does*. The greater the tension, the more audi-ences love it—as long as you deliver."

Thus there were signs all around the city of Largo advertising Ella as THE FLAMING VENUS or THE INTERNATIONAL THRILL GIRL, though she was well past what anyone might reasonably call girlhood.

Toni peeked around the curvature of the tank and saw an audience of perhaps one hundred crowding the bleachers: people munching on popcorn or hot dogs, women holding babies in their laps, older children gazing up in wonder at the diving tower even as Toni had done at their age, at Palisades Park. That wasn't the only thing that reminded her of Palisades—the smell of cotton candy wafted in from a nearby concession, as did the stutter of pellet guns at a shooting gallery and the sound of people laughing on the Tilt-a-Whirl as gravity whipped them crazily around in circles.

"Ladies and gentlemen," boomed an announcer's voice, *"shortly, from this ninety-foot tower, Ella Carver, a fifty-seven-year-old mother of two grown children, will dive headfirst into a tank filled with only five feet of water!"*

Through this, Ella came up behind Toni, put a maternal hand on her shoulder, and whispered, "Break a leg, hon—just don't take that literally."

"But before she does, her lovely assistant, a young lady not yet out of her teens, will thrill you with her astounding midair gymnastics! Pinellas County Fair presents that sensational duo, Ella Carver and Toni Stopka!"

Hearing her name announced for the first time in these electric tones galvanized Toni, as did the round of applause that welcomed her entrance. She raced out from behind the tank, made a small bow to the audience, then ran to the tower and began climbing—practically propelled up the ladder by the driving, pulsing rhythms of Khachaturian's "Sabre Dance." She reached her goal quickly—she would not be diving from the ninety-foot platform this afternoon, but from the forty-foot platform. She was, after all, only the warm-up act—she had to give Ella something to "top."

She stood on the platform, looking down at the tank. Everything seemed so different from the practice dive she'd taken that morning— the presence of the crowd changed everything, the sound, the motion, even the temperature of the air. Ella had warned her to be observant of anything unusual before she jumped—all it took was some idiot to trip over a guy wire, jostling the platform, to turn a routine dive into a fatal plunge. She scanned the crowd for possible hazards, gauged her distances, then—as "Sabre Dance" faded out over the loudspeakers, leaving a dramatic silence—she turned around on the platform, standing with her back to the audience.

Below her she heard gasps from the crowd, which made her smile.

She pushed herself off the platform backward, as she had watched Bee Kyle do years ago, and at the pinnacle of her jump she pulled her knees up to her chin, clasped her thighs tightly with her hands, threw her head back, and somersaulted as she fell—catching glimpses of the sky, the tank, the crowd below, pinwheeling like the shards of color in a kaleidoscope. Then she straightened her body and did a full gainer, feet-first, into the tank.

She flutter-kicked to the surface, climbed up the side ladder, and a wave of applause washed over her, as warm as the waters of Tampa Bay.

She took her bows, instantly addicted to the sound.

Then, just as quickly, it was her job to step back out of the limelight, jumping off the catwalk as the announcer introduced the top half of the bill: *"Now, the International Thrill Girl herself—Ella Carver!"*

Ella passed Toni briefly on her way to the tower, gave her a smile and wink of approval, then began climbing the ladder all the way to the top.

Ella performed her flawless swan dive from ninety feet up, which brought an even bigger round of applause and cheering from the crowd.

That evening, Toni performed a backward somersault from ninety feet, took her applause, then began sprinkling gasoline on the water in preparation for Ella's fire dive. She lit the gas with a torch, hoping no one would notice the way she kept her arm rigid and the flame as far away from her as possible. A ring of flames erupted like a lit fuse around the tank, eliciting gasps from the audience, as Ella ascended the tower and, at the top, ignited the gasoline packs on her back. She burst into flame, leaped into the air, plummeting down into the middle of the flaming tank. The waterspout from Ella's entry doused the flames—and the crowd went wild, cheering, hooting, applauding, as the lithe diver climbed up the ladder and onto the catwalk around the tank.

In a lovely gesture, she took Toni's hand and held it aloft with hers, sharing the audience's approbation with her assistant.

Even more touching was at the end of their five-day engagement, when Ella, behind the wheel of the truck, said, "Oh, by the by," reached into her pocket, and handed Toni a thick wad of cash. "Here's your share of the take. Ten dives at twenty-five dollars a pop."

Toni stared at the money—mostly twenty-dollar bills—and had no trouble believing there was two hundred and fifty dollars in her hand.

"I can't take this," she objected. "*I'm* supposed to be paying *you.*"

"You've graduated, honey, you're a working part of the act. The fair wasn't paying for one diver but for two, and I made sure they paid for two. You're a professional now, and professionals get paid. If they're lucky."

Toni sat there, stunned, looking at more money than she had ever earned at one time before, and managed a soft, "Thank you."

Ella tossed her a smile. "Not a bad racket, is it?"

Toni grinned and said, "Strictly delish."

There were a *lot* of winter fairs in Florida alone, and after Largo, they went straight to the Florida State Fair in Tampa, followed by the Florida Citrus Exhibition in Winter Haven, the Indian River Orange Jubilee in Cocoa Beach, and the Lake County Fair and Sportsmen's Exposition in Eustis. It was at the state fair that Ella introduced Toni to the concept of press notices, in this case a small review from the *Tampa Tribune* mainly praising Ella but also mentioning "her assistant, teenage Toni Stopka, and her aerial gymnastics." Toni immediately bought her own copy of the paper.

The diving was not nearly as tiring as the driving and the assembling, disassembling, and reassembling of equipment. After a long day of driving and rigging, Ella often had more energy left over than Toni, who would wolf down dinner and crawl into bed like a whipped dog. So Toni was surprised by Ella's announcement that next month, when they started touring with a carnival, Ella would be hiring a professional rigger: "I wanted you to get your hands dirty, like every diver's got to do sometimes. But with all the jumps a carnival makes, we're hiring a rigger—even I can only take so much of this."

She ran an ad in *The Billboard* and wound up hiring a former sideshow strongman, a forty-two-year-old Norwegian gone slightly to seed . . . though his still-staggering biceps could pound in axle stakes with three quick hammer blows. His name was Arlan and he seemed content just to still be working in the outdoor amusement business. He took over the driving, called Ella "ma'am" and Toni "missy," and was happy to sleep in a corner of the truck, which Ella had comfortably outfitted with a mattress, sheets, pillow, and a small battery-powered light.

After a few days' rest in St. Petersburg, they hit the road again. For the past few years Ella had been performing, at least part of the time, with the Central States Shows, a medium-size (fourteen rides, ten shows, forty concessions) truck carnival whose crowded schedule began in Kansas in April, ran through the Midwest in summer, then in September headed "south to the cotton"—Texas and beyond.

Ella met up with the carnival in mid-April in Wellington, Kansas, a small town surrounded by acres of golden wheat as bright and beautiful as the Florida sun. Arlan proved himself a good, fast rigger, freeing Ella and Toni to focus on their performances. Central States Shows was managed by W. W. "Scobey" Moser, who back in '42 had patriotically enlisted in the Army and put his carnival in cold storage for the duration. The midways were anchored by familiar rides like the Ferris wheel, the Spitfire, and a roller coaster, and populated by grind men hawking familiar concessions—Penny Arcade, String Game, Fish Pond, Hoop-la, Guess Your Weight, Cat Rack—and grab stands offering corn dogs, hamburgers, and Coca-Cola.

Ella's and Toni's first performance drew praise not only from the audience but from a fellow performer as well. After the evening show, as Ella was in the truck stripping off her slightly singed woolen tights, a young man wearing a red, white, and blue jumpsuit came up to Toni as she finished helping Arlan throw a tarp over the tank. "Great show," he told her.

"Thanks." He seemed a few years shy of thirty, dark-haired, with the lean frame and chiseled good looks of a Frank Sinatra. He spoke with a Midwestern twang, the *o* in *show* being a dead giveaway.

He extended a hand. "Cliff Bowles. I do a human cannonball act at the other end of the midway."

"Toni Stopka. Nice to meet you."

"You've got great control over your body. I say that as not a masher but as someone who also flies through the air and has to make a soft landing—in my case, in a net—a hundred feet away."

She laughed. "I'd like to see that."

"I'm on in fifteen minutes. Come on over if you get a chance."

He threw her a lopsided smile as he walked away, and she knew there was absolutely no way she would not go to that show tonight.

She walked down the midway to where posters announced, and just in case you couldn't read, an outside talker repeated:

JETMAN, THE HUMAN MISSILE!
SHOT FROM A CANNON AT 60 MILES PER HOUR
OVER NOT ONE BUT FOUR CARS TO A NET
100 FEET AWAY!
WILL TODAY BE THE DAY HE DOESN'T MAKE IT?

Toni took a seat in the stands with the crowd, taking in the huge flag-painted cannon tilted at a forty-five-degree angle into the sky, a ladder propped up against the muzzle. A few yards down, four Chevy sedans were lined up end to end, at least sixty feet of automotive metal; and about five yards beyond that a large horizontal net was stretched out, secured to the ground in all four corners by thirty-five-foot guy wires.

"Ladies and gentlemen, here he is—Jetman, the Human Missile!"

Cliff made his entrance in his red, white, and blue jumpsuit, matching crash helmet, and a pair of aviator goggles that made him look like a cross between a jet pilot and a Fourth of July parade marshal. The crowd cheered as he gave them a wave before climbing up a short ladder and into the two-foot-wide mouth of the cannon. His head disappeared below the rim of the barrel, a drum roll played over the loudspeakers, and Cliff's "trigger puller," Phil, a young man about Toni's age, made a great show of lighting the fuse.

"Five—four—three—two—one—FIRE!"

BOOM! With a thunderous crack and a cloud of smoke, the cannon fired, propelling the red, white, and blue figure of "Jetman" out at tremendous speed—head up, arms at his side. He flew in a parabolic arc above the first car . . . the second . . . the third . . . the fourth . . . and at the last minute, as he reached the net, Toni saw him do a half-somersault, turning his body over in time so that he landed safely on his back.

Toni had seen Victoria Zacchini of the Zacchini cannonball troupe perform at Palisades during the war, so she knew it wasn't a real cannon and that Cliff was ejected by a blast of compressed air, with some gunpowder ignited for smoke and sound effects—but it was still an impressive feat.

The crowd, unaware of how the act worked, cheered as Cliff got out of the net and waved triumphantly.

Afterward, Toni lingered and approached him. "You've got a pretty slick act yourself," she said. "That was a nice half-somersault into the net."

"Aw, that's the only part that takes any real skill," Cliff said. "For the first part of it you're literally unconscious."

"You're kidding!"

"Nope. That compressed air carries so much kick you're zooming out of there at seven or eight times the force of gravity. It literally pushes the blood from your brain down to your feet with such force that you black out for a few seconds. Hey, can I buy you a beer?"

He asked her with the same casual tone as when he spoke of blacking out in the middle of his act. This guy was a cool customer. "I'm nineteen, I'm not sure I'm old enough to drink in this state," she said.

"I'll buy it for you. This is a carny, no one's gonna arrest you."

At a grab stand, Cliff bought them a couple of bottles of Pabst Blue Ribbon and pretzels with mustard. As they sat munching and drinking at a picnic table, Toni said she found the four-car flyover very impressive.

"Aw, that's kid's stuff, really," Cliff said, washing down a bite of pretzel with a swig of beer. "Ever hear of a cannonballer called the Great Wilno? I was his trigger puller for two years. At the New York World's Fair he cannonballed over a gigantic Ferris wheel and into his net. The guy he's got working for him now, Hank DuBois, catapults over *two* Ferris wheels."

"Wow!"

"Scobey Moser won't let me jump over his Ferris wheel—he's afraid I'll kill myself and someone on the ride, too—so I go for distance instead. I've been in this game for five years, I may not be the best but I was taught by one of the best—Wilno—and someday I *will* be the best." He took a swallow of beer. "Ella Carver's one of the best too, you've got a great teacher."

"I know it." She finished her pretzel and said, "What got you into it?"

"Wanted to be a trapeze artist. Wanted to fly. First time I saw Wilno, I thought: Man, that's like flying a V-2 rocket! The speed hooked me, and the challenge of going higher, farther, faster—that's what keeps me hooked.

"But higher and faster also brings in bigger dough and gets you booked on better circuits," he said. "I don't want to end up as a forty-miler."

"What's that?"

"A carny who never travels farther than forty miles from home," he said with disdain. "I want to see the world and I want the world to see *me*."

They talked for a little while longer, then Toni looked at the time—was it really almost midnight?—and said her goodbyes. "It's been really nice meeting you," she said, "but I better be turning in."

"Yeah, me too," Cliff said. "Nice meeting you too, Toni."

Toni watched him go. Cliff had big ambitions—and he was also kind of delish. But after Slim she wasn't about to jump into anything.

After Wellington the Central show jumped to Great Bend, then to Dodge City for its annual Boot Hill Celebration. The carnival was torn down and resurrected every five to six days in a succession of small towns, and Toni continued collecting press clippings from newspapers like the *Emporia Gazette,* the *Belleville Telescope,* the *Iola Register,* and the *Arkansas Valley Home.* She mailed these to her father along with her letters from the road, partly out of pride and partly to reassure him she was alive and unhurt.

She was having the time of her life.

Also pleasant was the continued attention she received from the quietly persistent Cliff. She'd finish a show and he'd be there, talking shop with Ella for a while before he and Toni would go grab some hot dogs, burgers, or coffee, talking about what they loved to do and dreaming about the time when they would make it big.

About the only drawback to carny life was the occasional after-closing party, which could get boisterous—Cliff dragged her to one, but Toni was not a party person and left after half an hour. Even Arlan, a quiet man most of the time, got a little boisterous when he brought company "home" to his corner mattress in the truck. It was always late at night, after Toni and Ella had gone to bed, and Toni never saw or heard any of the women, just Arlan's grunts and groans; but the vibrations from the bucking mattress were prodigious and traveled through the trailer hitch and into the motor home, causing the aluminum flooring to oscillate with desire.

First Toni and then Ella—lying in their bunks, trying to get some sleep—broke into a fit of the giggles. Ella chuckled and said softly, "I'm glad the Lord made him such a strong, healthy man, but—if that floor doesn't stop tremblin' like this, I may have to go to confession tomorrow." Toni whooped; this was the first remotely dirty thing she had ever heard Ella say. "Hush up, you. First thing tomorrow I'm unhooking that towbar."

That seemed to solve the problem, and the act moved on to county fairs in Scott City and Goodland, Kansas.

In mid-June, on a cloudy, drizzly morning in Goodland, Toni was making a practice dive from ninety feet when a spray of rain blew in on a gust of wind just as Toni was launching herself off the platform. She didn't notice anything dire at first, but as she came out of her somersault she saw that the tank below was moving *away* from her: the wind had rattled the tower and sent her off at the wrong angle.

Fighting panic, Toni twisted her body to the left, trying to reverse her trajectory. It was only this that saved her from an even worse fate: she straightened her body as best she could, entering the water mere inches from the tank wall. She missed colliding with it, but entered the water at an eighty-degree angle—it felt as though her entire left side had been slammed against a concrete wall, she heard very clearly the sound of her ribs cracking, a fiery lancet of pain stabbing from her waist to her armpit. Between the pain and the crash into the water she had no breath left in her as she sank like a brick to the bottom, bruising her right hip in the bargain.

She thought of Anne Booker Ringens, and then she blacked out.

When she came to, she was being carried out of the water by Arlan, who had her slung over his shoulder as he climbed the ladder. On the catwalk he set her down on her back as she began coughing up water and Ella squatted down to examine her.

"I—I'm okay," Toni stammered, but when she tried to sit up the fire in her side flared up and she fell back down.

"Hell you are," Ella said. "Can you breathe all right?"

Toni took a breath. "My side hurts when I breathe."

"Try it again." This time Ella put her ear to Toni's chest, listening, then brought her head up. "No rattle, I think you managed to avoid puncturing a lung. But you've broken at least a couple of ribs." She turned to Arlan. "Find out if there's a hospital in this little burg, she'll need X-rays."

"Oh God," Toni whispered, "I'm sorry . . ."

"Wasn't your fault," Ella said, "it was the wind. Wind's the only thing I'm scared of, and this is why. Lord, I hate wind."

Cliff quickly got word of what had happened and rushed to the scene, offering to take Toni and Ella to the hospital in one of the Chevy sedans he used in his act. Toni readily agreed, only to find herself hurtling across the Great Plains at ninety miles an hour. Cliff liked speed, all right. "For God's sake, Cliff," Ella told him, "she's just got a couple of cracked ribs! If we spin out in this hot rod of yours she'll crack her skull open too!"

"Sorry, sorry." Cliff eased off the accelerator and they arrived safely at Boothroy Memorial Hospital, a two-story, redbrick building that looked more like a school than a hospital. But everyone there knew their business, X-rays were taken, and a doctor confirmed to Toni that she had fractured two ribs and severely bruised the cartilage surrounding three more. The doctor iced the ribs to get the swelling down as best he could, then taped the ribs with surgical gauze. "When you get home, ice the ribs, twenty minutes on, twenty minutes off, for the next few hours," he told her, "and take two aspirin every six hours. If the pain becomes too severe, call me, I can prescribe you something stronger."

"How long will it take to heal, Doctor?" Toni asked hopefully.

"Usually? About six weeks."

"Six weeks!" Toni said in horror.

"Sorry. Get as much rest as you can, no exertion, no jumping off ninety-foot ladders, and you should be fine in about a month and a half."

Toni didn't know whether she should be depressed at being sidelined again, or just grateful to be alive. Though she grumbled when Ella told her, back at the carnival, to lay down in the trailer and get some rest, she fell almost instantly asleep and didn't wake up until that evening, well after Ella's fire dive. Arlan helped her outside and they sat at a card table eating grab-stand hamburgers, French fries, and root beer. Then, to Toni's surprise, Ella came out of the trailer holding a cupcake with a single lit candle in it, and placed it in front of Toni.

"What's this for?" Toni asked.

"Congratulations, you've just passed your baptism of fire as a high diver: your first broken bones. I've cracked ribs, broken legs, gotten second- and third-degree burns on my hands, and can't count the number of times I've had to wear beefsteak on my eyes to take out black-and-blue marks before I could perform. I lived to dive again, and so will you."

Toni felt a bit better hearing this, and the cupcake wasn't bad either.

But it was frustrating to sit on the sidelines as Ella performed alone. Toni got the rest her doctor ordered, but the time she spent napping in the trailer was equal to the tense hours she spent inside listening, on the radio, to the unfolding crisis in Korea. On June 25, Communist North Korea had, without warning, invaded its neighbor to the south, the democratic Republic of Korea. Within four days the South Korean capital, Seoul, had fallen. A day later, under the auspices of a United Nations mandate to repel the invaders, President Truman announced he was sending American troops to aid South Korea in driving the North Koreans back above the 38th Parallel. Toni grew fearful that her father, a member of the Naval Reserves, might be ordered back to duty in this latest war, and placed a long-distance telephone call one morning to find out whether he was all right.

But Eddie just laughed and said, "They're not reactivating old farts like me pushing forty, especially not when we have children to support.

Don't worry about it. Hey, those clippings you sent are mighty impressive. I'm glad to see you're doing so well, and all in one piece, too."

Toni laughed nervously, which only made her ribs hurt more, a literal stab of irony. "Yeah, everything's going great," she lied.

"Been a few weeks since I got the last one, you too busy to write Dad?"

"Yeah, busy," she said, then, making a quick verbal U-turn, "So, are you back at Palisades this season?"

"Yeah, one more season and I figure I'll have enough in the bank to open that—thing we discussed."

"How's Jack?"

"He's right here, want to talk to him?"

Jack came on the phone, breathless: "Holy cow, Sis, have you seen what's going on in Korea? These dirty Reds launched a sneak attack, just like the Japs did at Pearl Harbor!"

"Yeah, sounds awful."

Then, with the same breathless excitement: "Toni, guess what? I've been accepted at the Pratt Art Institute in Brooklyn! All the big-name artists have gone there, even cartoonists like Jack Kirby and Gus Edson—"

"That's terrific, Jack, congratulations!"

They talked awhile longer and Toni hung up, vastly relieved that her father would not be going off to war.

Now she was able to relax, at least. Cliff visited at least once a day, sometimes spiriting her off—always at something approaching the speed of sound—in his Chevy for lunch at one of the town restaurants. After lunch he would kiss her goodbye, the kisses becoming ever more ardent; either I'm going stir-crazy, Toni thought, or I'm starting to fall for this guy. Luckily her fractured ribs prevented things from getting out of hand—but they didn't prevent her from *thinking* about things getting out of hand.

At other times Toni would just sit outside Ella's trailer with her or Arlan, who had played Coney Island's Luna Park in its heyday and was a sideshow star with Barnum & Bailey for years. It seemed to Toni like quite a comedown from Barnum and Luna Park, and she asked him delicately, "Do you ever miss being a performer?"

"I still am performer," he declared without batting an eye. "I perform so *you* can perform, you and Miss Ella. Everyone is performer in a carny."

Toni smiled. "I guess they are, at that."

"I like working shows. Show people don't care where you come from. Don't care what your real name is, what you did before, who you take to bed with you. They only care you do your job."

All at once, it clicked—the bucking mattress, the grunts and groans: there were two *men* in bed.

And like a true carny, Toni didn't care.

She smiled and said, "And sometimes more than your job—like rescuing waterlogged high divers."

"Ah," he said, waving a hand, "you do the same for me."

Yes, Toni thought again, this was very much like Palisades.

By August Toni's pain was gone and the show doctor pronounced her ribs healed. Gingerly, she began practicing her routines in the morning from a cautious forty-foot height, and when after a few days she felt no ill effects, she climbed up to the full ninety feet. She had a moment's fear standing on the platform, the panic of the botched dive still raw in her memory, but reminded herself that that had been the fault of an errant wind and not anything she had done wrong—and there wasn't a breath of wind, at the moment, on the great plains surrounding Phillipsburg, Kansas. She looked down, gauged her distance, then leapt into the air, tucking herself into a ball and tumbling end-over-end before straightening her legs. As she plummeted toward the tank she felt a calm exhilaration, the spinning Ferris wheel a garish blur of color and motion that thrilled and comforted her with its presence; she hit the water and entered her safe, quiet place of triumph.

She dove that afternoon during Ella's first performance, repeating her routine flawlessly, surfacing to the cheers of the crowd. She hadn't realized how much she had missed that sound until now.

Perhaps it was her exhilaration at performing again, or simply the growing sexual tension between them, but when, after dinner in town that night, Cliff asked Toni, "Would you like to come back to my trailer?"—she looked at him, at his sparkling eyes, and found herself say-ing, nervously, "I'd like to, but—first—you should know, I've . . . never done this before."

"There's a first time for everybody, hon," he said gently. "If you can dive into a Dixie cup, you can do this."

"And second, the last thing this show needs is a pregnant high diver."

Cliff slipped a hand into his pocket and pulled out—discreetly, so that only she could see—a paper-wrapped Deer Skin brand prophylactic.

"I always wear a helmet," he said, "before I take a flying jump."

She laughed, kissed him hard, then went with him to the trailer.

There she discovered that Ella was wrong about those "best damn three seconds of your life." This lasted considerably more than three sec-onds, and diving was at best a close second.

After five days at Phillipsburg the show moved on to the Nebraska State Rodeo in Burwell, Nebraska, for five days; a fair in Norton, Kansas, for another five days; and then Abilene, Kansas, for an eight-day engage-ment ending August 29. There were seven more major fairs on the schedule in Texas and Oklahoma, but Ella had promised to appear at the St. Petersburg Lions Club's Labor Day Festival on September 6 as she had the past two years, and she was not about to disappoint the hometown crowd. So as Central States Shows made the jump to its own Labor Day commitment in Holzington, Kansas, Toni kissed Cliff good-bye and she, Ella, and Arlan headed south to Florida. Ella would play the St. Pete Festival on the sixth, then hit the road and head west, meet-ing up with the Central show in time for the Cimarron Territory Cele-bration and Fair in Beaver, Oklahoma.

They arrived in St. Petersburg on September 2 and began erecting the tower and tank amidst the carnival-like rides and concessions the Lions Club had set up on Sunset Beach. The next day, word came in that a "baby hurricane," as some in the press were calling it, was entering the Gulf of Mexico. Storm warnings for Hurricane Easy—soon to belie its name— were issued from Key West to Pensacola. Ella gazed nervously at the ocean as the tide in Tampa Bay rose six and a half feet, a thirty-year high.

"Son of a bitch," she muttered to herself. But it was too late to do anything about it.

Hurricane Easy blew haphazardly up the coast, causing among other disasters a dam rupture that flooded the north Tampa community of Sulphur Springs with two feet of water, destroying some forty homes. Tides of between six and eight feet, fed by raging winds, immersed beachfront property from St. Petersburg to Clearwater to Sarasota, turning roads into rivers, smashing beach homes to splinters, and sinking boats.

Ella, Toni, and Arlan drove the truck and trailer inland and rode out the storm in a public shelter. By September 8, the hurricane departed Florida as a tropical storm, dying out over Georgia, and Ella returned to Sunset Beach to find that Hurricane Easy had been anything but on her equipment. The diving tower had been blown off its feet, the winds snapping it apart section by section, mangling and twisting them like licorice sticks. The tank had rolled on its side some distance before it, too, burst apart, some pieces vaguely identifiable while others had simply vanished, washed into the sea.

"Oh my God," Toni said softly.

"Jesus Kristus," Arlan murmured under his breath.

Ella stared at the wreckage with a mixture of shock, grief, and anger. "Didn't I tell you?" She shook her head disgustedly. "I *hate* wind."

The hurricane had destroyed three thousand dollars' worth of equipment, and Ella wasn't sure how much, if anything, her insurance would cover. The Lions Club announced it would hold a benefit on November 9 to raise funds for Ella to replace her equipment, but even if enough money was raised, it would take her months, maybe a year, to put her act back together.

"You're welcome to come back and join me when I do," she told Toni, "but you're a damn good diver. You'll find work." She promised to recommend her to her agent in Miami.

Toni hugged Ella and thanked her for everything she had done for her, then went to the nearest Western Union office and sent off two telegrams: the first one went to Cliff, c/o the Central States Shows, saying:

ELLAS EQUIPMENT DESTROYED BY HURRICANE.
WONT BE RETURNING TO SHOW THIS SEASON.
WILL WRITE MORE LATER. TONI

The second telegram went to her father, telling him she was returning home. The next morning she boarded the *Florida Special*, this time
as a paying passenger all the way to Newark.

Eddie met her at the train station on Monday. If Toni had any
doubts that her ribs were fully healed, Eddie's bear hug dispelled them.
"It's good to see you, Dad."

"Good to see you too, honey. Look at you, a veteran carny now! I'm
proud of you, Toni. I haven't stopped worrying, but I'm proud of you."

"Thanks, Dad." She hugged him again, then Eddie picked up her bags
and they started outside. "Jack's in Brooklyn, we found him a nice room in
a boardinghouse on DeKalb Avenue. He starts classes next week."

"That's great," Toni said with a smile, "I'm happy for him."

"By the way," Eddie said as they went to his parked car on the street,
"you mind if we make a stop? There's something I'd like you to show you."

When they reached Fort Lee, instead of turning right on Route 5 toward Edgewater, Eddie continued down Palisade Avenue until they
pulled into the parking lot of a small, one-story structure—a boarded-
up roadstand, with a marquee sign stripped of its name—squatting on a
tiny parcel of land about two miles north of the amusement park.

They got out of the car, Eddie pulled out a key from his hip pocket
and inserted it in the door lock. "It's just about the perfect size for what
I need," he said. He walked in, Toni following. "So what do you think?"

It was hard for Toni to tell anything in the dimly lit room, the electricity having been turned off; but Eddie, looking more animated than
Toni had seen him in years, hurried to the only window not boarded up,
rolled up the shade, and let as much sunlight in as he could. "It doesn't
look like much now," he admitted, "but it's got real potential."

Toni looked around at the old roadhouse with its dark wood paneling and floors. It was essentially one room, maybe eight hundred square feet, with about a dozen sets of tables and chairs (the chairs now resting upside down on the tabletops) and a wooden bar about twenty feet long. The barstools had seen better days, as had the mirror—cracked in several places—behind the bar. The empty shelves that had once contained bottles of liquor sagged even with no weight on them. Toni thought it looked small and kind of depressing, but by the smile on her father's face she could see he clearly thought otherwise.

"It used to serve hot dogs and hamburgers, like Hiram's," Eddie said, pointing toward a pair of swinging doors next to the bar, "so it's got a small kitchen, but big enough for me to make *pūpūs.*"

"Poo whats?"

"Appetizers, Hawaiian style, like *kālua* pork spareribs. People will mainly come for the drinks at first, but I want the food to be good too, and maybe in time we can expand to a full dinner menu."

She peeked into the kitchen, the stove looking more grease-encrusted than the one at the French fry stand, and smiled wanly.

"Dad, don't you think it'll take a lot of—work—to remodel . . . ?"

"Oh hell yes," he agreed. "This is just a dump now, I know that. I'll have to strip the wood floor, lighten it—replace as much of it with bamboo as I can—fill in the windows with drywall and plaster . . ."

"What? You can barely see in here as it is!"

"No no, you don't want windows looking out onto Palisade Avenue, it'll spoil the illusion that you're in the tropics."

Right now it looked about as tropical as the inside of Grant's Tomb, but her father looked so excited—and it had been so long, it seemed, that he had *been* excited by anything—that Toni was reluctant to dampen his enthusiasm. "How much rent do they want for this?" she asked.

"Oh, I'm not renting," Eddie said blithely. "I bought it."

Toni felt as if she had been pushed, backward, at ninety feet up.

"You . . . bought it?"

"You bet. It was only twelve grand! Hell, there's a gas station down the road that sold at close-out prices for eighteen, this was a steal."

One of the concession agents at the Central Show, a gentile with a nonetheless vast command of Yiddish, sometimes used a hybrid exclamation that Toni found amusing: *"Oy* dear," a combination of *"Oy vey"* and "Oh dear."

Toni looked around the grimy little tavern and thought: *Oy dear.*

She tried desperately to see it as her father did: decorated with wicker tables, adorned with ferns, an exotic, charming, tropical retreat.

Nope. She saw only a dank, narrow, costly little shoebox of a tavern that would need months of scrubbing, repairing, painting, and God knew what else before anyone would step willingly through its dark doorway.

But he'd actually purchased the place—what else could she do? She couldn't let him lose his life's savings without trying to make it a success.

"Well, I'm 'at liberty,' as they say, for the winter," she said, feigning enthusiasm and a bright smile. "So let's get to work."

But inside she was still thinking: *Oy dear.*

19

THAT NIGHT, TONI WROTE a short letter to Cliff, telling him she'd returned to New Jersey and was helping her dad start up a new business. She talked about the hurricane and how it knocked apart Ella's equipment like a petulant child smashing his Tinkertoys. And she ended by saying *I miss you, wish I could be with you. Please write soon, Love, Toni.*

She agonized before signing it—"Sincerely" seemed ridiculous and "Best Wishes" sounded like a birthday card—finally deciding to hell with it, and wrote *Love.* If that scared him off, then it wasn't meant to be.

According to Central States' tour schedule, the show would open at the Cimarron Territory Celebration this Thursday, September 14—and so she addressed the envelope to Cliff at the Central States Shows, c/o General Delivery at Beaver, Oklahoma, and mailed it first thing the next morning.

After the post office she and her dad returned to work on the tavern. The power was now turned on, but to Toni's dismay, electricity only served to illuminate how truly dirty and dingy the place was. Toni hauled all the heavy walnut-stained tables and chairs out back, then called the Salvation Army to come take it all away. With Eddie's okay she threw in what was left of the glassware, particularly the big beer steins that conjured images not of the South Seas but of the Sudetanland. Eddie swept the bare floors, kicking up dust devils big enough to carry them both to

Oz, but didn't bother to do so to the faded linoleum because he immediately began tearing it up. Toni scrubbed down the mahogany bar, since Eddie planned to strip off the dark stain, lighten the countertop, and add a bamboo facade to the front.

"So where do we get bamboo in New Jersey?" Toni asked.

"Bill Holahan at the lumberyard can order it for us from a supplier in the Philippines. They also carry rattan, which we're going to need too."

It was a long week—Toni and Eddie spent an entire day scrubbing years of accumulated grease off the kitchen stove, cleaning the oven, which was caked black with burnt food drippings, and scouring the sink and counters with Ajax. She was bone tired at the end of the day, but it was a vacation compared to the next, when they attacked the restrooms. The sight of the filthy urinals made her gag and she told her father, "This one's yours, I'll take the ladies' room," and Eddie didn't object. Toni went through two bottles of Lysol and a can of Ajax before the little girls' room looked remotely like a place a little girl could enter without contracting scabies.

By the end of the week, all Toni could think was that she had gone from an exciting new career as a high diver to an unpaid janitor's position. She was careful never to show her dismay to her father, who even as he mopped the men's room floor was enthusiastically telling her about the rattan wallpaper that would spruce up the room's dank-looking walls. But try as she may, she couldn't imagine how this squalid little place was going to be transformed into the thing of beauty her father envisioned.

Jack arrived on Friday after a long bus ride from Brooklyn, excited to hear about his sister's adventures on the midway and eager to tell her about his first semester of classes at the Pratt Institute. He was majoring in illustration but, like all first-year students, was required to take "foundation" courses—Creative Design, Structural Representation, Color, Fine Arts, and, for some unfathomable reason, Physical Education. "I thought my last game of softball was long behind me," he said, bemused, "but maybe getting picked last for a team prepares you psychologically for an artist's life."

After dinner they watched *The Camel News Caravan,* NBC's nightly fifteen-minute newscast with John Cameron Swayze, who announced the first good news from the war in Korea: U.S. Marines had landed at Inchon, one of the Communist North's most vital ports, and were in the process of securing it. "Finally," Jack said, "something's going *right* for the U.S."

Toni discovered there was more to this family reunion when after the news Jack opened his art portfolio and said, "I've done a few sketches for the murals—see if you like any of these . . ."

This was news to Toni. "Murals?"

"I want a couple of wall murals," Eddie explained. "A Hawaiian garden, maybe, or a stand of palm trees—something bright and tropical."

"Here's one I worked up," Jack said, flipping over the pages of a large sketchbook, "for behind the bar." He tilted the sketchbook to show Eddie and Toni a rough sketch of a long beach bordered by tall coconut palms—shown in perspective, so that the nearest tree showed only the base of the trunk and the farthest, tallest ones sported feathery palm fronds—as on the right of the page, frothy ocean waves lapped up the beach.

"Jack, that's perfect!" Eddie said with enthusiasm. "It's got everything— the palm trees, the beach, the ocean . . ."

"It'll have the same dimensions as the mirror behind the bar," Jack said. "Toss the mirror, but keep the frame—it'll help sell the illusion that the customer's looking through an imaginary window at a faraway beach."

"Jack, this is really good," Toni said, though wondering to herself if they weren't a little bit crazy talking about imaginary windows into the South Seas. "But will this really make anybody think, even for a moment, that they're anywhere but in Fort Lee, New Jersey?"

"I don't blame you for being a little skeptical," Eddie said. "That's why I'm taking you both out to dinner tomorrow night—in Merchantville."

"Merchantville!" Toni blurted. "Isn't that practically in Pennsylvania?"

"Yeah, pretty close. It's a two-hour drive."

"What's in Merchantville?" Jack asked.

"Something you have to see" was all Eddie said, and they couldn't get a peep out of him until they actually arrived there.

Growing up in New Jersey, Toni and Jack had a native fondness for the sometimes gigantic, often whimsical roadside attractions—signs, statuary, odd-shaped buildings—that fruited on the Jersey landscape as giant redwoods did in Northern California, or as towering derricks forested the Texas oil fields. Aside from the colossal attractions at Palisades, the first one Toni remembered seeing was the sixty-foot bottle of Hoffman's Dry Ginger Ale Soda—a water tower remodeled into a twenty-five-ton bottle of pop—that sat atop the Hoffman beverage brewery in Newark. (It had, five years ago, been upgraded from ginger ale to beer, which Hoffman also brewed.) There was the two-story-tall green brontosaurus on Route 9 in Bayville, which once advertised a taxidermy shop. There was a house shaped like a windmill in Barnegat and another in the form of a pirate ship that had dropped anchor in Old Bridge. But the undisputed queen of New Jersey gigantism was Lucy the Elephant, a sixty-five-foot gray elephant—with contradictory male tusks—bearing a howdah carriage on her back, built in 1881 as a realty office-cum-tourist attraction. Whenever Toni or Jack would spy one of these colossi on vacation with their parents, the sight of them would give them a little shiver of wonder that such grandly eccentric creations flourished in their own backyard.

So now, as Eddie drove down Route 38 into Merchantville, Toni was surprised to find herself getting that same little shiver she had as a child. Up ahead was a restaurant, most of it a long, low building with orange walls and a pitched roof of neutral color. What made the establishment unique was a round annex with a yellow domed roof scored in a repeated diamond pattern, with a crown of green "leaves" projecting up out of the roof.

"Holy Hannah, it's a giant pineapple!" Toni cried in delight.

"Two stories tall," Jack said, echoing her delight.

"So it is," Eddie noted with a smile.

In front of the giant pineapple was a sign identifying it as the HAWAIIAN COTTAGE—DINNERS—COCKTAILS—LUNCHEON.

"Look, there are even windows on the ground floor of the pineapple!"

"This beats the hell out of the windmill house," Jack decided.

"This place was built back in '38," Eddie said with a smile as he pulled into the parking lot. "I think the pineapple used to be a coconut. I've been to every South Seas place in the tri-state area—Hawai'i Kai in Manhattan, the Hawaiian Room at the Hotel Lexington, even another Hawaiian Room at the Teterboro Country Club—but I like this place the best."

He led them inside, where a hostess in a sarong ushered them into the main dining room. The interior decor was just as impressive: bamboo tables and chairs upholstered with colorful Hawaiian floral designs; ersatz palm trees, tall bamboo poles topped with fake ferns; and farther down, what looked like fishing floats hanging in nets from the ceiling. The walls were covered with rattan, along with several large murals of South Pacific and Hawaiian scenery. There was a bandstand, empty for the moment, and a rectangular bar topped by a round thatched roof that looked like a grass hat. Soft Hawaiian music was playing over the PA system.

The dinner menu consisted mostly of seafood platters, pasta, prime rib, steaks, salads, and sandwiches, though they also offered some Chinese fare like chicken chow mein and a Chinese pepper steak. "The food's not very Hawaiian," Eddie admitted, "but everything else is pretty authentic."

Now, as a saronged waitress took their dinner orders—Eddie ordered prime rib, Jack the exotic-sounding pepper steak, and Toni the chow mein—the light in the dining room changed and bright tropical day gave way to a sultry island night. The fishing floats hanging from the ceiling began to glow red and white, casting the room in rosy tones of sunset that gradually deepened to a lush crimson; it felt as if they were sitting inside a volcano, painted by the light of fiery lava. Waitresses lit the candle holders on each table, the rows and rows of white glowing candles reminding Toni of votive candles in church—but the statuary the candles illuminated here were not of saints, but the kind of strange pagan gods her father liked to carve.

Then, as their dinners arrived, the crowning touch: hundreds of previously invisible lights, strung from the ceiling, sparked to life, and Toni and Jack looked up to find the ceiling awash with "stars." The heavens had descended from the sky, constellations from another hemisphere floating just a few feet above them, close enough to reach out and touch.

"Oh, wow," Toni said in hushed tones. "*Now* I get it."

A band of genuine Hawaiian musicians ascended to the bandstand; the twang of steel guitars being tuned, unlike any instrument Toni had ever heard, echoed in the sunset light and sent shivers of unexpected pleasure through Toni's body. Their voices were almost like whispers as the band began playing a traditional island melody, "Hawai'i Aloha."

Sitting under starlight that seemed nearly as magical as any Eddie had seen in island skies, he and his children took in the same sort of sweet music and sensuous beauty that had entranced him seven years ago—and for the first time, Toni and Jack understood.

Dinner was delicious, and on the drive back home, Toni asked, "So what are you planning to call this tropic isle in exotic Fort Lee?"

Eddie hesitated, then admitted, "I've been thinking of calling it 'Eddie's Polynesia on the Palisades.'"

Jack smiled.

Toni said, "I like it."

"It's alliterative," Jack noted.

"It's perfect," Toni said with a smile that warmed her father's heart.

Before the weather grew too cold, Eddie started work on the bar's wooden exterior. He couldn't perform miracles—it would never be a little grass shack—but he could repaint the wooden facade, choosing a light tropical green for the walls and a dark brown for the pitched roof. He replaced the old entrance door with a new one made of polished *koa* wood, decorated with *tiki* designs. Toni had no idea what he was up to when he began constructing a short arbored walkway in front of the entrance. The roof of the arbor he built in an A-frame shape, which both echoed the shape of the pitched roof and was inspired by the grass huts Eddie had seen in the South Pacific. But it wasn't until the roofing materials arrived from Mexico that Toni saw the similarity: Eddie covered the peaked arbor with the kind of thatch grass that formed the roof of the bar in the Hawaiian Cottage.

The Cottage's owners, Michael and Mary Egidi, generously shared with Eddie their supplier for this and other decorations. Toni pored over wallpaper catalogs until she found a rattan pattern her father liked, measured the square footage of wall space, then placed an order for three double-roll bolts. When Eddie's bamboo arrived from the Philippines, he sawed the bamboo sticks in half lengthwise and glued them to the base of the bar; the resulting facade looked like one of the bamboo thickets on Espíritu Santo. He used a thicker piece of bamboo for the bar railing. Then he filled in the tavern's three windows with drywall, plastered them over, and papered them with rattan.

Eddie had a huge collection of *tikis*, of course, with which to decorate the interior, and a few *tiki* mugs of his own design. But he wanted some of those colorful ceramic hula girl glasses he had seen at Trader Vic's, and so last year had written them in Honolulu asking where they obtained those swell glasses and was it possible for him to purchase some for his little bar in New Jersey? With typical Hawaiian hospitality the owner, Granville Abbott, wrote back saying that their hula mugs and other Hawaiian tableware were manufactured by a company called Vernon Kilns, in California, and that though they were an exclusive license, Eddie was welcome to buy a half a dozen cases from the manufacturer if they had some in stock.

The kiln was not only happy to accommodate Eddie, but ran those hundred-plus hula mugs off the assembly line without the "Trader Vic's Ltd., Honolulu, Hawaii" imprimatur on the bottom. When the mugs arrived, Eddie was delighted to find they were the same long glasses with bas-reliefs of a black-haired, bare-breasted hula girl in a *lei* and grass skirt on one side, while on the other another Hawaiian maiden knelt on the grass reaching up for some forbidden island fruit.

At Palisades, Eddie had also taken note of some little chalk hula girl figurines being given away as prizes in one of Harry Frankel's concessions, and bought a few dozen from him to be used as table and bar ornaments.

Meanwhile, six weeks had passed without Toni receiving a response to her letter from Cliff. Now she asked Minette, "Should I write him again?"

Minette shook her head. "You sent him a telegram, wrote him a letter—if he wanted to write he would. Don't go chasing after him, forgiving him for how he's ignoring you, like I did with Jay all those years." Gently she said, "It happens, honey. Carny romances seem so real and passionate when you're on the road, but off the midway, they tend to fade away. I'm sorry."

Toni nodded, bravely coming to terms with the loss; then in early November came an envelope in the mailbox return-addressed *Central States Shows c/o General Delivery, Tampa, Florida.* She tore it open and read:

Hey, Toni—

I miss the hell out of you too, the circuit's been no fun without you. Sorry to hear about Ella's equipment—that sounds like some storm!

I'll try to get up your way after the show returns to winter quarters in a month. But if I can't, we won't be apart long, I promise!

Listen, not to step on Ella's toes, but I took the liberty of talking with Scobey Moser about you. He saw you perform and thinks you're pretty damn swell. If Ella can't return to the circuit by next spring, Scobey's of a mind to have you replace her. He knows you don't do the fancy fire dive, but he thinks you're pretty, a helluva gymnast, and the crowds love you. He'll pay twenty bucks a dive, three dives daily—not bad, and we'll be together again!

Talk to Ella, see what's what. If she's coming back, great, you can come back as her assistant; if not, you can headline your own act! What do you think about "Terrific Toni Stopka" for a handle? 'Cause I happen to think you're pretty terrific.

Love and kisses,
Cliff

Her heart beating like one of those Polynesian drums at the Hawaiian Cottage, Toni immediately ran to her father and asked, "Dad, is it all right if I make a long-distance call to Florida? I need to talk with Ella Carver."

"Sure, go ahead."

Toni called Ella, whose motor home was still firmly rooted in St. Petersburg, and asked how she was coming along replacing her equipment.

"Ah, not so great," Ella said. "The Lions Club held a benefit to raise money for me, bless 'em, but it wasn't enough to replace all I lost. Looks like I've got to take a nine-to-five job to raise more funds."

"I have a thousand dollars saved up, would that help?"

"That's sweet of you, honey, but I can't take your money. You worked your fanny off to earn it, you should get to keep it."

"So you won't be going on the road with Central States next year?"

Ella laughed ruefully. "Maybe not even the year after that."

Trying not to sound too delighted at her friend's misfortune, Toni told her about Cliff's conversation with Scobey Moser and his offer to let Toni headline next season. To her relief, Ella wasn't annoyed at all:

"That's great, honey, I'm proud of you. Scobey wouldn't make that offer if he didn't think you were ready, and I think he's right."

"And I'm going to send you part of my salary," Toni offered, "to help with buying your new equipment."

"Before you do that, hon, you given any thought to where you're getting *your* equipment?"

Toni's spirits plunged as quickly as if she'd taken a ninety-foot dive. "No," she admitted. "It never crossed my mind."

"I can put you in touch with the right suppliers," Ella offered, "but the equipment's not cheap—it'll set you back about three grand. Plus you'll need a truck to haul it, money to pay a rigger . . ."

"Damn it, I don't have that kind of money."

"Can your father help out?"

"He wouldn't last time, I can't ask him again. Besides, he's in the middle of his own project, and it isn't cheap."

"Then do what I did," Ella said. "You're starting a business—go get a bank loan. I'd do it again if I weren't still paying off my last loan."

Toni didn't want to go to her father's bank in Edgewater, so she picked one out of a phone book—the Hudson Trust Company on Palisade Avenue in Cliffside Park—walked right in, and asked to see a loan officer. She expected a fat, balding, prosperous-looking man like the bankers you saw in movies, but was instead led to the desk of a young, broad-shouldered man in his mid-twenties with a full head of hair—fiery red hair, at that. He stood, smiled, extended a hand: "Hi, Jimmy Russo. Nice to meet you."

"Toni Stopka. Pleased to meet you too."

"Please, have a seat."

As he pulled out a chair for her, she couldn't help but stare curiously at his hair. Finally she asked, "Russo—isn't that Italian?"

He grinned, quite unlike the sober banker she had pictured in her mind. "Italian father, Irish mother. I got her hair and his shoulders, which is probably better than the other way around."

She laughed. "I was wondering."

"When I was a kid they called me 'the red guinea.' I turned it into a noble title, like the Scarlet Pimpernel: 'Don't trifle with the Red Guinea.'" She laughed again. "There's my childhood in so many words. So what can I do for you, Miss Stopka?"

"I need a loan. I'm starting up a business."

He took a loan application form, began to fill it in. "S-T-O-P-K-A?"

"That's right. And Toni with an *i*. Legally, it's Antoinette."

"Age? Sorry, this is required information . . ."

"I'll be twenty next March."

He looked surprised but said nothing, just lowered his head and made another notation. "And what kind of business is it you want to start?"

"High diving."

His head popped up, and his eyes—they were hazel, a genetic compromise—stared at her in complete bafflement. "Come again?"

"I'm a high diver. I jump from the top of a ninety-foot ladder into a tank of water six feet deep."

A smile tugged at his mouth. "And you do this without dying?"

"Haven't yet," she said. Toni opened her purse and pulled out a handful of her press clippings and handed them to him. "Here. I apprenticed with Ella Carver, the best female high diver in the world."

He studied the clippings and his smile of skepticism became one of bemusement. "Wow. You're not kidding. You really jump off ninety-foot ladders." He looked up. "I didn't think girls did things like this."

Ignoring her irritation at that, she said, "Some of us do."

"And you make a living at this?"

"I've got an offer from a carnival to pay me twenty dollars a dive, three dives a day. You spend about ten days out of each month traveling, so it averages out to about three hundred dollars a week, April through October."

Doing the math, Jimmy Russo paused, then noted, a bit nonplussed, "Over eight thousand dollars for seven months' work—that's twice my annual salary. I knew I should've run off to the circus when I was a kid." They both laughed at that. "So you have a contract with this carnival?"

"Uh, no. But they're an established company—Central States Shows."

"Try to get at least a letter of intent. Have you held any other jobs?"

She told him about working her father's concession at Palisades Park and her salary there, and at the mention of Palisades, a broad smile crinkled the freckles on Russo's nose. "I used to *love* the annual Cliffside Park school picnic to Palisades," he said fondly. "I attended School No. 5 and we'd march down Palisade Avenue with the school band in front, picking up kids from other schools along the way. Did you go on those?"

"Only once, in kindergarten. Then I transferred to Edgewater."

"Two thousand kids, overrunning the park like Munchkins in Oz. Man, that was fun. I loved riding the old steel Cyclone." Then, forcing himself to return to business: "All right—so what exactly do you need in the way of a loan? What *are* the start-up costs for a high diver?"

"Three thousand dollars to purchase my equipment—the tank, tower, rigging—and maybe another fifteen hundred for a truck to carry it."

"Forty-five hundred total, okay. What kind of collateral do you have?"

She blinked. "Uh . . . what's that?"

"Real estate, savings, stocks and bonds—to secure the loan."

Embarrassed, she admitted, "Well, I've got about a thousand dollars saved from my work with Ella, but . . . that's about it."

He wrote that down, tapped the pencil on the paper for a moment as he studied the figures, then looked up and said, "Well, first of all, let me say that I've never had a more unusual loan application than this, from a more remarkable young woman. But I've got to tell you, I see a few pitfalls: your age, the fact you've just started in this line of work, lack of collateral . . ."

"But I only need less than five thousand dollars, and I'll make eight thousand by the end of next year!"

"That's true, the income to debt ratio works to your advantage. But you have *yet* to earn that much—usually we require an applicant to show two years' worth of tax returns corroborating their income." He looked thoughtfully at her. "Does your father own property?"

"Well, not a house. But he owns his French fry stand at Palisades, and he just bought a tavern, and . . . what does this have to do with me?"

"If your father agreed to cosign the loan," Russo said, "it would stand a better chance of being approved."

"No," Toni said emphatically. "He won't do that, trust me."

Russo sighed. "Well, I can give it a try. We're no strangers here to showpeople, we do business with several concessionaires from the park. But I can't guarantee anything." He handed her the application.

"I understand." She signed the application, handed it back to him.

"It's been great meeting you, Miss Stopka," he said, extending a hand. "I'll do my best. I'd like to have you as a customer."

She took his hand and said, "Call me Toni."

"I'm Jimmy. I'll be in touch." He held on to her hand a bit longer than felt businesslike. Flustered, she slipped out of his grip, mumbled a thank you, and hurried out of the bank, feeling Cliff's eyes on her from a thousand miles away.

Predictably, the Hudson Trust Company turned down her loan request despite Jimmy Russo's best efforts, though Toni was told they would reconsider if her father were to cosign. She put aside the letter from the bank and tried without success to think of other ways to earn the money.

When Jack came home for Thanksgiving, he finished the mural behind the bar. It was beautiful. He used watercolors on plasterboard—there was a pastel lightness to the colors, as if illuminated by a bright tropic sun. The palm trees appeared bent by a nearly palpable trade wind, their fronds billowing in the unfelt breeze. The sky was robin's-egg blue, the ocean an exquisite turquoise, white breakers rolling into shore—as waves that had already reached the shore spread fingers of foam up the sandy beach.

"Aw, Jack, this is fantastic!" Eddie said. "It's like you said, a window into the tropics. I couldn't be happier!"

Jack seemed pleased but distracted. Even over Thanksgiving dinner he insisted on listening to the radio for the latest war news—things were going badly for U.N. forces since the entry of Communist Chinese troops into the war on the side of North Korea. Over the long weekend, things got even worse with the defeat of the U.S. Second and Twenty-Fifth Divisions and a general retreat by the Eighth Army. Finally, Eddie asked why the war news was so upsetting to him—he had a deferment, after all, from the draft.

"My friend Johnny Lamarr, from grade school, was drafted earlier this year," Jack admitted, "and last month so was a high school buddy of mine, Rick DeJulio. Every time I hear about the Reds decimating a division, I wonder if Rick or Johnny were in that unit—and whether they're still alive."

"I'd be worried too," Eddie said. "But there's nothing you can do about it, Jack, except keep a prayer in your thoughts for them."

Jack nodded, but hardly seemed consoled.

Also that weekend, Toni was surprised when her father came up to her holding the letter from Hudson Trust Company and said, "Honey, I found this on the dining room hutch. Why didn't you tell me about this? I can loan you forty-five hundred bucks if you need it."

Toni was floored by that. "But you—you told me you couldn't. That if you gave me money and something went wrong, you'd never—"

"That was before you proved yourself," Eddie said. "Okay, sure, I'm still nervous about what you do, but . . . I can't argue that you don't know your stuff. Ella sure thinks so. You're a responsible adult, even if your dad will always think of you as a little girl climbing the Palisades—and part of me will always worry. I'd be happy to give you the cash."

She surprised him by saying, "No. This bar is costing you a fortune, I've seen the bills. All I want is to take on a loan like an adult and pay it off myself. If you cosign it with me, I promise, that's what I'll do."

When Eddie readily agreed, Toni hugged him, and felt quietly proud that she had earned his trust—even if she hadn't told him about the broken ribs. Or even the torn ligament, for that matter . . .

Several days later, the loan was approved. Jimmy Russo was pleased to deposit the money in Toni's new checking account, and said casually, "I've never seen a girl dive off a ninety-foot tower before—any chance I might be able to catch one of your performances in person?"

"That depends. You plan on being in Kansas in April?"

He laughed. "'Fraid not. Maybe you'll play Palisades Park someday?"

"I doubt that," Toni said, so dismissively it startled Jimmy.

When Toni told her father of the exchange he said, "Actually, I hear Irving finally came to some kind of agreement with those people from CORE, and has agreed to let Negroes and Puerto Ricans into the pool."

"I'll believe it when I see it," she said. As far as she was concerned, Palisades was the past; for now, for the future, she had equipment to buy, a career to build—and a boyfriend waiting for her in Kansas.

Toward the end of 1950, as one establishment on Palisade Avenue prepared to open, an old one closed its doors forever—not for want of patronage or word of mouth, but for too *much* publicity.

Beginning in March, when Senator Estes Kefauver began his hearings on Crime in Interstate Commerce, the nation was riveted to its radio and television sets, listening to testimony from both law enforcement officials and alleged mobsters about the extent of underworld operations across the country. Most of the mobsters said little—with the exception of the over-talkative Willie Moretti—but for the first time the public saw the faces of men like Joe Adonis and Frank Costello. The hearings were conducted in fourteen American cities, documenting the deep penetration into all aspects of commerce by the organization known variously as the Syndicate, the Combination, and the Mafia.

In October, in executive session in New York City, Chief Frank Borrell was called to testify and among other things explain how he came by his rich bank account balance—about eighty thousand; he couldn't recall exactly—on a police chief's salary. Borrell claimed it was income from his concessions at Palisades Amusement Park. And even after the committee had heard vast amounts of testimony about Frank Erickson's illegal bookmaking network in Cliffside Park, Borrell insisted, "I can't say there is any gambling in Cliffside," and that he had never had to make a gambling arrest in his town.

Testimony also revealed that the New York authorities had had Joe Adonis's headquarters, Duke's Bar and Grill, under periodic surveillance—including telephone wiretaps—since 1941. Once Adonis and his associates learned they were vulnerable even at Duke's, it was of no further use to them. The restaurant quickly went into bankruptcy, closing late in 1950.

It couldn't save Adonis, who was convicted on gambling charges and sentenced to two to three years in prison in May of the following year. And he would not be the last to find his life upended—or ended.

Ever since 1946, when the real "Trader Vic," Victor Bergeron, published his *Trader Vic's Book of Food and Drink*—followed two years later by *Trader Vic's Bartender's Guide*—Eddie had begun teaching himself the fundamentals of being a bartender. Each book offered hundreds of recipes for such appetizers as crab rangoon and Chinese potstickers, as well as drinks like the Mai Tai, the Zombie, the Fog Cutter, the Scorpion, even Eddie's beloved Singapore Slings. Most required copious amounts of rum, light and dark, but Eddie also stocked up on vodka, sloe gin, brandy, grenadine syrup, curaçao, pineapple juice, and passion fruit nectar.

By now he felt qualified to tend bar, but had neither the skill nor the time to staff his kitchen as well. So at the recommendation of Yuan Chen, who once ran the chop suey restaurant at Palisades, he hired a young Chinese-American cook, Tom Li, to be his chef. They decided on an appetizer menu of traditional Chinese and Cantonese fare like egg rolls and won tons, as well as Hawaiian *pūpūs* like *kālua* pork spareribs and shrimp grilled in coconut oil, *da kine* Eddie had eaten on Hotel Street in Honolulu.

But for Eddie the moment his dream finally became real came in January with the delivery of the new sign, designed by Eddie and made to his specifications: the base, rather than a simple wooden post, resembled the swaybacked trunk of a palm tree; sprouting from the top of the marquee was a spiky silhouette of palm fronds. Enhancing this image was green neon tubing that outlined the trunk and crown of the tree, while the name of the bar itself glowed in sunset-rose neon cursive:

Eddie's Polynesia on the Palisades

The first time he lit the sign, Eddie stared up at it with a mix of pride and wonder that it was real. Up there, emblazoned in light, was his name—along with the two places, wedded here in unlikely combination, that had touched him most deeply in his life. It felt as though the two halves of his heart, once separate, were united at last.

Eddie insisted on opening in February, in the dead of winter—"the perfect time for people looking for a place to warm themselves." And so, on February 7, 1951, Eddie's Polynesia on the Palisades opened with a party of invited guests: Bunty Hill, Minette Dobson, Roscoe and Dorothy Schwarz, and other close friends from Palisades, as well as Eddie's sister Viola and her husband, Hal, and their two kids. They all shook the snow off their boots under the thatch-grass arbor and found themselves being given the once-over by a goggle-eyed Kāne, god of creation, and a scowling Kū, god of war. As the guests crossed the threshold into the bar, the temperature rose to a sultry seventy-two degrees. Then they stopped short at the hostess station—the hostess being Toni, a bit self-conscious in her two-piece floral sarong—and gaped at what they saw around them.

The walls and ceiling of the little tavern were covered in rattan and the floors were hardwood—like the inside of a large and comfortable basket. Bamboo poles vertically accented the walls and crisscrossed the ceiling, from which were suspended floats hung in fishing nets. Everywhere there were plants—ferns and kentia palms, mostly—hanging from the rafters in wicker baskets or forming a jungle line along one of the walls. The furniture was all bamboo, with chairs upholstered in a lush green-and-white Hawaiian floral pattern; each table boasted a chalk figurine of a hula dancer, wicker placemats, and an unlit candle in a white bowl. Behind the bamboo bar were shelves containing every kind of liquor imaginable, arranged around a rectangular frame in which the image of a tropical beach, lapping ocean waves, and swaying palm trees beckoned dreamily. Playing from a speaker was the dulcet melody of Harry Owens's "Sweet Leilani."

Bunty, arm-in-arm with a statuesque brunette, took it all in and said, "Wow. Can I come live here?"

"No, but we can rent you a table for a few hours," Toni said with a grin, picking up a menu. "And it's an open bar today."

"Lead the way," Bunty said, as Toni escorted them to a table.

"Wow." Viola and Hal entered and looked around them in delighted astonishment, as Eddie, wearing a gaudy Hawaiian shirt, greeted them: *"Aloha.* Welcome to Eddie's Polynesia on the Palisades."

He hugged Vi, shook Hal's hand. "Thanks for coming, Vi."

"Eddie, it's beautiful. You did this all yourself?"

"I had some help." He led them to a table. "Drinks are on the house—here's a menu, take a look and see what you'd like."

Hal, intrigued by the picture of a large bowl with two straws on the menu, said, "What's a . . . Scorpion?"

"Pure trouble," Eddie said. "Did you drive over?"

"No, we took the ferry."

"One Scorpion, coming up."

At the bar he combined Puerto Rican rum, gin, brandy, *orgeat,* orange and lemon juices, white wine, a sprig of mint—then put them in the blender, where they all became very good friends indeed. He poured the mixture over cracked ice in the largest drink bowl he had been able to find, and garnished it with a gardenia blossom.

By this time Toni was back at the hostess station and heard someone entering make the customary exclamation of "Wow."

She looked up to find Jimmy Russo grinning at her. And he wasn't looking around in wonder at the bar.

"For a high diver," he told her, still smiling, "you make one beautiful island princess."

Toni blushed to match her sarong.

"Uh—thanks," she said with a nervous laugh. The admiring look in Jimmy's eyes was not unwelcome, but she had to fan herself with the menu as she stepped from behind the hostess station. "Nice to see you too."

Was it getting even warmer in here?

While Toni escorted Jimmy to a table, Eddie delivered the Scorpion to Vi and Hal, then looked up and saw another familiar face entering the bar: Jackie Bloom, wearing his finest white linen suit and Panama hat.

"I thought I might as well come dressed for the occasion," Jackie said with a smile. He took a good look around and said, "Eddie, in all the years I've known you, I never suspected. You're one helluva showman."

"Thanks, buddy, coming from you that means a lot. C'mon, let me buy you a drink."

Jack Stopka, also wearing a loud Hawaiian shirt, went from table to table taking orders for *pūpūs*. The food turned out to be as popular as the drinks, and Tom was kept busy in the kitchen preparing potstickers and *kālua* pork ribs. Even if the clientele today was largely a home-team crowd, the positive response still pleased Eddie.

At six P.M. he flipped a switch and the lighting in the bar dimmed from conventional white to the kind of sunset glow that had permeated the Hawaiian Cottage at night. He too had strung small white lights from the ceiling, and now they sparkled above. It was as if the ceiling had been pulled back, exposing a night sky splashed with stars. But Eddie went the Egidis one better: he'd rigged a couple of bright lights on tracks, hidden by bamboo struts in the ceiling, and now, powered by small motors, they streaked across the night sky like comets circling the sun.

There were gasps, sighs, and spontaneous applause from the veteran showpeople as they suddenly found themselves sitting under island skies.

As satisfying as that was, the gesture that touched Eddie the most came from his sister Vi, who got up from her table and—a little tipsy on her feet—put her arm around her brother and said, "Mama was so wrong, Eddie. You are *far* from an ordinary boy."

Tears welled in his eyes and, unable to find the words to thank her, he embraced her in a bear hug.

Eddie had been right in opening in February: the sight of a neon palm tree standing beside a thatched-roof entryway drew dozens of curiosity-seekers, tired of the long winter and yearning for some sun, to the Polynesia on the Palisades. Inside they were charmed by the atmosphere and warmed by the drinks and the food. Fort Lee was a small town and word of mouth traveled fast. By the end of Eddie's first month in business, each weekend every table was full, as was the bar. Toni and Jack had been temporary help, filling in until Eddie knew whether he had a going concern. By the time Toni left for the Central States Shows in late March, it was apparent that he did, and he hired a full-time waitress who also doubled as a hostess.

For the next two months, Eddie was in his glory: the vision he had nurtured in his mind for years had become real, and people were responding to it as he hoped they would. He loved going to work every day, leaving behind the chill of a New Jersey winter for his balmy tropical grotto. All the pain in his life—his father's death, Sergei's brutality, his mother's betrayal, Adele's abandonment—was left behind when he walked in here. As he had once imagined it, here it was always warm, always paradise.

He also made a point never to have a radio playing unless it was a ball game or *Hawaii Calls*—nothing to intrude on the idyllic illusion. As a result he was often several days behind on current events. In April, when Chinese troops began a spring offensive that smashed the U.N. line and drove through five infantry divisions on their way to retake Seoul, Eddie didn't hear about it from the TV or radio, but from Jack . . . who surprised his father by showing up at the bar one afternoon in the middle of the week.

"Hey, I thought you had classes on Wednesdays," Eddie said.

"Not anymore," Jack said. He paused a moment, then declared, "Dad, I've got something to tell you. I joined the Army."

For the first time, Eddie felt a chill inside his tropic retreat. "What are you talking about? You've got a student deferment."

"I enlisted, Dad. I couldn't take it anymore, knowing I had friends fighting over there, maybe dying, and me safe and doing nothing at home."

Eddie came out from behind the bar, trying not to show the panic he was feeling, and gripped Jack by the arm. "You're not doing 'nothing,' you're learning your craft! You're an artist."

"I draw pictures," Jack said. "You and Toni, you *do* things. She jumps off ninety-foot towers, for God's sake, into a shot glass. You left home at sixteen, traveled the country, joined the Navy—"

"Yeah, and you saw how great that turned out," Eddie said.

"If you hadn't joined," Jack countered, "this place wouldn't exist."

Eddie had no response for that. Jack looked at him searchingly, as though trying to reach inside him, trying to make him understand:

"I don't do anything *real*, Dad. I sit and I draw pictures. And for that I get a deferment while guys like Johnny and Rick get their asses sent to Korea. Can you imagine how guilty that makes me feel?"

Eddie remembered well the frustration of being a male civilian on the homefront in World War II—the guilt he felt that eighteen-year-old Laurent Schwarz was going to war and he wasn't.

"Yeah," Eddie said quietly. "I can."

But Laurent never came back.

"It's just something I've got to do," Jack said. "I leave for Fort Dix on Friday. So what do you say, why don't you make us a couple of Singapore Slings and we'll toast to it, okay?"

Smiling wanly, Eddie noted, "You're only eighteen. I could lose my liquor license, y'know." He laughed a mordant laugh. "Fuck it."

He prepared the Slings in a blender, poured them into hula glasses, handed one to Jack, and took the other himself. He raised his glass.

"Here's to you winning the war," Eddie said, "and coming back, like I did, to tell the tale."

"You bet," Jack said. They clinked glasses, then drank.

Eddie never drank on the job, but this time he drained the glass.

Eddie saw Jack off at the train station in Newark on Friday morning, realizing for the first time what Adele must have been feeling on the day he had left for war. He felt sick to his stomach, felt a loss worse than when his father died, or when Adele left him for Lorenzo.

He drove back to open Eddie's Polynesia as he had each day for the past two and a half months. But now it was different inside. It was still warm, still tropical, but even this perfect piece of paradise could no longer muffle the distant echoes of war, or assuage the fear and foreboding Eddie felt for his only son.

20

Wichita, Kansas, 1951

TONI STOOD ON THE TOP platform of the tower and gazed down at the crowd—though perhaps that was too generous a term—sitting in the bleachers below. Maybe twenty or thirty people, tops, barely filling up half the seating—a far cry from the crowds she'd enjoyed as part of Ella Carver's act. And this was Wichita, not some small bump on the prairie like Goodland or Iola. In Toni's first three months as a headliner, she had yet to perform for an audience larger than her first-grade class in Edgewater. But they had paid for a show, and a show was what Toni was going to give them.

Down below Arlan was making a last check of the guy wires. He gave her a thumbs-up, and Toni moved to the edge of the platform, gauging the distance, the wind, x factors on the ground—and then she turned her back to the audience. A small murmur of surprise floated up from the crowd, and before the sound drifted away she sprang backward off the platform and into space, at her pinnacle drawing her knees to her chest and somersaulting as the world tumbled dizzily around her. Coming out of the tuck-and-roll, her body went rigid and she splashed into the water, straight as an anchor tossed from a boat. Quickly she relaxed her body into a curve, broke the surface, and climbed up the side ladder to the applause of the crowd.

Applause was always a thrill, even as thin and scattered as this.

As she took her bow, her outside talker announced over the PA, *"Don't miss Terrific Toni when she performs another stupendous dive again at three P.M. today and seven tonight!"*

As the crowd filed out of the bleachers, Toni toweled herself off, then helped Arlan secure the equipment. "Good show," he said, as he always did.

"Why can't I build a tip, Arlan?" she said wistfully.

"Takes time, missy. Don't worry, everybody start somewhere."

She smiled wanly, walked past the bleachers and the small ticket booth where Toby Gilcrist—a young man with a good bally who she'd hired as her outside talker—called out, "Hey, boss? Can I ask you something?"

"Sure, Toby, what?"

"Nice show, by the way. Listen, Toni, I hate to ask, but—I've got to send some money back to my mom in Chicago and I'm embarrassed to say I blew through last week's salary already. Can you give me a lift"— lift being carny for *loan*—"as an advance against my next paycheck?"

"How much do you need?"

"Half a yard?"

Toni almost gulped. Fifty bucks: that *was* his next paycheck. "If I front you that, what'll you live on next week?"

"I'll get by on leftovers from Floyd's Franks, don't worry about me."

Toni earned twenty bucks a dive, three dives a day—when it didn't rain, or wasn't too windy to dive—about two hundred and fifty a week. Good money, but after she paid Arlan's and Toby's salaries, between taxes, gasoline, hotels, and food, she wasn't making a dime on this game.

But Toby was a good guy and a good grind man—she couldn't bring herself to say no. "Sure, I'll bring it by after I get dressed."

"Thanks, boss."

Still in her bathing suit, she headed down the midway to Cliff's trailer. To save money Toni hadn't purchased one of her own but used Cliff's to change in during the day, then rented a cheap hotel room in whatever town they were in. Cliff had offered to share his trailer with her for the run of the show, but Toni held back from committing to cohabit with him—bad enough, the Catholic in her chided, that they were having premarital sex.

She slipped into his trailer, got into a pair of dungarees and a T-shirt, and was out in time to watch Cliff being launched out of his cannon, over four cars parked end to end, and into the cupped hand of his safety net.

Afterward, Toni came up and kissed him. "Ready for some lunch?"

"I'm hungry for something else," Cliff said with a grin.

Toni laughed. "What, now?"

"Why not?"

"It's the middle of the day, and your trailer's not far off the midway," she pointed out. "People passing by might hear us."

"Yeah," he agreed, still grinning, "they might."

"You *do* like to take risks, don't you?"

"Says the girl who jumps ninety feet into six feet of water."

"Okay, fair point," Toni said, feeling a little frisson of excitement despite herself. She smiled mischievously. "Just try not to be so . . . vocal."

"*Me* try? *You* try!" He grabbed her hand and led her into the trailer, where they pulled down the blinds and started undressing. Toni stepped out of her jeans and slipped off her shirt. Though she'd done this many times before at night, standing there in her bra and panties in the middle of the afternoon, about to have a tryst with her boyfriend, it felt—different. And as Cliff moved close and kissed her, she suddenly knew why: she'd been here before, but on the other side of the trailer window, looking in.

But Toni was quick to remind herself that she wasn't cheating on anyone, and as far as the rest of the analogy went, the idea that someone found her as *attractive* as her mother—

She kissed Cliff back, hard, and they fell onto his bunk.

After an especially dismal turnout for the evening performance, Toni wasn't particularly surprised to find Scobey Moser striding toward her before she had even finished drying off. She slapped on a smile, but Moser looked sober as a judge—and she knew that she was in the docket.

"Toni," he said heavily, draping an arm across her broad shoulders, "we've given it, what, three months for word of mouth to get out?"

Toni's stomach churned. "Yes, sir, I know."

"It's not your talker's fault, Toby turns a good tip, but . . . people just are not coming back for that evening show the way they did for Ella's fire dive, and they're sure not telling everybody back in town how great that carnival high diver was and how they should go out and see her for themselves."

Toni nodded. He was right.

"The way I see it, you've got two problems. One's your billing. People gravitate to carnival acts with big adjectives in the names—words like 'Incredible,' 'Impossible,' or 'Amazing.' 'Terrific Toni' sounds like a radio show about that perky girl next door. No grandiosity."

"I see your point, Mr. Moser."

"Second, you're not upping the stakes for the audience. They watched Ella swan dive into five feet of water in the afternoon, then her talker says, *'Be sure to come back tonight at seven when Ella lights herself on fire and dives into a tank of flames!'* Man, we couldn't keep 'em away! *You* do a forward somersault at one o'clock, a piked somersault at three, and a backward somersault at seven. How does your bally man tease the crowd back? *'Come back tonight at seven and watch Terrific Toni do basically the same thing'*? You need to top yourself, girl, that's what builds a tip!"

"I know," Toni said. "I've been thinking about varying my routine—"

"Maybe three dives a day was too much to start with," Moser said. "Why don't we scale back to two—one o'clock and seven—and see if you can come up with something that'll be a real ass-kicker for an evening show."

"But . . . if I do that, will I only get paid for two dives a day?"

"Honey," Moser said, "I think you're a talented gal and someday you may be a big star in this business . . . but you aren't yet, and it's costing me money. Two dives a day, take it or leave it."

Toni definitely felt the chilly implications of "leave it." "I'll take it," she said, "and I'll come up with a better act, I promise."

"Attagirl!" He slapped her on the back and walked away smiling. But all Toni could think about was that her income had just shrunk from two-fifty a week to one-fifty, with the same expenses. She had gone from not making a dime to being in the hole every week. Even if she ate every meal at the cook shack, ordering the seventy-five-cent pork chops for dinner, she would run out of money before she ran out of appetite.

Five minutes later she went up to Cliff before he got shot out of his cannon and asked, "Is that offer of sharing a trailer still open?"

"Hell yes."

She kissed him and said, "Let me just get my clothes from my motel in town, and starting tonight, you've got yourself a roommate."

The next morning she and Cliff went to the cook shack—a big tent with two long tables running down the middle, the air sizzling with the smell of bacon, ham, eggs, and sausage—and as they stood in line to order Toni overheard a man behind her say, "If that son of a bitch Toby ever shows his face again, you can bet I'll—"

She turned around and asked, "Did you say . . . Toby? Gilcrist?"

"You bet I did," the man said. "SOB borrowed a double sawbuck from me yesterday and this morning his car's gone—he's skipped."

Noting the pallor in Toni's cheeks, Cliff said, "You didn't . . . ?"

She nodded. "Fifty bucks." There were almost tears in her eyes. That fifty could've paid half of Arlan's salary, or food for her for a week, or . . .

"Never loan money to a carny, hon," Cliff said. "I'm sorry. Bastard."

No one at Palisades would ever have done something like this, Toni thought, suddenly and exquisitely homesick. She shook her head sadly.

"He's not a bastard," she said. "Just a rat. Deserting a sinking ship."

Long after spring arrived and the need for a winter oasis melted away, Eddie's Polynesia continued to thrive—so much so that his waitress, Sharon, had her hands full waiting on the bar's twelve tables. Eddie placed classified ads in the *Bergen Record* and *Newark Star-Ledger* for a "Hostess/waitress for Hawaiian/South Seas restaurant-bar. Apply Eddie's Polynesia on the Palisades, 1120 Palisade Avenue, Fort Lee, N.J. Phone: Fort Lee 8-0070."

Within the week he received six letters and three phone calls from women inquiring about the position. All of them had previous work experience and good references, and he determined to interview each one before making a decision; but one applicant, even on her résumé, stood out.

Her name was Lehua Concepćion and her first place of employment was listed as "Dole Pineapple Cannery, Honolulu, T.H." She had a number of waitressing positions to her credit, a few in Manhattan and the most recent being "Hawaiian Room, Teterboro Country Club, Teterboro, N.J."

What Eddie saw when she walked through the door was an attractive woman in her late thirties, wearing a cream-colored dress that accented her café au lait skin and jet-black hair. She had a wide, warm, open face, as had so many of the Hawaiians he had met in Honolulu.

Eddie stood, extending a hand. *"Aloha.* I'm Eddie Stopka."

"Lehua Concepćion. Pleased to meet you." She had that distinctive "local" accent Eddie had heard in Hawai'i—a distillation of linguistic influences from Hawaiian to English, Portuguese, Chinese, and Japanese.

As she took a seat, Eddie asked curiously, "'Concepćion' is hardly a Hawaiian name, is it?"

She shook her head. "My late husband was Puerto Rican—came to Hawai'i in 1915. We met, married, but he thought we could do better on the mainland. So we moved here, twenty years ago—first New York City, then New Jersey—where we raised two *keiki,* children."

"How old are your . . . *keiki*?" He hoped he'd pronounced that right.

"Mary is eighteen, Virginia is sixteen."

"Virginia Concepćion," Eddie said. "That's a lot to live up to."

Lehua laughed. "It was her father's idea, not mine. Maybe that's why she prefers to be called Ginny, 'ey?"

He smiled. "So it says here you worked as a . . . 'waitress/musician' at the Hawaiian Room? What's a waitress/musician?"

"I played ukulele and sang with a Hawaiian band there. When they decided to move back to the islands, I stayed on as a waitress."

"Why?"

"My children have visited Hawai'i, but they've never known a home other than New Jersey. They're so settled here, I can't bring myself to uproot them just because I miss my *'ohana*—my family."

Eddie was impressed by her openness and her obvious strength—a widow raising two girls on her own.

"Mrs. Concepćion, how would you like a job here, as a . . . 'hostess/ musician'? You'd greet customers, take up the slack for my waitress when the place is full, and a few days a week you could sing some island melodies. What do you say?"

She liked that just fine, and she started as soon as Eddie could obtain a sarong for her in a size ten.

Around this time, in July, Jack Stopka, done with basic training in Fort Dix, was sent cross country by rail to California, where he boarded the U.S. Military Ship Transport USS *General M. C. Meigs*, bound for Yokohama, Japan, and then on to Pusan, Korea. Once he was stationed in Korea he sent Eddie a mordantly funny letter about the eighteen-day Pacific crossing:

Remembering your letters about your passage aboard the Lurline, *I sat back and waited expectantly for a moonlit Pacific voyage through idyllic blue seas. There were eight hundred Army troops aboard the* Meigs, *crammed in tiered bunks four feet high. The air belowdecks smelled like the inside of somebody's underwear, the seas bucked like a bronco, and almost everybody got seasick. They either threw up or they crapped themselves. It was a relief to be chosen for guard duty on one of the upper decks—it was windy, rainy, and cold, but at least there was no smell, probably since officers were quartered on the upper decks and we all know their shit don't stink . . .*

At least Jack seemed to be coping with things with his usual humor. And the war news was somewhat encouraging: in late June the Soviet delegate to the United Nations had proposed a truce in Korea, and on July 10, peace talks with North Korea began in Kaesong. Perhaps, Eddie thought, this whole thing would be over before Jack ever saw any action.

"I think I've got the solution to both our problems," Cliff announced excitedly one night as he and Toni lay in bed. In a few days the show was making the jump to Omaha, Nebraska—the biggest city they'd played so far. "It's sure-fire, and it'll make a name for both of us."

"Do tell," Toni said, just drifting off to sleep.

"Scobey won't let me fly over Ferris wheels or other rides 'cause he's afraid of liability, accidentally hitting a passenger, right? So what if I fly over an attraction that doesn't *have* any passengers?"

"Like what?" Toni asked. "Even the sideshow has people inside."

Cliff grinned and said, "Like you."

She sat bolt upright in bed. *"What?"*

"Picture this: When we get to Omaha, I set up my cannon in front of some bleachers, like always. But then, about a hundred feet in front of that, *you* set up your tower and tank. On the far side of that, I set up my safety net. Showtime comes, you climb up your tower, wave to the crowd, then the talker says, *'For the first time anywhere, two daredevils cross paths in the sky!'*—and BOOM!, I shoot out of the cannon, over your head, and into the net. You do your dive, I climb out of the net, we take our bows together. The world's first high diver–human cannonball team! It's a natural."

She gaped. "Are you nuts? What if you hit *me*? So *ends* the world's first high diver–human cannonball team!"

"Nah. You see how high I shoot out of that cannon—I'll miss you by a mile," he said calmly. "But the crowd won't know that, and they'll be on the edge of their seats! It'll be a sensation. Here, I'll show you."

He jumped out of bed, ran to the trailer's little dining table, and handed her some papers. They were filled with diagrams, parabolas, and equations like $x(t) = v_x(0)t$ and $y(t) = y(0) + v_y(0)t - \_gt^2$.

"This is calculus," she said, surprised.

"Sure. I worked it all out mathematically. If I set the firing angle of the cannon at forty-eight degrees, with two hundred pounds of air per square foot, I'll reach a zenith of one hundred feet high—ten feet higher than your diving tower—and two hundred feet in distance."

Toni, though still skeptical, was impressed by the forethought he had put into this. "What happens if you go off course and hit one of the guy wires? How could we even rehearse this without risking our necks?"

"We rehearse it with a weighted dummy we shoot over the tower. We can do a few practice tries here tomorrow morning—easy enough to move my cannon over to your setup. In Omaha we'll set up the net and I'll take a few solo passes over the tower. If I clear that okay, you go up, stand there, and I'll fly over you. If, after that, for *any* reason you don't feel comfortable with it, we'll forget the whole thing. But I think it can work, and work big!

"This could put us on the *map*, Toni." The excitement in his face was apparent even in the dim light of the sleeping carnival. "We'll be turning away customers. We'll never have to worry about being forty-milers again!"

Toni had to admit, if it was a success, it could draw the kind of tip she needed to stay afloat. "Have you told Mr. Moser about this?"

"No, I wanted to run it past you first. If Moser nixes it, well, that's it."

Toni thought long and hard a moment. "If Moser gives it his okay," she said, "we'll try the stunt with the dummy. But if the dummy doesn't clear the top of the tower, or hits a guy wire, that's as far as it goes—okay?"

His face broke into a smile. "Baby, you're the greatest! I love you."

And as she was reeling from those words, he kissed her, and more.

The next morning, Toni listened as Cliff sold his idea to Scobey Moser, showing him the diagrams and calculations. Moser mulled it over, then allowed, "Well, it *might* work . . ." He echoed Toni's concerns, but gave the okay to try the dummy test. "But if it does any damage to this lady's equipment, Bowles," he warned, "it's coming out of your pocket, not hers."

Cliff agreed, drove his truck-mounted cannon over to Toni's setup, and positioned it a hundred feet from the diving tower. He introduced her to his dummy, Mort—after Edgar Bergen's Mortimer Snerd—which he then stuffed into the barrel of the cannon. He set the cannon at a forty-eight-degree angle, the muzzle aimed well above the diving tower. Then he spun the controls that drew the piston down into the barrel of the cannon, releasing a blast of compressed air that sent Mort rocketing out.

The dummy flew up, up . . . and over the top of the diving tower, clearing it by at least ten feet. Mort then arced earthward like a pop fly, landing with a dusty thud in a sandlot behind the carnival.

Toni and Arlan had been standing beside the tower and one of the guy wires as Mort was shot out. Neither the tower nor the guy wire was jostled significantly by the wind of Mort's passing on his way over the top. Toni and Arlan looked at each other in relief. "So far," she said, "so good."

The next morning the roustabouts began tearing down the show and soon the caravan of trucks was on the road, making the jump to Omaha—or more accurately, a mile or two outside Omaha.

By late afternoon Cliff and Toni had carefully supervised the placing of Cliff's cannon and safety net, each one hundred feet on either side of Toni's tank and tower. As soon as everything was set up, Cliff again fired Mort out of the cannon, over the tower, and into the safety net.

"My turn," Cliff said. "Go get Scobey. It either works or it doesn't."

Cliff kissed her, put on his crash helmet and flight suit, and dusted himself with talcum powder to reduce friction inside the cannon.

Toni came back with Scobey just as the waning sun was causing the sky over the plains to blush. Moser looked at it and said, "God, they do have beautiful sunsets out here." He turned to Cliff. "Okay, Jetboy, show me."

"Jet*man*," Cliff muttered, climbing into the cannon's muzzle. His assistant, Phil, spun the controls and drew down the piston, along with Cliff.

From inside the cannon Cliff called, "Fire!"

Cliff went up like a shooting star in reverse. Toni held her breath as he rocketed up and then over the tower, clearing it by ten feet, then began a half-somersault that landed him on his back in the safety net.

He bounced around the net a few times, then jumped jauntily out and onto the ground. Toni ran to him and threw her arms around his neck.

"Thank God! I thought for sure you were going to smash your stupid, silly, beautiful face into my diving platform." She kissed him, hard. "And I did *not* want to have to clean that up." He laughed.

Arlan came over and told her, "Tower was solid. Maybe it jiggles a little up top, but hard to say from down here."

Scobey said to Toni, "What about it, honey? You're the one who's gonna be standing up there. You feel safe doing it?"

"I'll go up first thing tomorrow," she said, "and get a feel for how much the tower sways as he goes over. Too much sway and I won't do it."

The next morning was cloudy and breezy—two knots, not enough to affect her dive, but Toni told Cliff, "If I look down at you and anything feels wrong—your angle, your altitude—I'll jump first and ask questions later. Got that?"

He nodded. As she started climbing the tower she felt as if there were a swarm of butterflies in her stomach, all beating a mamba with their wings. At the top she looked up at the six inches of ladder above her head, which, she reminded herself, Cliff had cleared twice yesterday. She looked down and saw Moser, Cliff and Phil at the cannon, Arlan standing by just in case anything went wrong—though Toni wasn't sure what he could do if it did.

She gave Cliff a thumbs-up.

Moments later, he came shooting up like a bullet out of a gun barrel, and in a half-breath's time he was arcing above her head.

She felt a light breeze on her face as he passed, but the tower stood steady and the platform below her feet didn't sway.

Cliff landed safely in the net and in moments was jumping out of it onto the ground. He called up to Toni, "How'd it feel?"

She gave him a thumbs-up and called back, "Let's try it again!"

They repeated it half a dozen times, each time Cliff clearing the tower by between eight and ten feet. After the last one, Toni climbed down, Cliff ran up, gave her a long kiss and said, "We're going to be famous! And famously in love!"

By afternoon, Toni was relieved that the weather had improved—bright and clear, not a cloud in the sky, with no wind. Perfect diving conditions. Meanwhile, Cliff's talker was building a tip with his bally:

"For the first time anywhere, two daredevil acts for the price of one! Watch as Jetman, the Human Missile, is shot out of a cannon and over the head of

that high-diving sensation, the Terrific Toni! Will he survive? Will she? Don't miss this death-defying duo, today at one o'clock!"

To Toni's delight, by one o'clock there was a capacity crowd gathering in the bleachers, bigger than either she or Cliff had ever drawn on their own. She gave him a kiss for good luck as he slipped on his crash helmet and goggles.

Toni climbed the ladder to her customary accompaniment of "Sabre Dance," the music stopping when she reached the top. Down below, Cliff's drum roll began its wind-up as he climbed into the muzzle of the cannon.

This time when it went off, there was also a small gunpowder explosion to give the illusion that this was a real cannon and not just a souped-up peashooter. Cliff came rocketing out and up toward Toni.

His angle seemed fine at first—it wasn't until he was already shooting up past her that she realized he was coming in lower than he had this morning. He arced over the tower, cutting it closer than he should have.

So close that his foot clipped the top of the tower as he passed over.

It didn't affect his trajectory, but his weight and velocity was like a fishing line that snagged and pulled the tower backward. Toni grabbed onto the ladder for support, trying not to panic.

Then she felt a *pop* beneath her feet and looked down.

To her horror, she saw that one of the axle staves securing the guy wires to the ground had come loose.

The tower shuddered and began to topple backward.

People in the audience gasped and screamed.

In the few seconds she had left, Toni considered her options: There was no possibility of diving into the tank. She could hold on and hope that the tower fell into the net and didn't crush her in the process, or . . .

She turned around on the platform, keeping hold on the tower even as it lurched backward at a terrifying new angle.

Cliff had landed safely in the net. There was only one thing she could think to do, one way to keep from getting killed.

She squatted down, trying to gather as much spring in her legs as she could, then launched herself off the platform—toward the safety net.

She didn't have anywhere near the velocity as Cliff, but the falling motion of the tower gave her some momentum and her legs added to it.

She straightened her body into a swan dive across hard, unforgiving ground. The edge of the safety net loomed ahead—the center of it exactly a hundred feet from her tower—and on a wing and a prayer she began a half-somersault, tumbling over so her back was level with the ground . . .

And she fell into the net. Nowhere near the center, dangerously close to the edge—but she was *in* it. She bounced three feet up on impact, and for a moment she was afraid she would fall against the steel frame and split open her skull . . . but she managed to twist her body and fall sideways instead.

One more light bounce, and she was safe. For the moment.

Cliff clambered across the net to her side. "Jesus! Are you *okay?*"

"Yeah," she said, breathless, "but—the tower—it's gonna—"

"Don't worry about the tower," Cliff said.

Toni looked back and saw to her astonishment that the tower was, impossibly, frozen in mid-fall—tilted at something like an eighty-five degree angle, looking like the leaning tower of Pisa. How the *hell?*

When she looked past it, into the distance, she saw Arlan—holding on to the guy wire that had popped out of the ground, the former strongman literally holding up the ninety-foot aluminum tower with his bare hands.

"Holy shit!" Toni shouted. "Arlan!"

As she and Cliff jumped out of the net, a dozen more carny hands and roustabouts joined Arlan in his tug-of-war with the tower, grabbing hold of the cable and, with their combined strength, slowly pulling the tower erect.

Toni and Cliff arrived just as Arlan had grabbed a hammer and began pounding the stave back into fresh ground.

"Arlan, that was incredible!" Toni cried. "Are you all right?"

"Yeah, sure." He finished pounding the stave into the earth, tossed the hammer aside—and Toni could now see his abraded, bleeding hands.

"My God, you need an ambulance!"

"Aw no, just some little cuts," Arlan said with a shrug.

"You saved us!" Toni hugged him as they were surrounded by a growing crowd of onlookers and show folk, including Cliff's assistant, Phil.

"You save yourself," Arlan said. "Nice dive."

Toni turned to Cliff. "How the hell did this happen?"

"I—I don't know," he said.

"I told you the barometric pressure was too high," Phil blurted.

Cliff snapped, "Shut up!"

"What do you mean, barometric pressure?" Toni asked.

"There's a high-pressure system over the plains today," Phil explained, uncowed by Cliff, "pushing down, creating air resistance. I *told* him."

"You're fired!" Cliff yelled at his assistant. Then, to Toni: "I thought it was safe! I'd done it before, under similar pressure."

"You knew about this?" Toni said, stunned. "And you didn't even *tell* me?"

"Toni, you saw the crowd, it was *huge,*" he said. "How could we turn them away? It's what we both needed! And I really thought I'd clear the tower by at least five feet. Hell, *most* of me did clear it!"

He grinned at that, but he was the only one smiling, especially after Scobey Moser ran up and boomed, "Are you two all right? And what in fucking *hell* went wrong?"

Cliff's ex-assistant was happy to tell him.

Toni's eyes filled with tears as she faced Cliff. "You son of a bitch," she said softly.

"Toni, I *love* you—I swear, I'd *never* intentionally put you in any danger—"

"What the hell do you call *this?*" she shouted.

"You wanted this too!"

"Yeah, but I want to stay alive more!"

She had trusted him with her life, all because she thought she loved him. What kind of reckless fool had *she* been?

"Get that goddamn cannon away from my tower," she snapped. "Arlan, c'mon, I'll drive you to the nearest hospital."

"I'll go that one better," Moser said. He told Cliff, "Get that goddamn cannon off my *lot*. Your contract's been terminated."

Cliff's eyes pleaded with her. "Toni, honey," he said desperately, "tell him, tell him how *careful* I was—don't go, please—"

But Toni just kept on walking. "You sure of this, missy?" Arlan asked. "Damn sure," she told him.

But there were tears streaming down her face as she said it.

Scobey canceled that evening's dive so Toni had time to pull herself together, but after she had rented another motel room she came back to the lot and to her tank and tower, encircled by darkness amid the flash and neon of the midway—the red spinning lights of the Chair-o-Plane as it tipped and whirled, the blazing gold spokes of the Ferris wheel turning like a wheel of chance. That was what she'd done today: she'd spun the wheel, desperate for a jackpot, and only by chance had it not cost her her life.

There were no floodlights on the tower, but there was enough light spill from the rest of the carnival for Toni to see the rungs of the ladder as she slowly climbed up to the top. Moser had had roustabouts working all afternoon on securing the axle staves that anchored the guy wires, and when Toni stepped onto the platform she felt a comforting and familiar solidity.

She looked down at the darkened tank, a few wriggling neon reflections rippling across the water's surface. She thought about something Peejay Ringens once told her at Palisades, about how he overcame his fear of doing the bicycle jump by standing each day on his tower and "taking an imaginary ride down" until he had conquered his fear and did it for real.

Toni looked down, imagined herself springing off the platform, tucking her body and somersaulting—but instead of coming out of the tuck, she pictured herself doing another revolution, just as calmly as she had the first one—no disorientation or panic—and after the second spin she straightened her imaginary legs and plunged safely into the water.

She took the same imaginary dive another ten times before climbing down and returning to her motel. She may have done a few in her sleep.

Unlike Peejay she didn't have a month to spare for her imaginary dives, but the next morning she climbed the tower again and—much to Arlan's puzzlement—stood up there for the better part of an hour, making dozens of double somersaults in her mind before she felt confident enough.

She launched herself off the platform and, at her pinnacle, went into her tuck-and-roll as she had hundreds of times before. As she came to the end of the somersault, she didn't let go of her knees, remembering the calm, easy way she had done this in her mind, and that was exactly how it played out: she spun a second time, no big deal, then came out of it with legs straight, plunging into the tank in quiet triumph.

She enjoyed the serenity of the water and thought she could hear Bee Kyle applauding. But when she surfaced she saw it wasn't Bee, but Arlan.

"Good dive," he said, grinning. "*Very* good dive."

She thanked him, toweled off and got into dry clothes, then went over to the thirty-foot trailer that served as Scobey Moser's office and knocked.

"How you feeling, honey?" he asked as she entered.

"I feel great. I've got a new evening show—a double somersault—and, I think, a snappy new name. An adult name."

He looked impressed and said, "So what do you want to call yourself?"

"The Amazing Antoinette," she said, and Moser's smile told her it was the right choice.

Lehua was both a fine ukulele player and a talented singer whose melodic voice added immeasurably to the atmosphere of Eddie's Polynesia. Whenever she sang, diners stopping talking, silverware stopped clattering, and Eddie paused in whatever he was doing to listen to her, to allow her voice to truly transport him to Hawai'i. She sang in Hawaiian and English, *hapa-haole* songs like "Sweet Leilani" as well as traditional standards like—a frequent request—"Aloha 'Oe." She told the crowd:

"This song has special meaning to me, since the first verse speaks of how the wind seeks out the *lehua* blossom—the flower I'm named after."

Aloha 'oe, farewell to you,
E ke onaona noho i ka lipo.
One fond embrace, a ho'i a'e au,
Until we meet again . . .

Eddie found tears welling in his eyes, quickly blinking them away as he returned to mixing a Fog Cutter for table five.

Later, at closing time, Lehua came up to him and noted, "You always cry during 'Aloha 'Oe,' don't you?"

He flushed with embarrassment. "Do I?"

"It's not really a song about farewells or funerals, you know," she explained. "The falling rain is supposed to be the seed of Wakea, the sky father, conjoining with Papa, the mother of all the Hawaiian people. It's actually a very romantic, passionate song."

"I never knew that."

"You miss the islands, don't you?"

"I've got to admit . . . I wasn't thinking about the islands," he said. "My son is in Korea."

"Oh, Lord. I'm sorry, I didn't know."

"Those damn peace talks broke down last week, and . . . he sent me this letter the other day."

"What did he say? Is he all right?"

"Yeah, for the moment." Eddie reached under the bar, took out Jack's latest letter. "He's got a way with words. He said, 'The first time my unit took a hill I heard this sound above me as I scrambled up—*snap snap snap,* like someone snapping their fingers. My buddy Dominguez said it sounded more like castanets to him. That's what the bullets sound like, and that's when you realize, 'Holy crap, there are people out there trying to kill me.'"

Eddie put the letter down and said, "Nobody took a single shot at me in World War Two, and it kills me that my son is going through this every day."

Lehua put a hand on his. "If he is anything like his father," she said with a smile, "I'm sure he's very resourceful."

God, Eddie thought, she has a beautiful smile.

"Mahalo," he said. "That's right, isn't it? Thank you?"

Reluctantly he pulled back his hand.

"Very good," she said. "You're becoming quite the *kama'āina,* 'ey?"

Eddie laughed. "I'm not even sure what that means."

"There are those of us who are Hawaiian by birth," she said, picking up her purse, "and there are those who are Hawaiian at heart." She smiled as she headed for the door. "See you tomorrow, boss."

He called after, "Yeah. See you tomorrow."

He smiled. Seeing her was one of the few things that could keep him from worrying about Jack.

Some months later, on a Thursday morning in October, Eddie was driving up Route 5 to Palisade Avenue when he saw a fleet of police cars parked across the street from Palisades Amusement Park. As he paused at the light Eddie could see a phalanx of policemen, including Chief Borrell, gathered outside Joe's Elbow Room. Once, Eddie might have stopped, gone up to Frank, and asked him what was going on. But he hadn't spoken to the Chief in years, and when the light changed he turned right on Palisade.

It wasn't long, though, before radio reports satisfied Eddie's curiosity: apparently the gangster Willie Moretti had been shot dead inside Joe's, an obvious gangland hit. Willie always had been too chatty for his own good.

Eddie didn't think much more about it until the following Saturday, when Bunty Hill stopped by Eddie's Polynesia, bellied up to the bar for an ale and asked Eddie, "You hear about Stengel?"

"Who?"

"Fred Stengel. The Fort Lee police chief."

"Oh, yeah," Eddie said, "I saw in yesterday's paper. He was indicted for corruption? Turning a blind eye to Joe Adonis's gambling network?"

"Old news," Bunty said grimly. "He committed suicide this morning."

Eddie was stunned . . . and a little saddened. "Aw, jeez, no."

"I ain't shedding any tears over a corrupt cop," Bunty said, "much less one who beat the crap out of a bunch of kids protesting for civil rights."

"Yeah," Eddie admitted, "that's all true. But . . ."

"But what?"

"He was also the guy who stopped Arthur Holden from jumping off the George Washington Bridge," Eddie said quietly. "He wasn't all bad."

"Maybe not all, but it was still more than he could live with. That's the line these guys walk. And now the birds are coming home to roost."

It was early November and the Central States Show was playing just outside Miami, Florida. The Amazing Antoinette had just performed her backward double somersault to a crowd of about a hundred, taken her bows, and was on her way to her truck when she heard a familiar voice:

"Toni!"

She turned to find a smiling leprechaun of a man and a tall, willowy blonde, weighted down with gold charm bracelets and carrying a tiny Chihuahua, walking toward her.

An instant later she recognized them as Irving Rosenthal and his wife, the composer Gladys Shelley.

"Mr. Rosenthal?" she said, stunned to see him here.

"Sweet act you've got there, Toni," he said, extending a hand. "Congratulations."

Politely, she took his hand. "Well, thank you."

"You remember my wife, Gladys? And our little one, Debussy?"

The dog barked at its name.

"Yes, of course," Toni said. "What—what are you doing in Miami?"

"We've been wintering down here the past several years," Rosenthal said. "I saw one of your show posters around town and thought, this has to be Eddie Stopka's daughter. How could I not come and see you?"

"You were amazing, hon," Gladys said warmly. "And beautiful."

Rosenthal nodded. "I believe Arthur Holden is resting well, knowing the torch has been passed to another Palisadian." The veteran diver had died three years before, at the age of seventy-one. "I think it would be only fitting if his successor played Palisades Park next season. What do you say?"

Toni was shocked and, despite herself, flattered, but . . . "I—don't know if I can do that, Mr. Rosenthal . . ."

"I don't blame you for being angry at how the whole picketing business was handled, but it's all been resolved. The pool is open to anyone who buys a ticket. Ask your friends at CORE if you don't believe me."

He handed her his business card. "What do you say to a month's engagement next summer? Two dives a day at the free-act stage at four hundred a week. Interested?"

Toni's jaw dropped. "I guess I might be," she said, "assuming the pool situation has been resolved."

"Good. We'll talk when you get back to New Jersey." He shook her hand again. "Your father must be very proud. I'll tell him I saw you."

My father has never even seen me perform, Toni thought as the Rosenthals walked away. But who knew? That might change soon.

Excitedly she ran for her truck to find Melba Valle's phone number.

21

Palisades, New Jersey, 1952

TONI STOOD AT THE GATE to the Palisades pool, taking in the briny air that smelled like home in a way nothing else did, and marveled at what she saw. The vast majority of pool patrons were still Caucasian, but today the onetime sea of white was peppered with two or three black faces and considerably more brown ones, mostly Puerto Ricans. They swam in the same waters as white swimmers; they lay atop blankets on the gray boards of the sundeck alongside white people paradoxically trying to darken their skin. They were relatively few in number—Melba had said that CORE distributed thousands of leaflets in Harlem announcing that Palisades was no longer segregated, urging Negroes to patronize the pool, though most were still hesitant to believe it—but according to CORE, Palisades was living up to its agreement and admitting all those who sought entry.

"I was a fool not to change the pool's policy years ago," Irving Rosenthal, standing beside Toni, admitted freely. "I was absolutely convinced that whites would never share a pool or a bathhouse with Negroes. I was hardly the only businessman who believed that, but I'm pleased to say that I was wrong—and you were right."

"Is that why you invited me to appear here?" Toni asked.

Rosenthal laughed. "If all I wanted to do was apologize for being wrong, I'd have sent you a telegram. I wouldn't pay my own mother four hundred a week unless I thought she was going to draw a tip."

Toni smiled. "I'll do my best. And thank you. For doing this."

"I wouldn't have if not for your friends at CORE, making my life miserable summer after summer. But it turned out to be a good business decision that happened to be the right thing to do." He started off, then turned back: "Oh, by the way—the DuMont Network is broadcasting three TV shows from the park this summer. A talent show called *The Strawhatters* is going to shoot here at the pool, using aquatic acts—would you be willing to do a few fancy dives off the boards, for publicity?"

"On *television*?" Toni said excitedly. "You bet I would."

"Excellent. I'll talk to you about the schedule later."

He moved off just as another familiar face came up to Toni.

"Hey," Bunty said, grinning, "don't let your head get so big you fall off the ladder going up."

She gave him a big hug. "That won't be hard. This all still feels like a dream, being back here as a headliner."

"Irving ask you to do some dives for the TV show? For 'publicity'?"

"Yeah, isn't it great?"

"You do know you just agreed to do it for free?"

Toni went over in her head what Rosenthal had said, then laughed. "Good old Uncle Irving. He's still that little kid selling pails and shovels, isn't he?"

"Yep. And you just bought one. So did I." He patted her on the back. "Break a leg today, kiddo."

Toni's afternoon performance was at one o'clock and it was only eleven thirty. She and Arlan had already checked the rigging, so she had time to wander the park, greet old friends, and take in the changes since she had last been here—my God, she thought, had it really been five years?

So much seemed new, but perhaps this was just window dressing: Anna Halpin had finally talked her uncles into adopting an all-pastel color scheme, the kind coming into vogue these days in fashion and interior decoration. There were new rides like the topically named Flying Saucer and Jet Bomb, as well as the park's biggest hit, the Tunnel of

Love—really just a new version of the Old Mill playing up the romance angle, but once Palisades had opened theirs to great success, Tunnels of Love suddenly bloomed like passionflowers at amusement parks across the country.

There was also a new Kiddieland with pony carts, airplane swings, a miniature train, and smaller versions of the Cyclone and Carousel. Kiddieland was itself the province of someone just out of childhood: John Rinaldi, the bright, capable eighteen-year-old son of Joe Rinaldi, who had begun working at Palisades three years earlier as a consultant, planning and overseeing programs for teenagers.

Many of the old concessionaires remained—Sadie Harris still had a teddy bear stand and a few palmistry booths, Jackie Bloom still lorded over the cat game as Curly Clifford did his canaries—but some franchises had been passed on to a new generation. Helen Cuny retired and sold her stands to her daughter and son-in-law, Norma and Peter Santanello. And Minette Dobson was managing two cigarette wheels now, plus the old "mouse game" once owned by the late Adolph Schwartz. Toni stopped by and asked her out to lunch; Minette told a handsome young man who worked for her that she'd be back in an hour.

Toni discovered that the old Grandview Restaurant overlooking the Hudson was now the red-and-white-striped Circus Restaurant. They took a seat in view of Toni's tank and tower on the adjacent free-act stage.

"That young guy who's working the wheel with you is one hunk of heartbreak," Toni noted. "What's his name?"

Minette winced and said, "Jay." Then added, "Junior."

Toni's eyes widened. "He's your old boyfriend's son?"

Minette nodded. "His father asked me to put him to work. Get him some experience."

"Isn't it a little—uncomfortable—having him around?"

"Yeah, you could say that. He's a good kid, but I'd like him better if he wasn't the spitting goddamn image of his old man." Minette's face only hinted at the pain she must have felt. She looked down at the menu and said, "Speaking of uncomfortable, is your mom coming to see you today?"

"Hope not. I didn't invite her."

Minette sighed. "Toni, you've got to see her sometime. Even your dad's made his peace with her . . . he's seeing that nice Lehua now, everything's worked out for the best, for him and for you."

"It wouldn't have worked out for me if not for you," Toni said. "You were there when I needed a mother. You're the one I want here today."

Minette seemed touched by that. "I was happy to do what I could. But showing you how to set your hair and do your makeup doesn't compare to the fourteen years Adele put into raising you. She led you and Jack out of here when the whole place was in flames, remember?"

Toni frowned at that, flagged a waiter, and ordered a salad.

An hour later, she was standing in her brightly colored swimsuit off to one side of the free-act stage. For the past fifteen minutes, the voice of park announcer Bob Paulson had been booming, every five minutes, throughout the park, *"Today on the free-act stage at one o'clock, see that high-diving sensation, the Amazing Antoinette, as she jumps from the top of a ninety-foot tower into a tank filled with less than six feet of water . . ."*

It was standing room only as Toni looked out at the crowd, but the audience who mattered most to her was sitting in the front row: her father, looking at once proud and terrified as his eyes went from Toni in the wings to the towering aluminum ladder on the stage. Sitting on either side of him were Bunty Hill and Minette Dobson, and standing at the end of the row was a grinning Irving Rosenthal, as Paulson's voice welcomed the crowd:

"Ladies and gentlemen, here's a young lady whose high-flying gymnastics have made her a sensation on the carnival circuit in the Midwest—but we're proud to say she took her very first dive, at the tender age of five, right here in our saltwater pool! Give a hometown welcome to Palisades Park's own Amazing Antoinette—Toni Stopka!"

The words, and the applause that followed, brought unexpected tears to Toni's eyes. She walked onto the stage, bowed to the audience, caught her father's eyes and gave him a thumbs-up—then, to the familiar percussion of "Sabre Dance," began scaling the ninety-foot tower.

Reaching the top, she stepped onto the platform just as the music faded. She looked down, gauging the distance, the wind, and factors on the ground, as usual . . . but this time was far from usual. She gazed out at the park spread out below her, and she wasn't looking down at some random collection of carnival tents and concession booths . . . she was looking at the place where she had grown up. On her right was the pool where she learned to swim, and next to it the midway where her family's French fry stand once stood. She saw Roscoe Schwarz's Funhouse, and the thirty-foot-high dome of the Carousel building, and the wooden peaks and valleys of the Cyclone coaster, all the familiar midways and marquees that had been, even more than Edgewater, the small-town streets of her childhood.

She was standing where Arthur Holden once stood. And Peejay Ringens. And Bee Kyle. She felt a rush of pride and accomplishment.

She pushed backward off the platform, drawing her knees to her chest as she began her first tuck-and-roll, and saw Palisades as she never had before—a blur of speed, color, sounds, and smells, tumbling under her like tilting funhouse floors and distorted mirrors.

She somersaulted twice before straightening her body and slicing into the water like a knife. She dawdled less under the surface than usual, coming eagerly to the surface; and as she climbed the side ladder, she basked in the approving roar of the audience.

She took her bows alongside Arthur Holden and Bee Kyle.

Afterward her father came up to her, his face shining with pride and relief, and hugged her. "That was amazing, honey. You *are* amazing."

After Uncle Irving had congratulated her, Toni was surprised to find herself staring into the face of the freckled, red-haired Jimmy Russo.

"Told you I'd come when you played Palisades," he said with a smile. "Got to look after the bank's investment, after all."

"Yes, of course. So what do you think, am I a good risk?"

"Hard to say 'good risk' about someone who does what you do for a living," he joked, "but I think we invested wisely. You've got a great act and a great future ahead of you."

"Thanks. From your lips to God's ears."

"I'll bring it up at Mass this Sunday," he said, smiling. "What do you say I take you out to dinner the night before and we can toast to the future?"

The debacle with Cliff, almost a year ago, faded in the bright promise of Jimmy's smile. "My last show is at seven. I can be ready by eight."

"My sister Grace takes twice that long to get ready, and she doesn't even jump off a tower," he said, impressed. "Shall I meet you here?"

"Yes, by the main gate."

"Great. See you then." He started off, then turned back. "You were beautiful up there," he said, and with a shy smile moved off into the crowd.

After her last show, Toni went over to Eddie's Polynesia, where she was finally old enough to order a drink—one of Trader Vic's "Florida daiquiris," which her father prepared as she sat at the bar and chatted. "Melba says that thanks to our protest, the New Jersey legislature changed the state civil rights law to include swimming pools," Toni noted proudly. "We really made a difference, and not just to Palisades."

"You did," Eddie agreed, pouring two ounces of Bacardi Carta Oro Rum into the blender, "but don't fool yourself into thinking we still don't have a long way to go on that score."

"Why do you say that?"

He added maraschino juice, lemon juice, sugar, and lime juice. "Couple weeks ago, Lehua and I went into New York to visit Vi and Hal. We took a little heat from some stupid kids on the street."

"What? Why?"

"Because we were a couple. Because they thought she was colored."

Toni sat stunned as her father switched on the blender for about ten seconds, then poured the contents into a tall glass. "But she's Hawaiian."

"Her skin was darker than theirs. To them she was colored. One called me a nigger lover." Toni shuddered. "I wanted to drop him headfirst into a garbage can where he belonged, but Lehua said, 'Just walk away.'"

As Eddie soberly placed the daiquiri on her cocktail napkin, Toni said, "Well . . . let's celebrate one small victory, at least." She raised her glass in a toast and took a sip. "Mm, this is delicious."

"We have a limit of one to every high diver who comes in."

She laughed and asked, "Have you heard from Jack?"

Eddie frowned. "He sent me a note last month. His letters have been getting shorter and shorter. He used to draw funny little figures in the margins, but he's even stopped that."

"I've tried writing him several times and all I get back are travelogues about Korea. I don't think he wants to tell me about being in battles."

"He's stopped writing about that to me too."

"Why the hell did he have to go and enlist?"

A second after she'd uttered them, Toni realized they were the same words her mother had used after her father entered the Navy.

Saturday night, after her evening dive, Toni used one of the rooms for visiting sideshow performers, did as much as she could reasonably do with her hair without pincurling, applied her makeup, then slipped into a blue two-piece peplum dress she had bought at Schwartz's just for the occasion. She met Jimmy outside the main gate, and as he rolled up to the curb in his shiny 1951 Buick, her efforts were rewarded by a look of pleased surprise as he got out to open the passenger-side door.

"Wow," he said. "I liked you in the swimsuit, but—wow."

Ella's maxim about confounding audience expectations worked both ways. Toni smiled as she slid into the passenger seat. "Thank you."

He took her to the posh Chimes Restaurant in Paramus, where they both ordered steaks and continued the conversation begun in the car. Jimmy wanted to know how her carnival engagement had gone, and she told him all the good, discreet parts. She asked about him, his family, and he told her he was the second-youngest of six children. "Must've been nice, being part of a big family," she said. "It was just me and Jack, growing up."

"Only two of you? You're sure your family is Catholic?"

"My mother is Presbyterian. After Jack came along she told my dad, 'I'm done having babies, feel free to have one yourself but two is my limit'—and from that point on they, ah, invested heavily in the rubber industry."

He laughed. "Heresy! My mother would never have spoken the word aloud, much less actually use one, for fear the Pope might strike her dead on the spot. Did your mom actually tell you this?"

"Oh yeah, we had a talk when I was thirteen. I'm glad she did, I—" She caught herself before revealing her own use of the heretical device with Cliff. "I know, at least, why there was only me and my brother," she said.

An unwelcome notion crept into her thoughts. "Is your family pretty . . . devout?"

He nodded. "Mass on Sundays, confession on Saturdays, Father Manz over for dinner once a month."

Toni was accustomed to the more relaxed moral standards of the amusement business, but here was a young man from a strict Catholic family. What would he think if he knew that the young woman he was courting was . . . well . . . not a virgin? It wasn't like she slept around, she'd only been to bed with Cliff—but would that still tarnish her in Jimmy's eyes?

The thought plagued her throughout dinner, turning what should have been a pleasant evening into a tense one. She tried not to betray her anxiety, and Jimmy didn't seem to pick up on it; after dinner, when the orchestra began to play, he even asked her to dance. She was not a practiced dancer but could follow along well enough, and as they slow-danced to someone else singing Nat King Cole's "Unforgettable" she allowed herself to finally relax, enjoying the warmth of his hand in hers, the other hand cupped around her waist. She liked his . . . solidity, for want of a better word, and took in the scent of his cologne as their faces brushed against each other's. She enjoyed it so much that she suggested they stay on the dance floor for the next tune, "Don't Let the Stars Get in Your Eyes."

But on the way home a new fear occurred to her—and she decided to gently determine whether she had anything to worry about on that score.

A discussion of the excellent cuisine at the Chimes gave her an opportunity to bring up Eddie's Polynesia: "It's doing really well, he's thinking about expanding it—more tables, a bigger menu. It's been a good thing for him . . . he'd been mooning over my mother for too long." She added casually, "Have you met the lady who works as a hostess there—Lehua?"

"The Hawaiian singer? Sure, she's good."

"Good for my dad too. They're, ah, seeing each other."

"Yeah?" Jimmy said. "That's swell."

"You really think so?" she said, perhaps a bit too earnestly.

"Well, sure," he said. "She's very pretty. They make a nice couple."

In the light of a passing car she studied his face, looking for any sign of dismay or dissembling—but found none. He seemed completely sincere.

She let out a breath and said, "I think so too."

The following week Toni and Bunty performed a series of acrobatic dives off the pool's diving board for *The Strawhatters,* the DuMont television series so far only airing locally on the New York station WABD-TV. The host, Bob Haymes, was a handsome young actor and singer who gave Toni a great introduction—*"Here's a beautiful young lady who flies through the air with the greatest of ease—but no trapeze"*—commenting enthusiastically as Toni performed a cupid dive, a flying tuck, a parasol dive, and others she had learned from Bunty. The producers liked her so much they decided to film Toni's high dive for the following week's show. As Bunty predicted, she wasn't getting paid anything extra for this—but just appearing on this new medium of television was thrilling enough compensation.

Afterward, she and Jimmy had a quick supper at the newest restaurant on Palisade Avenue—Callahan's Roadstand, which had opened right next door to long-standing local favorite Hiram's, which also served the same basic menu of frankfurters, hamburgers, and French fries. Jimmy was a devotee of Hiram's deep-fried franks, crispy on the outside and succulent on the inside; but Toni was quickly won over by Callahan's nearly foot-long hot dogs, thick, juicy, and grilled to within an inch of their lives, nearly exploding from their sausage casings.

"This place," Jimmy predicted, "won't last long next to Hiram's."

He would only be off by about fifty years.

At the end of Toni's month-long engagement at Palisades, Irving Rosenthal extended an invitation to return next year. Toni accepted at once, then left for a series of shorter gigs her agent had set up here in New Jersey: Olympic Park in Maplewood for a weekend, the Steel Pier in Atlantic City for five days, and the Sportland Pier in Wildwood.

She kept in touch with Jimmy by phone and on weekends he drove down to the shore to see her. "How many towns did you play in Kansas?" he asked over fried seafood in Wildwood.

"All of them, I think," Toni said, laughing. "At least it felt that way."

"Doesn't all that traveling wear you down?"

"No, it was exciting. But being a forty-miler isn't all that bad, either. I'm happy to be back in Jersey. I love living in Edgewater and seeing the Hudson from my front window. It's nice to just drive home after a gig."

"Sounds like you can have more of a life that way, too. A home, family . . ." He quickly added, "Assuming that's what you want, of course—"

"Oh—sure," she said, just as quickly. "I want a family, someday, kids. But I also want to keep diving."

"You mean . . . even after having kids?"

"Sure. Even if it's only playing summers at Palisades. Why not?"

Jimmy smiled and said, "Well, you *do* have a loan to repay." They laughed, quickly returning their attentions to their fried shrimp and cod.

The relationship became more passionate with the proximity of hotel rooms, though always just stopping at the door, with Jimmy driving home afterward. One night, though, in the midst of a blinding thunderstorm that canceled Toni's evening show, they decided that driving back was too dicey, so Toni invited Jimmy to sleep on the couch in her hotel room.

Toni got into her pajamas in the bathroom as Jimmy, in boxers and undershirt, threw a blanket and pillow onto the lumpy couch. They smiled awkwardly at each other, then she said, "Well . . . g'night, I guess."

"G'night." He gave her what started out as a light goodnight kiss. But they both quickly became more amorous, Toni wrapping her fingers around the nape of Jimmy's neck—

And then a little voice inside told her *Stop,* and she suddenly pulled away. "Wait—no," she said, breathless, "maybe this isn't a—good idea . . ."

"Uh . . . okay," Jimmy said, confused.

"I mean . . . maybe it's too soon. Maybe we should . . ." She stopped, sighed, then decided on the truth: "Jimmy, I'm just . . . afraid. That you'll be disappointed when I tell you that I'm not a . . . a virgin."

She said this last so softly he strained to hear it.

He gazed at her soberly and she braced herself for rejection.

"Toni . . . I'm sorry, but . . ." *Oh God, here it comes,* she thought. "I'm afraid you may be disappointed to learn . . . neither am I."

She looked at him, nonplussed, until he broke into a laugh. She happily laughed along with him, and then he cupped his hands around her waist, pulled her to him, and they took up where they had left off.

The last "bird," as Bunty Hill had put it, came home to roost in January of 1953, when a convicted gunman serving time in state prison testified before the State Crime Commission that in 1935, after being wounded in a waterfront shootout, he was given shelter from pursuing authorities by Chief Frank Borrell of Cliffside Park. The accusation was page-one news in *The New York Times*; Borrell denied ever knowing the man.

Then, on the morning of March 12, Toni was at home reading the morning paper as her father was bringing in the mail. "Hey, Dad," she said, not without a certain glee, "the Chief's been indicted."

Looking distracted, Eddie said, "What?"

She read aloud: "'Frank Borrell, the easygoing police chief of Cliffside Park, New Jersey, was indicted yesterday, along with a cousin and two members of his police force, by the Bergen County rackets grand jury . . . charged with having protected the gambling empire of Frank Erickson, who is serving eighteen months in prison, and lying to the grand jury.'" She whooped. "Get this: Erickson rented two buildings from Borrell's cousin, Patsy, yet the Chief says he never knew about them and Patsy claims he's never even spoken to Erickson . . . even though his son collects Erickson's rent. Hah!"

Eddie appeared to barely listen to any of this. He sat down at the kitchen table and tossed down one of the envelopes he had just brought in. "Look at this," he said tonelessly, and Toni glanced over at it.

The return address read UNITED STATES ARMY, WASHINGTON, D.C.

"Oh my God," Toni whispered.

Eddie stared at it as if it were a venomous snake coiled an inch away.

"Aren't you going to open it?" Toni said.

Numbly, Eddie picked up the envelope, tore it open, and took out a letter. Toni watched as his face seemed to show first relief, then shock.

"What? What does it say?" she asked.

"It says that . . . Jack is coming home," he said flatly. Before Toni could react, he added softly, "On a medical discharge."

22

EDDIE AND TONI WAITED as Jack's train pulled into Newark's Central Station, not knowing what to expect when its doors opened and Jack walked out. Would he even be able to walk? "Medical discharge" could mean anything, and in the week since Eddie received the Army's cryptic letter he had feared the worst. Would he be crippled? Blind? Disfigured? In a wheelchair, on crutches, or missing an arm, a leg, an eye? The fact that they hadn't received a letter from Jack himself only amplified his anxiety.

"At least he's still alive," Toni said, reading her father's face perfectly.

The train braked to a halt and within minutes was disgorging passengers, largely civilian with a scattering of khaki-clad soldiers or white-uniformed naval personnel. Some of these did, in fact, wear visible badges of injury: an eye patch, crutches, a face half swathed in bandages, the absence of a limb. Eddie braced himself for the worst.

"Look!" Toni cried, pointing. "There he is!"

Emerging from a train door about fifty feet down the track was Jack, carrying a duffel bag and wearing his khaki-and-olive-drab Army uniform and garrison cap. From what Eddie could see, he still had two legs, two arms, two eyes, and walked with no perceptible limp.

"Jack!" Toni called as she took off like a bullet toward him. "Jack!"

He turned and looked in Toni's direction, saw her, and seemed to smile. Eddie, following, thought it a thin smile at best—as thin as Jack himself appeared. Toni ran up to him, threw her arms around him, and hugged him. "Oh God, Jack, thank God you're okay!"

Jack didn't return the hug and even seemed a little uncomfortable with it. "Hey, Sis," he said quietly. "Thanks, but—gimme a little air, okay?"

"Oh. Sure," she said, letting go. "God, it's good to see you again."

"Good to see you too," he said, a little weakly.

Eddie came up, outstretched a hand. "Welcome home, son."

Jack just stared at Eddie's hand, his eyes betraying something like panic, and did not take his father's hand.

"Thanks, Dad," he said, hefting his bag nervously from his left hand to his right. "It's . . . good to see you. Good to be . . . back."

The way he said it, it sounded almost as if he wasn't sure of either.

"Well, let's get you home," Eddie said, reflexively taking Jack's bag from him. Startled, Jack stuck his hands in his pants pockets.

Jack spoke little as they made their way through the terminal and out to the car, so Eddie and Toni filled the silence by updating him on doings at the park and the bar. Jack slid into the backseat, Eddie and Toni in front. As Eddie keyed the ignition he said, "Hey, they finally finished the turnpike. It goes all the way up to the George Washington Bridge."

"Uh-huh," Jack said, leaning his head back on the seat. "God, I'm tired. Feels like I haven't slept in days."

He closed his eyes, and within minutes he was out for the count, sleeping through the manifold wonders of the New Jersey Turnpike.

Eddie had left Lehua in charge of the bar for the night, so when they reached home, he and Toni prepared the kind of dinner they figured Jack hadn't had in a while—grilled steak, baked potato with sour cream and chives, and homemade split-pea soup. While they were cooking, Jack settled back into his old room, then walked around the house, looking out the windows at the Manhattan skyline or at the Palisades. He turned on the television set, watching *Howdy Doody* for a minute or two with a look of bemused wonder on his face—the same look he gave to everything in the house, including the kitchen where Eddie and Toni were working. He stood in the doorway, hands in pockets, and said quietly:

"I can't believe this is all—real."

Eddie looked up from stirring the soup. "What do you mean, Jack?"

"A few weeks ago, I was in a—a snowy foxhole in Korea, my feet freezing, ducking low to avoid burp gun fire while I took potshots at Chinese troops up the hill. *That* was real. All this—just doesn't seem real to me."

"It will," Eddie assured him. "Takes time. Is it really as cold over there as they say it is?"

"Colder. Forty below on a good day. So cold your canteen bursts. Your feet never get warm because they sweat inside their Army-issue, Mickey Mouse rubber boots, and then the sweat freezes in the boot."

"My God," Toni said.

"Frostbite kills as many men as enemy fire," Jack said. "And when a man dies in that kind of cold, his body just—freezes solid. Stiff as an ironing board. I saw men stacked up like—"

He caught himself. "This—this isn't dinnertime conversation. Sorry."

"It's okay," Eddie said. "Sounds like you saw some . . . awful things."

Jack made no reply.

"Soup's on," Toni announced. "Let's eat."

They sat down to dinner, Jack last, and for several moments he stared at his plate with a mixture of longing and hesitation. Then, slowly, he took his hands out of his pockets and reached for a spoon with his right hand.

Toni noticed first: Jack's hand was trembling like a leaf in a storm, so badly it appeared to be an effort to even lower his spoon into the soup. And when he did raise it, the spoon shook off half the soup before it could reach his mouth. Toni didn't want to stare but couldn't help herself.

Eddie felt as if he'd had a stake driven into his chest.

Jack switched the spoon to his other hand, and this time he was able to get something close to a full spoonful of soup to his mouth. "Left hand's a—a little better than the right," he said.

"Jack, my God, what happened?" Eddie said softly. "Some kind of . . . nerve damage?"

"Something like that," Jack said, eyes downcast, concentrating on trying to finish his soup without spilling half of it.

"Were you . . . shot?" Toni asked in an atypically small voice.

Jack shook his head.

"Mortar strike?" Eddie asked.

Jack looked pained to speak of it. "A mortar was involved."

"But there's something they can do for that, right?" Toni asked, ever the optimist. "They can operate on the nerves?"

Jack put down his spoon, picked up a fork with his right hand and a knife with his left. He used his trembling right hand to anchor the steak as best he could, then sliced off a small piece of meat with his left hand. It clearly took an effort; perspiration beaded his forehead.

"No," he said in response to Toni's question. "But they say it—may get better with time, and rest."

He chewed his steak with nothing like the pleasure Eddie and Toni had hoped he would. Eddie's heart was breaking.

"You know, Jack Rosenthal—Irving's brother—has Parkinson's disease," Eddie said. "I'll ask Irving for the name of Jack's doctor. Maybe he can suggest something—"

"I've seen enough doctors, thanks," Jack said flatly. He managed another piece of steak, then, embarrassed, let his knife and fork drop back on the table. He stood up. "I'm not really hungry. I'm sorry, I know you went to a lot of trouble. But I'm just going to go lie down for a while."

He hurried away from the table and out of the kitchen.

For a long moment there was silence in the room . . . then Toni began to cry. She made no sound, but tears streamed down her cheeks and her chest was wracked with sobs she couldn't vocalize. Eddie went to her, wrapped his arms around his daughter, and let his own tears fall.

Toni woke around one A.M. to the sound of floorboards creaking in the hallway. She got up, passed her father's bedroom—he was sound asleep, nothing short of a tree falling on the house could wake him—then past her brother's, which was empty. Hearing footfalls on the back steps outside, she returned to her bedroom, pulled on a winter robe and slippers, then opened the back door and hurried down the steps.

She peered around the corner of the house into the side yard, where she saw Jack, fully dressed, standing in front of a metal barrel in which their landlords, the Murphys, would burn leaves. Jack threw a handful of oak leaves into the barrel—even from here Toni could see his hand tremble, giving the leaves a shaky spin as they spiraled into the big metal drum. After a few more handfuls he reached into a pocket—and took out a book of matches. He held the book in his left hand as his right tore off a match, then struggled to strike it against the matchbook. He missed it once, twice, swore softly, then finally got the match to ignite and tossed it in.

The leaves burst into flames, which spouted up, sucking oxygen from the air with a fiery inhalation. Toni, concerned, started toward him. At her approach he started, spun round, then saw it was her and let out a breath.

"Jack?" she said, coming to his side. "What are you doing out here?"

"Getting rid of stuff," he said, and bent over to pick something off the ground. He came up with a handful of comic books—*Captain America, Sub-Mariner, Plastic Man, Detective Comics, Superman.*

"What?" Toni said. "You're not going to—"

But he did, tossing the half-dozen or so comics onto the fire, which crackled and surged as it fed on the old, dry pulp paper.

He bent down to pick up another handful, but Toni stopped him, gently putting a hand on his arm. "Jack, don't. You'll be able to draw again someday, I *know* it—we'll get you the best doctors in the country—"

"This isn't about that," he said, shrugging off her hand. He stooped to pick up more comics and pulp magazines: *The Shadow, Doc Savage, Human Torch, USA Comics, All-Winners Comics, Blackhawk.* They shook for a moment in his hand, then he tossed them into the fire.

"Jack, *why?*" Toni asked as his old four-color dreams turned ashen.

"They're all lies," Jack said tonelessly, watching the corners of *Blackhawk* and *The Shadow* blacken and curl. "That's all they are—lies."

Toni stared helplessly as he threw the last of his comics onto the pyre.

"Jack," she said softly, "what the hell happened over there?"

"If I tell you, Sis," he said, "then it's not just in my head anymore, it's in yours. And I'm not about to do that to you."

He waited until the flames died down, then returned to the house.

Toni stayed behind, staring without comprehension into the dying embers of Jack's childhood.

The next morning, as Jack slept, Toni shared what happened with her father, and they decided that if Jack wanted to talk about his experiences he would, and if he didn't, that was his business. "He needs for home to start feeling 'real' to him again," Eddie said, "and I think that's the best thing—maybe the only thing—we can do for him right now."

That first day all Jack seemed to want to do was sleep, which was understandable, but on his second day home Toni talked him into a walk along the riverfront. They bundled up in winter clothes and strolled along the banks of the frigid Hudson, toward the George Washington Bridge. "Remember when we found the 'dinosaur bone' here?" Toni said, pointing out the slippery rocks they had clambered over in grade school.

Jack smiled. "Yeah. Johnny Lamarr was there that day. I never did manage to meet up with him in Korea. Hope he's okay."

Toni took him to lunch at Callahan's, where his trembling hands needed no utensils to grip one of the gigantic franks. As he wolfed it down, something of the old Jack glimmered in his tired eyes. "Man, these are *great*. After a year and a half of Army chow, this is like eating at the Ritz."

When he finished that one he promptly ordered another, as well as a second Yoo-Hoo to wash it down. Toni was glad to see him so happy.

After lunch they dropped by Eddie's Polynesia, where a light afternoon crowd was gathered to graze on the day's appetizers: Mandarin dumplings, Tahitian fruit *poi,* and shrimp grilled in coconut oil. Jack sampled one of each, even after the two hot dogs, but passed on Eddie's offer of a Singapore Sling: "After the injury, I drank a lot of beer, hoping it would help, or at least help me forget." He shook his head. "All it did was make me feel even less in control of my body."

When he first sat down at the bar, he stared at the mural behind it—*his* mural—with an intensity that alarmed Toni. Too late, she realized it might be a mocking reminder of what his once-healthy hands could do. But a small smile crept onto his face and he said, "There *is* something peaceful about it . . . isn't there? Almost like a window into the past, into Gauguin's South Seas—not that it comes close to Gauguin. I was afraid I wouldn't be able to bear the sight of it, but . . . it's nice to sit here and imagine I could step through it into another time, another place. Another me."

Jack seemed to feel so at ease in the bar that after a couple of days Eddie suggested he help out there, to give him something to do. "Dad, are you nuts?" he asked. "I can barely hold on to a fork, can you imagine how many mugs and glasses I'd break?"

"I was thinking you could work the cash register. You were always good with math and numbers. What do you say?"

Jack agreed to give it a try, and the next day came to work wearing one of the gaudy Hawaiian shirts Eddie kept for fill-in personnel. Jack had little trouble operating the cash register; his fingers were shaky, but they could press a key all right. The trickier part was taking money—directly from customers, Eddie, or Lehua—placing it in the cash drawer, then dispensing change. His hands shook as he tried to separate dollar bills from fives and tens, putting them in separate compartments, but he managed.

Worse were the coins, which he could barely pick up one at a time, much less hand back to Eddie or Lehua. Even his left hand would shake so violently that he would spill the coins all over the counter, his frustration mounting. Finally, after three hours, it came to a head when he tried to open a roll of quarters and wound up scattering them all over the floor.

He looked ready to burst into tears.

"That's it. This was a crappy idea from the start," he told Eddie, and got out from behind the counter. "I'm going home."

"Jack, wait—"

But Jack ignored him and hurried out the door. Eddie ran after, catching up to him in the parking lot. "Jack, I'm sorry, I shouldn't have—Will you *stop*, for Chrissake, and let me *talk* to you?"

"There's nothing to say!" Jack snapped, but he did slow and let his father approach. "I'm just a goddamned spastic cripple."

"Let me find out the name of Jack Rosenthal's doctor," Eddie pleaded. "There's *got* to be something they can do for you."

"Dad, there's nothing they *can* do, because it isn't a physical injury!" Jack blurted.

"What? What do you mean?"

"It's a psychiatric problem, all right? I cracked up! I broke down. I'm a goddamn coward, Dad—is *that* what you wanted to hear?"

Eddie was too stunned to respond. His face red with shame, Jack turned and started to run away.

Eddie shook off his stupor and ran after him, grabbing him by the arm before he could cross Palisade Avenue to the nearest bus stop.

"Jack, there are still doctors who may be able to help you—"

"Shrinks? In Korea they've got traveling psychiatric detachments, ready to fix you up and send you right back to the front. I was so fucked up, they sent me home. I've seen enough shrinks for one lifetime, thanks."

He pulled loose from Eddie, who made no further effort to stop him. The truth was, Eddie didn't know what to say to him—this was so far outside his experience, he was afraid anything he said might make things worse.

Eddie's eyes filled with tears as he watched his wounded son hurrying down Palisade Avenue toward Route 5 and Edgewater. Goddamn it, he thought, it wasn't fair. Why had Eddie, with a hardier constitution, been spared the horrors of war, while his son—sensitive, physically slighter—was sent straight into hell?

Worst of all—Jack had been following his father's example by volunteering to go to war. Eddie knew in the pit of his soul that this was all *his* fault—and he would never forgive himself for it.

On Saturday night, Jimmy took Toni back to the Chimes Restaurant, but all the way there and into the meal, all Toni could talk about was

Jack and how worried she was for him. Jimmy, who had started the evening out jovial if a bit nervous, slowly deflated in enthusiasm as Toni
related the story of Jack burning his comic books in the dead of night—
until finally she looked into Jimmy's face, saw the dismay in it, and said,
"Oh God, I'm sorry, this must be so depressing to you. I'll shut up now."

"No, this is what I love about you. You love your family, like I love
mine. It's just . . ." He sighed. "I wanted this night to be special. Don't
you remember? It was exactly nine months ago we came here on our first
date."

"Oh, that's so sweet. You're so much more romantic than I am."

"I thought it would be a good time to . . . oh, hell, it still is. Why
not?"

He reached into his jacket pocket, took out a small velvet-covered
box, placed it on the table, and opened it.

Inside was a gold ring inset with a small cluster of diamonds.

"I love you, Toni," he said, taking her hand. "Will you marry me?"

Toni stared at the ring—this had been the furthest thing from her
mind when the evening started—and then her face lit with a smile.

"Of course I will," she said, and kissed him with a ferocity not quite
befitting a public place.

The next morning she told her father and brother, who were both
delighted for her. But as Eddie and Toni washed the breakfast dishes
together, Eddie said gingerly, "Honey, I know you don't want to hear
this, but . . . I think you should seriously consider inviting your mother
to the wedding."

She looked up, startled. "Okay, I bite. Why?"

"You can't keep your mom out of your life forever."

"You did."

"Yeah. I did." Eddie's face darkened. "And it was only after she
passed away a few years ago that I learned from Viola how hurt she was
that she hadn't been there to see me get married, or to play with her
grandchildren. I thought I was doing the right thing by you kids, but I
realize now I was just doing it selfishly, for me."

"So you think I'm being selfish?" Toni said, a bit tartly.

"Look, I know how you feel—I was pissed off that my mom married

Sergei so soon after my dad died, but now I realize she didn't have any choice. She had three kids to feed and could barely do it working as a steam press operator. Sergei offered security. I just didn't get along with him, that's all, so I scrammed."

Sarcastically Toni asked, "You think Mom has some real good reason to tell me why she abandoned us to run off with Mr. Brylcreem of 1945?"

"She did have her reasons. But you don't even have to listen to them, especially not on your wedding day. Just invite her. Let her back into your life for that one thing, and see where it goes from there. And at least that won't be on your conscience, when you're my age."

Toni hated the idea. But she agreed to think about it.

Sunday was laundry day in the Stopka household, and everyone but Eddie seemed to clear out early that morning and find things to do, leaving their father to do the washing, drying, and folding. Toni took Jack to Callahan's for lunch, so it was left to Eddie to carry the laundry basket up from the laundry room and then, as Adele had done for years and for which Eddie was beginning to realize she had not received adequate esteem, deliver the clean clothing to the appropriate closet or chest of drawers.

This being the first laundry day since Jack's return, Eddie had to open several drawers in his son's bureau in order to figure out what went where. The third one was Jack's underwear drawer, but as Eddie opened it and began to make room for a stack of undershirts, his hand brushed against something that was both hard and soft. In the back, tucked in a corner behind some clean socks and jockey shorts, were two small, felt-covered boxes. Eddie took them out and opened the first, which contained a ribbon of red attached to a bronze star. The second held a purple ribbon attached to a gold heart-shaped medal.

A Purple Heart—and a Bronze Star, awarded for valor in combat.

Eddie was astonished. Jack called himself a coward—but here were two medals he'd been awarded for heroism.

What the hell was going on?

Eddie returned the medals to Jack's hiding place and waited the rest of the week, trying to figure out what to say and when to say it. On Saturday, when he returned home from the bar, it was half past midnight and Toni was fast asleep. But Jack was sitting on the couch in the living room, watching, of all things, *Wrestling from the Marigold Arena* on Du-Mont. On the nine-inch screen it appeared that Lou Thesz was fighting "Farmer" Don Marlin. "You're still up," Eddie said.

"Couldn't sleep."

"Why are you watching this? You hate wrestling."

"I hated high school wrestling. These are professional thespians."

Eddie came over and said, "Can I talk to you about something?"

"Sure, go ahead."

Eddie drew a short breath. "Jack, I didn't set out to do this, but—when I was putting away your laundry last weekend, I found your—your medals."

Jack stiffened but said nothing, just kept watching Farmer Don Marlin grunt and groan as Lou Thesz pinned him briefly to the canvas.

"Why didn't you tell us about them?" Eddie asked.

"Because they don't mean anything, that's why."

"You must've done something to merit them."

"They're a joke!" Jack snapped.

"The Army didn't think so."

Jack's temper flared. "Fine! You want to hear the joke? It's a damn funny one, you'll laugh your ass off. You really want to hear it?"

He glared as if daring Eddie to listen. Eddie turned down the volume on the TV, and as the tiny black-and-white figures silently grappled with each other, Eddie sat down on the couch. "Okay. I could use a good laugh."

"Fine," Jack said. "I've already told you about how the cold turned men into Popsicles. Did I mention the guy who slept in his combat boots? Inside his sleeping bag?"

"No."

"That's not what got him kicked out of the Army, though. See, the frostbite in his boots was so bad that when the doc took them off, there was no skin left, just a few pounds of ground meat."

He looked at Eddie as if to say, Heard enough?

Eddie said, deadpan: "You call that funny? What else you got?"

Jack let out a breath, resigned to telling this now.

"Okay. So it's forty below and my regiment's been marching for five straight days. We were told to take this hill—somebody named it Hamhock Hill because he said it looked like a pig's ass. I remember Bernstein asked the second looie if he could sit this one out: 'This hill ain't kosher,' he said."

Eddie laughed. "Now *that's* funny."

Jack allowed himself a thin smile. "Yeah, the lieutenant laughed too, then told him to get his ass in gear. The Chinese were dug in on the hill, so our tanks went in first, trying to soften up their artillery, to be followed by grunts like me. Well, if that artillery was soft I'd hate to see the hard stuff. The damn mortars went right over the heads of the tanks and exploded all around us. You know one's coming your way because the shell cuts through the air like a banshee. Went on like that for half a fucking hour."

"Jesus," Eddie said, "how did you stand it?"

"Oh, I wanted to shit my pants plenty of times," Jack admitted. "But then you look like a pussy to your pals, so you suck in your gut and take it. 'Course, they're all doing the same thing. Ninety percent of bravery in combat is trying not to look like a pussy in front of your friends.

"Finally, the tanks take out one of the enemy positions and the looie tells us to get going. So we charge up the hill, firing our burp guns at enemy positions, hoping one out of four bullets does some damage.

"My buddy Dominguez was on my left as we went up, and then out of my left ear I hear a banshee shriek, louder and closer than before. It was just a knee-jerk reaction—I grabbed Dom by the arm, yanked him toward me, and a few seconds later the spot where he'd been standing is a smoldering crater. We dive to the ground as dirt, rock, and shrapnel go flying over our heads. When we're finally clear of it, we get up.

"Dominguez says to me, 'Jesus Christ, man, thanks.' There's a raw recruit on my right who's seen the whole thing, and he says, 'Good work, man,' and reaches out to shake my hand. I take it and start to say something, but before I can finish there's another loud wail, and—"

He paused, staring at something a thousand miles away.

"The recruit just—explodes. In a red fog. Some goddamn mortar shell just—tore him to ribbons. The concussion threw me to the ground, and when the smoke cleared I opened my eyes. I'm covered with blood and skin and—guts. And my hand's still holding something.

"I look down and see—I'm still holding the recruit's hand. His arm's been severed at the elbow. And I'm holding it. I'm covered in blood and bile and bits of intestine, and *I'm holding his goddamned arm.*" His face was harrowed; anguished. "I started to scream. Had to be carried off the field. They tell me I didn't stop screaming for twenty minutes." He gazed down at his hands twitching in his lap. "My hands haven't stopped trembling since."

Eddie, overwhelmed, could only say, "Oh, Jesus, Jack—I'm *sorry . . .*"

On the tiny television screen, the silvery image of one of the wrestlers slung the other across his shoulders, then threw him to the canvas. Jack got up suddenly, went to the TV, and switched it off.

"So that's the joke," he said. "I save my buddy's life—another guy gets blown to hell for congratulating me—and I come apart as completely as if the mortar hit *me.* What a riot, huh? The psych detachment tried to patch me back together, and they did to a point, but—a soldier who can't hold a gun isn't much use to the Army, and I was due for rotation soon anyway, so they sent me home with a couple of medals that don't mean shit."

"That's not true," Eddie said. "You saved Dom's life. You're a hero."

At that there was fire and shame in Jack's eyes. "For Chrissake, don't use that word!" he snapped. "All those stupid comic books I used to read—all the heroes would save the girl, fight battle after battle, month after month—and me, I save one person's life, then crack like an egg!"

"Comic characters aren't *real*, Jack, you know that."

"Then how about the men I served with? All those guys who climbed hill after hill, charged into the thick of it, saw shit a hundred times worse than I saw—and went right back on the front lines the next day! But me, *I* fell apart." He sank into a chair. "I couldn't take it like they could. I cracked like an egg," he repeated, breaking down into sobs.

Eddie came over, stood in front of him, and said: "So what?"

Jack looked up, uncomprehending.

"So fucking *what* that you cracked? Everybody's got their limits, Jack, and you reached yours. After charging up hills into enemy fire for—what, over a year?—you save your buddy's life, see some poor bastard die horribly in front of you—and you broke down. Hell, I might've done the same."

"No you wouldn't. Not you."

"Bullshit," Eddie said. "I worked on planes that had the tailgunner's brains splattered across the canopy. The first time I saw it—had to hose it out, like cleaning out a horse stall—I threw up in the toilet. I did that every day for the next week. Now, that's nothing compared to what you went through. I was never tested like you were, Jack, so I don't know where my breaking point would be—but I'm damn sure I've got one. Everybody does.

"Heroes don't have to go *on* proving they're heroes, like Sergeant York or Superman," Eddie said gently. "Once is all it takes. You're my hero, Jack."

Jack looked gratefully into his father's face—and began to weep. Eddie squatted down and draped his arms across Jack's shoulders, comforting him as he had when as a boy he'd come home after falling off his bicycle, or sporting a bloody nose after a fight with a bully. He let him cry then, and he let him cry now. Eddie knew that he himself had kept too many things bottled up inside him for too long, and he wouldn't let Jack do the same. "Let it out, son," he said gently. "Let it out before it poisons you."

On a sunny, breezy day in June, within the elegant nave of the Epiphany Catholic Church in Cliffside Park, Toni and Jimmy—she in a white taffeta wedding dress, he in a black suit and red tie—stood expectantly before the altar as Father Joseph Manz told them, "Please join your right hands together." Then, to Jimmy: "Repeat after me: I, James Robert Russo, take thee, Antoinette Cherie Stopka, for my lawful wife—"

Jimmy looked into Toni's eyes and repeated, "I, James Robert Russo, take thee, Antoinette Cherie Stopka, for my lawful wife . . . to have and to hold, from this day forward, for better, for worse, for richer, for poorer, in sickness and in health . . . until death do us part."

Father Manz turned to Toni, had her recite the same vow, then declared, "I join you together in marriage in the name of the Father, and of the Son, and of the Holy Ghost. Amen."

He sprinkled the couple with holy water, then took the wedding ring from the outstretched palm of Jimmy's best man, his brother Tim.

"Bless, O Lord, this ring, which we bless in Thy name, that she who shall wear it, keeping true faith unto her spouse, may abide in Thy peace and in obedience to Thy will, and ever live in mutual love. Through Christ our Lord. Amen."

Manz sprinkled the ring with holy water in the form of a cross, then handed it to the groom, who placed it on the third finger of Toni's left hand and said, "With this ring I thee wed and I plight unto thee my troth."

"In the name of the Father, and the Son, and the Holy Ghost, amen."

After this came the Nuptial Blessing, followed by Mass for the bride and bridegroom. During the processional to the altar, Toni had been too overwhelmed and elated to take much notice of who was sitting in the pews; and once at the altar she had been facing first the priest, then Jimmy. Now, during the Mass, she was able to look out into the congregation and pick out familiar faces on the bride's side of the aisle: Minette Dobson, Bunty Hill, her father, Lehua, Aunt Vi and Uncle Hal and their kids, Grandma Marie . . . and beside her grandmother, someone she had not seen for eight years.

Her mother.

Adele was now forty-two years old, but Toni was surprised to see how little she had changed. Her hair was still long, wavy, and blonde— Miss Clairol might have had something to do with that—and she looked stunning in a creamy pastel sweater and halter-neck dress with a full circle skirt and matching hat. Even from here Toni could see the proud, pleased smile on her face, making Toni suddenly happy that she had invited her.

Later, at the wedding reception, Toni, Jimmy, and the rest of the wedding party stood in a receiving line at the door, shaking hands with guests as they entered. When it was Adele's turn she cupped Toni's hand in hers and said, "You look so beautiful, honey. Thank you so much for inviting me." She kissed Toni on the cheek and moved on. "I'll see you later," Toni called after. Adele smiled and nodded.

An hour later, after the toasts and the dinner and the cutting of the cake, Toni was able to mingle with the guests, going from table to table to chat briefly at each one. She spoke first with her father, Lehua, Jack, Minette, and Bunty, but made a point to go next to the table where Adele sat with Grandma Marie, Uncle James and Uncle Ralph, and their families.

Toni sat next down to her mother, took her hand and said, "I'm glad you could come. You look pretty beautiful yourself."

"Thanks. It takes a lot more work than it used to." Adele laughed, then said, "You know, this isn't the first time I've seen you since . . . I left."

Toni blinked. "It isn't?"

"I saw you perform at the Steel Pier last year," Adele said. "I was in the crowd. You were amazing, Toni, just amazing. I was so proud of you."

Surprised, Toni said, "Well, thanks. Were you and Lorenzo playing Atlantic City too?"

Adele laughed. "I haven't been with Lorenzo for years. I'm performing solo now."

"Solo? As what?"

"A magician—a lady magician. I met one years ago, at Palisades, and never forgot her. There are some of us around—Dell O'Dell, Suzy Wandas, Celeste Evans . . ."

"I had no idea there were any at all."

"We're a select few. Like lady high divers." She leaned in to Toni. "You're a born performer, Toni. You got that from me."

Toni found herself bristling at that. "You never wanted me to dive. You didn't think it *was* ladylike."

"I know. I was so foolish, I'm sorry . . ."

"Dad and Bunty are the ones who encouraged me," Toni said, "and now *you're* trying to take credit for my success?"

"No—no, honey, I didn't mean to imply that—"

Toni stood.

"I'm sure you're a great magician, Mom," Toni said in a sudden fit of temper. "You're terrific at making yourself disappear."

"*Toni* . . ." Adele said plaintively.

But it was too late—Toni had turned on her heel and was walking, quickly but coolly, on to the next table.

Marie put a hand on her daughter's arm consolingly. "She's under stress. It's her wedding day."

"No, she's right," Adele said quietly. "I do a great vanishing act. So great"—her eyes misted over—"she'll never forget it."

23

Palisades, New Jersey, 1962

In 1956 Palisades' publicist, Sol Abrams, engineered what was arguably the grandest public relations stunt in the park's history: a fifteen-hundred-pound circus elephant water-skiing on pontoons, towed across the Hudson by motorboat to promote the park's April opening. The sheer audacity of it landed the elephant in newsreels, magazines, and newspapers across the country. But the best publicity by far the park ever received was a gift that arrived in March of 1962 from Swan Records, singer Freddy Cannon, and a young songwriter named Chuck Barris:

> *Last night I took a walk in the park*
> *A swingin' place called Palisades Park . . .*

"Palisades Park," intended to be the B side of Cannon's single, was a breakout hit, quickly rising to number three on *Billboard*'s music charts. The bouncy, up-tempo tune, punctuated by the sound of a calliope and the rattle and roar of a real roller coaster, told of a young man who comes to Palisades looking for girls and rides the shoot-the-chute beside a cute one, with whom, in short order, he finds himself holding hands.

It was a story that had played out countless times at the real park, and its breezy rhythms captured the spirit of excitement, fun, and romance that generations of teenagers had come to associate with Palisades:

You'll never know how great a kiss can feel
When you stop at the top of a Ferris wheel
When I fell in love . . . . down at Palisades Park.

Even music fans who had never before heard of Palisades Park could identify with it, and the song quickly became an international success—selling two million copies by the end of that summer—and was welcomed with open arms by Irving Rosenthal as the sweetest "gag" he never had to pay for. He invited Cannon to sing "Palisades Park" *at* Palisades Park over the Fourth of July weekend, where thousands would turn out to hear him.

And by this time, Palisades Amusement Park had really become the "swingin' place" of which Cannon sang. Starting in the mid-1950s, the Rosenthals began to capitalize on the burgeoning popularity of rock and roll, hiring local radio deejays Murray Kaufman, better known as "Murray the K," and Bruce Morrow, "Cousin Brucie," to host concerts on the free-act stage by such rising young stars as Bobby Rydell, Fabian, the Shirelles, Bill Haley and His Comets, Frankie Avalon, and a local Tenafly girl made good named Lesley Gore, singing her hit "It's My Party." For one season, singer Clay Cole hosted his own daily television show broadcast from Palisades, featuring bright new names like Chubby Checker (who performed the "Twist" for the first time on the show), Frankie Valli, Brian Hyland, and Neil Sedaka.

Palisades Amusement Park was not just popular—it was *hip*.

But the park also continued to feature more traditional attractions like the Hunt Brothers Circus, the Little Miss America and Miss American Teenager pageants, as well as a variety of high-flying aerial acts that included Palisade Park's own high-diving sensation, the Amazing Antoinette.

"Dawn," Toni asked her daughter, "where's your brother? Doesn't he know we're leaving?"

Seven-year-old Dawn looked up from playing with her Barbie doll, blew a long strand of reddish-blonde hair out of her eyes, and said, "I think I saw him take his go-cart out of the garage."

Toni sighed. "I told him we were leaving for the park. Wait here."

Toni walked out of the two-story white clapboard house she and Jimmy had purchased three years ago. Valley Place was a narrow, sloping street that ran from Undercliff Avenue to the dead-end of Hudson Terrace; reaching the curb she could hear the approaching rattle of metal wheels.

She looked up the street to see her son, Jeffrey, dark-haired, eight years old, hurtling down the hill on a go-cart he had built himself by hammering an orange crate to a plank, then nailing a pair of old roller skates to the plank—singing the theme to some puppet show he watched on TV:

"Supercar! Sooopercar!" he cried as he rattled past her, then, just before reaching the fencing at the end of the street, veering to the right and skidding to a stop in front of the last house on the block. Toni worried that one of these days he would collide with a car turning right from Hudson Terrace, or jump the fence onto Route 5; thankfully most of the go-cart races he took part in were held on dead-end streets.

"Jeff, we're leaving, put your cart away and get into the car!"

"Just one more ride down, Mom?"

"Mommy has a big tank of water to jump into, pal, so get in the car."

Jeff pushed the cart past her, muttering, "I never get to have any fun."

"We're going to an *amusement* park, remember?"

"Oh, yeah," he said, mood swinging to sunny. "Is Dad meeting us?"

"Yes, at showtime, when he's on lunch break."

It was a short drive up Route 5 to Palisade Avenue and the park, where Toni parked in the employee parking lot on this, the first day of her annual month-long engagement—always the highlight of her year.

There were changes this season at Palisades, as ever, as the Rosenthals kept up with the beat of the times. Toni loved the rock-and-roll acts that played the free-act stage, even if Jimmy said, "Ah, they can't compare to Glenn Miller," and her children were a little too young to enjoy them. There were new rides like the Atomic Boats, the Roto-Jet, and the Wild Mouse.

There were also changes behind the scenes. Anna Halpin was now

Anna Cook, having wed businessman Fred Cook in '55. Candyland was still here, but the man who once owned it, Chief Borrell, died in disgrace in '57 after serving a prison term for perjury. And sadly, just a few weeks before, Superintendent Joe McKee passed away; the park's assistant superintendent for twenty years, Joe Rinaldi, was quickly named to replace him.

Toni took the kids to the free-act stage where she and Arlan had put up her tank and tower the day before. Already waiting for them there was . . .

"Uncle Jack!" Jeff and Dawn ran up to him and he squatted down and wrapped his arms around both of them. His hands, though they still trembled, became much stronger and steadier when he held his niece and nephew, whom he doted on.

"There you are! I was just about to ride the Roto-Jet without you!"

"No no, take us with you!" Jeff pleaded.

"I want to see Noah's Ark," Dawn said. This was a new exhibit showcasing a hundred different varieties of animals, many of which, like baby lambs, could be petted.

"That's boring," Jeff said. "I want to see the cow with two heads." Jeff couldn't get enough of Arch and Maie McAskill's Freak Animal Show.

"We'll go to as many of 'em as we can before coming back to see your Mom," Jack promised. "And remember, there's always tomorrow."

"Do we have to?" Jeff complained. "We've seen Mom jump a thousand million times, but I've only seen the two-headed cow once before!"

"If the public were as blasé about my act as you two are," Toni said, smiling, "I'd be out of a job. Try not to yawn when I make the dive." She gave them each a kiss. "Thanks for taking them, Jack."

"What are uncles for?" he said with a grin, and led the kids away.

Toni and Arlan checked her equipment, the weather and wind speed, then Toni used one of the performer rooms at the sideshow (now known as "Hell's Belles and the Palace of Wonder") to slip into her swimsuit.

A little before one P.M., Jimmy arrived to wish her luck as a crowd gathered at the free-act stage. Eddie and Lehua—celebrating their fifth wedding anniversary this month—arrived hand in hand shortly after. Minette Dobson, on lunch break from her concession, slid onto a bench.

Then, at the last minute, a willowy blonde in a red Jackie Kennedy dress slipped in, sat down beside Minette, and began chatting with her.

"Your mom's here," Jimmy said.

"She was invited," Toni said, "but I kind of hoped she'd have a gig of her own in Atlantic City."

"I thought you two put all that behind you."

Toni frowned. "More like we put it aside. For the kids' sake."

At that, the voice of Bob Paulson announced, *"Ladies and gentlemen, Palisades Park is proud to welcome back its prodigal daughter, Toni Stopka. Here now the death-defying gymnastic diving of—the Amazing Antoinette!"*

Jimmy kissed Toni for luck and she ascended the ladder.

In the audience, Adele told Minette, "I really am in awe of what she does. The timing, the precision, the skill it requires. . . ."

"Have you told her that?"

"Yes. But I'm not sure she believes me."

Minette hesitated a moment, then asked, "Adele, if you had it to do over . . . would you still have left them?"

"You mean, do I regret leaving my children?" Adele said hotly. "Of course I do! But Minette, I'm fifty-one years old. My best years in the business may be behind me, but what I would also have regretted is to have reached this age . . . and never to have *tried*."

Toni launched herself off the platform and into a cutaway double somersault, piked—one of the most difficult dives for any high diver—before plunging safely into the water.

She emerged from the tank to the cheers and applause of the crowd—all but Jeffrey and Dawn, otherwise occupied consuming clouds of cotton candy bigger than their heads. Jack always bought them too much food.

Once Toni had changed into dry clothes, the whole family drove down the street for a celebratory lunch at Eddie's Polynesia on the Palisades.

Eddie's was no longer just a bar, but a full-service restaurant; after three years in the black he expanded the kitchen and dining room to accommodate up to a hundred customers nightly. At the same time he added a new, six-foot *tiki* at the front entrance, which was now bracketed by two flaming torches fed by a small gas pipe. As Eddie was fond of saying, you could see the place a mile away and think, "What the hell is *that*?"

Since Hawai'i had become the fiftieth state—and the advent of jet travel had brought the islands closer to the mainland—business at Eddie's had nearly doubled. He and Lehua had added three waitresses and two more cooks to the staff. Eddie still liked working the bar, though he now employed another bartender to take up the slack. Eddie asked Toni and Jimmy, "So what can I get for the Amazing Antoinette and the Red Guinea?"

Jimmy laughed. "Red wine for the Red Guinea—Merlot if you got it."

"We got everything. Toni?"

"Banana daiquiri."

"Coming right up."

They sat down at a table where Jack, off the clock from his job as the restaurant bookkeeper, was entertaining Jeffrey and Dawn. Jack's hands still trembled enough that he couldn't draw, but he'd discovered that he could work an adding machine and a typewriter just fine—and had even started using the latter to write stories about his experiences in Korea, which his VA psychiatrist had recommended as a way of coming to terms with them.

Adele entered the restaurant, as always a little amazed by it. She had never suspected that Eddie had anything like this place in him—he was more of a showman than she had ever credited him. Despite what she told Minette, part of her couldn't help wondering what might have happened had she given in to that last plea of his to put together an act and go on the road together. Where might they be today?

"*Aloha*, Adele," Eddie greeted her.

She smiled. "*Aloha*, Eddie."

"What'll you have?"

"Gin and tonic."

"Done. Take a seat and I'll have your drink in a jiff."

She went to the table, kissed and greeted Toni, then Jack, then Toni's husband and the kids. "Hi, Grandma!" they each said. They were beautiful children, as beautiful as Jack and Toni had been at their age.

She sat down next to Dawn, and realized when she looked up she was directly opposite Lehua. "*Aloha,* Lehua, how've you been?"

"Fine, Adele, and yourself?"

"Still pulling rabbits out of my hat," she said, which always made everyone laugh and took the place of potentially awkward conversation.

Within a few minutes Eddie brought a tray of drinks to the table, took a seat beside Lehua, and proposed a toast: "To another day in which my death-defying daughter remembered to fill the tank with water."

Everyone laughed and drank to it.

Lunch was a delicious buffet of Hawaiian *kālua* spareribs, Mandarin duck, Tahitian lime fish, pineapple rice, and for dessert, Hawaiian *haupia* (coconut) pudding, the recipe for which Eddie had obtained from Lehua's mother on their last trip to Oʻahu to visit her family.

Seeing Eddie married to Lehua, Adele felt caught in a thorny tangle of emotions. She was glad he was happy—she had treated him badly, no two ways about it, despite what he had done to her by enlisting—she only wished that her last boyfriend hadn't recently skipped town, as she once had, with a showgirl. Not that she had been all that crazy about him, but it would have been nice to have someone sitting beside her right now.

As soon as she reasonably could, Adele found a reason to leave for Atlantic City. Dawn asked, "You're still coming to my birthday party next month, aren't you, Grandma?"

"Of course."

"Will you show us some tricks?"

"Try and stop me," Adele said, kissing her and Jeffrey, then exiting. Toni was silently relieved to see her go.

"Mom, can we stop at Pitkof's for the new comic books?" Jeff asked. Toni smiled. "Absolutely."

Pitkof's Candy Store was still at 310 Palisade Avenue, still selling candy, ice-cream sodas, toys, cards and magazines, and above all, comic books. Jeffrey and Dawn ran for the spinner rack as Toni and Jack had twenty years before; Dawn was interested only in titles like *Casper, Baby Huey,* and *L'il Dot,* while Jeff snapped up the new issues of *Justice League of America* and *The Fantastic Four.* Flipping through the *JLA,* he spotted a familiar half-page ad featuring Superman himself, inviting the reader to

Be my guest at Palisades Amusement Park, New Jersey. This coupon entitles you to FREE admission plus 2 FREE RIDES . . . acts And Parking!

Jeff was always thrilled when he saw these ads, which elevated Palisades from just their local amusement park to a place where Superman might hang out on his days off as Clark Kent.

Jack Pitkof was in his late sixties now, his hair as gray as the service jacket he still wore, patient as ever with the kids who thronged his store. His eight-year-old niece Miriam, whose job it was to open the packs of comics and put them on the racks, often read the comics aloud with Jeffrey.

Toni marveled at how little the store had changed: the yellowed greeting cards on display could have dated from the 1940s, and here and there, on a back shelf, was an old toy that time seemed to have passed by. She slid onto a stool at the soda fountain and ordered a chocolate soda.

"So, Jack, how's Rachel?" Toni asked, referring to Pitkof's wife.

"Good, good. Miriam has a cold or else she'd be here today."

"And how are Kamal and his family doing?" Although he seldom mentioned it, the elderly Jewish shopkeeper, living his faith, had taken an immigrant Egyptian family under his wing, renting them a small apartment which, at first, they couldn't afford to pay for—an issue Jack never pressed.

"Ah," he said, "very well. Kamal is going to open an insurance office next door, he's got enough saved now for the rent."

"They owe you a lot," Toni said.

He shook his head. "They owe me nothing. I know how hard it is, to come with nothing to a new country. All I did was give them a little push."

Toni looked at him and thought: To receive hate and to give back kindness—that was not "nothing."

After Pitkof's, Toni took the kids back home, by which time Jimmy was home. Toni cooked dinner and was out of the house by six o'clock. Her evening performance—a double somersault, tucked, with a half-twist—went well, the crowd quite vocal in their approval. But as good as it was to be back at Palisades, there was someone important missing from the park, and Toni would make a point to seek him out tomorrow morning.

Five years earlier, Bunty Hill, a fixture at the Palisades pool for twenty-three years, left to take a job as a lifeguard at the Colony Swim Club in Chatham. He worked there for two years, but by '62 he was largely retired, working only odd jobs, living alone in his apartment on Hoefleys Lane—though still taking his daily swims in the Hudson, and still serving as swim instructor to the gaggles of Fort Lee kids who followed him like geese to the riverfront to learn from the master.

Toni couldn't help but worry for her friend—was he really getting by all right? Was he happy?

Leaving Jeffrey and Dawn in a neighbor's care, Toni drove down Henry Hudson Drive to Hazard's Dock—where Bunty, as always during the summer, was showing young students how to swim safely in the Hudson (when he wasn't sitting on the shore, reading his racing form and sharing his crackers, cheese, and liverwurst with the exhausted pupils). When Bunty looked up and saw Toni he smiled, the corners of his eyes crinkling with pleasure. "Hey, kid, where you been? It's been a while."

"I had some gigs in Florida," she said, sitting down on the dock alongside the kids. "February's a big month for county fairs in Florida."

"And Jimmy takes care of the kids while you're away? Man, you married a saint."

"Well, it helps that I work four months a year and earn a little bit more than he does all year at the bank," Toni said.

"Bunty," one of the kids asked, "my grandpa says people used to spend summers down here, is that true?"

"Hell, yes. About half a mile south of here"—he pointed, and every head snapped in that direction—"at Carpenters Landing, there'd be hundreds of tents and summer homes—vacationing New Yorkers, mostly . . ."

Toni sat back and enjoyed the sun, the salt air, Bunty's soothing voice as he told his stories of days gone by. And even if his hair had grayed and his face wrinkled some, he was still in remarkably good shape for a sixty-one-year-old man—that triangular swimmer's body of his looked as sturdy as it had a decade ago, broad shoulders, thin waist, lean muscular legs. Bunty hadn't stopped time, but here at Hazard's he seemed to have at least slowed it down.

Later, after the kids had gone home, Toni asked what he was up to these days.

"You remember Tommy Meyers—he was a lifeguard at Palisades?" Bunty said. "He just bought a run-down old house in Coytesville and I'm helping him fix it up. He wanted to pay me for it and when I said no, he said, 'Okay, then, when this place is finished, you're coming over every Sunday for dinner with me and my family.' Well, I'm no fool—I may turn down money, but never food."

They both laughed. Then after a moment, Toni worked up the nerve to ask something she had wondered about these past few years:

"Bunty? Do you ever . . . regret not getting married? I mean, you obviously love kids—didn't you ever want any of your own?"

Bunty thought a moment and said, "Yeah, sure, sometimes I regret it. But I had so many sweethearts at the pool, I just couldn't bring myself to pick one and hurt the feelings of the rest. And if I had, I'd have had to get a regular job, pay a mortgage—and then I couldn't come down here and swim the river every day. I've got plenty of kids, Toni—all of you are my kids, and I couldn't ask for better ones. Look how beautiful it is out here today. Look at the friends I have. I've got everything a man could want."

The smile on his face was genuine—he chose this life, and he loved it. And if he was truly happy, that was all that mattered to Toni.

The highlight of Dawn's eighth birthday party in August was a performance by "The Magical Adele," who started out her routine by showing Dawn and her friends a square bag made of felt, turning it inside out to demonstrate that it was empty, then zipping it shut. "You see, this is no ordinary bag," Adele explained. "It produces eggs, as many as you can eat. Like so." She unzipped it, reached into the seemingly empty bag, and took out a hard-boiled egg, which she then passed around to the children.

"Wow!" a boy said. "How many are in there?"

"Let's find out," Adele said with a smile, then reached in and took out a second egg, which she handed to the boy. Then a third egg, and a fourth, and a fifth. There were gasps of delight from the kids as they examined them, then Adele said, "But since none of you are hungry after all that birthday cake, we'll put the eggs back in the bag and make them disappear until someone—probably me—needs to make an omelet. All right?"

She took back the eggs, placed them in the bag, then zipped it, spoke a magical incantation, then unzipped it and held it upside down.

It was empty.

More gasps of awe and delight from the kids.

"But really, it's not such a good idea to make omelets out of disappearing eggs," she noted, "because when the omelet reaches your stomach, it disappears again—and you're still hungry!"

They all laughed at that.

She went on to make a series of coins, taken from the pockets of the children themselves, disappear from the palm of her hand, then reappear. And when they came back, there were now *two* coins for each child.

"This is called getting a return on your investment," she quipped.

Toni watched from the doorway, impressed not so much by the magic tricks—she knew that the coins had been "palmed" and that the eggs actually disappeared into secret pockets in the bag—as by Adele's patter, the way she kept the kids entertained and misdirected their attention when necessary. She had only seen her mother perform her act once, at the Steel Pier in '58, and she had been good then too.

At the end, when Adele literally produced a rabbit out of her hat, the kids applauded enthusiastically and the bunny was passed among them to be fondled. Toni saw the bright smile on her mother's face and knew exactly what she was feeling: the satisfaction of having performed the routine well, the pleasure of approbation, the quiet pride that you could do something few people could. She had told herself a thousand times that these were the same reasons her mother had abandoned them, that she had been driven by childhood dreams even as Toni had . . . but despite this, she still couldn't manage to open her heart to her.

Later, after Dawn's guests had left and it was just family, Adele spent an hour playing dolls with Dawn as they chatted about hairstyles and dresses and shoes. Toni watched this too, and felt a twinge of guilt and sorrow that she hadn't been the kind of daughter her mother had so desperately wanted. But at least she had given her a granddaughter whose face would light up when Adele gave her the latest doll, or a new comb for her hair. She was happy that she could do that, at least, for her mother. It hadn't all been Adele's fault; Toni had been just as stubborn, resisting her help, rejecting everything she held dear. She'd been a brat at times—she could admit that to herself, if not to Adele.

Go on, Toni told herself. After she's done with Dawn, talk shop with her, compare war stories, life on the road. Maybe now you *are* the kind of daughter she can be proud of. Her mother had said as much, but Toni never quite believed it. She was too afraid it would turn out to be a lie.

Like all the other lies.

Anger at those lies held her back, and kept her heart closed.

She turned away and left Adele and Dawn to play their girlish games and laugh their girlish laughter. As a child Toni would have mocked them. As an adult she longed to join them. But she knew it was too late for that.

Toni had a three-day engagement at the Steel Pier in Atlantic City the last week of August, before the annual Miss America Pageant took over the town. She and Arlan drove down on a Tuesday and had the equipment set up the next day. She knew she would have to call her mother at some point, but for now she put it off to take in one of the pier's most famous attractions. The diving horse act conceived by Ella Carver's adopted father continued to this day, as a horse named Shiloh dove headfirst into a huge tank of water, a young woman astride him. Toni marveled at their virtuosity but couldn't help feeling sorry for the horse—Toni had freely chosen her career, these animals had had no say in their dangerous profession.

Other than the horses the mid-week attractions at the Pier were "Skip Sigel's Steel Pier Jazz Dancers," a troupe of twelve young women dancing to jazzed-up melodies like "Who's Sorry Now?", and a young singer named Barbara Ann Mack, who had parlayed appearances on an Albany, New York, television show called *The Teenage Barn* into a twenty-four-day gig here.

At Toni's performances the next day, she offered the afternoon crowd the backward somersault with a half twist and the evening crowd got the topper, the cutaway double somersault, piked. After the last show she decided to walk across the boards to Abe's Oyster House—an Atlantic City tradition—for a nice hot bowl of chowder. But as she stepped up to the old two-story brick building to look at the menu posted in the window, her attention was caught by one of the waitresses inside, serving a table about twenty feet away from Toni. The woman was laying down a plate of steamed clams and another bearing a whole Maine lobster. As she did, her wavy blonde hair fell into her eyes, and with her hands occupied, she blew the hair out of her vision.

Toni felt a chill colder than the wind off the ocean.

It was Adele.

Toni stared a long moment, hoping that she was mistaken, but—no. It was her. It was her mother.

And it wasn't even the off-season yet.

Toni quickly turned away before Adele could see her, and began hurrying down Atlantic Avenue. She walked all the way to Maine Avenue, losing herself in Hackney's Restaurant, whose vast dining room, it was said, could accommodate three thousand guests. There weren't anywhere near that many tonight, but there were enough to make her feel safe in a crowd.

Once again she had looked through a window and seen something she wished she hadn't—but this time, instead of reacting with fear and anger, she felt only shock and sadness. A terrible, piercing sadness that could not be warmed or blunted by the hot coffee or clam chowder she held in her hands. And for the first time in almost twenty years, her eyes filled with tears for her mother—not for her mother's abandonment of her, but for her mother herself, and the heartbreak that she was surely feeling.

24

Palisades, New Jersey, 1966

GLADYS SHELLEY, IN ADDITION to being Mrs. Irving Rosenthal, was a talented, successful composer of popular songs and Broadway show tunes who had made several attempts over the years to compose a theme song for her husband's beloved park. All, sadly, were of fleeting posterity: few visitors ever left Palisades humming "Sunnin' in the Summer Sun," "Amusement Park Waltz," or "Color It Palisades Amusement Park."

And then came Freddy Cannon's "Palisades Park." Whether inspired creatively or competitively, Miss Shelley, asked in 1965 to write a jingle for the park to be played on local radio stations, finally struck gold:

Palisades has the rides,
Palisades has the fun,
Come on over . . .

The melody, like that of "Palisades Park," was bouncy, fun, and highly contagious: this one you *did* hum (or sing) after hearing singer Steve Clayton's breezy delivery. All summer, every summer, it ran on radio and TV in the New York metropolitan area, and for local children growing up at that time—Baby Boomers—it would forever become part of the soundtrack of their childhoods.

Palisades from coast to coast
Where a dime buys the most
Palisades Amusement Park
Swings all day and after dark!

If "Palisades Park" was the song that made Palisades famous around the world, "Come On Over" was the hometown anthem that would be fondly recalled, even in adulthood, by millions of children who grew up in New York and New Jersey:

Ride the coaster, get cool,
In the waves of the pool
You'll have fun, so—come on over!

Meanwhile, another literary achievement was celebrated at Eddie's Polynesia on the Palisades, when an elated Jack Stopka rushed in one day carrying an envelope and a magazine and announced: "I sold a story!"

Eddie had not seen him looking so animated, so excited, since before he joined the Army. Lehua asked, "What story, Jack?"

"It was one I wrote for my shrink, about taking my first hill in Korea," Jack said, almost breathless. "I called it 'The First Day Up,' but the publisher is retitling it 'My First Day in Hell,' which I guess is punchier."

"My God, Jack, that's fantastic!" Eddie said, coming out from behind the bar. "Who's publishing it?"

"*Argosy* magazine. Here, this is last month's issue." He handed his father a copy of the former pulp, which now billed itself as "The No. 1 Men's Service Magazine" and featured stories like "Hitler's Solid Gold Pistol" and "Vietnam: Air Cavalry's Bloody Debut."

"It's not *The Saturday Evening Post*," Jack admitted, "but it's not *Man's Illustrated* either, which is where I probably would've sent it next."

"Congratulations, Jack," Lehua said, giving him a hug. "That's quite an accomplishment."

"Hell yes! Congratulations, Jack." Without thinking, Eddie outstretched a hand. For the first time in years, Jack didn't flinch from it, and his grip was surprisingly steady.

He proudly displayed the acceptance letter and a check, admitting a little sheepishly, "They only paid me thirty-five bucks for it. But it's a start."

"You're damn right it is. Being a published author—that's as good as being a movie star in my book. I couldn't be prouder of you, son."

"Too bad Sis isn't here," Jack said. "I'll have to call and tell her."

At that moment, Jack's sister was sitting in the shade of a palm tree outside Ella Carver's trailer, which now shared space with her tank and tower on a lot in Dania, Florida, near Fort Lauderdale. In August of 1966 Ella would turn seventy-three, and she looked the archetypal grandmother: a nest of snow-white hair framing a tanned, weathered face, her eyes still keen and lively behind white horn-rimmed spectacles. "My eyes are the reason I stopped daytime diving," she explained to Toni as she sat knitting a scarf for her granddaughter. "The glare of the sun on the water practically blinded me. Now I only do night dives. That's just common sense."

Toni, fresh from a series of Southern engagements in May and June, just smiled. "Where are you performing these days?"

"Wherever I can. Not as many carnivals around these days, so I do a lot of drive-in theaters—fire diving in between showings of *Darby's Rangers* and *The Yellow Mountain*. Also shopping centers and supermarkets."

"I saw how you stumped the panel on *What's My Line?*"

She laughed. "Like I told you once, it's all about expectations. Nice little white-haired grandma, who's gonna think she does what I do for a living? Yeah, that show was a hoot."

"So no plans to retire?"

"And do what? Sit and knit? If I stopped diving, I'd die. I wouldn't be happy settled down in one place for too long. We old-time entertainers . . . we just live in a world alone, by ourselves."

Toni thought of Bunty and was supremely grateful for her family.

Ella said, "I hear you wowed 'em at the Jacksonville Fair."

"Yeah, I started with a backward double somersault, then in the evenings I did a cutaway double somersault, piked. The usual routine."

"You know," Ella said slowly, "there's a feature you should consider adding to your act. Ever thought about doing a fire dive?"

Toni started at the word *fire*. "But—that's your specialty."

"Oh, hell, I didn't invent it, Bee Kyle was doing it before me. And Billy Outten does a male human torch act. But I won't be around forever and there ought to be *some* woman I can pass the torch on to, so to speak."

"Ella, I'm flattered, but . . . fire *scares* me, you know that—"

"All the more reason to do it," Ella insisted. "You can't live your whole life afraid of something that happened twenty years ago. Back in '53 I was adjusting some guy wires when the wind blew a high-tension wire against them, sending seven thousand volts through my body. Knocked me cold. But you don't see me cringing from light sockets, now do you?"

Toni couldn't help but laugh. It was true, every time she overcame her fears she had come out stronger in the end.

"I suppose I could . . . try it once," she allowed.

"That's the spirit. C'mon, I'll get you outfitted right now."

"You mean—right this moment?"

"Why not? Wind's calm and neither of us are getting any younger."

Inside the trailer, Ella rummaged through her closet and pulled out a pair of gray woolen tights and a wool shirt. "Here, try these on. You're a few inches taller'n me, but these tights have stretched some over the years."

"Can I leave on my underwear?"

"Sure, protect the dainty bits if you want. Your hair's longer than mine, I'd put on this cap too."

Toni stripped to her undies, pulled on the wool tights—a little snug, but they did the job of covering her exposed skin—then the shirt, then stuffed her hair under the wool cap. She looked into the nearest mirror.

"I look like the world's most pathetic cat burglar."

Ella smiled. "Here, put this on."

Toni slipped into one of Ella's canvas jackets. "I always keep two or three of these handy. The canvas gives you an added layer of protection, but they do occasionally get a bit scorched. This is all deductible, y'know."

"Along with my hospital bills?"

"Quit bellyaching. I've been doing this fifty years and all I've gotten is a few burns on my hands. C'mon, I keep the gasoline packs out back."

Holy shit, Toni thought, I guess I'm really *doing* this.

Outside, Ella opened a metal case containing two gasoline packs. She strapped them onto Toni's back and showed her how to ignite them.

"You've got to gauge the wind—you can't have a stiff breeze blowing the flames every which way. When the packs ignite, it's going to feel like there's a fireball on your back, 'cause there *is*. Don't let the sudden heat panic you. Don't seize up. Just look down at the tank and jump."

"What happens if the flames set my clothes on fire?"

"They won't. They're too busy consuming the oxygen around you, and you're protected, for a little while, by that canvas jacket. The trip takes only three seconds and the water extinguishes the flames."

Toni took a deep breath and began climbing up Ella's tower.

This is crazy, she thought. I'd rather have Cliff Bowles shoot himself out of a cannon over my head! But she kept climbing, listening to the slosh of the gasoline even as she accustomed herself to its extra weight and how it altered her center of gravity—she'd have to adjust her posture accordingly when she was preparing to jump.

Once on the top platform, she looked down into the tank and saw Ella standing on the side. "Gauge the wind, honey," she called up.

Toni focused on the wind direction and speed—the fronds of palm trees below her were barely moving. "Light wind, two knots at the most."

"Then light the fuse and jump."

Toni took several deep breaths, then ignited the packs.

There was a WHOOOSH of air that rocked her on her heels—she struggled to keep her footing firm—as her back was enveloped in hot flame, *tremendously* hot. She felt it more than she saw it—a few angry orange flickers at the corners of her vision—and, with a quick assessment of distance, she immediately jumped off the platform.

She plummeted straight down, trailing fire, the air around her rippling with heat. The fall felt longer than it ever had, then she dropped like a hot coal into the water. The flames sizzled as the water quenched them and turned to steam, raising the water temperature by thirty degrees.

Once the shock of it had worn off, she was ecstatic: she *did* it—a fire dive! She'd been a genuine human torch. Jack would have been so impressed! She swam excitedly over to the ladder, climbed up and out of the tank, and found Ella waiting for her as she descended the other side.

"How'd I do?" Toni asked.

"Not bad, for a first-timer," Ella said. "By the end of the week we'll have you jumping into a tank full of flames."

Toni felt as if her stomach had just plummeted another ninety feet.

"Okay, let me get this straight," Jimmy said, an obvious strain in his voice. "You strap a couple of gasoline packs on your back, set them on *fire*, then jump into a tank filled with gasoline that's *also* on fire. That about cover it?"

They were sitting in their living room, it was past ten in the evening, and the kids were in bed—the first chance they'd had to discuss this since Toni had driven her truck and trailer into the driveway late that afternoon.

"The flames are in a ring around the rim of the tank," Toni explained. "There's plenty of open water for me to jump into."

"Define plenty."

"At least six feet. And the waterspout extinguishes all the flames."

"You better hope."

"Honey, I've done this now about fifty times down at Ella's place," Toni said. "Sure, it sounds dangerous, and it is, but not if you practice the same kind of precautions I do when I'm making a regular dive."

Jimmy, looking equal parts frustrated, annoyed, and scared, said, "Goddamn it, I think I've been pretty open-minded about these stunts of yours, but it doesn't stop me from worrying that you'll miss the tank, or break your back, every time you climb that damn ladder. Now you want me to worry about you burning to death, too?"

"You knew what I did for a living before you married me, Jimmy," she said, adding with a smile, "You even invested money in me."

His tone softened. "I've got a lot more invested now."

"Honey, I swear, I never take any risk that might take me from you and the kids. I've performed this stunt safely dozens of times, and I was taught by someone who's done it *thousands* of times."

He sighed. "All right, all right. You'll do it eventually no matter what I say, you might as well do it at Palisades where I can be there if anything—"

His voice caught. He touched a hand to her face. "I love you. Promise me this is safe."

"I promise. I love you too—and I have no intention of leaving you."

Toni was surprised to find the temperature in Jersey actually higher than it had been in Florida. According to the U.S. Weather Service, there was a "persistent continental anticyclone" producing higher temperatures across most of the Mid-Atlantic states. You could certainly feel it in Cliffside Park, where it reached ninety-one degrees on June 21, the day Toni decided to go to Palisades and tell Irving Rosenthal about her new act. The idea of bursting into flames in weather this warm wasn't exactly appealing, but at least fire dives were usually done at night, when temperatures were cooler.

The park was definitely benefiting from the heat—Palisade Avenue was jammed with traffic all the way back to the George Washington Bridge. It took Toni twenty minutes just to turn right off Route 5 onto Palisade. No wonder there was so much squawking from the cities of Cliffside and Fort Lee about traffic congestion. It took another ten minutes just to get into the parking lot, partly due to traffic having to detour around a police car inside the lot, where an officer was taking information from a distressed woman whose car had been broken into while she had been in the park. This, too, unfortunately, was becoming more common.

Before seeking out Irving Rosenthal, Toni took a detour to one of the park's most popular attractions—the sideshow building, crowned with its brightly colored sunburst marquee, which hosted the Freak Animal Show and the Palace of Illusions. Maie McAskill was managing it while her husband, Arch, handled their other attractions touring the country. "Hey, Toni," she said from the ticket window, "welcome back. How was Florida?"

"Went great. Okay if I pop in for a second?"

Maie waved her inside. The Palace of Illusions featured standard illusion-show fare like the Headless Woman—the living body of a woman who appeared to be sitting there *sans* head, with tubes and wires arching out of the stump of her neck—and its opposite, the Decapitated Head of a woman sitting on a pedestal, chattering away as if nothing were amiss.

But what Toni had come to see was the Blade Box Illusion, the same trick that had so thrilled her and her brother back in the '40s. As Toni drew closer she heard the voice of a magician doing the standard patter:

"—hate to think of what might happen if anything goes wrong. Let's have a hand for this brave young woman."

Toni stood at the back of the audience and looked up at the figure standing beside the blade box.

The Magical Adele was dressed in a white tuxedo shirt, black tie and jacket with tails, black silk stockings—her legs still shapely as a dancer's, even in her mid-fifties—and three-inch-high heels, which helped give her a commanding presence onstage. She took the first of the razor-sharp blades and plunged it casually into the lid of the box and out through the bottom, which brought a small gasp from the audience. "Good, no blood," she said. "Let's see if her luck holds up." She lifted an even bigger, heavier blade and plunged it straight into the middle of the box and out the bottom—where the tip of the blade seemed to have picked something up along the way.

"What's this?" Adele wondered, bending down to pick off the sharp tip of the blade what appeared to be a scrap of white clothing. "Oh, dear. Part of an undergarment. That *was* close," Adele said with a grin.

Toni had never let on to her mother that she'd seen her waitressing in Atlantic City, but when she returned to Palisades she asked the McAskills whether they needed a magician for their sideshow. As it happened one of their traveling illusion shows needed someone to do a Blade Box, so at Toni's suggestion they called Adele's agent directly, auditioned her, and soon had her on the road. She played state fairs in Milwaukee, Detroit, Memphis, and Dallas; then, when the '63 summer season began, she performed with one of the McAskills' Palace of Wonders units at Riverside Park in Agawam, Massachusetts. Postcards from the road barely contained her happiness at being back on the circuit again, and for the next two years, when she wasn't playing Riverside Park, she was sending Jeffrey and Dawn little presents from Sulphur, Louisiana; Amarillo, Texas; and the Pike amusement pier at Long Beach, California.

But this was her first season at the Palisades unit—perhaps she had asked the McAskills whether she could spend a season closer to home—and Toni found it strange and uncomfortable having her here, and performing this particular illusion, no less. No matter how much she admired her mother's skill and dexterity in doing the Blade Box, it couldn't help but dredge up unhappy memories. Already she saw Lorenzo's smirking face again, saw the two of them in bed, felt the old anger bubble to the surface.

Quickly she slipped out of the sideshow before Adele spotted her.

Crossing the main midway on her way to the administration building, Toni noted another familiar figure: a seven-year-old boy with a tight blond crewcut who was scrambling up one of the hills on the miniature golf course and, while no one was looking, snapping up golf balls that had gone astray in the water hazard. Eagerly he dipped his arms in up to the elbows, scooping out a clutch of slime-covered golf balls. Now, as he sneaked back down the hill, Toni walked up to him, blocking his path, and smiled. "Morning, John-John," she said. "Whatcha got there?"

John Rinaldi, Jr., arms dripping wet, caught red-handed, smiled a hundred-watt smile. "Oh, hi, Mrs. Russo," he said cheerily. "You mean these? Nobody'll miss 'em, and I need 'em for my ball collection at home."

"Yeah, I've seen you sneaking around the batting cages too. What does your dad think about you doing this?" Upon the unexpected death of Joe Rinaldi after only one year as superintendent of Palisades, Irving Rosenthal had promoted Joe's son, John Sr., to the position—making him, at twenty-nine, the youngest amusement park superintendent in the country.

"Oh, he doesn't mind," John Jr. maintained.

"You mean he doesn't know."

"That too."

"Didn't I see you a while back sneaking a teddy bear out of Sadie Harris's stockroom?"

"Oh, but that wasn't for me," John protested. "A little kid was crying and crying 'cause he couldn't win a prize, so I went and got one for him, and boy was he happy!"

Toni had to smile. This kid regularly got away with murder because his dad ran the park and no one wanted to get on his bad side—but you couldn't say his heart wasn't in the right place. Like the time he had released all of Curly Clifford's parakeets from their cages so they could have a better quality of life, but which only resulted in them dive-bombing hapless customers in the Penny Arcade. It took hours for Curly to round them up, and almost as long for the Mazzocchis to clean up all the bird shit.

"Okay, I never saw any of this," Toni told him. "Just stay away from my water tank once it's up, okay?"

"What's in your water tank?"

"Seventy thousand gallons of water. And I'd like to keep it there."

"Deal. Thanks, Mrs. Russo. Hey, you wanna come down to the free-act stage with me? I'm gonna hang out with Cousin Brucie, he told me Bozo the Clown and Soupy Sales were coming today."

"Can't, I'm looking for Uncle Irving."

"He's on patrol. I just saw him down at the Antique Car ride."

"Thanks." As John Jr. started off down the midway she added, "Enjoy the show and stay out of trouble!"

"Sure thing," he assured her, but somehow Toni was not convinced.

The Antique Cars were a short walk up the midway, and Toni indeed found Irving there, looking it over. When she called out a hello, he turned, face brightening. "Ah, the Amazing Antoinette. Back to amaze us again?"

"Maybe more so than usual," Toni said. "I have a new routine."

Now she noticed that the Antique Car ride was shut down, with workmen repairing several of the old-timey, Model T–like roadsters, which had had their tires slashed and seats defaced. "What happened here?"

"Petty vandalism. Some riffraff's idea of a good time. A while back we even caught two young punks stealing a pair of human skulls from the sideshow—go figure. The price of success, I suppose." He greeted her with a warm hug. "Walk with me, would you like something cold to drink?"

"I'd love it. It's hotter here than it was down in Tampa."

Irving bought her a birch beer—he never failed to pay, never cadged free food from anyone—and they moved on down the midway. "I've added a new stunt to my act. Ella Carver showed me how to do it. A fire dive."

Rosenthal smiled. "Audiences always love a good fire dive. I think the last one we had here was Billy Outten. Do you dive into a flaming tank, too?"

"That's the idea."

"We could bill you as 'Antoinette, the Blazing Beauty—Watch Her Dive Into the Flames of Hell!'"

"That's about what it's going to feel like in this heat."

His imagination fired, Irving snapped his fingers. "Here's a sweet wrinkle: What if I arrange for one of the fire engines from the Fort Lee Fire Department to park itself not far away from where you're diving? Have them station a fire captain right next to it, and we announce, 'This act is so dangerous, the fire department insists we have equipment on the premises to put out Antoinette's flames should anything go wrong!'"

Toni laughed. "That is some high grade of bullshit you're selling, Irving. I like it."

"I'll run it past Sol Abrams, he'll love it. Jack would've loved it too."

A shadow eclipsed Rosenthal's bright mood at the mention of his brother, who had died from Parkinson's disease last year.

"I was sorry to hear about your brother," Toni said gently. "I was out of town, I didn't hear of it until I got back."

"You know, I didn't think it would be this hard, running the park without him," Rosenthal admitted. "He was in pretty bad shape the past

few years, he wasn't that actively involved. But I'd been working alongside him for almost sixty years—he was always there if I needed advice,
or to just listen to me blow my top over something. I feel like my right
arm's been cut off." He sighed. "And I'd hoped one of his kids might
want to take over Palisades after we retired. But none have any ambitions to run an amusement park."

"What about your niece Anna?"

"Her least of all. She's been doing it as long as I have. And I can't sell
Palisades to just anybody. A place like this—it's like a living thing, the
way people interact with it, how they think of it. For kids like you who
grew up around here, it's always been a part of your lives—it's personal.
Sell it to someone like Walt Disney, and it's no longer the same park. I
want it to be the same, to go on living, after I'm gone. We're at the top
of our game now, Toni—Palisades has never been more popular, more
famous. What's wrong with wanting that to go on? Nobody wants summer to end."

Touched by the longing in his voice, Toni said, "You're going to be
here to keep summer going for lots more years, Uncle Irving."

He smiled, took out his wallet, and handed her a dollar bill. "I never
get tired of being called that. Here you go. Don't spend it all in one place."

Toni laughed and took the dollar with good grace, a pleasant reminder of her childhood when these dollars seemed like ingots of gold.

Irving waved and moved off down the midway, continuing his daily
health inspection, like a parent checking the temperature of a child.

Posters soon went up all over Palisades, as well as Cliffside Park and
Fort Lee, proclaiming the imminent appearance of

AMAZING ANTOINETTE, THE BLAZING BEAUTY—SHE DIVES FROM A HEIGHT OF NINETY FEET INTO THE FLAMES OF HELL!

It was accompanied by an illustration of a woman wrapped in fire,
diving headlong into an inferno of flames at least ten feet high.

Toni's children now displayed an interest and excitement in her career for the first time in years. Jeff bragged to all his friends that his mother was going to turn herself into a Human Torch. "Yeah, sure—and your sister's the Invisible Girl," one of them scoffed. But when Jeff showed them the poster, their skepticism evaporated.

The Atlantic heat wave continued, making Toni's and Arlan's job of erecting her tower and tank all the more arduous. The rising temperature sapped their strength and caused a constant drip of perspiration into their eyes as they worked under a brutal sun. They took frequent breaks and drank as much water as they could to avoid getting dehydrated, and it took longer than usual to raise the tower—close to two days of exhausting work.

The temperature soared to a hundred degrees by July 2, the first day of the Fourth of July weekend and the day Irving wanted Toni to debut her fire dive. And he insisted on her doing it not at night, but at one in the afternoon—peak attendance, but also peak temperature as well. "It'll get more press coverage, too," he explained, "because the photographers will be able to get a better shot. After that you can go to night dives, all right?"

She agreed as long as the winds remained light: "Anything higher than eight knots and I'll scrub the dive, I'm not taking that chance."

The night before the dive, Toni slept fitfully, and not from the heat. She seemed to float through a series of disturbing dreams, none of which she could remember afterward; and when morning finally came she woke with a feeling of dread and anxiety. She never had feelings like this before a dive, and to allay them she checked again with the Weather Service and was told the local temperature would top out at a hundred degrees, with the wind speed between five or six knots. She felt a little better after that—wind was what worried her most, and six knots was nothing to worry about.

Even so, the atmosphere at the park was hot and muggy and she wasn't thrilled to be pulling on a woolen leotard and shirt for her first show. She checked and rechecked the equipment; everything was in working order. She licked her finger and tested the wind, which remained light.

About forty-five minutes before showtime, an engine company from the Fort Lee Fire Department parked one of its trucks outside the northern border of the park, off Route 5—exactly where many of the fire engines had parked back in '44—and unrolled several hundred feet of fire hose, which two firemen carried into the park, snaking it behind the bathhouses and all the way to the free-act stage. They struck a suitably dramatic pose as Bob Paulson's voice issued from the loudspeakers:

"In just fifteen minutes on the free-act stage, for the first time at Palisades, the Amazing Antoinette will dive from the top of a ninety-foot tower, her body set on fire, into a tank filled with flames! And because this is the Blazing Beauty's most daring and dangerous dive ever, a fire engine has been posted outside the park, and firemen from the Fort Lee Fire Department stand ready to assist should anything go terribly wrong!"

Arlan, helping Toni into her jacket with its backpack of gasoline, pointed out, "Lotta help they'll be—fire hose isn't even hooked up."

Toni should have found that funny, but didn't.

Arlan picked up a gasoline can, went to the tank, and carefully sprinkled the circumference with gasoline.

As the audience gathered, Toni adjusted her canvas jacket and the gasoline packs. From behind the stage she saw her cheering gallery being seated: Jimmy and the kids, Eddie, Lehua, Jack, Bunty, Minette, Irving . . . and, still wearing her black-and-white magician's costume, Adele, taking a seat next to Jack. This shouldn't have surprised Toni, but it only added to the anxiety she had been unable to shake all morning.

"Ladies and gentlemen, performing the most daring of all high dives, Palisades Park is proud to present . . . Antoinette, the Blazing Beauty!"

Toni's music started and she began to ascend the ladder. In her woolen costume she was sweating like a pig before she had even cleared the halfway point. By the time she reached the top she licked her lips, sorry she hadn't taken another swig of water from her thermos bottle.

Down below, Arlan struck a match and tossed it into the tank.

A spear of flame erupted from the tank, the crowd gasping as the flames circled all the way around in less than ten seconds.

Toni walked out to the edge of the platform. She gauged the wind speed—five knots, tops—and looked down.

The flames danced around the edges of the tank and Toni felt a surge of sudden fear, despite the calm wind and absence of anything threatening on the ground. She looked farther afield, just to be sure—taking in the audience, the saltwater pool and bathhouses in the distance, and behind them, a single fire engine parked on the curb outside the park.

She felt another jab of fear, for no apparent reason. *Stop it*, she told herself. Everything was fine, and the audience was waiting.

She reached behind her, lit the fuse on the gasoline packs, which burst into flame with a WHOOSH—the fireball generating a blast of heat so intense it staggered her, took her breath away.

As she gasped for air she looked down and saw—

Flames across the midway, consuming her parents' French fry concession as if it were no more than an appetizer before a really good meal. WHOOSH, and then it was gone! Sparks flew like spittle across the midway and ignited the Funhouse, the exterior walls gobbled up like a snack, exposing bones of dry tinder, which were then devoured in turn . . .

A frightened voice inside Toni said, No, no, not again—

The heat was overpowering and the skies above her glowed red, the air around her choked with acrid smoke. The bathhouse was next for the fire to feast upon, and Toni on her high perch found herself nearly surrounded by the hungry flames. She told herself to jump, but fear paralyzed her—fear of falling, of hitting the water the wrong way, her body snapping like a twig . . .

Terrified, unable to move, Toni felt the ferocious heat on her back growing even hotter, saw livid flares at the periphery of her vision and knew they would soon consume her if she didn't jump.

She was staring down into a sea of fire. Her body was covered in sweat, she shook with fear and wanted to call for help . . .

But still she couldn't move. Gripped by panic, she barely heard the murmurs of alarm and apprehension floating up from the crowd.

No one was more alarmed than Adele, who saw her daughter standing there swathed in flame and *knew* something was wrong. In all the times she had seen Toni perform, she had never seen her hesitate more than a few seconds before diving. And yet here she was, nearly engulfed in flame, and still she didn't move. What was wrong, what was she think—

Oh, God. Suddenly, Adele knew exactly what Toni was thinking.

By now Toni's body was drenched with perspiration, the sweat dripping down her forehead and into her eyes. She wiped it away with her sleeve, but it was the only movement she seemed capable of.

Where was the Human Torch? Where was Bee Kyle? She could command these flames to retreat, couldn't she? But there was no one to come to her aid, and her nose twitched at the smell of burning canvas . . .

"Toni!" came a voice from below. "TONI!"

She looked down.

Her mother was standing by the tank, calling up to her: "Jump, Toni! You have to jump! Do it now, Toni! *Go!*"

The cars in the parking lot exploded like firecrackers and her mother said, "Let's go!"

Toni finally shook off her nightmare and jumped.

She plummeted straight down, dragging a comet's tail behind her, the bubble of heat surrounding her almost unbearable as, below, a tank of writhing flame beckoned . . . with just six feet of open water in the middle.

Threading the fiery needle, she plunged safely into the water, the flames on her back sizzling and sputtering, a steaming waterspout dousing the ring of fire. Toni relaxed her body, threw back her head and arms, slowing her descent into the now tropically warm waters.

She was alive—but no thanks to herself.

She flutter-kicked upward, and as her head broke the surface she was greeted by cheers and applause from the crowd.

She knew she didn't deserve it. She had screwed up, almost fatally.

Arlan stood on the walkway, and beside him was Adele, conspicuous in her magician's costume (*sans* high heels, which she had kicked off).

"Honey, are you *okay?*" her mother called out over the applause.

Toni swam over to the ladder.

"You—you saved me," Toni said wonderingly. "*Again.*"

Arlan offered her a hand up the ladder, and on reaching the walkway Toni embraced her mother with tears in her eyes.

"Thank you," she said softly. "I thought I saw—"

"I know," Adele said. "Believe me, I know." Even though her daughter was sopping wet, Adele never wanted to let go. But she smiled and said, "We've got to make the crowd think this was all part of the act."

Toni nodded. "Follow my lead."

She took her mother's hand and led her to the front of the walkway surrounding the tank. Then she raised Adele's hand in a victory salute.

"If you think *this* was miraculous," Toni called out, "go straight to the Palace of Illusions to catch the next performance of—the Magical Adele!"

The crowd laughed—it was all a stunt, after all. They hooted and cheered, Toni took her bows, then she and her mother climbed down the ladder and hurried behind the stage.

Arlan had a bottle of water for Toni as soon as she got there, and she chugged it down almost in one gulp.

"My God," she said softly, "I could've died."

"But you didn't," Adele said. "Thank God."

"Ella can have her damn fire dive—I am *never* trying that again."

Adele looked her square in the eye and said, "Don't you dare."

Toni blinked in confusion. "What?"

"Don't you dare give up," Adele told her. "You can do anything you set your mind to, Toni. You can *be* anything you want to be. Don't you *ever* think you can't."

Toni hugged her mother and held her tight, as she had on that fiery day twenty-two years ago, the years between vanishing in a puff of smoke.

The Last Days of Palisades

BY

JACK STOPKA

THE PARK SLUMBERS through the long winter, weighted down by ice and snow, dreaming of spring. It dreams of its infancy before the turn of the century, of the trolley cars that came clanging up the hill to The Park on the Palisades and the passengers who came to enjoy its gardens, picnic groves, and shaded paths overlooking the Hudson. It dreams of its childhood in the first years of the new century, and of the visitors who now sought out more worldly attractions like a Ferris wheel, games of chance, balloon flights, a dancing pavilion, and a high diver named Arthur Holden. The park grew along with the century, reaching adolescence in the 'teens with the Big Scenic Railway and saltwater pool, and adulthood in the twenties with the addition of a sideshow, two new coasters, even an opera company.

As it drowses beneath its quilt of snow, it dreams of all the people who flocked to its midways: men, women, and especially children, the joy the park brought them, the laughter that was like oxygen for the park, which breathed it in as it floated up from the Cyclone, the Funhouse, the Wild Mouse, the Carousel. But there are dark moments, too—fires, accidents, deaths, robberies—as there are in anyone's life.

Shaking off sleep, the park wakes to the familiar sounds of workmen repairing, repainting, and remodeling the rides and concessions. By April, visitors are again thronging the midways, flying high above the park on the Sky Ride, being whipped around the steel curves of the Wild Cat, or piloting a rocketship on a Flight to Mars. In May the park pool opens, officially marking the start of summer. On the surface there is nothing to indicate that this summer of 1971—the seventy-fourth summer in the park's life—will be any different from the ones that preceded it.

Nothing except the faltering heartbeat of Irving Rosenthal, who has for the past thirty-five years *been* the heart of Palisades Park. But the increasing crime, the recent accidents in which two youngsters died—a girl thrown from a ride, a boy gruesomely drowned, trapped beneath a toy boat in a shallow channel—all these things are a weight on his heart. The towns of Cliffside Park and Fort Lee want the park gone, along with the thefts, noise, and traffic congestion it attracts, and in 1967 they rezoned the land it sits on for residential development. Rosenthal's faith in himself and in the park has always been strong enough to keep the towns at bay, but now his heart is failing and his faith has faded. He longs for the son or daughter he never had, someone to take over Palisades, to make it new again.

But there is no one, and even before the final season begins, in March of 1971, Rosenthal has made his decision.

And so at the end of the 1971 season in September, Irving Rosenthal announces that he has sold Palisades Amusement Park, for twelve and a half million dollars, to a real estate developer from Texas who will raze it to the ground to build high-rise condominiums.

Everyone but the park is shocked.

Irving Rosenthal is only two years older than Palisades itself; they have grown old together, grown accustomed to the rhythm of each other's heart, and each somehow knows that the time left to them is brief.

Concessionaires who have worked here for decades now strip bare their display cases for the last time and empty the stock in their storerooms. Palisades has been more than just a livelihood for them, it's been a family, and for some, a family business for generations. So they mourn its death as they would one of their own, along with thousands of heartbroken children and adults for whom Palisades was also part of their family.

If laughter is the park's oxygen, grief is an opiate, numbing and dulling the surgery that is soon under way.

Ride operators begin dismantling rides they have lovingly tended for years—dismembering the arms of the Octopus, stripping the canopy of green skin from the Caterpillar, using a giant crane to pull the steel ribs out of the Ferris wheel three at a time. The magnificent Philadelphia Toboggan Company Carousel, Irving's pride and joy, is painstakingly taken apart and preserved—from the antique paintings, mirrors, and "gingerbread" woodwork atop the carousel to the hand-carved horses embedded with rhinestones. Rosenthal refuses lucrative offers for it, hoping to find a buyer who will keep it intact and operative for a new generation of riders.

Many of the rides will be sold off, in whole or in part, to other amusement venues: the Flight to Mars will rocket to Gaslight Village in Lake George, New York; the Roto-Jet flies to Whalom Park in Massachusetts; the Love Bugs find a new home at the Canadian National Exhibition; and the coaster cars from the Cyclone will again carry passengers around hairpin curves at Williams Grove Amusement Park in Pennsylvania.

So far the dismantling has been done with surgical precision, but the biggest and most beloved of the rides will experience the most brutal end.

John Rinaldi, the park's most recent superintendent, finds new employment with a local construction company. Rinaldi's first job: to tear down Palisades Park.

As the heavy demolition equipment begins to roll in, sending threatening tremors into the park grounds, the numbness of grief gives way to something new, as the park understands for the first time the fear that every human being already knows: the fear of death.

The Cyclone, seventy-nine feet tall and two blocks long, has been Palisades' most defining feature for decades—the backbone of the park. At first Rinaldi tries to respectfully dismantle it, track by track, timber by timber—but the Cyclone literally refuses to bend to his will and the old lumber made from white pine simply falls apart in the attempt. The wooden colossus built by Joe McKee is not so easily dismembered, clinging to life as stubbornly as any human.

In the end, John Rinaldi does what he has to do. He attaches thick steel cables to the Cyclone at three different locations, then hooks the cables up to the biggest bulldozers he can find. When he gives the signal, the bulldozers rumble off in three different directions.

The bulldozers literally pull the Cyclone down, breaking its back, its wooden skeleton collapsing in on itself. Metal track that has survived for decades tumbles to the ground along with the shattered uprights that once held it aloft. Chains that once pulled the roller coaster's cars come rattling down like falling shackles on an executed prisoner. The Cyclone crashes to earth amid an enormous cloud of sawdust, dirt, debris, and dreams.

The park's spine has been broken. It can no longer feel anything.

In this painless limbo, it dreams again. It dreams of music. Opera. Swing. Rock and roll. *Last night I took a walk in the park.* It dreams of young people dancing—fox trotting, jitterbugging, twisting. *A swingin' place called Palisades Park.* It remembers every burst of laughter that escaped every passenger on every ride, now only memories to give it breath. *We took a ride on a shoot-the-chute.* Every daredevil who ever drew a gasp from an audience, every boy who ever stole a kiss in the Tunnel of Love or at the top of a Ferris wheel. *That's where the girls are!* It remembers the orphans for whom the park was not just a diversion but a miracle, and the girls who died on the Virginia Reel, and an eleven-year-old boy in 1922 who had never been as happy as he had been at Palisades Park.

> *Palisades has the rides,*
> *Palisades has the fun,*
> *Come on over . . .*

Eight days after the Cyclone falls, a fire erupts in the pool's bathhouses; no one will ever know why. Within minutes the park is ablaze for the last time, hundred-foot daggers of flame piercing the sky, consuming the bathhouses, pool, and Circus restaurant. Embers blow in burning clouds over the cliffs, commanding attention from across the Hudson as the towering PALISADES sign once had. It takes three hours and six engine companies to contain the fire, and at the end of it, the park is no more—just a blackened, demolished shell of an enchanted island that brought so much joy to so many. Palisades Amusement Park has gone out in a blaze of glory, put on its final show, and taken its final bows.

The following year, its impresario, Irving Rosenthal, takes his.

CLOSING BALLY

Hazard's Dock, 1974

IT WAS A CLEAR, sunny morning in April, and from the driveway of her house on Valley Place Toni could see a light wind combing the surface of the Hudson, the whitecaps catching the sun the way it used to glint off the tiny crucifix he wore pinned to the collar of his T-shirt. The Hudson had begun its daily tidal push north and back, its cycle of centuries. "I follow the river," he once told her. "The river never has plans either." She wanted to cry.

High above, on the summit of the Palisades above Edgewater, construction crews were erecting twin monstrosities, high-rise condominiums, on the bluffs where Palisades Amusement Park once stood. Toni thought of her brother's wistful eulogy to the park published in the *Bergen Record*'s "Voice of the People" column after Irving Rosenthal's death last year. Irving might have been the heart of Palisades, but for Toni, the soul of Palisades had been Bunty Hill, and now he, too, was gone.

She got into her car and began the short drive to Hazard's Beach.

The news had stunned everyone; Bunty had always been the very embodiment of robust health, and last September, on his seventy-second birthday, he had again commemorated it by making his sixtieth crossing of the Hudson. Then just weeks ago, what seemed like a bad cold took a turn for the worse and into the hospital, where he passed away of pneumonia.

Toni couldn't believe it when she first heard. Not Bunty—he seemed eternal, everlasting, like the river he loved. It seemed even more of a mistake at John G. Heus & Son's Funeral Parlor in Fort Lee, where the name on the guest book read: JOHN HUBSCHMAN. She didn't know anybody named John Hubschman—she knew Bunty Hill, and he couldn't be dead.

But as the wake got under way and Toni approached the casket and saw his creased face, like worn granite, in unnatural repose, she knew the truth—that only the river was eternal.

It was a simple, modest service, like the life the man himself chose. Among the small group of mourners were friends like Toni and Eddie, Tommy Meyers and his family, as well as a Hubschman cousin named Betty. At one point a group of about fifteen youngsters came in: thirteen, fourteen years old, they were the latest graduates of Bunty's college of swimming, Hudson River history, the picking of racehorses, and above all, learning the importance of doing your best, of becoming your best self. They filed up to the casket one by one, each murmured a prayer, then left.

About halfway through the wake a young woman of about thirty entered, walked up to the casket, knelt to say a prayer, then placed a single red rose on the casket and left. No one knew who she was and no one asked. Tommy Meyers thought she might have been one of the thousands of people Bunty had saved from drowning over his forty-one years as a lifeguard, someone who might not be walking the earth today but for him.

Toni said a prayer over her friend too. This would be the last time she would ever see him like this, but not her last opportunity to say good-bye.

That came today, on this bright, warm April morning.

Toni parked her car off Henry Hudson Drive and made the short hike along a dirt path that ran beneath the George Washington Bridge to Hazard's Dock—Bunty's dock, where he spent each day in the sun, at times entertaining and teaching youngsters, at times sitting alone reading, enjoying the beauty of the Palisades and the Hudson, but always watchful.

Already gathered at Hazard's were Tommy Meyers, Eddie, and a few of Bunty's other pals from Palisades and Fort Lee.

"I guess this is all of us," Tommy said as Toni joined the group. "As you all know, Bunty asked to be cremated and have his ashes scattered in the Hudson—partly because the river had been so much of his life, and partly because over the years he'd seen too many kids sneak down to the river to swim and he'd have to pull them out when something went wrong.

"He told me, 'I want my ashes in the river in case any kids from town have trouble there—so maybe I can be there, in a way, to help.'"

His voice broke a little as he said it. Toni had tears in her eyes.

"Since the Hudson's a tidal river," he went on, "Bunty's ashes, just scattered every which way, could end up as far north as Albany or as far south as Tierra del Fuego. So we got this idea for a special kind of . . . anchor."

Tommy held up the small cloth bag containing Bunty's ashes—and tied to it was a bottle of his favorite Ballantine Ale.

Eddie laughed. Toni laughed. They all did.

"Perfect," Eddie said. "All that's missing is crackers and cheese."

"And a racing form," someone else suggested.

One by one Bunty's pals came up, briefly held his ashes in their hands, and said a few words of farewell.

When it came Toni's turn, her eyes brimmed with tears. "Follow the river, Bunty," she said. "You showed me how to follow mine."

She handed it back to Tommy to do the honors.

Tommy turned to face the river, tossing the bag and its anchor of ale into the welcoming waters of the Hudson. Bunty vanished under the waves, returning to the river he loved, of which he would now always be a part.

Eddie, his arm draped across Toni's shoulders, walked his daughter back to her car as she sought to compose herself. "You going to be okay?"

"Yeah. I just need a minute."

"Want to come back to the restaurant? We'll drink a toast to Bunty."

"Another time, okay? I'm doing a fire dive tonight at Coney Island. Arlan's set up the equipment but I need to go over and check the rigging with him."

"Jeff and Dawn doing okay?" he asked.

"Dawn loves her new acting teacher at NYU, but Jeff's still a little unsettled at Rutgers. He's thinking about changing majors."

"Late bloomers run in the Stopka family," Eddie said. "Except for you. You knew what you wanted to do right from the start."

"How could I not," she said, "growing up at Palisades?"

They had reached her car, parked on the side of the road next to his.

"Minette says hi, by the way," Eddie said. "She and her sister Mary are going great guns with that dress shop they opened in Point Pleasant. And they can still dance the rumba on a tabletop."

"Send her my love." She kissed her father on the cheek. "Jack too. Tell him I'll see him on Sunday for dinner, and I want a copy of that Ellery Queen mystery magazine with his new story."

"I will."

Toni slid behind the wheel of her car, keyed the ignition. She took a last look at Bunty's dock in the distance and thought: Goodbye, dear friend.

Traffic in New York was the usual nightmare and it took more than an hour to get to Coney Island. She and Arlan wolfed down a couple of Nathan's hot dogs and French fries—they really couldn't compare to her dad's, though the franks were as good as Callahan's—and then set about checking the rigging and other equipment for Toni's eight o'clock show. At forty-three, her joints might be getting a little stiff, but she fully intended to keep doing this at least as long as Arthur Holden, if not Ella Carver, who had remained active almost up to her death last year at the age of eighty.

Toni changed into her woolen bodysuit and canvas jacket bearing what Jeffrey had once jokingly, if inaccurately, dubbed her "rocket pants."

She liked Coney, it reminded her of Palisades—especially once she had begun her act and climbed to the top of the tower. She stood on the tiny platform, taking in the sights and sounds and smells all around her: the briny air blown in off the surf, the Wonder Wheel revolving majestically on one side of her, and on the other, the rattle of winches and screams of passengers plunging down the steep drops of the Cyclone—the original wooden coaster of that name, the one Jack and Irving Rosenthal had built here back in 1927.

And as she stood there, in those calm moments of silent expectation from the audience below, Toni realized:

Irving's not gone. Bunty's not gone. Palisades is not gone.

They're all here, in me, a child of the park—one of millions of children who found joy, escape, thrills, and inspiration from Palisades Park. Every time she made her dive, Palisades lived in her wake of flames—written against the night as brightly as Irving's million-watt marquee on the cliffs.

She smiled at the thought, igniting the gasoline packs on her back as, wrapping herself in fire, she leapt into the air.

AUTHOR'S NOTE

This novel is a love letter to a cherished part of my childhood. I grew up in the towns of Cliffside Park, Palisades Park, and Edgewater, always living within a mile of Palisades Amusement Park. Some of my fondest childhood memories are of Palisades: swimming in the pool, riding the kiddie Cyclone with my dad, the night in 1961 when my Aunt Eleanor spent an hour (and untold numbers of coins) letting me pitch ball after ball at a concession stand so I could win a stuffed dog nearly bigger than I was. But I couldn't have written this book on my memories alone, and I am indebted to a great many people who shared with me their own memories, work experience, and knowledge.

Foremost among them is Vince Gargiulo, author of the definitive nonfiction history *Palisades Amusement Park: A Century of Fond Memories* and writer/co-producer of the PBS documentary of the same name. Apart from the wealth of information in his book and film, Vince generously answered my every question about Palisades and even shared some of his still-unpublished research, which was key in helping me visualize the park at different points in its history. Thanks, Vin, for your expertise, your patience, and your unstinting support.

Vince also introduced me to John Rinaldi, whose father, John, and grandfather, Joe, both served as superintendent of the park. John drove me all over Cliffside Park and Fort Lee, pointing out locations relevant to Palisades history, showed me his collection of park memorabilia, spoke at length about park history and his family's involvement with it, and gave me a great sense of the physical operation of the park. Thanks, John, for your invaluable assistance. (Yes, that's him doing a walk-on in chapter 24.)

Norma Cuny Santanello actually grew up playing in wooden crates filled with straw, which once contained china given as prizes at one of her mom's concession stands. In the course of two phone interviews, Norma offered a treasure trove of information about the park from the days of her mother's involvement through her own years working at Palisades. She spoke knowledgeably and passionately about the *people* who made the park what it was—staff, concessionaires, ride operators— who came alive in her recollections, and who I have tried to make come alive for the reader. Norma, thank you for your time, humor, and fantastically good memory.

Ann Meyers Picirillo generously shared her memories of her friend Bunty Hill, as did her brother Tom Meyers, who as a curator at the Fort Lee Museum also gave me access to Bunty's personal scrapbooks, let me hold his old shillelagh in my hand, and took me to Hazard's Dock, which still stands today in the shadow of the George Washington Bridge. Both Ann and Tom have written fine reminiscences of Bunty at www .fortlee.patch.com. I've drawn upon these for my portrayal of Bunty, as well as a profile/obituary by George Richards printed in the *Bergen Record* in 1974, and a long letter from one S. B. Schaffer, also from the *Record*. Lou Paolina spoke to me at length about his friendship with Bunty and I've used one of his anecdotes—about how Lou swam halfway across the Hudson, only to turn back to Bunty's chagrin—as a crisis point in Toni's life. And a shout-out to Tom Bennett and Chuck Griffin, who also related to me their encounters with Bunty.

My deep appreciation to Georgia L. Haneke and Gary Lesnevich, who shared stories, photos, and press clippings about their aunt, Minette Dobson, their father, Gus Lesnevich, and their mother, Frances Georgiana Warner. Susan Hutcherson provided biographical information about her grand-uncle, Peter "Peejay" Ringens. My uncle, Edgar Wittmer, shared details of his tour of duty during World War II on Espíritu Santo, on which I based Eddie Stopka's wartime experiences, while my friend Richard Kyle's combat service in the Korean War helped me shape Jack Stopka's. George Kellinger Jr. shared memories and photos of his father. Roscoe Schwarz Jr. was kind enough to answer my questions about his father and his brother Laurent. Jim Tolomeo, a former Palisades lifeguard, advised me about the particulars of lifeguarding (as did the gracious and knowledgeable Mary Donahue of DeAnza College). Linden Clark told me everything I could possibly want to know about operating a Saratoga French fry stand and making those delicious fries. James Donnelly added to my knowledge of his grandmother, Anna (Halpin) Cook. Miriam Kotsonis revealed a side of her grandfather, Jack Pitkof, of which I was unaware back when she and I were in first grade, reading comic books from his candy store. My thanks also to Corinne Rinaldi, Guy Brennert, Mary Ederle Ward, Charles Freericks, and Marc Hartzman (author of the excellent book *American Sideshow*).

Special thanks to Carol Horn and Susan Luse, who shared memories of their aunt, Gladys Shelley, and graciously granted me permission to use lyrics from her song "Come On Over."

Sally Sullivan spoke to me about her days on the picket line with CORE at Palisades Park. I only wish I could have spoken with the late Melba Valle Rosa, whose simple request to swim in the Palisades pool sparked the battle against segregation there. In a life of seventy-seven years Melba was a model, flamenco dancer, actress, and an artist who received her bachelor's of fine arts at the age of seventy-one. To get a sense of her as a person I drew upon articles in *The New York Daily News*, *Jet* magazine, and a portion of Walter Dean Myers's book *Bad Boy: A Memoir*. The details of CORE's protest at Palisades is based in large part on the "Alabama in New Jersey" chapter from James Peck's memoir *Freedom Ride*, with additional information from *The New York Times*, the *Bergen Record*, *The Crisis*, the *CORE-lator*, *New York Amsterdam News*, *People's Voice*, and *The Baltimore Afro-American*.

Much of the dialogue in which Bee Kyle and Ella Carver talk about high diving and their lives is quoted from articles in *The Daily Northwestern*, the *Lethbridge Herald*, the *St. Petersburg Times*, the *Daily Inter Lake*, the *Memphis Press-Scimitar*, the *Montreal Gazette*, and other newspapers.

I lack room to list all my reference sources, but most valuable were the "Palisades Notes" column that ran in *The Billboard* from the 1920s–1950s, as well as: *Step Right Up!* by Dan Mannix, *Monster Midway* by William Lindsay Gresham, *Eyeing the Flash* by Peter Fenton, *On the Midway* and *Bally!* by Wayne Keiser, *Side Show: My Life with Geeks, Freaks & Vagabonds in the Carny Trade* by Howard Bone, *On the Road with Walt Hudson* by Walt Hudson, *Sh-Boom! The Explosion of Rock 'N' Roll 1953–1968* by Clay Cole, *Defying Gravity* by Garrett Soden, *Circus Dreams* by Kathleen Cushman and Montana Miller, "High Dive" by Montana Miller *(Radcliffe Quarterly,* Spring 1998*)*, "You Have to Hit the Dime" by Billy Outten as told to Don Dwiggins *(For Men Only,* October 1955), "The Thrill Hunters" *(Popular Mechanics,* March 1937), *Operation Drumbeat* by Michael Gannon, *Riding the Rails* by Errol Lincoln Uys, *Hopping Freight Trains in America* by Duffy Littlejohn.

Also, *Fort Lee: The Film Town* by Richard Koszarski, *Fort Lee, Birthplace of the Motion Picture Industry* by the Fort Lee Film Commission, *A Chronological and Picturesque History of Cliffside Park* by Lawrence Matthias, *America, the Dream of My Life* edited by David Steven Cohen, the transcript of Congress's "Investigations of Organized Crime in Interstate Commerce," *The Secret Rulers* by Fred J. Cook, *Home Front America: Popular Culture of the World War II Era* by Robert Heide and John Gilman, *Women at War With America: Private Lives in a Patriotic Era* by D'Ann Campbell, *"Daddy's Gone to War": The Second World War in the Lives of America's Children* by William M. Tuttle Jr., *The First Strange Place: Race and Sex in World War II Hawaii* by Beth Bailey and David Farber, *Hawai'i Homefront: Life in the Islands During World War II* by MacKinnon Simpson, *Return to Paradise* by James A. Michener, *Desert Sailor: Growing Up in the Pacific Fleet 1941–1946,* by James W. Fitch, FC 1/c USN, *Waikīkī Tiki: Art, History and Photographs* by Phillip S. Roberts, *Tiki of Hawai'i: A History of Gods and Dreams* by Sophia V. Schweitzer, and the Discovery Channel documentary *Our Time in Hell: The Korean War.*

For their research assistance, my appreciation to Arlene Sahraie of the Cliffside Park (NJ) Public Library, Andrea Romano of the Cliffside Park High School Library, Susan Schwartz of the Oshkosh (WI) Public

Library, as well as the staffs of the Edgewater (NJ) Public Library, the Fort Lee (NJ) Public Library, the Bergen County Historical Society, the New Jersey Historical Society, the New York Public Library (in particular the Schomberg Center for Research in Black Culture, in Harlem), the Special Collections department at Rutgers University Library (NJ), and the UCLA Music Library.

For advice, criticism, suggestions, and support, I am grateful to my friends and fellow writers Carter Scholz, Amy Adelson, and Greg Bear; my editor, Hope Dellon; my agent, Molly Friedrich; and my wife, Paulette.

Singer Marian Mastrorilli has composed a lovely song, "At Palisades," whose chorus is: *"Oh, what I wouldn't trade / for another day at Palisades . . ."* Writing this book has given me another day at Palisades, and I hope it's done the same for readers who were once park visitors. And for those who never were, I hope it provides a glimmer of what it was that made Palisades Amusement Park such a special place for those of us who knew and loved it.